Secrets of the Unborn

WAR OF THE UNBORN

C.H. LYN

thank you!
Hope you enjoy

C.H. Lyn

Barski-Lyn Adventures

CONTENTS

To my superman.

Without you, none of this would be possible.

I love you.

1

CONCRETE JUNGLE

T HE CITY GLINTED AT night. Not the way it used to, before the world plunged into a war that took decades and super soldiers to end. But it glinted all the same.

Jamie's jaw clenched as she rode the clear exterior elevator up the side of one of the only lingering habitable skyscrapers. The remains of dozens more reflected the light from the halfmoon, the stars, the fires lit to keep people from freezing during cold east coast nights. Some of the massive structures had crumbled entirely, others were half-fallen, the rest stood as taunts for those brave and stupid enough to enter. Floors and ceilings caved in at the lightest breezes.

It was a good thing she hadn't grown up here. Jamie's lips curled as she pondered the trouble she'd have gotten in with a concrete jungle like this to play in.

She probably would have broken her neck.

The muscles in her back tensed as the elevator slowed to a stop nearly thirty stories up. The glass didn't seem to keep out the chill, and she pulled up the zipper of her cropped sand-colored jacket, stuffing her hands into the pockets. Jamie cracked her neck to the side, the pop drawing the attention of Thick and Squat.

Those weren't their real names, of course, but she barely cared enough to remember Carter's name, let alone his numerous henchmen.

A rush of nerves cramped her stomach. Or maybe it was hunger. She'd been at the gym most of the day, staying fresh for the next two weeks of fights. The big tournament ended soon. She and Alice would have a healthy payday that might get them out of the city. If not, it would at least keep them fed and warm through the winter.

The elevator dinged.

Thick stepped off first. Jamie winced at the groan of metal as the man lumbered out of the death chamber. She made a mental note to take the stairs back down and followed him.

However dingy the rest of the city was, Carter kept his territory clean. There were only four skyscrapers left. The military owned one, the supposed government another, some old tech mogul was cooped up in the third, and Carter claimed the last.

Jamie inhaled the stale scent of too much incense and nearly sneezed. "No windows this far up?" she asked Squat as he waddled onto the plush hallway carpet. "Sure is stuffy in here."

Thick glowered and gestured for her to continue down the corridor. Fancy tables lined the walls, lights in brackets—wasting energy—every few feet, and collections of vibrant paintings that Jamie tried to avoid looking at.

What was the point of admiring something you couldn't have?

The three reached an arch, and Thick held up a finger. Jamie rolled her eyes.

Every time.

Carter liked to make a show of being a busy man. It was no surprise when Jamie ducked her head into the room and saw him finishing a solo dinner at his ornate table. He stood quickly, swallowing a final bite of what smelled like perfectly seasoned steak—a delicacy Jamie had only tried once, on V-Day—and turned to face her.

"Ahh, my prize fighter."

Jamie held back the urge to roll her eyes again, thinking about Alice and the possibility of eating steak sometime in the next year.

"Carter, it's an honor." It was harder to keep the dry irritation out of her voice, but she put up a good effort. At least there wasn't any malice audible.

Carter smiled. His teeth were too white, too straight, and too brittle. Those eyes, dark blue with bushy brows that jumped around when he got excited, narrowed in on her own, different ones.

"It gets me every time," he said with a sigh. He pulled a suit jacket from the back of his chair, stuffing his thick arms into the sleeves and leaving it unbuttoned, draped over his protruding stomach. Carter pointed a finger at her. "Silver eyes. The color means something, right?"

Jamie blinked.

Silver did mean something. It meant when she was created, grown in a glass bottle much like the elevator for the first nine months of her life and then ejected into a sterile room with a dozen beds, they'd designed her to be a leader. They'd built her to be unbreakable. They'd trained her to be the best.

Well, second best. But Gold was rare and almost a different breed. She'd only met one in her time at war.

"Not really." Jamie shrugged. "Just wanted to make sure we didn't get mistaken for Adams."

Carter, an Adam, grimaced at the term. "Hah, an unnecessary addition to your otherwise perfect physique. Besides, anyone who watches you Unborn fight knows you're not human."

She bristled. "What did you need from me, Carter? Changing the line up again?"

"Tone, Jamie." His own tone was cold.

She reminded herself to keep a civil tongue. It would have been easier with Alice there. "Course, boss. Just tired from the gym. Looking to get some rest before tomorrow night."

Carter's mouth slid into a smug smile that made her wish he'd step into the ring every now and then. Hell, just once and she'd show him exactly what his fighters went through to earn him a dime.

He strode around the table toward a cigar humidifier in the corner.

This room was much like the hall. Decorated beyond the means of every other person in the city. Maybe a handful of the manors near the river were like this. Maybe there were some rich folks with smaller homes that had chandeliers, and cushy seats, and three kinds of forks, and steak, but Jamie doubted any of them flaunted it like this.

"About the fight..."

Jamie scowled.

"Not tomorrow's." Carter waved off her expression with a clipper in his hand before he cut the end of his cigar and tucked it into the corner of his mouth. "I'm talking about next week. The big one. You're first on the roster, going up against, what? Six opponents?"

Jamie shrugged. Her fists remained in her pockets, where they couldn't give away how tightly they were clenched. "Nothing I can't handle, Carter. You know that."

"Yeah, well I have a name I'd like to see get to the top of that list."

She remained quiet.

"If you know what I mean," he said with a grin, lighting his cigar and puffing acrid smoke into the room.

"I don't." Jamie inhaled through her nose, chanting an internal mantra of *calm* like Alice told her to do every time their landlord demanded extra rent.

"You fight Travers that night. It would be beneficial to me if he didn't go down."

Jamie closed her eyes and cracked her neck again. She took her hands out, planting them on the table in front of her and leaning forward. "Listen, Carter. I do a lot for you, but I'm not taking a fall. If you don't want him going down, put him in with someone else."

Carter sneered. "Don't get uppity now, Jamie. Not when we've worked so well together."

On either side of her, Thick and Squat stepped forward.

Jamie's tight expression slid into a smile. "I fight for you, Carter. I'll keep fighting. But I'm not taking a fall." She tensed her core, subtly shifting her weight as the henchmen waited for their orders.

If these flesh bags wanted to fight, she'd show them a fight. A real one, not the bullshit half-showboating she did in the ring.

They'd find out just how high this monstrosity of a building was when they went out the damn window.

Carter hesitated. He watched her with those blue eyes, beady and angry. Then he smiled. "Well, let's see how this week treats you. It may be you come 'round before the finale."

Jamie's chin lifted half an inch. "Anything else?"

His nose pinched again, but he gave a dismissive nod and gestured to his men. Thick reached for Jamie's arm. She whirled, moving toward the corridor fast enough that it took the men jogging to catch up.

"Stairs?"

Thick grunted. "We take the elevator."

Jamie snapped her glare toward Squat. "*Stairs.*"

The man swallowed and pointed to a door a few yards from the big glass bubble that had carried them nearly thirty stories from the ground floor.

"See you boys on the ground."

She jammed the door open with her shoulder and hurried into the dark stairwell.

"So, how'd it go?"

Jamie's expression was answer enough, and Alice stepped back, pulling the door open to let her into their tiny apartment. Jamie kicked off her shoes, tossed her jacket over the back of their torn and raggedy couch, and leaned against the closed front door.

"Carter sucks."

Alice nodded sympathetically. "We've known this for a while now."

Jamie grimaced. She heaved a sigh. "He wants me to throw a fight."

Alice's eyes, silver and glinting even in the low light of their apartment, went wide. "That's..."

"Yeah. I told him to shove it."

Alice pursed her lips, glaring. "Please tell me you didn't *actually* say it like that?"

Jamie pushed away from the wall and trudged into the kitchenette. "No, I was nice about it. Nice-ish."

Alice snorted.

"What is there to eat?" Jamie tugged open the door to their mini fridge. Apparently, there was a time when people had full sized ones.

Big-ass hulking things that ate up electricity and held weeks' worth of food. The idea was simultaneously enticing and appalling.

Her question was answered by the utterly empty shelves looking up at her.

"Never mind." Jamie ignored Alice's appraising eyes as she turned away from the counter. She pulled the little brown elastic band from the end of her long blonde braid. Running her fingers through her hair felt so good—almost as good as a fat sandwich in her stomach would have felt.

Alice grinned.

Jamie caught the look from her peripheral vision as she shook her head, loosening the tight braid she wore for training. "What?"

Alice shrugged.

"You've never had a good poker face, Alice. What are you smiling about?"

Her sister in all but blood crossed the space, opened a usually empty cupboard, and pulled out a loaf of bread.

Jamie's jaw dropped. "Where the hell did you get that?" she demanded, wondering how her nose had missed the scent. Then again, her nostrils were still plugged with smoke from Carter's cigar and incense.

"You know Joey? From 7E?"

Jamie's hungry look turned to a scowl. "The Adam?"

"The *baker*," Alice said, her tone dry.

Organic was the polite term for regular people; many were offended when called Adams. Not that it stopped them calling Unborn everything from hybrids to robots.

"Anyway," Alice continued. "We ran into each other on his way to work this morning, and he said he'd bring us back a loaf if I helped him move a massive dresser in his apartment."

A smirk pulled at Jamie's lips, even as mistrust stirred in her chest. "You've gotta be careful with them, Alice."

"Bakers?" Alice asked, her voice overly innocent as she turned away. She laid out a wood block, pulled a knife from a drawer, and began cutting slices. "I've got some butter hiding in that one." She gestured with the sharp end of the blade, and Jamie followed the hint to pull butter and—to her shock—a jar of strawberry jam from where they'd been hiding.

"Why hide these?" she demanded.

Alice grinned again, whirling with two slices of bread on one plate and three on another. She danced toward Jamie, fluid and graceful, pecked her on the cheek, and continued toward the couch. "We never have nice surprises," she sang. "I wanted to give you a nice surprise."

Jamie snagged a spoon from their sparse cutlery drawer and followed with a smile. The two settled onto the couch, legs crisscrossed as they smothered fresh sourdough with butter and jam.

"Remember Five-Cal?" Alice asked, a wistful hint to her tone as she leaned her head back against the couch. Her hair, corkscrew curls in dark brown except for a single white lock on the front right side, was streaked with dust. She'd spent most of the day at their side-gig, drilling through old cement to clear space for farming closer to the city proper. It was hard work. Tiring, even for Unborn.

"Remember?" Jamie scoffed. "I dream about those days."

Alice chuckled. Five-Cal, as they called it, was a period of time from their youth. Unborn developed faster than humans—a necessity when building soldiers from scratch to fight in an already decades-long war. Some of Jamie's earliest memories were the days when she, Alice, Vic (the third member of their pseudo-sisterhood), and the others had been fed upwards of five-thousand calories a day.

They'd grown fast enough to stretch their skin, bones pulling tendons tight, pain pills sometimes not enough to ease the unnatural strain on their nerves and muscles. Even with the pain, Jamie missed those days. She missed the three of them, drenched in sweat, hands trembling from training with weapons half their size, sitting cross-legged on their cots and slamming through half a dozen massive bowls of Cook's spaghetti and meatballs.

In human years, they'd been around twelve when their growth had slowed. Mind followed body and—though the rotation of the earth around the sun would suggest they were only in their early twenties—all the Unborn left from their squad were closer to thirty by the time the war ended.

Jamie wasn't sure how it all worked. Had never really cared, especially those nights when Vic got in everyone's head about the logic behind it. She'd learned to tune out her older sister when the "Unborn role" preaching started. Jamie had already known they were soldiers; she hadn't needed the reminders from Miss Goodie-Two-Shoes.

Though, thinking back, most of those reminders had happened after Jamie had been demoted... again.

She heaved a sigh and set her plate on the ground. It was days like this, when she was tired and hungry and dealing with people like Carter, that she wished Vic was with them. Most of the time she could brush it aside, remind herself of Vic's words when the war had ended, when the brass had handed down orders saying the three of them were getting split. After over a decade growing and fighting together, losing their friends, losing territory, and gaining it back, killing countless enemies, and someone up top had decided the three of them didn't deserve to stay together.

Jamie had nearly burned down the barracks.

Still, she and Alice had found each other. They knew Vic was somewhere out west. Past crumbling cities, towering mountains, and a vast wasteland. Beyond their reach.

"What are you going to do about the fight?" Alice asked, her voice soft.

Jamie closed her eyes. "I'm not taking a fall."

"I know *that*." Alice's voice carried a smirk.

"I'll worry about it when I get there," Jamie muttered, sleep coming quickly now that her stomach was moderately satisfied and her body relaxed. "It's not till next week anyway. I have to get through this weekend before I'm guaranteed to be in the finals."

"Right." A sardonic sound now, almost a chuckle, came from her friend. "Like there's a chance you don't make it to finals with me."

Alice had made it through her bracket the week before.

"You never know," Jamie said through a yawn. "I could go up against a gorilla or something."

"Shit, *I'd* pay to see that fight."

Jamie snorted, shifted her butt to avoid a spring in the couch, and fell asleep.

2

VALHALLA

S WEAT.

It was the constant scent of Jamie's life. Sweat on the battlefield. Sweat in those damn transport planes. Sweat on the site jackhammering concrete.

Sweat dripping from her furrowed brow as she stared down the tree trunk of a Copper in front of her. Her opponent was massive, nearly four times her weight and taller by a foot.

Jamie wiped away the trickle of salty liquid with the back of her knuckle wraps. It came away with a streak of the paint she wore for each official bout. A layer of black lines patterned into her tightly braided hair crawled down her forehead and ended just below her sharp cheekbones. She glanced at the stained cloth covering her hands and squared up again.

Sound surrounded her, kept at bay by the force of her concentration. She had eyes for one focus. Her ears were listening for the shift of the man's feet on the mat, the grunt that would mean she hit a weak spot, and the increase in cheers that would mean the crowd was still on her side.

That had taken some getting used to... getting the crowd on her side. She'd spent her life taking orders from one group of Adams and killing another. It was still odd needing their admiration—however twisted it was with their disdain for her kind.

A bell chimed.

Jamie struck.

Her fist slammed hard into the Copper's gut and met a wall of muscley resistance. She grimaced. Darted to the side and swept her leg. The man snatched at her.

Too slow.

His fist rammed into her thigh.

She grunted, sucking air through gritted teeth and whirled. A lucky blow. Concentrate.

Jamie was faster than a Copper, faster than an Adam. Faster than just about everyone in her squad. Alice had been the only one able to beat her in a foot race.

She circled the trunk of the man, jabbing into his sides, his back. She kicked, snapping her foot into the side of his knee and drawing a screech from him like a wounded animal.

He swung wild, startling her from her form, and connected with her chest.

Jamie flew back, ramming into the steel cage that protected on-lookers from bodies getting knocked out of the ring.

She straightened and got her hands up, ready for his next swing. Pain yowled in her chest with each breath.

The Copper moved slowly. His eyes were unfocused, his mind distracted by the pain that showed in the limp of his leg, the way he couldn't quite catch his breath.

She grinned. The crowd howled around her. Cheers and jeers blended together as a handful of people realized they were about to win or lose big.

She strode forward, ignoring the pain and pumping her arms for the crowd. "Valhalla!" she called out.

"*Unfallen!*" returned the throng of onlookers.

"*Valhalla!*" she shouted louder, half jumping as she exaggerated her walk. The Copper's gaze followed her movement, his whole body swaying unsteadily.

"UNFALLEN," they screamed.

She swung.

Her fist connected with the man's cheek. Blood burst from his mouth. There was a pause, that split second of time she relished when her opponent was done but not down. That brief breath where their body drifted through the air before it slammed into the mat.

The Copper went down. The whole ring shook as his body thudded against the ground.

Jamie looked up, wiping her sweat away again as she stared out at the crowd.

She blinked.

Her smile fell. Disbelief and heat plunged into her stomach.

A pair of silver eyes stared at her from the front of the crowd. Hooded by thick, dark brows that rested on golden-brown skin.

Oliver had lost none of his build. His arms were crossed over his chest, biceps just visible against the shadows that covered most of the crowd. His full lips were pursed; that initial rush of attraction in Jamie was replaced almost instantly with irritation at the judgmental way he looked at her.

Jamie's skin buzzed with nerves. The lights above her were suddenly too bright. She stood too exposed to the crowd of Adams and the single Silver watching her.

The announcer declared her the victor, and she turned from Oliver, marching out of the ring and into the locker room.

"Nice!" Alice bounded toward Jamie as she strode into the locker room. "You took him down quick."

Jamie said nothing, her heart still pounding and breath coming quickly. Not from the fight, but from the surprise of her past standing on the other side of the ring.

"What the hell is he doing here?" Jamie demanded in a low mutter. She ripped at her wraps. The unwinding process sped up as Alice stepped forward and took over.

"Carter comes to every fight in the final," Alice said with a raised eyebrow. Her gentle hands eased the cuts across Jamie's knuckles as she unstuck the fabric from the bloody skin.

The wounds would heal quick enough. People paid more to watch Unborn go rounds without gloves.

"Not Carter," Jamie growled after a pause to wince.

Alice dumped the wad of bloody cloth onto the bench and raised her hands. "I'm lost. Who are you talking about?"

Jamie put a hand to her ribs just under her left breast and sat down, trying to keep her torso straight. The bones were bruised. She knew it from the familiar sting, and the fortunate lack of intensity that would have meant they were cracked.

For a human, this kind of thing would take weeks to heal. For Jamie it would take a few days, less if she stretched right and didn't irritate it with rapid movement.

A difficult task as Oliver pushed open the locker room doors a few yards ahead of her.

Jamie sprang to her feet, a scowl fixed on her face.

Alice's silver eyes went wide. Then her smile did the same. "Oliver!" She ran to him, tossing her arms around his neck and clinging to him like he was a long-lost brother.

Which... technically.

Jamie grimaced. Oliver may have been like a brother to Alice, but he was about the farthest from it to her. Sure, they'd grown up together, but they'd never been siblings.

"What the hell are you doing here?" Alice asked, her tone the opposite of what Jamie's had been when she'd asked that very question a few minutes before.

Oliver chuckled and set the petite warrior down. "I came to see you two." He looked at Jamie. "That was quite a fight."

She scoffed. "You've seen me take down Coppers before. Nothing special."

Silver flashed as his eyes widened a smidgeon before returning to their normal alert but steady gaze. His lips twitched into a grin. "Sure."

The back of Jamie's neck was marked with ink, but the little hairs stood up all the same, giving fur to the phoenix that had been tattooed there a year before the war ended. He was teasing her. Making fun of her. Either.

"What do you want?" Jamie asked, her voice dry.

"Oohh." Alice grinned, still clinging to Oliver's arm like he would disappear if she let him go. "Let's do dinner!"

"Alice," Jamie growled. Her friend ignored her.

"Give us a few minutes to get cleaned up. That was the last fight for Jamie tonight; we're good to go."

Oliver's sardonic expression melted into a grateful, warm smile as he put a hand over Alice's slim fingers. "That would be lovely, thank you."

Jamie's eyes rolled so hard she almost gave herself a headache. "Fine. But get out. You're not supposed to be in here anyway."

Alice blushed, her hand going to her mouth to cover her giggles. "She's right. This is the women's."

Oliver met Jamie's eye and that smirk reappeared. "Nothing I haven't seen before. I'll be waiting outside."

Heat surged through Jamie's chest like a grenade had gone off. She opened her mouth, but he was already gone, the rusty, dented door clanging shut behind him.

His words were true. They'd all grown up together, trained together, learned together, showered together. The remains of his unit had joined Jamie, Alice, and Vic once the numbers lined up. It made sense to put survivors in the same wing of the base; freed up more space that way.

The Silver Base they'd been stationed on had started with six rooms, each holding a dozen bunks. By the end of the war there had only been one room left. Only twelve Silvers.

So, sure, Oliver had seen them all naked. And they him. But the fire at the bottom of Jamie's stomach proved that wasn't what he was talking about.

She bit her tongue to keep the flush from reaching her cheeks and rounded on Alice. "Why did you invite him over?"

Alice took half a step back, surprise on her face. Then she pushed a lock of curls back from her forehead and narrowed her brows. "Excuse me? Because he's our friend, because he's the only other Silver we've seen in years, because he came to *see* us? Take your pick."

Jamie's hands trembled with frustration. Her knuckles, already swollen and bruised, went white as she clenched her hand into a fist. A few seconds later, with no ease in the tension within, she sank a fist-sized dent into one of the dark green lockers.

"Fine."

She ignored Alice's suspicious expression, grabbed her clothes, and made for the showers. If she was going to deal with Oliver all night—with bruised ribs on top of her already frayed temper—she was going to make him wait. Besides, this was the only time she could score hot water.

3

Broken Cities

"Valhalla, huh?" Oliver asked as the three Silver Unborn moved through the city.

They caught more than a couple stares. Some curious, some malicious, some watching because they knew Carter, knew Jamie and Alice worked for the man, and knew if anything happened, they'd get a fine reward for snitching.

"Alice came up with it," Jamie said. She tucked her hands into the pockets of her cropped jacket, wishing she'd worked harder to get the paint out of her hair. The pale strands were naturally darker at the roots and looked almost black now. The hot water in her shower had only lasted a few minutes.

Alice shrugged, stepping over a pile of coals still burning low. The metal garbage bin they'd come from rolled gently down the crumbling asphalt. Whether the people with nowhere to go had fled their warmth earlier, or if it was because they'd seen the Silvers coming, Jamie didn't know.

"It fits." Alice gestured to her own shoulders and neck. She had a handful of tattoos as well—they all did—but Jamie boasted the most. "You're rocking a whole Viking thing."

Oliver nodded. "Especially with the braids."

Jamie's stomach lurched. "The braids are utility," she snapped. "They're slicked so they're hard to grab, and they keep my hair out of my face."

Alice chuckled. "And they're hot."

Jamie's lips twitched at that. She couldn't deny her friend the smile she'd earned, and flashed Alice a quick smirk when Oliver wasn't looking.

His attention kept catching on the dark alleys, burnt-out houses, and broken shopfronts, the glass from their windows crunching underfoot.

"Is it... all like this?" he asked.

Alice perked up and glanced around. Dim light from the full moon above showed them the way, though Jamie and Alice both carried wind-up flashlights at this time of night. Streetlights still stood tall in many parts of the city. A few were solar-powered, and those came on occasionally. But most of them were obsolete, statuesque reminders of the old days.

"Not all," Alice laughed. "We're in the Strip."

"What?"

Jamie snorted at his confusion.

Alice explained. "So there's the main part of the city, the Core." She gestured behind them, where the four functioning skyscrapers gleamed like dull candles, burning electricity. "That's where wealthier Organics live, and where a lot of business runs."

"Like the fights." Oliver's tone sent another burst of irritation through Jamie.

"Yeah," she said with a scowl. "The fights, and everything else. The main market is in the center, the courthouse, jail, police precinct, hospital, mail depot..."

"Why live out here then?"

Alice laughed. "We don't. This is the Strip. It got burned up and looted really bad maybe a decade ago?" She turned to Jamie for confirmation.

Jamie shrugged.

"Right, about a decade ago, according to Mrs. Zalinsky." Alice continued, "We're on the other side of the Strip."

They passed the unspoken boundary at that moment, striding through a narrow alley and coming out on a street with functioning homes and buildings. It was late enough that most things were closed, but a few stragglers wandered the streets.

Alice did a twirl, gesturing like she was showing him something grand. "This is the *Crescent*."

Oliver glanced at Jamie.

"It's shaped like a crescent around the Strip and the Core." Her wary gaze scanned the street.

This was a more populated area, which meant they needed to be on the lookout. In the Strip, danger came from drugged out vagrants or gangs of Adams looking to prove themselves against an Unborn. They usually turned tail at the realization that she and Alice were Silvers.

The Crescent was different. Police lived here with their families. Military personnel who weren't sequestered to their tower had homes here. Civilians surrounded them. It was the kind of place where Jamie made herself small and unseen. Lashing out would get her and Alice kicked out of their apartment and possibly flagged as problem Unborn.

She'd worked too damn hard to get them to this point for her own temper to destroy what they'd built. Of course, depending on how things went with Carter and the finale next week...

She shook her head, focusing on Alice's descriptions of how things in the city worked. Oliver listened with rapt attention. He picked up information the same way the rest of them did, locking away key details and connecting her words to the things he saw around them.

Jamie watched Oliver's face as they came upon their apartment building. It was a shabby thing—like most of the Crescent. Made of brick and stone, three stories tall, with a big bulletin board in the front lobby where people tacked up notices and flyers.

His expression didn't change from mild interest as they climbed the stairs to the second floor. Alice led the way, taking him right to their door as Jamie braced herself for an evening of mundane questions when all she wanted to do was sleep.

"Nice place," Oliver said after they all shuffled into the petite sitting area.

A tiny hallway led down to one bedroom and a bathroom. Jamie and Alice had been bunk mates their entire lives, so being unable to find a two-bedroom in their price range wasn't a problem.

The kitchenette was separated from the living room via the couch. Sparse was a correct adjective to describe the space, but it was significantly more decorated than anything they'd had before. Alice had a habit of using their left-over rent money to buy random assortments of things to display on the walls.

Jamie shifted uncomfortably as Oliver stepped around the room, surveying the trinkets. He'd come to see them, sure. But there had to be something else. Travel wasn't something people did these days. Trips were a thing of the past or reserved for the disproportionately wealthy.

"Popcorn?" Alice asked, turning to look at them both from the counter. Her hand was in a cupboard, pulling out a jar of one of the only things they currently had on hand. Yellow kernels shook around inside.

"Sounds great," Oliver said. He moved his gaze from a collection of spoons, each with their own design, bent together to form a weird heart. His silver eyes met Jamie's.

She turned away, strode down the hall, and snatched a hand towel from the bathroom. It was only a few paces to the sink where Alice was pouring popcorn into a deep pot. Butter, which had cost them nearly a day's shift at the construction site, was already melted on the bottom.

Jamie waited for Alice to finish, then ran cold water over the rag and began scrubbing the roots of her hair.

"So." She didn't look at him as she spoke. "What are you doing here?"

"Jamie," Alice snapped.

"No." Jamie shot her a warning look. "He's got a reason. I want to hear it."

Oliver's steady gaze, one of the most irritating things about him in Jamie's opinion, didn't waver. He gave Alice an appreciative smile, then turned to Jamie. "I need your help."

"There it is," she muttered. "Knew you didn't come all this way to say hi."

Oliver sighed. "It wasn't far. I'm up north. Boston area."

At this, Jamie's rough cleaning of her scalp hesitated. He'd been so close. This whole time, only a few hours north. She pinched her lips together.

"How'd you know where we are?" Alice asked mildly. She poured hot popcorn into three chipped wooden bowls and carried them deftly to the couch.

Jamie followed, sitting cross-legged in her usual spot. Alice settled next to her, which left Oliver on the fold out chair. Jamie almost smiled at how he had to contort his body to fit.

The man was tall.

"I called in a favor. If I'd known sooner, I'd have..."

"Come to visit?" Jamie drawled.

"Well, maybe not," Oliver admitted. "But there's some bad stuff going on, Jamie."

Her whole body reacted to the sound of her name on his lips. She covered the jerk of her fingers by scooping a handful of popcorn and stuffing it into her face. Which would hopefully also disguise the heat that had rushed to her cheeks and the roots of her hair.

She waved the hand holding the cloth around the air. "Yeah, Oli," she said with her mouth overflowing. "There's lotsa bad stuff. Kinda all the time."

He grimaced, both at her words and the nickname she knew he hated. Smug humor pushed aside the memories that had surfaced when he'd said her name.

Alice nudged her with a shoulder and gave a "knock it off" look, which Jamie ignored.

"Have you heard what happened on the west coast?" Oliver asked.

Jamie's brow furrowed. Taking the nickname in stride without a comeback was concerning. "No."

Alice shook her head.

"An Unborn settlement was destroyed."

A storm of cold washed over Jamie's shoulders. Fear gripped her chest like an icy hand, constricting her lungs and limiting her next inhale.

"Vic?" The question escaped her as a whisper, but the other two had the same hearing she did.

Oli's piercing gaze met hers. "They only found one Silver... a man. From what I was told it was a village of mostly Coppers. Torn apart."

Jamie's stomach lurched. Alice put a hand to her lips with a slight whimper.

Oliver continued, his voice tight. "Uniforms found the mess. Every building was burned. The people just... turned on each other. It was brutal."

"We wouldn't do that," Jamie growled through gritted teeth. She tossed the now ashen rag on the floor, wanting to do the same with her bowl of popcorn but knew Alice would be the one to clean it up. So she set it down instead, the thunk reverberating around the room.

Alice shivered. "Are they sure it was Unborn attacking each other?"

Jamie scowled.

"Yeah." Oliver swallowed. "I saw some pictures from the scene. Only other Unborn could... could do that to our kind."

Alice stood. The popcorn bowl rolled, a few remaining kernels scattering onto the ragged carpet. "I need to—"

She hurried down the hall. The bathroom door slammed shut, and Jamie tried to block out the sound of Alice's stomach rejecting everything she'd eaten that day.

"You didn't have to be so—"

"Graphic?" He shook his head, hands clenched before him. "Shit, Jamie, that was the light version. The pictures were... it was like the war again. But all Unborn. Even some..." He fell silent again.

Her very bones seemed to go cold. Oliver'd always had nerves of steel. He could go through anything and, with a hot shower, come out the other side unscathed.

She'd only seen him this rattled one time before. About a year before the war had officially ended. When they'd been evacuating a small village on the edge of the hot zone. The enemy hadn't been completely cleared beforehand. Oli had been the one driving the school bus full of kids. He'd been the only survivor, blasted through the front windshield when an RPG slammed through the back of the bus. Being stuck in the medical wing for three weeks had done wonders for his wounds, but his nightmares had lasted a lot longer.

"Kids," she finished for him, her voice low. "Unborn?"

He shrugged. "Hard to tell. I don't know if anyone's figured out if we can even have them. No one I know does. They could have been orphans the Coppers took in."

She had no response to this, so she flicked the edge of Alice's bowl with her toes, knocking it upright. Down the hall the bathroom door opened, soft steps padded across the floor, and the bedroom door closed.

"She won't come back out tonight," Jamie murmured. "You can have the couch."

He nodded his thanks, and they sat a while longer, silence heavy between them like it had been the day they'd ended things.

We didn't build you to love. We built you to kill. There's no time for romance in a war.

That's what Command had said.

Jamie's back grew stiff with how tight her muscles were clenched. Her ribs still ached. Her thigh hurt more and more until she finally had to shift, had to elevate her leg to increase the blood flow and speed up the healing. Her skin was tender under her sweats. There'd be a massive bruise there, the size of her fist and as purple as the violets that grew on the side of the road in the spring.

"There's…"

She looked up.

Oliver's elbows were on his knees, his hands cradling his head. He spoke to the floor. "There's something else. Cade is dead."

4

Old Friends

ASH AND SMOKE CLOGGED *the air. Jamie staggered up, pushing off an upturned car. She yanked her hand from the hot metal, her palm red and blistering.*

Ambush.

It was supposed to be an ambush. A quick mission. Just her and a few other Silvers handling things.

Oliver.

Her heart slammed against her chest, and she whirled in the middle of the road, squinting through the haze. She couldn't hear much beyond the crackle of flames where the convoy had exploded.

She gritted her teeth and stepped forward, ignoring the biting pain in her foot. Voices reached her as she made her way off the road and between the cluster of buildings her squad had been camped at for the past three days. Waiting.

"Stop."

It was Oliver's voice. Jamie sped up, relief momentarily forming a lump in her throat.

"Cade," he said again.

There was a thud, fist against flesh, and a whimper.

Jamie hesitated. She leaned against a brick wall to her left. They were just around the corner.

"I'm doing the job," Cade responded. His voice was rough, gritty from the cigarettes he stole or traded from their handlers.

"This isn't the job." Oliver's anger seeped into his words. "We were sent for the Minister, not his entourage."

Jamie exhaled, closing her eyes for a second and gritting her teeth. This was why Vic should have been on the mission. She always kept Cade in check. But she was halfway across the continent. Jamie had hoped Oliver would be able to rein in his friend.

She squared up, all seventeen years of training in the rigidity of her back, the furrow of her brow, and stepped into the open.

Jamie swallowed, fear curling her fingers into fists. "How?"

He shook his head. "He was hunted down by Uniforms and executed."

"Why?" Jamie asked, her voice dark.

He didn't respond.

"Why, Oliver?"

He stood abruptly, running a hand across his cropped hair and heaving a sigh. "They said he killed someone. Some state official."

"What happened?" Jamie scowled. "Still can't keep a leash on him?"

Oliver snarled, and Jamie grinned. There it was, the hint of ruthless fury she'd always known they shared. It was part of the draw back then, part of what brought them together. Not just romantically, but as friends. It was something he'd never had to hide around her. She sure as hell never bothered to hide it.

Oliver took one look at her expression and turned away. He strode across the small room. His voice was quiet, and she thought it might have been to spare Alice's sensitive ears from the tale.

"He'd been having blackouts. I thought it was drugs. He... he got into some stuff he shouldn't have."

Jamie barely caught the sharp words that danced at the tip of her tongue. Oliver's voice carried enough pain; he didn't need her voicing her opinion of his closest friend. He turned around and met her gaze, and she was glad she'd held her tongue.

Tears glinted in his eyes. "I got him out of it. Like I always did, right?"

She dipped her head in a shallow nod. Her confirmation did nothing to ease the hurt in his expression.

"He was past it, Jamie. Turned things around. We were working the docks, making enough to live, saving up for something better."

She covered her grimace by shifting her braid to the front and beginning the work of undoing it. She could see them in her mind's eye. Oliver and Cade hefting boxes on some fish-smelling dock. Going back to a dingy apartment every night, the same way she and Alice did. Cade, flirting with some dairy trader the same way Alice did the baker. Mirrored lives.

"He kept coming home late. Didn't remember where he'd been. Then, one night, he came back covered in blood."

Jamie winced.

"He ran," Oliver muttered.

She shook her head. "Might have worked with regular cops, but Uniforms aren't built to let anyone escape. They've been patrolling more and more around here. Even the Adams don't like it."

"They tore him to pieces, Jamie." His voice was just above a whisper. His hands, as rough looking as she remembered, clenched into fists.

A shiver went down her spine. The room fell silent for a few long minutes. Jamie pondered Cade's death. He'd always been wild. Worse than her by a mile, and that was saying something. But she'd never killed innocents—on purpose.

She could see him as a gun for hire. A hitman for some greased-up gang-lord living on the outskirts of what was left of their society.

What she couldn't see was him getting caught.

Cade was a prick and a violent son-of-a-bitch. But he was also a Silver Unborn.

"What do you think happened?"

Oliver glanced up. His jaw loosened slightly. "I don't know. But it has to have something to do with the village out west. Reports say the Unborn there lost all sense. All reason." He rubbed his fingers across his forehead. "They went savage."

Jamie's lips twitched as she—yet again—held a handful of sharp words from slicing him apart. Instead, she tilted her head. "Why are you here, Oli? You didn't come find us just to tell us Cade died. And it's not like you need help preparing a funeral."

He shook his head. "No." He inhaled, the air filling his chest in a way that drew Jamie's gaze before she focused back on his face. "I came to get your help finding out what killed him."

Jamie rose from the couch, her movements stiff, pain flaring in her bruised ribs. "You already know what killed him."

"No, I don't." Oliver tracked her movements as she stooped and picked up Alice's popcorn bowl.

With a muffled groan, she carried her and Alice's bowls to the kitchenette. When she turned, Oliver was standing a few feet from her, his gaze intense.

"We need to find out what happened to the Unborn in that village. We need—"

"No," Jamie cut across his words. Her body ached, her stomach growled, and her heart hurt. "There is no *we*, Oliver. Alice and I have a life here. We have jobs, a roof over our heads, and enough to fill our bellies. That's my *we*. Me and her, carving out a life best we can with what we've got."

He sneered. "This is the best the great Jamie Rodina can do, huh?"

Furious heat chased the hunger from her stomach, both at his tone and his use of her chosen last name. As though he were mocking it. Her hands clenched into fists.

"You always were a fighter." Oliver stuck his hands into his pockets and leaned up against the paint-peeling wall. The nonchalant motion did not cover his bristling frustration. "Never thought you'd fight for someone else's entertainment, though."

At that, she took half a step forward, her teeth bared. "I'm about to kick your ass for my own."

"Jamie."

Alice's small voice made them turn, surprise cooling both their tempers. She'd snuck up on them. On accident, judging by the widening of her eyes as they took her in. She'd always been able to do that, to walk lighter than a feather, make no noise even as tears dripped down her cheeks.

Jamie had never met anyone else—Unborn or Adam—who cried without any sound.

"Alice." Jamie hurried forward, putting a hand on her shoulder. "You okay?"

She nodded. "I wanted to see if Oliver needs a bed."

"He can sleep on the couch," Jamie growled. "Just tonight." She gave Oliver a furious look and gently urged Alice down the hallway toward their room.

"I came to you because you've never followed the rules, Jamie." Oliver's smooth voice was low, but it carried. "I need someone willing to break them to get answers."

"Yeah?" Jamie turned, a snarl curling her lips. "Find someone else."

She ignored Alice's questions as she shut the bedroom door, slipped out of her clothes, and pulled on an old knit sweater laying on her bed. By the time she slid under the thin covers of her bottom bunk, Alice had given up. Jamie closed her eyes, trying not to picture the slaughter Oliver had described.

Trying and failing.

5

Grown in a Bottle

Payment came for the first half of the final fights. Alice's bouts went longer; she liked to stretch them out, extend the drama, so she got paid more. Jamie was certain Carter had taken more than his usual cut from the last set of her own fights, but it was enough to fill their tiny fridge and stock up on dry goods. After putting the usual amount aside to prepare for heating their apartment in the winter she didn't have the credits to buy new wraps for the coming weekend.

Alice bought them for her.

Jamie gave her friend a light shove as Alice handed over the package. It was roughly wrapped, old newspaper she'd almost certainly gotten from the baker. Jamie could count on one hand the number of presents she'd received in her life, and it took biting the inside of her cheek hard enough to bleed to stop herself from tearing up in public.

When they got home, she swept Alice into a tight squeeze as a few tears slid down her cheeks.

Oliver was gone. He'd stayed three nights, two longer than Jamie had been okay with. When they'd woken on the fourth day of his visit, he'd vanished. The spare blanket neatly folded at the end of the couch was the only sign he'd been there.

"You could have been nicer," Alice grumbled as she whipped powdered eggs with some water to get their breakfast going.

"I could have," Jamie agreed with a wicked grin.

Alice rolled her eyes. "I think we should have let him stay longer."

"Hey." Jamie reached into a cupboard and pulled out a loaf of slightly burned bread. She chopped two slices from the end, put them on plates, and set them beside the single-burner stove. "I didn't tell him to leave."

"You didn't invite him to stay either."

"No, I didn't." Jamie's joking tone went somber. "We have a life here, Alice. We don't need the kind of trouble he wanted to bring."

Silence fell for a moment, only the gentle scraping of a wooden spoon stirring eggs on the pan permeating the heavy lack of sound. Then Alice shut off the heat, moved the pan onto a thick slab of wood they used as a cutting board, and faced Jamie.

"Uniforms killed his best friend, Jamie. An entire village of Unborn was torn apart. And we have no idea if Vic—"

Jamie's stomach twinged. She pressed her lips together, fighting the burning in her eyes. "Vic can handle herself. There are thousands of Unborn on the west coast. We have no reason to think she was there."

Alice shook her head. "I'm only saying... I don't think it was unfair of him to come to us."

"He only came because he thinks I'll break the rules for him. Again."

Alice's neatly shaped eyebrows rose, incredulity in the thin line of her lips. "Wouldn't you?"

Jamie ground her teeth. "No." She swallowed. "As much of a prick Carter is, I don't mind the fights." A shadow of a grin eased her jaw.

"I *like* the fights. And I like our apartment. And I like," she tilted her head, "*most* of this city. We fit here."

Alice looked down at her hands. Her knuckles were smooth, bruises and cuts from the fights a week before already healed. Jamie's ribs were the same, the bruises she'd sustained fully faded. It paid to be a Silver. Not even Coppers healed so fast.

"I think we fit, too," Alice murmured. "But sometimes I feel like something is missing."

Jamie stepped forward and took her hands. "Me too. But we're never going to have everything, Alice. I'm not willing to lose *this* by chasing something more."

The two ate a filling breakfast and headed to the last day of their construction gigs before they took a few days off for the finals. The Organics running the site bet on the fights as much as everyone else with any spare credits in the city. They didn't mind Unborn taking a rest before fight nights.

Jamie enjoyed this work as much, if not more, than the fights. On an empty stomach it was brutal, but the repetition with which she swung the sledgehammer into massive slabs of concrete, cracking them to dust, was soothing. The steady thud, thud, thud echoed the memories of choppers above, Jamie and Alice flanking Vic, the eldest—the leader—of their squad. Weapons drawn, raised. Muzzles flashing with heat and light. Screams choked in smoke.

She slammed them all down with each stroke of the hammer.

"Valhalla."

Jamie jerked away from the wall she was breaking down, subconsciously shifting the hammer and choking up her grip for more accurate aim.

Her heart pounded as she caught sight of the man who'd spoken.

"Carter." She gritted her teeth. "Didn't think I'd see you down here. You'll get dust on your boots."

The man flashed his bright white teeth. Thick and Squat flanked him, weapons poorly hidden under their clothes.

Jamie knew Carter had influence—he'd have to with the kind of money the fights brought him—but she didn't realize he had walking-around-strapped kind of influence. It took serious work to get access to guns. And even more to pay off the police to let him keep them.

"I wanted to continue our conversation," Carter said.

The little hairs on the phoenix at the back of Jamie's neck stood on end. She flexed her forearms; the tattoo of her serial number—not quite disguised by the pattern of thorny ivy crawling up her inner left arm—rippled with the movement of her skin.

"Thought I made myself pretty clear." Jamie inhaled, concentrating on keeping her voice even. "I'm not taking a fall."

Carter scowled. His henchmen seemed to swell as they puffed their chests and bulged their biceps. It was almost laughable.

Jamie eased her grip on the hammer. She knew people on this continent—the one that saw the least amount of actual fighting during the decades-long war—didn't have a full grasp of how strong Unborn were, but these men had seen her fight. Surely, they didn't think they could take her on.

Then again, Thick and Squat weren't Carter's men because of their brains.

Carter stepped forward, distancing himself from his goons and putting his face too close to her.

Heat flared in Jamie's chest. Her limbs tensed automatically, her feet shifting to find purchase on the loose gravel she'd turned a solid wall into over the last hour of work.

Part of her fought the instinct. Knew it was built in, designed, engineered to mimic the most dangerous of beasts that thrashed and bit when cornered. She wasn't a wild animal. Yet an itch in the back of her mind reminded her that survival was part of her programming.

If Carter tried anything, she'd end him.

"You work for me, Jamie," he hissed, and she realized part of his reaction came from her words.

They weren't surrounded, but it was an active work site. There were people all around, mostly Adams, mostly men who enjoyed betting on legitimate fights.

She cocked her head, a malicious grin twisting her lips. "What's a matter?" she asked in a soft voice. "Don't want these fine folks knowing you're a cheat?"

He moved.

It was sudden, his hand coming toward her cheek. A thunk as she dropped the hammer and caught Carter's wrist instead. Surprise splattered across his face as she held him, her fingers tightening just enough that he'd lose feeling in his hand within a few seconds.

His henchmen darted forward. Jamie released Carter, taking half a step back until she butted against the wall behind her.

Squat and Thick reached for weapons.

Jamie growled her frustration. There were too many people. This place was too public for her to take them down with lethal force, and she wasn't feeling particularly merciful at the moment.

Carter seemed to have realized the same thing, or at least the part about too many people. He called off his dogs, a scowl twisting his lips. "You're too proud, Jamie." He huffed, cradling his wrist as though she'd snapped it. It might bruise, but she'd managed serious restraint on her strength. He was lucky.

She said nothing, piercing silver eyes staring him down while she kept note of the men in her peripheral vision.

"Too proud for someone grown in a damn bottle."

She kept her face bland, but as he turned and strode away through the rubble, she felt the chafe of his words. Thick and Squat followed their master like good little dogs.

Jamie spat on the ground, aware of the handful of eyes on her. She expected a conversation with the foreman would come during her break. Trouble wasn't something anyone wanted in a construction site. Especially not with someone like Carter.

Jamie bounced on the balls of her feet, fists hovering protectively in front of her face. Ahead of her, a mammoth of a woman grinned.

Blood, a gift from Jamie in the first round, seeped between the Copper's teeth. She fixed her eyes on Jamie, overconfident because of her stature. She weighed nearly three times as much, stood a full foot taller, and her biceps were the size of Jamie's thighs.

The crowd howled their approval as the two entered the third round.

"You're a big girl," Jamie taunted, pitching her voice to carry to the onlookers. "You got a big man keeping you company?"

The Copper—Hammer—grinned back. "Yeah, big man, warm hands, keeps me fed." She gave Jamie a once over, exaggerating her scornful gaze as the audience cackled. "Looks like you could use a good meal."

Jamie wiped a trickle of sweat from her brow. Hammer was good at this, better than the last Copper she faced who barely stirred the crowd at all.

"Maybe your man can take me to dinner," Jamie said with a laugh.

Hammer's expression darkened. She and Jamie circled, ensuring everyone around them caught the building tension.

"They call you Valhalla," Hammer spat. "You can eat in the halls of the dead when I'm done with you."

She swung.

Jamie dodged, using her size and speed to pummel under Hammer's arms, battling the bigger opponent's body into submission. They went another two rounds before Jamie dealt the final blow across Hammer's jaw. The big woman went down hard.

The crowd cheered. Jamie sucked in a breath and pushed down the ache in her limbs.

She raised her fists into the air. "*Valhalla!*"

"Unfallen!"

She shouted it again, louder, so they'd remember her the next night. She'd made it through to the semi-finals. Travers had been her first fight that evening, and he'd gone down like a sack of potatoes.

Maybe putting on a show like this would get Carter off her back.

"*VALHALLA!*"

The crowd screamed "*Unfallen*" loud enough that Jamie was sure the throng of people wanting to get into the building heard.

She smirked and headed to the locker room.

6

THE RING

J AMIE PACED THE LOCKER room, flexing her hands and drinking water. If Alice won this bout, the two of them would go head-to-head for the semi-finals. Then one of them would face the Tank.

The room was thick with the sticky scent of sweat. The rumble of the crowd reached her, but the sound was low, not enough to pull her attention.

She leaned against the dark green lockers, stretching her sore legs. The fluorescent lights above flickered.

She heard footsteps before the door opened. Her heartbeat remained steady, but she slinked into a corner.

"Jamie?"

She blinked at the sound of Oli's voice and stepped into view. He moved into the locker room, letting the door fall shut behind him.

"Thought you left town," Jamie said, aiming for a casual tone. Her fear, that Carter would come with dangerous intent and she'd have to kill the man who controlled the fights, faded. But tension was still tight in her chest.

Oliver raised an eyebrow. He strode to the door that took fighters to the ring and glanced through the foggy window. "Nope. Still hoping you'll change that stubborn mind."

Jamie snorted. "You know me better than that. I'm not interested in your mystery, Oli."

"Oliver."

She pursed her lips, amused. "Ahh, so you *do* still mind the nickname."

His nostrils flared, full lips curling into a scowl. "I came to *you*, Jamie. There are other Silvers out there. Other captains with cleaner records who are just as capable as you are."

Jamie's hands flexed instinctively. The words were true, and he didn't have malice in his voice, but they stung nonetheless. "So go find one of them to help you."

Oliver rolled his eyes, turning in a wide circle before leaning a shoulder on the lockers and crossing his arms. The stance was so familiar, his tensed shoulders, furrowed brow, lower lip nearly disappeared as he chewed the left side, that Jamie had a split second of time where she saw a different version of him. Younger, hair longer and in need of a trim, fewer tattoos and scars, smoother skin.

Then she blinked and the current version returned. His eyes bored into her, their gazes locked for a few seconds.

A cheer went up from the crowd beyond their little room. Oliver shook his head. "I came to *you*. Because I thought you'd care that something is happening to our people. I thought you'd want to find the truth, like you used to, no matter the cost."

Jamie ran a hand across her jaw, bitter anger rising. "Curiosity kills the captain, Oliver, remember? Maybe I've finally learned my lesson. Maybe I know how to keep my head down now."

His chuckle surprised her. The sound brought a pang of longing that she shoved down harder than any ounce of fear she'd ever felt the need to bury. She didn't *need* him. She'd never *needed* him. And missing something she didn't need—or want—was as foolish as fighting without wraps.

His grin also brought a flash of rage.

"What's so funny?" she snapped.

He shrugged, pushing off the lockers as another round of cheers went up, loud enough this time that someone clearly won the match. "If a decade at war and getting busted down to LT half a dozen times didn't teach you to follow the rules, I doubt a few years of civilized life did the trick."

"Hey Oli," Jamie growled, stepping until she was toe to toe, looking up at him with fury etched across her face. "Go fu—"

"I *won!*" Alice sang as she burst through the door from the ring.

Her happy tone faded. She looked from Oliver to Jamie, a disapproving frown—startlingly akin to Vic's—furrowing her brow.

Jamie stepped away from one of their oldest friends, heat burning her cheeks. "That's great. You and me next, Valhalla versus the Hummingbird."

Alice's raised eyebrow, and the scolding expression eased a little. She chuckled and turned to Oliver. "Now that's a nickname to make fun of. Hummingbird doesn't exactly pump fear into the enemy."

"Seems fitting though," Oliver said, his voice stiff. "You've always been the fastest."

She shrugged. "Glad you're back. Got time to have a snack with us? We have a bit of a break before we go out."

Jamie turned away, trying to mask the still present anger rippling through her veins.

"Nah." Oliver shook his head. "I'll pick something up on my way out."

"You're not staying to watch the fight?" Alice's voice matched the pouting of her lips.

"I've seen you two spar often enough."

Jamie closed her eyes, inhaling to ease the trembling in her fists. "Leaving town this time?" She wasn't facing him, but almost felt him bristle, and certainly heard the tension in his voice.

"Not just yet."

Jamie swung a leg over the bench in the center of the aisle of lockers, facing them in time to watch Alice dart over and give Oli a brief hug.

"Okay, well make sure you say goodbye before you leave."

He nodded, gave Jamie one last indecipherable look, and left.

Alice turned on Jamie and opened her mouth.

Jamie held up a hand. "Not right now, please?"

Her friend hesitated, then rolled her eyes and strode away. She returned a moment later with a plate of bread, meat, cheese, and a bowl of cherry tomatoes.

"Eat up. We only have ten minutes."

They entered the ring one at a time. Jamie went first, lifting her hands and screaming Valhalla until her throat burned. She grinned, the bruises on her face easy to ignore while the crowd chanted her name. She moved to her corner as the announcer did his bit for Alice.

"Should've done what I said."

The voice came from her lower right. She glanced down and spotted Carter looking up at her. She crouched.

"You can't tell me you didn't make a bundle last night with or without Travers. Hammer is three times my size, and we put on a show."

The man shook his head. "Too much pride. You should learn your place, Jamie."

She opened her mouth to retort, but he was already following his goons as they pushed through the crowd, taking him to his fancy box in the top row of the arena.

Jamie rolled her eyes, straightened, and turned her focus to Alice. The announcer finished listing the numerous fights Alice had won that ended with Coppers needing urgent medical attention. He nodded to Jamie, who nodded back, and hurried from the ring.

Jamie shook her head clear of thoughts of Oli, Carter, and how she and Alice would pay rent if she lost this and the construction crew gig. She inhaled.

Burnt popcorn, sweat, urine, perfume... the amalgamation of scents burned her nose. She concentrated. Narrowed the focus until all she saw was Alice's mischievous grin. All she smelled was her friend's lilac perfume. All she heard was the steady in and out of her own breath.

The crowd knew both fighters. Knew they were friends. The trick here wouldn't be riling anyone up, it would be making sure neither of them held back enough to make a boring fight.

The bell rang.

They sprang forward.

Alice landed the first blow. A punch to Jamie's head that blurred her vision for a few perilous seconds. She recovered quickly, circling as Alice darted around the mat faster than should have been possible. She was a dancer, weaving in and out of Jamie's swings and slamming punches and kicks into her each time there was an opening.

Jamie landed a few as well, harder blows designed to stun her opponent and give her a moment to breathe.

The bell rang. The first round ended.

Alice grinned at her from across the ring, blood dripping from her nose.

Jamie stuck out her tongue. The crowd laughed and cheered.

The two squared up again. The bell rang.

Alice froze.

Jamie, about to leap in with a right hook, hesitated. Her friend was still as a statue, eyes fixed straight ahead. A full three seconds passed. The crowd grew restless.

"Alice?" Jamie hissed.

The silver of Alice's eyes dimmed.

Icy fear gripped Jamie's chest. She put her arm up, ready to call the fight a draw and get help.

Alice's head twitched.

Her face was smooth, expressionless as porcelain as her gaze focused on Jamie. Her eyes... her eyes were so dark. The black of her pupil had claimed the silver, leaving no trace of the Unborn heritage they shared.

Jamie's hands moved on instinct, settling in front of her, ready to defend. She opened her mouth again, Alice's name on the tip of her tongue.

Alice swung.

Jamie blocked. Again and again as Alice moved with speed Jamie had only seen on the battlefield. This wasn't right. This wasn't the fight they were supposed to have.

"Alice," Jamie said, uncaring of who heard now. "Get it together. What's going on?"

A blow knocked her low. She staggered. Alice swiped with a leg, her face blank as she took Jamie's feet out from under her. Jamie hit the mat with both hands, yelping at the way her wrist twisted under her weight.

"Stop," Jamie called out. "There's something—"

Her words were cut short by a knee to her face. Blood spurted in her mouth. She'd bitten through her tongue.

She reeled. Scrambled backward as Alice stomped down where her ankle had been seconds before. Jamie rolled. A kick breezed past her braids.

With a grunt of pain, Jamie twisted on her shoulder, using her legs to knock Alice's feet from under her.

Jamie stood quickly, panting.

"Alice." Desperation filled her voice. Her vision wasn't right, things were blurred. One too many blows to the head. "Please. *Alice, snap out of it.*"

There was no expression. No fury or malice to be found as Alice rose from the mat and rushed her yet again.

Alice cornered her. Small fists rained down on Jamie as she put her arms over her head, curling into herself to stop Alice hitting a vital organ.

Training—survival—kicked in.

Jamie stopped holding back. She snuck past Alice's speed and landed a few blows, dodging twice as many as she took.

She whirled around, shoving Alice into the cage. Alice slammed against the metal grate and turned back, a slice bleeding across her forehead.

Jamie grimaced. Fear thundered through her. Sweat ran with the paint on her forehead, dripping down her temples and mingling with the blood from various slices across her face.

She had to end this. Had to stop Alice and figure out what the hell was going on with her.

Jamie feinted, twisting at the last second and throwing her arm around Alice's neck, locking it in place with her wounded wrist. She held fast. Tightened her grip and winced through the elbow slams Alice aimed at her ribs.

"Stop," Jamie grunted. "Alice, stop."

She squeezed harder. Cut off circulation. Knock her out. Get her help.

But Alice thrashed even harder.

"Alice." Jamie's wrist, already aching from the way she'd landed, grew weak. She shifted, putting her back against the cage for extra leverage. "*Please.*"

Alice's nails dug into her arms. The smaller woman kicked, rearing back and forth in her drive to escape.

Time slowed as something cracked.

The snap reverberated through Jamie's arms. She recognized the sound. Had heard it a handful of times on close quarter missions. Had heard it each time she'd ripped someone's head the wrong way. Broken their neck. But she hadn't...

The effort Jamie put into keeping Alice at bay now went to holding her up. Holding her body up.

Realization hit.

Jamie let go, and Alice's body fell. Drifted in slow-motion. Her back hit the mat with a thud.

Jamie only noticed she'd stopped breathing when her lungs cramped. She gasped in air, staring down at her friend. Her sister. Her family.

Alice stared back, eyes silver again. Silver and unblinking and empty. Her neck was twisted all wrong.

Tears pooled in Jamie's eyes. Pain screamed in every inch of her, loss driving so far past the physical hurt it was as if her body was numb.

Slowly, Jamie came back to her senses. The crowd was silent. Or her ears weren't working. Her head rose, eyes moving past Alice's body.

Her body...

Across the ring, a set of silver eyes flashed in the light. Jamie followed the glint.

Oliver stood at the edge of the cage, his expression as broken as she felt, tears streaming down his cheeks. He met her eye, his lips trembling.

Emptiness encompassed Jamie's insides. She looked back at Alice's graceful body. It was bloodied and bruised from the fight.

Jamie's gaze stuck on the awkward angle of her sister's neck.

Nausea built and crested before she had a chance to recognize it. She spun, put a hand against the cage to hold herself up, and wretched.

7

ECHOES

REVERBERATIONS OF THE SNAP echoed in Jamie's bones. She flexed, unable to shake the ghost pressure of Alice's neck along her forearm.

She sat in the locker room where she and Alice had shared a snack less than thirty minutes before. Her vision couldn't seem to focus; her mind buzzed with a low thrum of a kind of horror she'd only lightly touched before now.

She'd taken lives. More than she could count—and she'd tried. The little X's, checkered across her left bicep, had kept track of her first hundred kills. When the space had filled and there were still enemies coming, comrades falling, and death plaguing their days, she'd given up the count.

This wasn't the same.

"You didn't kill her."

Jamie blinked away the haze taking her vision. She looked up as Oliver said it again.

"It wasn't you. You didn't do this."

Paint streaked down Jamie's forehead, though she'd gone cold enough that the sweat on her body made her shiver. She didn't respond.

"They moved her." Oliver sat beside her on the bench, folding his hands together as he leaned his forearms onto his legs. "Cleared the ring for the finale."

The numb sheet of ice protecting Jamie from the brunt of her feelings cracked. Fury spiked through. At his words. At the thought that they expected her to fight after what had happened. At the realization that no one in the crowd cared that Alice was...

"We need to go," Jamie said in a low, rumbling growl that carried none of the pain she felt within.

"Jam—"

She stood, interrupting his words with her abrupt movements. She crossed to her locker, pulled it open, tugged on her jacket, and began piling things into her bag. "I'm not doing the finale, Oliver."

"I know." His voice was soft, but enough to make her pause.

She glanced at him. Grief was laced into the crinkle of his brow, the pinch of his lips, and the faint traces of white where his salty tears had dried on his dark skin.

He nodded. "Whatever you need. Whatever comes next. I'm in."

Guilt stirred in her belly, barely noticeable compared to the all-encompassing remorse and blame she felt for Alice's death. She bit her tongue, fighting down the memory of her dismissal of Oliver's worries. Now was not the time or place to echo his sentiment. Nor were they far enough from prying ears for her to ask where they needed to go to get the revenge she sought.

Alice's locker was next. Jamie emptied it with the same cold callousness she'd seen on Vic's face each time they'd had to clear out a fallen friend from their squad. The only time that stoic expression had faltered was when her sister tattooed the losses on her arm. She blamed the pain for her tears the few times they'd caught her crying.

It was a rare thing.

"Come on."

Oliver followed her quick pace out of the room. "Are they going to just let you leave? There's a lot of money riding on this next fight."

She continued without looking back. Barely contained rage simmered on her skin, a blazing heat slowly burning away everything she'd thought she was. Everything she'd built. She pulled her hood up, covering her ash-painted braids.

"They can try to stop me."

No one tried.

Either because the bustling throng of people were too busy getting drinks, placing bets, and talking about the scandal of death to recognize her. Or because anyone who did recognize her was smart enough to keep their distance.

Fragments of conversation hit her as she pushed through the crowd to the exit. Muttered conspiracies, condolences, and contemptuous remarks about Alice's sudden death only served to stoke the flames of rage within Jamie.

They made it to the street, then to the Strip. Darkness surrounded them, and Jamie was grateful. The lack of light felt appropriate. There was no light in her life anymore, why should there be in the sky?

"Jamie..." Oliver had begun a sentence many times in the past twenty minutes. He'd not gotten past her name. "I—"

"Was it the same?" she asked.

He hesitated. Jamie wheeled, looking at him for the first time since they'd left the locker room.

"What happened to Alice, was it the same thing that happened to Cade? To the Unborn in that village out west?"

He ran a hand over his head, his face scrunching in a grimace. "I think so. It'd be one helluva coincidence if not. And I've... I've never seen Alice like that."

Jamie nodded, her suspicion confirmed. "What do you have?"

"What?"

"You came to me for help. What do you have to go on?"

Oliver sighed. "Not much. Best I can tell the big stuff has only happened on the west coast. I was... I was going to try to get to the scene."

Jamie closed her eyes, snapping them open almost immediately at the sight burned into her eyelids. Nope, no closing her eyes for a while. "Okay."

"Okay?"

"Okay," she repeated, her tone filled with the frustration within. "We get to the west coast. Across the wasteland, around, however it needs to be done."

"We have very little to go on," Oliver murmured.

Jamie nodded. Her brow furrowed. "Carter."

"What?"

"Carter," she said again; their conversation moments before the fight fluttered to the front of her mind. "He wanted me to take a fall. I refused. He definitely had something up his sleeve. Do you think—"

"An Organic with no military ties was behind whatever happened to Alice?"

Jamie scowled. "It's possible."

Oliver nodded. "Possible, but not all that likely. Alice had me do some digging—"

"What?" She stumbled on a bit of rubble, turning back to look at him again.

He shrugged a shoulder, the movement nearly lost in the darkness. "She was looking out for you. Wanted to make sure Carter didn't have bigger things going on."

Pain rippled through Jamie's stomach as she clenched every muscle to avoid letting out her grief.

"And?"

His silver eyes landed on her for a brief second, and she felt the calculations in his appraisal. "Nothing. He's a big fish here, but that's it. A few trading contacts, some nasty human trafficking—Unborn trafficking," he corrected with a snarl, "but nothing connected to the military. Nothing that would suggest any kind of power to make something like... like whatever that was."

Jamie nodded, making her way to the gap between burnt out buildings that would lead them to the Crescent and her and Alice's apartment.

The roads were quiet. For a few blocks.

Muffled shouts and an all too familiar crackling reached Jamie's ears two turns from their building. Dread ate a pit in her stomach.

She moved faster, jogging down a dim street and turning—

"Oh shit," Oliver huffed behind her.

Her apartment was on fire. Not just hers, of course, the whole building was lit with flames. But it was clear from the roaring on the second floor that the blaze had started there. Her neighbors had poured onto the street. Tears flowed in abundance, parents cradled their children, people ran for sand and water.

Stockpiles were stored every few blocks. They had to be, with the city falling apart and no real fire department around to handle disasters.

Community handled them instead.

Lines had already formed, sweaty Coppers alongside Adams as they passed buckets toward the blaze. Handfuls of watchers waited with bins to put out any sparks that might attack the neighboring buildings.

Oli leapt into action. He brushed past Jamie, hurrying to the men and women giving commands. Through the buzz of nearly unbearable fury, Jamie caught him asking if anyone was left in the building.

The answer was no.

He asked if they were sure.

And Jamie's fury grew. She clenched her hands so tight her nails cut into her palms.

The people running the volunteer fire-crew knew the building was empty. Because Carter's men had evacuated it before they'd lit Jamie and Alice's apartment. They'd made sure every one of their neighbors knew who was responsible for the loss of their homes.

She felt the eyes on her, even as she closed her own. Felt the burn of their gazes almost as strong as the flames that consumed the last dregs of the life she'd built, fitting together pieces of a broken world to create a home.

"Jamie?"

She snapped open her eyes, taking half a step back and lifting her fists. A young man stood before her, the innocence in his eyes simultaneously reassuring and infuriating.

She recognized him. He had burns on his hands, soot in his dusty blond hair, and scorch marks on his apron. Alice's baker.

Her heart lurched.

He must have noted the recognition in her gaze because he nodded, a flash of relief cutting across his worried expression. He reached toward her.

Jamie took another step back, her lip curling in anger, until she realized he held a folded paper out to her.

"I was so worried you and Alice were in there," he said with a grin.

Buzzing, like a mild electric shock, ran through her arms and chest. She said nothing.

"I, uh." He hesitated, looking around. "I have this for Alice. The post came this afternoon, and I wanted to..." He flushed and stuck his hand out even further.

Jamie took the letter with stiff hands. Her knuckles were bruised. Was it Alice's blood cracking across the creases in her skin or her own?

"I'm, uh, I'm gonna go help." He shuffled his feet, still not moving. After a second, he looked up at her. "I know they're trying to blame you, but you should know that most of us understand it's more complicated than that. We know Carter is responsible for this. Not you."

The words reached her, as much as she tried to shunt them from her mind. Jamie's jaw tightened, her teeth grinding against each other. Eventually, to get him to leave, she nodded.

He dashed back to the line.

Oliver returned to her side a moment later. "The building was empty when the fire started. I think we can—"

Jamie cut across his words by holding up the sheet of paper folded in her hand. "We should leave."

The muscles in his neck and jaw tightened. "We can help."

"They have it handled," Jamie snapped.

It was true enough. There were a dozen Copper Unborn who lived in the building; they had plenty of manpower. The flames were already starting to go down.

Still, the heat of the blaze was minimal compared to Oliver's gaze as Jamie turned and stalked away. The bags, hers and Alice's, were heavy on her shoulders.

Jamie hesitated at the intersection. She knew the way out of the city vaguely but well enough to get them on their way toward the Wasteland. However, there was unfinished business to attend to.

Carter didn't get Alice killed... probably. But he sure as hell destroyed the homes of just about everyone Alice had been friendly with. The sounds of the children, sobbing and scared as their parents watched everything go up in flames, briefly drove the sound of the snap from Jamie's mind.

There was the slip of paper in her hand as well. A message for Alice.

Jamie glanced down, realization and curiosity clicking at the same time. She moved to the side, where a beam of light fell from one of the few remaining light posts in the city. Oliver hurried behind her.

"Jamie, what—"

"Alice got a letter."

He raised an eyebrow. "From who?"

"Exactly," Jamie growled. She unfolded the wrinkled parchment and stared down at the blocky typed words.

It took a few seconds for the beginning to click. The presence of her name as well as Alice's. The numbers and letters next to them. Digits, which matched the tattoo on her inner left elbow. They were a way to label her. Her and every other Unborn: Gold, Silver, and Copper alike.

It had been a long time since she'd seen them written out beside her name like this.

The words under the identification were even harder to process.

"Was in the Unborn town, you might have heard by now. Escaped. Be careful. Unborn hacked. Working on it. Found a safe place. Get here."

A set of coordinates and the name of a town Jamie had never heard of, and then the final chunk of words.

"Miss you. I'm sorry.

Vic."

Whatever had been left of Jamie's heart before reading her eldest sister's words shattered. Tears ran down her cheeks, slow and salty and hot against the cool night air.

"She..." Oliver stumbled over the words, tears clogging his throat. "She *was* there. Jamie, Vic might know who we're fighting."

Jamie closed her hand around the paper, scrunching it into a tight ball. Her anger wasn't so blinding that she threw it away, but she stuffed it into her bag more aggressively than was necessary.

"Great," she said through barely open lips. "That's the next stop then."

Her simmering anger built to a boil. Vic knew where they were. For how long? The whole time? She could've come to find them years ago.

And this letter. Jamie's chest constricted. She struggled to inhale, to push down the rage that came with the knowledge that if this had come a day sooner...

"Next stop?" Oliver's hesitant voice interrupted her thoughts.

"Yeah." Jamie shouldered her bag again. "After I take care of something here. You don't have to come. I can meet you outside the city."

Oli shifted his muscular frame, positioning himself in her eye-line. She scowled.

"I'm not going anywhere, Jamie."

She met his gaze, silver on silver, for a few seconds. There was too much emotion in her.

Not the way of a soldier.

Jamie's scowl deepened at the unwanted memory of one of their handlers growing up.

Sympathy, empathy, love. Emotions. Unnecessary and dangerous. Not the way of a soldier.

"Good," Jamie snapped, drawing her mind back to the present. "This guy has muscle. Look big."

Oliver squinted with a somewhat bemused expression, glancing down at his 6 foot 2 inch, tree-trunk of a frame, and cocked his head at her. "What, exactly, are we going to take care of?"

Jamie didn't answer him. She picked up a brisk pace toward the Core, knowing exactly where Carter would be right now, and knowing exactly what she wanted to do when she found him.

8

Supers

T HOUGHTS OF ALICE WERE out of her mind for the time being, and Jamie fed on the rage burning inside her like a starving dog. Wanting to hurt Carter kept the crashing tidal wave of pain at bay.

"He can't think he can do this," she said as Oliver followed her into the bright lights of the Core. "Burn down an apartment building with no repercussions."

"Jamie." The warning in his tone almost made her laugh. That tone had never worked on her.

"If he gets away with this, what stops him next time? What stops him doing it again without warning the residents? It was only him wanting everyone to turn on me that saved their lives this time."

Oliver sighed but continued after her as she turned and stalked into the nightlife district. They were near where the fights took place, and a brief twinge of nerves went through Jamie. They'd have shut down the finale by now, without her there to compete. Or they called up some poor schmuck she'd already beaten to go up against the reigning champ. If that was the case, it was likely the fight was already over anyway.

Which meant spectators would be moving on to other evening events, increasing the chances that they'd see her. The silver in her eyes would prevent most from attempting to get their money's worth of blood. But it wouldn't stop them all, and she wanted to be quick.

"Here," Jamie said. She took an abrupt left, stepping under the awning of a gaudy neon lit building. Another waste of electricity by the wealthy while the poor spent most nights in the dark.

Oliver stopped at the curb, glancing up with a blush rising in his dark cheeks. "This is—"

"A strip club," Jamie finished with an eye roll. "Yeah, it's where Carter is after just about every fight night. Let's go."

She didn't wait for him, pushing through the glass double-doors and past the bouncer whose name she'd never bothered to learn. The Adam tried to stop her, but one snarl was all it took for him to back off.

"Don't cause trouble," he said in a weak attempt to maintain his status as she strode down the short velvet hallway.

Jamie shrugged off her bags, handing them back without a glance. Oliver took them. She heard his intake of breath as they stepped into the vast main room of Supers, the strip club owned and operated by Carter.

Booths lined the walls, little stands before each of them for women to dance on. The main stage stuck out like a knife, allowing dancers to catwalk up and down it in their barely-there outfits.

The room was lit with red lights and stank of cigars and alcohol. It wasn't the kind of place Jamie expected to find any of the men from the construction site. This was a high-end establishment with the type of liquor that didn't come cheap.

"What the hell..." Oliver's tone was filled with the same disgust Jamie had felt the first time she'd set foot in the place.

Carter had offered her and Alice jobs at Supers when they'd started joining fights. One look at the cages dangling throughout the room, with Copper Unborn wearing next to nothing inside, and she'd nearly ripped his head off. Only Alice's cool temper and strong grip had kept Jamie from killing the man then and there.

She followed Oliver's gaze to the twin cages near the stage. Stunningly beautiful Unborn swayed to the easy music filling the break between main-stage dancers. Their copper eyes glinted in the ruddy light. Smiles dazzled their faces.

Jamie knew better than to believe the expressions.

"They're on drugs," she said in a low voice. She yanked her jacket zipper all the way up in an attempt to keep some of the revulsion at bay.

A waitress wearing a pink mini-skirt and a white lace bra raised an eyebrow at them as she passed.

Jamie did a quick count. The room wasn't overly crowded, but she had no way of knowing how many men were counting cash or getting lap dances in the side rooms.

Oliver glanced at her. "What?"

She jerked her chin at the cage nearest them as she walked toward the largest booth in the farthest corner. "The Unborn. We weren't built to be center of attention like this. A lot of them are on something to cut the stress of it."

Oliver's jaw twitched, the muscles in his neck bulging at her words and the sights before them. "Can't we do something about this?" he demanded softly, an echo of the way he'd always followed the chain of command during the war.

Questioning her, but always quietly, always without alerting the Unborn under her command.

"No." Jamie's gaze found her prey, and the rest of their conversation faded to the back of her mind. "Not unless you've got jobs for them all."

He didn't respond, but his footsteps followed her across the awful maroon carpet toward the booth where Carter sat.

Jamie came to a stop in front of his table, just beside the little dais where a young woman—barely more than a teenager—danced. Jamie turned to the girl, a brunette with a pixie cut and bright blue eyes. "Leave."

The girl, one of the few Adams currently working, shot a scared look toward Carter. The man waved a lazy hand, and she scurried away.

Thick and some other Organic muscle she didn't recognize sat in the booth with their boss, one on either side to stop random people sliding in. A pair of girls sat squeezed beside Carter. They looked everywhere but at Jamie.

The henchmen kept their gazes on Oliver, who had come up behind Jamie seething with barely contained anger. It came off him like waves.

Carter was the only one looking at her. The scornful derision on his face did nothing to further her fury; it was already at a peak.

They stared at each other for a long moment. Then he took the cigar from his lips and spoke: "I told you to take the fall."

Jamie leaned forward, planting her palms on the table as Carter's goons pulled guns from under their jackets. "I told you to find someone else." Her voice was low, a murmur meant for that table alone.

"You cost me a lot of money, Jamie. Even more when you walked."

"Alice is dead," she hissed, spit flying from between her teeth. "That wasn't enough for you? You had to burn down our home?"

He shrugged. A vain attempt to mask the fear that flashed across his face as Jamie's rage began to show. "That was put in place before she went nuts."

Pain flickered through Jamie's chest. She sucked in a breath to stop herself launching across the table at his throat. "Did you have anything to do with it?"

Carter frowned, true confusion clouding his gaze. "The fire? You needed to be taught a lesson, Jamie. I can't have people disobey me with no repercussions."

"Not the fire." She leaned closer, the shallow table doing little to block her from him. "Alice. Did you have something to do with Alice? And keep in mind, I'll know if you're lying."

Carter swallowed. His henchmen raised their guns, but he cast a glance at Oliver, still standing guard behind Jamie, and shook his head. "I... no. I didn't."

Jamie nodded. The fear on his face, and Oliver's previous digging, was enough to convince her that Carter didn't have the connections to cause whatever had made Alice go berserk.

She remained silent for a long moment. The table was frozen in limbo, the girls trembling with nerves, the guards unsure of how to respond to two Silvers in front of them, and Carter staring at Jamie with his ever-present scorn underneath the fear.

"Tell me," Jamie said, her voice back to a normal volume. "Did you order your men to evacuate the building? Or did they do that themselves?"

"I—" The confusion on Carter's face was enough. He hadn't known. He'd planned on burning the apartments down with no care for the people inside. It was only the mercy of his minions that had spared her neighbors.

It was likely the men he'd sent would be punished for warning them.

Jamie reached across the short gap between them. Faster than the human eye could track, she latched onto Carter's wrist. The cigar fell from his fingers as he let out a yell.

It took mere seconds to snap his wrist backward, the crack drawing screams from the girls. The henchmen pointed their guns at Jamie, and she heard the tell-tale sound of someone racking the slide.

The idiots wanted to shoot her.

She bared her teeth at Carter. "Tighten your leash, or I'll remove the hand."

The man was pale as a sheet, sweat dripping from his brow as he sobbed ragged breaths. His voice came in a low grunt.

Jamie smiled at the audible pain laced in his words.

"Put 'em down."

She didn't have to look to know they'd obeyed. Their guns thunked onto the wooden table.

"You're a rich man, Carter," she whispered.

He heard it. Through his own moaning and the chattering teeth of the terrified girls next to him, the way he looked at her told her he heard her voice.

"You'll be in a cast for a while, but you have the money to get this fixed."

She snapped his pointer finger.

Another scream split from Carter's lips. The girls were sobbing now, curled into themselves as they cried. The goons shifted. There was a thud of fist on flesh, and Jamie figured Oli was handling any resistance from Thick and the other one.

"The people whose homes you destroyed aren't rich. They don't have the same opportunity to heal that you do." She met his eye. Tears streamed down his ruddy cheeks. The cigar burned slowly on the table, flecks of ash falling onto the dark wood.

"Think about that, next time you try to teach someone a lesson."

She snapped his middle finger at the knuckle joint. There was no scream this time, only desperate moaning as Carter nodded, begging her to stop.

Jamie released his hand.

She straightened. Oliver stood to the right, the bags on the ground next to him and a fresh bruise reddening his knuckles.

The nameless henchman was on the ground, unconscious. Thick had stayed in his seat, now staring fixedly at the table.

Jamie looked up at Oliver, wanting to thank him but not knowing how. The words wouldn't come out right. Not with everything roiling so furiously in her mind.

"Let's go."

He followed her from Supers, sparing one last glance at the comrades dancing seductively in ornate wire cages. Jamie's stomach churned at leaving them behind.

It's not about saving everyone.

Another uninspiring speech they'd been given after a failed mission. Failed in the sense that they hadn't completed their objective. Vic had brought them all back alive.

It's about defeating the enemy. No matter the cost.

Jamie breathed in the words as she strode out of the Core with Oliver by her side.

She moved through the Stripe and the Crescent, past the occupied homes and into the remains of suburbs. The adrenaline of hurting Carter fueled her for a ways, but eventually each step radiated pain, internal and external, from wounds on her body and her heart.

She didn't care. None of it mattered.

Not Carter burning down her apartment. Not the fight she'd walked away from, guaranteeing more than a handful of enemies if she ever returned. Not the letter crumpled in her bag.

She'd lost everything except Alice five years ago when the war ended. She'd thought they'd built something, but it had been hollow. A shell of a life with only Alice holding it together.

Dawn broke over the bombed out remains of the sprawling neighborhoods. And still, they walked.

Jamie didn't know who, or how, or why this had happened. She didn't know where to go, or when she'd come face to face with the person or people responsible.

But she knew she would. She'd look them in the eyes when she killed them. She'd mark a final X on her arm, a final tally to prove she'd avenged Alice.

9

A SHIFT

SHOTS RANG OUT. DISTANT, *but getting closer. Vic put an arm over Jamie's torso, keeping her pinned to the wall while the mission lead stuck her head out to check for enemies. Beside Jamie, also coated in ash and dust, Alice huddled close.*

The three wore heavy gear, but it felt like nothing compared to the weights they'd worn during training. They carried guns longer than Alice's forearm, each piece as familiar as their own hands. They'd trained for months just for this mission, yet it had all gone wrong.

It kept all going wrong.

Vic was determined. Jamie read it on her face as easily as she could count to ten. Came from growing up together.

Alice was scared, Jamie was angry, and Vic was determined. They'd make it out of this one; that much was true just from the expression on Vic's face as she turned back to them. Whether or not they'd survive their punishment for failing to capture the city with only them and a dozen coppers each... that was a different question.

Jamie jolted awake.

Exhaustion weighed on her, begged her to lie back down and rest her bones.

She would not. Could not.

The memory her mind had pulled up was one she was used to dreaming about. Little nightmare scenarios that were only brought to the surface when she was asleep. In consciousness Jamie was usually able to keep her memories happier, or at least less excruciating.

But it wasn't that memory that had jerked her from sleep. It was the crack. The snap of Alice's neck, felt in every nerve of Jamie's arms, in every vestibule of her heart, in every breath she took that her sister didn't.

The snap was what woke her, and as she rubbed sleep from her eyes, her ears caught the sound again.

Jamie didn't freeze. She continued her movements as though she'd heard nothing, but every sense heightened to pinpoint the potential threat.

She and Oliver had traveled west through the day. They'd left the city behind and found a main road that was once an interstate. Back when everyone owned a car and traveling more than thirty miles wasn't a ridiculous notion for the rich.

By nightfall, after nearly thirty-six hours of being awake, they'd come to a much smaller town. Oliver had suggested sleeping in the woods a fair distance away, and Jamie agreed. Neither were certain how the Adams here would react to a pair of Silver Unborn. One of whom still had blood stains on her skin.

Jamie didn't know if the person skulking through the woods was there for them or was perhaps a hunter looking for an early morning kill. Or if it was something else entirely—a hungry beast tired of feeding on rabbits. Each option meant danger.

She crouched, using a long stick to stir the embers of their fire. At the same time, she clicked her tongue against her teeth in a familiar pattern. Two, a pause, and a third.

Oliver's eyes opened where he lay, his breath as steady as it had been seconds ago, but his whole body was alert now. He met her gaze.

The two waited a few minutes, Oli laying as though he were still asleep, Jamie packing up their things as though nothing was wrong. The person, or people, or creatures in the woods didn't move again. Once Jamie had everything ready, she pretended to wake Oliver, and the two made their way back to the road.

"A deer?" Oliver asked in a low voice as their boots found purchase on crumbling asphalt.

Jamie shook her head. "Maybe. Sure as hell sounded like footsteps."

"Maybe raiders. Saw what we are and decided not to risk it."

Jamie snorted. "Yeah. That tracks. Bad news for the town though."

He nodded, looking out at the little cluster of homes and shops making up a decent sized village still a couple miles away.

The Wasteland was days away, if not longer. Walking nonstop wasn't an issue for them, but even a Gold wouldn't make it across the several hundred mile stretch of toxic land and air that split America in two. Not on foot.

Putting aside transportation issues, there was also the challenge of avoiding raiders—groups of asshole Adams who decided working for credits wasn't good enough for them.

There was a lot of terrain between them and Vic's coordinates. The distance felt almost insurmountable.

"What's the plan, Cap?" Oliver asked.

Jamie rolled her eyes. "Not a captain, remember? I got bumped again just before the surrender."

He shrugged.

She went quiet for a moment, biting down the fury that threatened to whip out at his lack of memory. Then again, he hadn't been there for the actual demotion.

He'd walked away before it had happened.

"The plan," Jamie said, exhaling her words as hunger gnawed a hole in her stomach, "is to get some food. We need a vehicle, or enough credits to book transport across."

"You don't want to go around?"

She scowled, her mind flashing to the crumpled-up note tucked in her bag. "No. That'll take too long. I want to get to Vic and find out what the hell is going on."

"Jamie." Oliver put a hand on her arm.

She stared at it for a few seconds before he removed it. Cold sank into her where his fingers had been. She'd almost forgotten how warm he was.

She raised an eyebrow. "What?"

"It's just... do you want to talk about—"

"No."

Oliver exhaled, a low growl rumbling in the back of his throat. Jamie heard it, noted the way his eyes narrowed, the muscles in his jaw clenching with annoyance.

The urge to walk away itched at the back of her neck. The desire to tell him to shut up, to leave her alone, to be quiet until she damn well wanted him to talk drove her to pick at one of the gnarled scars on the back of her hand. A painful habit she'd had since she'd thrown herself in front of a dropped frag grenade when she was eleven.

That would be beyond unfair. She knew it. Knew it deep enough in her broken heart that she resisted the urge and met his eye instead.

"I don't, Oliver. I don't want to talk about it. I don't want to think about it. The only thing I want to do is kill the person responsible in the most painful way possible."

His eyes didn't widen. There was no surprise or fear or judgment in his gaze as he gave a slow nod. "I understand."

Jamie gritted her teeth. He'd lost Cade, that was true, but none of the other Unborn had been as close as she, Alice, and Vic had been. Their creator had made a point of turning the three of them into a family. Into sisters.

"Maybe when it's done," she said in a low voice. "Maybe then we can talk about it. But right now I need revenge, not a therapy session."

The bite in her words made his mouth twitch, but the rest of his expression remained smooth. "All right, then. Let's find a way to cross the Wasteland and kill these bastards."

There was little to be found in the village. Oliver had a few credits saved up, so he was able to buy them sandwiches at a small deli. Longer lasting provisions would need to be found elsewhere. There was no general store to speak of.

Jamie stretched her shoulders and neck as she waited for Oliver to use an actual bathroom before they continued on. Small as the town was, there were still people going about their business.

Lingering dark looks had her on edge. A few too many Adams whispering amongst each other brought a nagging worry to the forefront of her mind.

A village out west had gone berserk. Oliver had told her and Alice about it before she'd heard anything from anyone else, but was it possible that rumors had gotten around?

They left as soon as Oliver was done. Jamie would have liked to collect some supplies, and perhaps trade some of the weight off of her back, but her gut told her they needed to move on.

They strode down the potholed road and made it past the final few houses without incident.

"I wonder if those weren't the footsteps you heard," Oli murmured, his breath warm against her ears as he leaned in while they were moving.

She followed his gaze to a cluster of young men watching them from the woods parallel to the street. One had a string of rabbits slung across his shoulder. The others wore hunting gear. No guns, but they had knives, sling-shots, and what looked like a crude wooden bow.

"Maybe." Jamie faced the road. "That town seem strange to you?"

"Stranger than the city? Yeah. Felt like there were more eyes on us."

She nodded. "I wonder if there's something we don't know going on."

"There's a lot we don't know." His bitter tone struck a chord within her.

She shot him a grimace. "Wish we had Christian here."

Oli chuckled, still a dark sound, but without the bitter edge. "Damn, he'd sure as hell come in handy right now."

Jamie's cheek jerked, a grin wanting to force its way out. Christian was a Copper and had served under the two of them on more than one occasion. The man had a knack for collecting information he wasn't supposed to have.

"Hell..."

They slowed to a stop, and Jamie watched Oli take in the vastness ahead of them as sadness clouded his features.

"I'd take any of the old crew." He shook his head, brushing a hand across his short, military style buzz cut. "It was just me and Cade in

Boston. We saw plenty of other Unborn, but no one we knew. No one we fought with."

Jamie waited a few seconds, then picked up the pace again. "It was the same in Philly. Loads of Coppers, even a Silver or two, but no one from any of our units."

They walked the remainder of the day. Oliver offered, once, to carry her or Alice's bag. After seeing the look on her face, he didn't bring it up again.

That evening they discussed the crossing. The Wasteland was still far. Far enough that if they'd had the fortune of running across a vehicle of any kind, Jamie would've had little regret stealing it.

The only cars they spotted along the way were rusted out junkers in packed lots.

"Going around takes..." Oli glanced up at the night sky. His silver eyes glinted with the moon and firelight. A second passed, his lips moving while he did the math. "A week and a half. And that's if we can go north. If we have to take the southern route—"

"A helluva lot longer." Jamie poked the fire with a stick. Her stomach gave an audible grumble.

She should eat. Fill her belly with the remaining half a sandwich in Oliver's bag. But it had tasted like ash when she'd made herself take small bites on the road.

Instead, she stacked hers and Alice's bags against the cluster of rocks at her back, leaned against them, and watched the stars move overhead until she finally fell asleep.

The next day saw them enter a larger town. Not as big as the city, but certainly large enough for a general goods store.

And possibly information.

"Better reception so far," Jamie murmured. The two strode up main street with a more standard number of glances—and only a handful of them suggesting animosity.

"Stay sharp," Oliver said with a nod.

Her lip curled, temper sparking at the unnecessary reminder. "See you in a bit."

They split up. Oliver headed to the general store to gather lasting provisions for the trek and ask about transport. Jamie went in search of information and a place to unload the heavy bags she'd been carrying for three days.

She passed a sheriff's truck and briefly pondered the possibility of causing a full-blown manhunt. Then she shook out of it. It was one thing to handle Carter, a crime-lord who had an already strained relationship with the police built mostly on bribes. Actively hijacking a police car was an entirely different situation.

One Alice would have punched her in the arm for considering.

Jamie's fingers drifted to her forearm, scratching the spot where she couldn't shake the invisible pressure of Alice's neck.

The sheriff strode out of a building and crossed to the truck. He offered a nod and, after a half-second to reel in her spiraling thoughts, she returned it.

She heaved a sigh and continued down the main thoroughfaire.

There were horses. Ranchers and farmers trotted in and out of the town, some pulling small wagons with goods, others simply using the beasts to get around.

But beyond the fact that she had incredibly limited experience with the creatures, horses wouldn't last in the Wasteland any longer than she and Oliver would. And the border was close enough now that it made more sense to keep walking than to court trouble.

At the far end of the main street, Jamie found a second-hand clothing shop. She hurried inside. Hopefully she'd get something for her filthy fighting gear. There was no point in keeping it, and they needed the credits.

She dumped her bags onto the counter and waited as the middle-aged brunette with a splattering of freckles and bony hands picked through the clothes.

"Do you know a crossing point near here?" Jamie asked.

Her heart gave a lurch as the seamstress tugged on the sleeve of the shirt Alice had worn before the fight. She looked away, pretending to inspect the store.

"No decent one," the woman said with a sneer. Her gaze smoothed over as she pulled out a pair of Alice's lucky socks. Dirty, but well made and fuzzy on the inside. "Oohh, these are nice."

She looked up, her mousey brown eyes meeting Jamie's and her face falling at the Unborn's expression.

"These *are* for sale?"

Jamie gave a curt nod.

The woman returned to inspecting Alice's clothes. "They finished the tram down south, but unless you have sixty-thousand credits that's not an option."

"That's not quite in the budget," Jamie said, her jaw tight. "Any other options?"

"It's another five days north to the closest crossing that won't kill you. It's closer to forty-thousand a head." She shuddered. "I'd never. Can't stand the thought of flying."

Jamie closed her eyes, teeth grinding together in frustration. She'd known it would be pricey, but—

"There's also..." The seamstress's hesitant voice cut across her thoughts.

Jamie met the woman's eye, noting a nervous twitch as she continued fidgeting with the clothes.

"I don't know if they're letting Unborn through right now, but..." She bent forward, her voice going to a near-whisper. "If you keep heading straight west, you'll get to the Switch."

"The Switch?" Jamie raised an eyebrow, leaning her hip on the low counter and watching the door with wary eyes.

The woman brushed a strand of hair out of her face and nodded. "It's something of a town, more a waystation, really. They help folks find a way to cross." Her gaze darted to the door and back to Jamie. "You know," she murmured. "Without going through an official checkpoint."

The seamstress straightened, laid the clothes out on the counter, and piled the ones she wanted to the side.

Jamie frowned, suspicion thick in the tension of her muscles. Why would this woman tell her about an illegal crossing? Why offer the help?

To trick her was the likely answer. To get an Unborn caught breaking the law.

But the fair price Jamie got for hers and Alice's unnecessary clothes made her question her own suspicion. The woman gave a nod as Jamie went to stuff the money and the remaining clothes back into her bag.

"Ask for Noah," she murmured. "Tell him Gloria sent you, and he'll be even more willing to help."

Jamie turned to the door but hesitated.

After a few seconds staring out at the road, she rounded, facing the counter again. "Why tell me? Why risk me alerting the police?"

Gloria's mouth twisted into a tight smile. "I'm not old enough to remember the war before you Unborn started fighting, but my papa was. He was overseas when the first bombs hit the coast. A lot of our family died when it happened." She shook her head. "He remembered the first time he saw Unborn in battle. Always told me they saved him, saved everything left of his generation. He said you were heroes."

Jamie's gut twisted at her words. What an unjust thing, to be called a hero for doing what she'd been built for. It hadn't been her job, or her desire, or her trying to save anyone. It had been her purpose. It had been kill or be killed. Fight or be destroyed.

"Anyway." Gloria cleared her throat, seeming to sense Jamie's uncomfortable tension. "Uniforms have been crawling all over lately." She shivered. "So be careful, whatever you decide to do."

Jamie swallowed. She tightened her grip on the strap of her bag. "Thanks."

She stepped outside. Oliver hurried up to her, kicking up dry dust with his heavy boots.

"We've got a problem."

She shook her head, trying to force the seamstress's words out before they sank too deep. Then she blinked and looked at him. "What?"

Oliver's lips curled into a scowl. "Unborn aren't allowed to cross. New regulations."

Jamie let out half a chuckle and half a sigh.

Oli crossed his arms, his shirt going tight around his biceps as he raised an eyebrow.

"Come on," Jamie said. "I'll explain on the road."

10

COWBOY

O LIVER HAD SECURED PROVISIONS and a map of the region but no form of transportation. There was a truck headed north to the checkpoint, but the driver had pointedly refused to carry Unborn with his cargo.

"What did he think we were going to do? Slaughter his chickens?" Jamie asked with gravel in her voice. As she said it, the thought of a chicken roasting over a fire made her stomach growl.

Oli shrugged, frustration tight in his shoulders. They had a full day of marching ahead of them. Part of Jamie knew he'd take it personally—he'd think it was his fault for not getting them a ride. He was like Vic in that way. Always taking responsibility for things that weren't his fault or weren't in his control.

When it came to things he *was* responsible for, he'd given up as easily as her sister had.

"We should have figured out a ride in the city," Jamie grunted. It was as close to an apology as she'd give. They might have bartered transportation if she hadn't made a permanent enemy of the man who basically ran things. And if she hadn't been so desperate to leave.

Oliver shook his head. "I wanted to get out of there too, Jamie." He repositioned his bag onto the other shoulder, his gaze scanning the patchy vegetation they walked through. "Did the same when Cade... When they killed him I left without looking back. I get it."

Jamie said nothing for a long time.

They stuck near the road. It would branch soon, and they'd take the middle fork, continuing as directly west as possible. Until then, asphalt turned gravel crunched under their boots. Weeds pushed through cracks in the black, reclaiming what had once been theirs. Woods encroached, no road teams to keep them in check anymore.

This was their home, their country, the place they'd been built and spent their lives fighting for. Yet Jamie was unfamiliar with much of their surroundings. She and Alice hadn't possessed the time or money for outings away from the city. When the military had dropped them, it had been further east.

A four-legged creature with a hard shell—turtle, Jamie recalled from those early days when the scientist and handlers had let them play school with normal things children would learn—made a slow trek across the road. Squirrels darted by them, so close it was ridiculous.

At the sight of a family of deer barely a quarter mile in the distance, Jamie scoffed.

Oliver glanced her way.

She threw up her arms, frustration heavy like the ghost weight of the gun she was so used to carrying on her hip. She still reached there sometimes, an automatic reaction to threat. An ingrained movement she couldn't shake after nearly five years away from the battlefield.

"If we had a damn weapon, we'd be eating like kings."

Oliver followed her angry gesture and grinned. "Yeah, wouldn't that be nice. You remember that antelope looking thing we took down in sector twelve?"

Jamie shook her head, the memory of crispy meat making her mouth water. "It was a clutch move, bringing salt and pepper on a recon mission."

He laughed. "I learned my lesson the first time. Once that base was gone, I figured they'd make us find our way back."

"Those onions Cade found," Jamie said with wistful hunger in her voice.

"Vic's stash of chocolates."

Jamie's heart swelled at the memory. The four of them hunkered down in a snow strewn forest, no exfil for three days, no rations beyond what they'd carried on their backs. No knowledge of whether or not their intel, their distraction, had let Alice do her job.

The swell grew to an ache. The food had made it a good day, ruined right after by one of her worst fights with Vic. Jamie, furiously demanding they raid the smoldering compound, find a vehicle, and go help Alice. Vic, explaining with an infuriating lack of emotion that they had a mission. They had orders.

"*Bullshit orders,*" Jamie had snapped as Oliver and Cade moved away. "*As much as you want to be, we aren't robots, Vic. We can break the rules sometimes. Alice needs our help.*"

She hadn't, of course. If they'd gone to her like Jamie wanted, they'd have blown the whole operation. That knowledge hadn't stitched together the wedge driven between her and Vic. If anything, it had opened it further.

Each time one of them was right, it meant the other was wrong. If there was anything the two shared beyond how they were created, it was a bone-deep hatred of being wrong.

The deer in the distance caught their scent and scattered. Their movement drove Jamie from her memories, and she refocused on Oliver.

"Have you been this way?"

He shook his head. "Cade and I were northeast of you. This is all new to me."

"Good thing we've got a map, then."

Oliver gave her a half-grin. "What, you don't want to get lost with me again?"

Jamie grimaced, heat flaring at his words. "We've done enough diving into the past for the day, Oliver. Let's stick to the present."

His brow furrowed, his grin sliding into a thin line as he gave a curt nod and picked up the pace.

They ate well that night. As careful as they knew to be with provisions, they also needed to retain their strength. Jamie's ribs were still slightly bruised, the skin on her knuckles had healed but was raw, and her jaw ached if she talked too much.

But she could taste again. Maybe the memory of their forest feast had driven the ash from her tongue.

Firelight crackled between them, bright against the growing darkness. They camped at the edge of a wood. Jamie had cleared it while Oliver set up and heated their meal.

Tree branches swayed above, the light from the fire reflecting on the underside of the leaves. The scents of woodsmoke, the spices from their pre-packaged noodle dinner, and the tangy musk of thick forest ground filled the air around them.

Jamie leaned against a tree trunk, mindlessly braiding her long hair into a single lock to keep it out of her face at night.

Her fingers hurt.

Her heart hurt.

Alice had done the braiding before missions. She'd learned it from Angela, the woman who had created the three of them, the one whose initials were inked onto their arms.

She'd been different from the other researchers, the other Organics who created Unborn. Jamie could still recall the early days. The woman's tender fingers brushing out her long hair, a motherly voice telling Vic to be gentle, Alice to be strong, and Jamie to be kind.

As they'd grown older, they saw her less often. Their training became more tactical and weapons based.

But the three of them still found a way to be teenage girls. Jamie and Vic would take sharpies to their nails, aiming for the shiny coat of color they so often saw on the female doctors who worked with them. The three would stay up past lights-out, their heightened vision helping them not get caught, and pretend they were in the real world. They'd share stories of what life would be like after the war. After they'd won and returned home as heroes.

Jamie secured her hair with an elastic band. Her gaze was stuck on the fire, watching the flames crackle as she spiraled in a crushing void of pain and guilt. If Vic had been there... if the three of them had been together...

But they hadn't, and as much as she wanted to blame the separation on Vic, she knew whose fault it really was.

Jamie and Oli had danced around their feelings for each other for over a year before she acted on them. Their little moments had stayed secret for a long time. Stolen kisses in the stairwell, holding hands in the transports, and then a quiet night just before the war ended. A night she'd never be able to forget, because of what it was, and what it caused.

They hadn't known the surrender was coming. Orders had come down for a big push on one of the enemy capitals. A siege. An incursion.

Those meant death. Meant losing soldiers, friends. When Jamie had told Oli what she wanted that night, he'd agreed.

She'd always wondered, after they'd been caught by one of the ranking commanders, after the punishment that left them both bruised and bleeding, after they'd been forced into separate units for that final siege, if he regretted it.

Jamie hadn't. She hadn't regretted a second of their time together. Not until the war was over and orders came down the line for her, Alice, and Vic's placements. What reason could Command possibly have had to separate them if not to punish her?

And sure, Vic could've fought harder. Could've used her pull as the goody-two-shoes favorite of the Organic commanders to get them at least on the same side of the continent. But when it came down to who was to blame for the separation, Jamie knew the fault was hers.

The fact that Vic knew where they were—the proof of which was in the letter that came a day too late for Alice—was something Jamie would swallow another time. It was too much right now.

She ripped her gaze from the fire, unable to stand the regret burrowing into her chest. She looked instead to Oliver. He sat a few paces away. Not quite across from her, but at a distance. His head was bowed. If she didn't know him so well, she might think he was dozing.

"Was it quick?"

He looked up, firelight dancing across his silver eyes and turning them gold for a brief moment.

Jamie swallowed to clear her throat. "Cade. Was it quick?"

Pain splashed across her old friend's face.

"I don't know." Oliver picked at his fingers without meeting her gaze. "I wasn't there."

"Why not?"

A flash of anger furrowed his brow, but it wasn't for her. He ran his hand across his head. "Uniforms took him after he ran. I only learned they found him after he was already taken."

Jamie's stomach churned.

"I tried to get to him. I had a plan. If they didn't release him..." He shook his head. "I was ready to get him out, go on the run. But he was gone before I got to the courthouse. It was all military. A private execution. At the hands of Uniforms." Oliver paused for a few seconds. "I had to bury what was left of him. They wouldn't let me burn the body."

The crackling of flames and rush of wind through the trees above them weren't quite enough to cover the hitch in Oliver's voice as a few tears slid down his cheeks.

"I'm..." Jamie clenched her hands, the new skin on her knuckles stretching past the point of comfort. "I'm sorry, Oliver. I'm sorry for what happened to him."

Oli swallowed and nodded, his jaw tight.

Jamie struggled to sleep that night. When she did drift out of consciousness, it was for short stints. The heavy sound of snapping, the feeling of Alice's body breaking in her arms, jolted her awake each time.

She was grateful for the sun when morning finally came.

The day passed with an odd ease. They walked, paces quick as an Adam jogging. Being a Silver sometimes had its perks.

The route was relatively clear. They passed a handful of homesteads, farmers and their families caring for land that would otherwise return to the wild. Low stone walls and raggedy wooden gates offered little protection for these people.

"If raiders came this way..." Oliver shook his head, voicing the concerns Jamie had just been thinking.

A child waved at them from afar, a stick in his hand and mud in his hair. A parent came to his side, shielded their eyes from the sun, and squinted at Jamie and Oliver.

Jamie read the recognition on their face as they blanched, wheeled, and tugged the child indoors by the scruff of his shirt.

"Yeah," Jamie murmured. She scanned the horizon. "We're still pretty far from the Wasteland, I think. I can't see it yet."

"Me neither," Oliver returned, cutting his gaze away from the small cottage home and looking west as well. "But, I wonder how often the law gets this far from the city."

She snorted and raised an eyebrow at him. "The law?" she repeated, incredulity in her tone. "Okay, cowboy."

Oli rolled his eyes, half a grin splitting his face. "You know what I mean."

"Sure." Jamie spat a laugh and took on a very bad southern accent. "The law hasn't been 'round these parts in a long time, sheriff."

He shook his head, but the trace of his smile didn't fade. "You pick a western for movie night two times and get branded a cowboy for life."

Jamie gave him a light shove. "It was four times, five if you count that one set in Australia."

"Fine, but if I'm a cowboy, that makes you a princess."

Her smile turned to a grimace, and she squinted at him. "Don't you dare."

Oli darted down the road, skipping over a wide pothole and laughing back at her. "Come on, highness, we have a lot of ground to cover."

Jamie growled, the humor still dancing in her belly. "It was *one* time!"

It felt so natural, laughing with him. And when he broke into song, jokingly hollering the lyrics to one of those stupid princess movies she and her sisters had enjoyed, she was taken back to those stairwell days. His voice echoing up the floors as he sang to her between tender kisses. His songs pulled not from memory, but from heart. The words putting every unsaid emotion the two of them shared into the world.

That night they finished most of their perishable provisions with the expectation that they'd be able to restock when they made it to the Switch. They'd chosen a burnt out building to spend the night and scouted the area to ensure privacy—and security.

They talked into the evening, discussing plans for getting across the Wasteland, finding Vic, and what they might have to do to stop the strange mind-control that had taken their friends' lives. It was late by the time they bedded down on opposite sides of the fire.

It would have been smart to try to get to sleep earlier, but Jamie's fear of feeling the snap in her dreams again kept her talking. A tiny voice in the back of her mind wondered if Oliver was doing the same, keeping the conversation going for the sake of holding his nightmares at bay.

11

THe SWITCH

J AMIE'S BREATH CAUGHT AS she and Oliver came over the last in a set of rolling foothills and the Switch became visible, along with the Wasteland.

"Well that's..."

"Unsettling?" Jamie finished.

"Yep."

The town was a good twenty miles from the edge of the nuclear fallout zone, but the towering cloud of smog was visible even from such a distance. The forested area they'd been traveling through faded into scattered scraggly trees and the occasional ruin as the miles stretched closer to the Wasteland.

The Switch itself was less a town or village and more a ramshackle collection of RVs, trucks, and thrown together hovels. There were a few gardens, the green of the plants not quite as vibrant as they should have been. The whole place gave Jamie a forlorn sense of hopelessness. She doubted they'd find any sort of useful help here.

"Is this it?" Oli asked, his voice low as they crested the hill and trudged down toward the only area that could have been considered a town square.

Jamie nodded. "Yeah. There's nothing else. The official checkpoint is several days north of here."

"Well, shit. Let's see what they've got."

Jamie half smiled at the resignation in his tone. She tugged at the edges of her sleeves, pulling them down over a series of fresh scratches and bruises marring her wrists and forearms. She wasn't certain how she got them. Maybe the trees. They weren't anything terrible, but she didn't like people asking questions she didn't have an answer for. And if Oliver saw them, that's exactly what he would do.

They followed a dusty road, too narrow for most vehicles and marked with dirt bike tracks, past a series of trailers. Silver cylindrical ones, scratched and dented with ragged curtains over the windows and janky cement blocks serving as stairs, white rectangular homes with dirt and stains emphasizing wear and time. Shadows moved as the two Unborn strode down the road, bodies shifting inside their homes to catch a glimpse of the newcomers.

Jamie's fingers itched towards her waist, and she cursed—yet again—the lack of a gun at her side. Even her blade would've been a comfort. Yet another thing lost in the fire. Another reason she felt no burn of guilt or regret over what she'd done to Carter's hand.

"Steady," Oliver murmured.

The two walked slowly. Curtains closed around them. Grandparents shooed their children indoors. Men and women emerged from the corners and alleys formed by the mobile homes.

"Tell them 'steady'," Jamie snapped quietly, her eyes on a man carrying a highly illegal shotgun a few yards away.

"No one has made a move yet, Jamie."

She growled. "It's only been a few years, Oli. I haven't forgotten my training."

"Thank goodness for that."

They both whirled. To Jamie's surprise, she caught sight of a knife clenched in Oliver's hand in her peripheral vision.

"Woah." A man stood a few yards from them, his hands up in a defensive posture, eyebrows raised. "Are we going to have a problem?"

Oliver cleared his throat and tucked the blade into the holster at the back of his waistband. Jamie gritted her teeth, wondering if he'd ever planned on letting her know he was armed. Her focus shifted as the man took a step toward them.

"I'm Noah," he said. For such a big man, he didn't have a very deep voice. He stood a few inches taller than Oliver's already impressive six-foot-two.

Noah wore a tight long-sleeve cream-colored shirt, but a sprawl of tattoos was just visible against the dark skin of his neck. Oli's caramel complexion looked nearly pale compared to the depth of auburn of the man.

"Jamie," Jamie said shortly. "And Oliver."

Noah nodded, as though he was already familiar, though Jamie knew for a fact they'd never met. Something about him stirred an uncomfortable feeling in her chest. Not quite unease, but certainly enough to put her on edge.

She frowned as he drew closer. His eyes were dark, nearly black, but there was something slightly off about them. She couldn't put her finger on it. Especially with her attention torn by the handful of Adams surrounding them.

Jamie clenched her hands at her sides. She and Oliver could easily handle the people around them, even with shotguns, but who knew how many more there were in this crappy town? Not to mention the danger of a stray shot hitting one of the many children who had scurried into the nearby homes.

"You came here for a reason, Silver." Noah turned in place as he spoke.

It almost looked as though he were giving a warning look to his people, but part of Jamie recognized the move. He was showing them he was unarmed. Sure, there could have been a blade in his boot or a pair of brass knuckles in his pocket. But he didn't have a gun or knife big enough to be a serious threat.

"We did," Jamie said, glancing at Oliver.

He nodded. "We were told there might be help here. For people like us."

"People," Noah repeated.

Frustration echoed in the low growl from the back of Jamie's throat at the humor in his tone.

"Yeah, people like us," she said again. "People trying to get across the Wasteland."

Noah lifted his chin, surveying her with a gaze that felt like she was being scanned. It was so familiar, the expression on his face when he finally nodded and raised a hand. The Adams around them relaxed. A few seconds passed with the soft sound of retreating footsteps.

"Can never be too careful," Noah said with a grin. He stepped forward again, and Oliver moved between him and Jamie.

She scowled at his protective instinct and sidestepped around him. "Why? Because we're Unborn?"

Noah laughed, the sound deeper than his voice as he stuck out his hand. "Absolutely. Everything to do with you being genetically engineered super soldiers and nothing to do with raiders, Uniforms, police, or general assholes trying to destroy everything we're building."

Jamie wasn't sure if Oliver chuckled at Noah's words or her expression. She wasn't used to her own level of sarcasm thrown back at her quite so succinctly.

Her friend took the stranger's hand and shook it. After a long pause with both men looking at her, Jamie did the same.

Noah walked with them, leading the way toward the few actual buildings in town. "So, who sent you to us?"

Jamie's nostrils flared. "Who said we were sent here?"

"Not many people find their way to the Switch on accident," Noah said with a grin. "We're far enough away from the legal checkpoints, and it takes a special kind of person to settle so close to the Wasteland."

Jamie clicked her tongue. "A woman, Gloria, told me to find you. She's in a town a few days east."

"That far?"

"A few days walking," Oliver supplied.

Noah raised his eyebrows. "You walked all this way?"

"How else do you think we got here?" Jamie demanded.

The man didn't react to her tone. He answered her question, directing his words at Oliver. "I figured you parked a ride in the hills to keep your goods discreet."

"This is everything we have." Oliver gestured to the bags slung over his and Jamie's shoulders.

Jamie scowled again, heat rising in her chest and cheeks.

Noah came to a halt at an intersection of sorts. The road they'd walked in on branched into a T. Two wood and brick buildings stood a few yards from them. One had a sign marked "General Goods," the other was blank, though the front door was wide open.

Jamie glared at Noah's back as he pointed to each.

"General will get you both whatever supplies you need. At a discount, if you don't have the credits. And next door you can find a room for the night."

Oliver met Jamie's eye. She dipped her chin.

Oli spoke, his voice low. "Noah, we were told you might have a way for us to cross the Wasteland without having to go through..."

"Legal channels?" Noah filled in with a chuckle.

Jamie bristled as another Organic walked past with a basket of laundry in tow. A soft scent of lilac lingered in the air behind her.

"Is there a more private place to discuss this?" Jamie asked through clenched teeth.

Noah looked at her again. Those dark eyes were appraising in a way that made her deeply uncomfortable. They felt almost alien. As though he knew more of her than he should just by looking.

"No one in the Switch is going to betray your trust."

"'Course not," Jamie said. "There has to be trust for it to be betrayed."

Oliver heaved a sigh and rolled his eyes. Stepping between Jamie and Noah, he addressed the larger man, "If we can take an hour to settle in, dust off, and grab something to eat, we'd like to discuss what's involved with getting transport. We need to cross as soon as possible."

For the first time since he'd introduced himself, Noah's expression darkened. A furrow creased his brow and his lips pressed into a straight line.

There was a long pause. Curiosity was heavy in the air, and Jamie almost thought he was going to ask why. Why they needed to cross, why they needed him for it, and why it needed to be quick. None were questions she was eager to share with anyone.

He didn't ask.

Noah gave Oliver a low nod, walked them to the open door, and told them he'd return in the evening to share a meal and discuss the trek.

Jamie waited at the threshold, watching Noah stride away down the dusty street. He plunged his hands into his pockets, ambling as though he hadn't a care in the world.

"Jamie," Oliver called from inside.

She shook her head and went to find him.

"How many nights are you thinking, dears?"

Jamie struggled to keep the wince off her face.

There was nothing inherently wrong with the young woman who stood behind the counter. She was petite and pretty, with long blonde braids and a baby on her hip. The child gnawed on his fist, staring at Jamie with the wide, unblinking eyes of an infant who had no understanding of how rude he was being.

Trisha, "call me Trish," seemed nice enough. She hadn't flinched at the silver in their eyes and had been happy to set them up with a room.

One room.

Jamie avoided sighing with frustration by turning to examine their surroundings. The building was an inn. The ground floor was wood furnished, roughly carved benches and tables that probably held maybe thirty people. A pair of swinging doors led to what Jamie assumed was a kitchen. It certainly smelled as though food was being prepared back there, and the scents drove a gurgle of hunger through her stomach.

Jamie's lips twitched into a smile at the three children hidden throughout the room. They snuck down the stairs one at a time, tiptoeing in vain before ducking between tables and behind benches.

Trish continued talking as though she hadn't seen them. "Dinner around 6, but there's no rush. We'll save plates for you if you come down late. We don't do much for breakfast, but if you're partial to strawberry jam we've got that and fresh bread. *Daniel Smith Watkins, get off that table right now.*"

Jamie almost snorted at the way Oliver's eyes widened at the woman's abrupt change in tone. Across the room, a small blond boy backed off a table, only looking at them all when his feet were on the floor. He met Jamie's gaze, squeaked, and darted over to stand behind Trish's leg.

"All yours?" Jamie asked as the others joined Daniel. They reminded her of the litter of kittens that had been found on base one time. All wide eyes and curious scampering.

Trish grinned. "Not quite. The three oldest are my sister's. She and her husband passed a while back so me and mine took them in."

A lump formed in Jamie's throat.

Oliver gave a shallow nod. "I'm sorry to hear that. It's good they had somewhere to go."

Trish shrugged, but there was an ache in her expression that was all too familiar. "She was my sister. I miss her, but I get to see her in the little ones. More and more as they grow."

Jamie opened her mouth to speak. To say how beautiful the children were, or to ask how much the room was, or to make some innocuous comment about the town. To her horror, tears burned the corners of her eyes.

She swallowed the lump and turned away from the counter. A gentle breeze came through the still open door. A few people walked by, going about their own business in the Switch.

Jamie's fingers trembled. She clenched her hands into fists. Her nose itched. A tear escaped, following the lines of her face and leaving a salty taste on her lips. Buzzing filled her ears. The shaking got worse.

"Hey."

She jerked as Oliver's hand closed around her arm. He released her as though her skin had burned him and cocked his head.

After an appraising look, he held up a set of keys. "We've got the room."

Jamie turned toward the stairs, wiping at her cheeks as she muttered, "Lead the way."

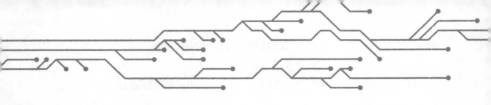

12

Familiar

"This town is strange."

Jamie didn't respond right away. She had a dripping wet cloth in one hand and was leaned over the ceramic bowl on the dresser, wiping away a layer of dust and grime from her face and neck. It wasn't a shower, but damn if it didn't feel about as good as one after several days on the road.

"As usual," she said, turning to him with water trailing down her neck and soaking into her shirt. "You're great at stating the obvious."

Oliver gave her a deadpan glare from his perch at the foot of the bed. "Why would a bunch of Organics help us?"

Jamie exhaled a sigh, dropped the rag into the bowl, and turned away from her attempt at relaxing. "I don't know, Oli. Same reason that woman told me about it? They've got a deluded idea that we're heroes." The words tasted acrid on her tongue, and she winced.

He shook his head. The dark buzz cut was growing a bit shaggy. Floppy locks of hair stuck at odd angles, though he'd tried to flatten it when he'd seen himself in the mirror.

"I don't think that's it. There's something off. Did that Noah guy seem—"

"Familiar? Yeah." Jamie wiped her hands on her jeans and crossed to lean against the doorframe. She'd have liked to sit, but Oliver was in the middle of the bed and there was no other furniture save the dresser. "Maybe because he's clearly in charge? Reminds me a bit of the commanders."

Oliver sucked in a breath and fell backward, sprawling onto the comforter. Jamie swallowed. She nibbled on the inside of her lip, trying not to notice the pull of his shirt over his muscular torso. Or the way his thighs stretched the limits of his pants.

"I guess."

Jamie stretched her arms and turned away. "If you want to rest a bit, I'll bring us up plates."

Oliver shot up. "I don't think either of us should go off alone."

She pursed her lips. "Maybe you could lend me that blade. I wouldn't be so alone if I had a weapon."

A flash of chagrin crossed his features. "Saw that, did you?"

Jamie clicked her tongue against her teeth. "When were you going to tell me about that?"

He shrugged.

"If those Adams had been a little jumpier you could have been shot pulling it out." She struggled to keep her voice even, and her pulse jolted at the thought, unnecessary dread flooding her veins for a moment.

Oliver briefly met her gaze. Then he looked away. "I'm sorry, Jamie. I should've let you know I had it."

She froze. That was not the response she'd expected, and the lack of an argument left her wanting a different kind of heat. Another handful of seconds ticked by. She breathed through parted lips, the ever-present roiling storm of rage and grief within momentarily calmed by the simple act of Oliver apologizing.

"I'm hungry," she finally said. "Are you coming?"

He studied her face, his brow furrowed in a familiar crease that was both comforting and frustrating. He was trying to figure her out. Trying to read past her words and get to the inside of her thoughts and emotions.

She half turned toward the door, and he darted from the bed to follow.

Dinner consisted of watery vegetable soup and fresh bread. It was heaven. Jamie savored each broth-soaked bite with her eyes half-closed, the sensation of a full belly and warm room both new and distantly familiar.

Her back was to a corner, another small bit of comfort. Oli had chosen to sit next to her rather than across, and most of his concentration was also on the meal before them. Like her, his gaze darted up and around every now and then, his head tilting at every sharp or sudden sound.

They didn't attract as many curious gazes as Jamie expected them to. Plenty of townsfolk wandered through the room. Some collected bowls and made their way back out, others sat at the various tables and talked amongst themselves. Trish came over–the baby in a sling on her chest, sleeping despite the commotion–to make sure they were doing well and offer a second portion that Jamie quickly accepted.

She ate slower with this one, her attention less focused on the food now that her stomach was satiated.

"Have you spotted a single Copper since we got here?" she muttered.

Oliver shook his head, his mouth full. He swallowed with a wince, then leaned close. "None. I thought we'd have seen some Unborn coming through here for a meal. There have to be some, right? Why would Organics help us otherwise?"

Jamie nodded. "Hiding, maybe? Or they live on the outskirts?"

"This town is the outskirts," he said in a dry voice.

Jamie snorted into her soup. "They eat well enough, though. I'm surprised they have so much access to water."

He nodded, sipping at the water in his glass. The dishes were a hodgepodge. Ceramic bowls of varying sizes and patterns, old glasses with faded logos of long-gone breweries, silverware of every shape.

He was right. Jamie had been wary of the water, especially this close to the wasteland. But her sensitive nose didn't pick up anything suspicious, nor did her tongue.

She sat back a bit, rubbing a hand over her extremely pleased belly and setting her spoon against the bowl for a moment.

The little blonde children that belonged to Trish scampered about. They were given as much attention as native rodents scurrying in the woods. Jamie chuckled as they darted under a table, causing the diners to lift their legs and allow the children to pass.

"What hit you the hardest when you landed?" Jamie asked, her gaze still on the little ones.

Oliver was silent, so she turned to look at him. He had an eyebrow raised, curiosity in his expression.

She elaborated. "After we got discharged. When you and Cade got off the transport. What was the biggest culture shock about being around civilians?"

"Ohh." He grinned. "We were looking for a place, got that dumb handout of 'Unborn Safe' options and completely ignored it. We wanted to see it all, the city, the people, the shops." He shook his head, the grin sliding to a bitter smile. "There wasn't much of that. Those assimilation movies didn't end up being all that helpful in the real world."

Jamie nodded, her mouth twisting at the memory of picket fences, boutique grocery stores, and shining brand new apartment buildings winking at her from a large screen in the mess hall. Whoever had put them together had no clue what the reality was for most Americans.

"Was that it?" she asked. "Finding out they lied about everything?"

"No, actually." He leaned back as well, folding his arms across his chest with a sigh. "There was a couple. One of the first things I saw off the plane. This man and woman, both Organics... they were hugging—kissing—right there in front of everyone. Cade had to pick my jaw up off the floor." He laughed.

The sound of it, his bemused laughter rumbling up from his belly and out his full lips, pulled her focus from the conversation. She was briefly teleported to a different time, a different place, that laughter echoing up an empty stairwell. Her cheeks hurt from smiling, from finding the right timing and punchline to earn that heartfelt guffaw.

He looked at her, his lips moving.

"What?" Her mind came crashing back to the moment, all the horror and heartache of the last several days settling once again like a blanket of thorns.

"How about you?" he asked again. His brow furrowed, and she looked away to avoid noticing his concern.

Her gaze landed on the children, now bouncing excitedly at a small table as Trish planted plates of food down for them.

"I remember when we first got into the city. Me and Alice, we saw a baby. A real one. A born one. Its mother was feeding it, and then it fell asleep and she just... she cradled it while it slept."

Jamie watched as the baby on Trish's chest stirred. The woman bounced a little as she walked, swaying side to side on her way back to the kitchen.

Jamie's words were quiet, and Oli leaned in a bit to hear, his shoulder brushing against hers. "I remember wondering how often we were held when we were that small."

A few seconds passed. Jamie continued to look away, her gaze blurred, not quite seeing what was in front of her. Then she felt the warmth and pressure of Oliver's arm leaning against hers. Most of her wanted to pull away. To leave him cold. Let him take a turn with that feeling. But a small piece of her resisted the urge just long enough for her to gain some strength from his presence. She leaned in, matching him, and they sat together in silence for a long moment.

A shadow passed in front of their table, and Oliver pulled away.

"Room for one more?" Noah's mild rumble was loud enough for them to hear, though no one else looked his way when he spoke.

Oliver nodded, gesturing to the seat across from him.

Noah sat and, almost instantly, Trish was there with a bowl of soup and a full loaf of fresh bread.

The big man whipped out a folded cloth and spread it across his lap. He scooted his chair forward and dug into the food.

Jamie worked to maintain a neutral expression. After a couple seconds of silently watching him eat, she went back to her own bowl and took a few bites. The soup had gone cold.

Her insides were chilly as well. She pulled her jacket tighter and picked at a scab on her wrist.

Oliver didn't touch his remaining crust of bread. Nor did he move when Noah ripped apart his loaf and offered a chunk to each of them.

"So," Noah finally said. He wiped his face with his napkin and leaned back in his chair.

His movements, mannerisms, were so familiar it was like an itch in Jamie's mind. Yet she was *certain* she'd never met the man. The feeling was simultaneously curious and infuriating. She wasn't one to forget a face.

"Two Silvers, wanting to cross the Wasteland... without attracting attention from the government?"

"That's why we're here, isn't it?" Jamie said with a curled lip.

Noah's eyes widened, his eyebrows shifting up in an amused expression. "It's not possible to be too careful these days. But we try our best. Tell me, why not get a pass from the military? Surely two captains have more access than regular civilians."

Jamie opened her mouth, but Oliver spoke first, glancing in her direction like he knew what she was about to say.

"We have no contact with any of our prior handlers or commanders." Oliver leaned forward and rested his forearms on the table. "If we had a legal way to cross, we wouldn't be here." He inhaled, his jaw going tight before he continued. "You may not have heard, but new restrictions were just passed. Unborn aren't allowed to cross."

Jamie swallowed. Her hand was clenched in a fist under the table. The other pressed too hard against the divot of her spoon, and the metal began to bend.

Noah's dark gaze slid from one to the other, and Jamie frowned as the gears in her mind shifted to a new track.

"We have ways across," the man said. "But each comes with risk, some more deadly than others."

Oliver nodded. "We're not unused to putting our lives in danger. We *have* to get across. As quickly as possible."

"I don't suppose you'd be willing to share why?"

Jamie's brow furrowed. "You gonna share why there are no Unborn in a town that supposedly helps our kind?"

"Would it be less suspicious if it weren't Organics offering assistance?"

Jamie let out a snort. He spoke mildly enough, but she didn't take him for a simple man. He knew what she was getting at, and if he wanted her to say the words, so be it.

"I'm sure you've heard of the Unborn trafficking going on." She sneered. "Who knows how many unsuspecting Coppers go to little towns with the offer of work or help, only to disappear without a trace."

At this, Noah's expression finally darkened. He lost the lackadaisical ease with which he sat, his imposing form looming larger when he leaned forward.

Oliver put a hand on Jamie's thigh as the big man's jaw went tight, his neck muscles bulging for a second.

Noah eased out a breath, smoothing his features again.

Jamie lifted her glass and sipped her water, still watching him. "So you have heard."

"We get less trouble from the law—"

Jamie side-eyed Oli, barely containing a sly grin.

"—when we only have Organics in town," Noah said.

Oliver nodded. "But you do work with Unborn."

Noah clicked his tongue against his teeth. He shifted in his seat as the door opened again, a few people coming in to eat.

The light from the fading sun streaked across his face.

Across his eyes.

Jamie's lips parted with a sharp inhale.

The door closed and Noah shifted his gaze to her, cocking his head. She met his eye.

She waited a few seconds, giving her heartbeat time to steady. Then she said, "Do the Organics living here know?"

Oliver glanced at her, then back to Noah. He addressed his question to Jamie. "Do they know what?"

Jamie jerked her head at their host, not taking her eyes from him.

Noah raised his eyebrows.

"Where did you get such realistic contacts?" Jamie asked, keeping her voice low in case she was wrong about her hypothesis and this whole town was being deceived.

Oliver shifted, his hand going to the blade at his side.

Jamie shook her head. She rested her fingers on Oli's arm to steady him. "Don't bother. We don't stand a chance against a Gold."

13

SUNSET

NOAH KEPT THE CONTACTS in as the three of them left the little inn. It seemed the entire town had decided to have dinner there, and Jamie was glad to be out of the noise.

The three Unborn strode west down the dusty road.

"Why keep it a secret?" Oliver asked. He met Jamie's quick look, no doubt thinking the same thing she was—where could they get a pair of contacts like that?

Noah puffed out a breath. "I didn't at first. I was dropped in DC, or what's left of it, and I had no reservations about showing my true self. But people were nervous around me." He shook his head with a rueful half-smile. "No one tried anything. There are educated ex-military in that region, and they knew what I was. But enough folks flinch when you walk by and it starts to get to you."

"Were there any others with you?" Jamie asked the question quietly. Her thoughts shifted away from the Gold strolling the evening with them and shot like a bullet to her sisters. She and Alice had been together. But Vic... She had something now, based on that damn letter. But what had the first few weeks–months–been? Had she been alone?

Noah cracked a bitter grin. "No. Golds are solitary creatures. Or so we were told. It's too dangerous for more than one of us to be in the same region."

Oliver frowned. "That's... insane. Even during the war?"

The Gold gave a light shake of his head like he wanted to chase away a memory. "It's done."

He picked up his pace, and the other two lengthened their strides to keep up. They left the central part of town, passing more rundown, ramshackle homes before they came to the open stretch of nothing between them and the Wasteland. Noah slowed to a stop, staring out at the dazzling array of color.

Rays of sunlight filtered through the towering haze of nuclear fall-out on the horizon. The horror of it, the silent screams of the millions who were destroyed in seconds, faded just a little in the face of the stunning view.

It reminded Jamie of an oil painting of a rainbow she'd once seen. All distorted, no clean lines or sharp edges. A gust of wind picked up in the distance, and the haze swayed. A mix of color that shifted in a way the painting hadn't.

She stared for more than a few seconds, entranced by the sight.

Alice might have seen this. If Jamie had listened to Oli in the first place. If they'd gone with him when he asked for their help. If she hadn't been so bitter about his mere presence.

Her heart hurt. Or maybe it didn't. Maybe Alice had taken such a large chunk of it when she died that Jamie didn't have a heart left. Maybe it was the empty space in her chest that ached. A gap of cold that seemed to grow with each passing day.

The feeling of the snap against her arm sent a wave of goosebumps across her skin. She closed her eyes, needing the conversation to continue so the sound of Alice's neck breaking would stop ringing through her ears.

"So they know," Jamie prompted.

Noah glanced down at her.

She jerked her head toward the town. "All the Adams you live with know you're a Gold?"

His mouth twitched at her vocabulary, but he nodded. "It didn't take long for me to leave the city. I found people who could use my help, and eventually people who'd take it without balking at my origins."

Oli huffed out half a chuckle. "Trish?"

Noah nodded. "Her family were farmers in the southeast. They didn't mind my eyes as long as I kept up with the chores. I was with them about a year before raiders took the home."

Jamie frowned. "Must've been a lot of them."

He grimaced. His features pinched at the memory. "I wasn't there. Trish's father and I were delivering goods a few towns over. The women managed to escape with the children, and we all hit the road together."

"You could've taken the farm back." It wasn't a question, but Jamie wanted to know why he hadn't.

"They didn't want me to," Noah said. He glanced at Oliver. "It took more restraint than I ever needed during the war. But Trish and her sister wanted nothing more than to be gone from that place."

Jamie's stomach rolled at his implication. Her hands clenched at her sides as fury bubbled in her stomach. "You should have killed them."

Oliver released a poorly contained sigh and attempted to give her a warning look. She ignored it.

Noah strode a few paces away, and she followed him. He plunked down on the edge of a wide cement strip and gazed out at the fading sun.

Jamie stood beside him for a moment, her teeth clenched together as she stared down at him.

Oliver sat down a few feet away.

"Why didn't—"

"I did," Noah interrupted, his eyes still trained on the sunset.

Jamie fell silent. Her heart raced, blood pumping with unwanted adrenaline. Her design didn't allow for her level of anger to just go away. The programing in her bones, muscles, veins demanded she protect. Destroy. The mental image of Trish, baby on her hip, little ones clutching to her skirts brought that instinct to the forefront. She inhaled, shunting aside the urge to find and kill something.

"We made good time. Trish's father had a truck. But I'm still faster."

Jamie shifted uncomfortably. With a glance at Oliver, she moved to sit between them.

Noah's voice was low. "I hope someone made use of the farm afterwards. Maybe there's a family there now, making new memories. But they'd have had quite the mess to clean up."

Jamie fiddled with the zipper of her jacket. "Does Trish know?"

The Gold shook his head. "I was back to our campsite by dawn. Her father knew, and her sister's husband. She hadn't met John yet. And I was able to wash off the blood before she saw."

Silence fell between them all, and Jamie let it. Oliver scooted closer, settling so their thighs were touching. Jamie barely noticed.

The story was familiar.

There were plenty of brutes in the war. She, Alice, and Vic had seen their share of what civilians went through at the hands of enemy soldiers—on both sides. They'd come upon a village that had been hit by what could be called raiders. In reality, they were Organic soldiers from both sides of the war. Men who had fled the battlefield and formed their own group. Bandits who stole to survive and killed whoever got in their way.

No one had escaped that village by the time the Silvers had arrived. And no one escaped after the sisters had seen what the men had done.

Jamie knew what it was to leave bodies in her wake.

"Why the contacts?" Oliver asked, bringing everyone back to their earlier conversation.

Noah looked his way. "Safety. We've had a handful of government inspections. Military folks claiming to check if our town is safe to live in. I hid the first time. Didn't want any trouble. But I'm the one running things for the most part, so it's easier if I'm there to answer questions."

Jamie picked at the edge of her nail, the rage within cooling as they moved away from battles here and abroad.

"Did you put in the paperwork to leave your region?" There was a hint of amusement in her voice. "As a Gold you'd have to, wouldn't you?"

Noah huffed out a laugh. "And you've never bent the rules, Captain Jamie AF:179?"

She didn't flinch at his knowledge, though it sparked a new set of questions in her mind. "It's Lieutenant. You keep the rank you leave with, and I was busted down right before discharge."

"Huh."

Jamie's gaze snapped to the Gold, her brow furrowed.

Noah shrugged. "Whoever did that forgot to put in the paperwork. You're still a captain according to my intel."

Something in her gut twisted. She studied the man's face, certain he was lying, or just messing with her. His intel was good—at least good enough to have her identification number. He might have seen it on her arm, if she'd ever taken her jacket off around him. But she hadn't. Someone in town had access to information.

Information that gave her back the highest rank a Silver could achieve. She'd told herself it didn't matter. That she wasn't like Vic, didn't care about rank.

The first time she'd been bumped down it had stung. The second time, she'd nearly busted her knuckles on the concrete wall behind her cot.

"Is that true?" Oliver leaned forward, darting a quick glance at Jamie before focusing on Noah. "She's still a captain?"

"Well, none of us is anything anymore, right?"

"Right." Jamie worked to loosen her jaw, forcing her eyeline back to the sunset as though the knowledge meant nothing to her. "We're all civilians now."

Silence fell for a moment. Oliver tried to catch her gaze, but she ignored him. The muscles in her neck and back ached. She ran her fingers along her forearms, pressing too hard on a bruise and wincing.

A headache was building. Jamie leaned over, resting her arms on her knees and rubbing the spot between her eyebrows.

Oliver heaved a sigh and rose to look down at the Gold. "Can you help us cross?"

"Are you going to tell me why?"

Jamie finally met Oliver's eye. She nodded.

"Probably best you know anyway," he said. He shook his head. "I don't want to know what would happen if a Gold turned."

Noah frowned, a deep crease marring his smooth features as he stood to join Oliver. "What do you mean, turned?"

Oliver explained while Jamie continued watching the sun go down. Cold came with the darkness. The first touches of it skimmed her skin as Oliver told Noah about the Unborn village out west. By the time he described what happened to Alice, she was shivering despite her jacket.

She tried to block out his words, to keep at bay that echoing crack that haunted her. Hearing the whole thing from someone who had watched it happen was almost as bad as her nightmares.

"This is…"

"Bad," she finished as Noah hesitated. "Really damn bad. And apparently my sister has a lead on stopping it. That's why we need to get across. We *have* to get to her before this happens again."

Noah inclined his head, though she noticed the way his expression shifted when she said *sister*.

"Let's get back. I have some things to show you both. There are fewer options for getting you across."

"Because we're Unborn." Oli's guess was proved correct as Noah nodded.

"I have some allies, but they won't risk taking you with those new regulations in place. Contact lenses would be an option, but they do thorough scans at the checkpoints, and they'd take a couple of weeks to secure good ones."

"And we'd need to rob a bank to get the crossing fee," Jamie muttered darkly.

Noah smiled. "Still, there are ways."

Ways, it turned out, were choosing between a tiny old car shaped like a beetle, or a pair of half-rusted dirt bikes. Jamie gaped at the interior of the small garage Thomas had taken them to.

The door clattered loud enough to wake the entire town as it rolled up into the ceiling. Splotches of oil stains coated the chipped concrete floor. Only the tools, hung neatly on the wall, looked clean and cared for.

"What part of either of these," she gestured between the vehicles with a limp hand, "will get us through the Wasteland unscathed?"

"Unscathed? That's a tall order. If you don't want to get hurt, you'll need to go around like Organics."

She scowled at his tone. "We don't have time for that."

Noah nodded, his features obscured with only the dangling light hanging above the bikes to brighten the space. "I know."

He stepped through the room, resting a hand on the hood of the little car. Upon closer inspection it was also very rusted, or maybe they'd meant to paint it orange.

"This will get you across with the least damage. Silvers can take a lot, including radiation poisoning. Prolonged exposure will kill you, but a few days with the windows taped up and some oxygen tanks and you should be fine."

"A few days." Oliver's expression sharpened. His jaw shunted to the side, matching Jamie's feeling on that timeframe.

"What about those?" She pointed to the pair of bikes.

Noah tilted his head with a nod. "Those'll be faster. Probably two days if you don't sleep, and I wouldn't. Not out there. I can get you masks, goggles, oxygen tanks. But they'll have to be small to fit on the bikes."

"Two days." Jamie walked over and rested a hand on one of the rubber grips on the handle of the blue bike. The red one appeared to be in *slightly* better condition. At least, the grips weren't entirely worn down.

Vic's face flashed through her mind. How much had she changed in the five years since they'd seen each other? Did their last conversation still echo in her head the way it did in Jamie's? Did she remember their hug? The brief graze of Jamie's fingers across the tattoo on Vic's ribs—their unspoken way of saying *I love you*? Or did she only remember the shouting that came before that?

She was startled from her own questions by Oliver placing a hand on her shoulder.

"I'm up for it if you are."

She nodded and turned to Noah. "We'll take the bikes."

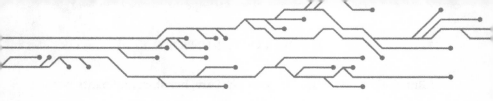

14

Sleep

HAVING A REAL BED to sleep in was like something from a dream. Having to share it with Oli might have been a dream once, but at the moment it was a nightmare. And, since he didn't offer first, Jamie ripped the comforter off the bed, grabbed a pillow, and chucked them both on the floor.

"I'll sleep down here. Closer to the door." She avoided looking at him. Her words were true—enough. There was a three-foot difference between where she'd dropped the blanket and the edge of the bed.

Oliver, who had been rinsing the dirt from their walk off his face, turned and raised an eyebrow at her. His hands were still in the ceramic bowl on the dresser. He shook them off and then wiped them on his pants.

His shirt had been removed the minute they'd returned to the room. A habit he'd gotten into in their training days. Most of them did it, stripping the top layer of sweat drenched clothing while they waited for a turn in the showers. Jamie had spent half of her training days in nothing but a sturdy sports-bra and military-issued pants.

But she'd grown out of it, dammit. Sure, her shirt and pants were coated with dust. Of course, she'd rather strip down like she used to at home, not sleep in full gear like she had on the road. Obviously she'd be more comfortable in her panties, on the cushy mattress, buried in covers and warmed by—

Nope.

Jamie shook her head as heat rushed down her chest to a much lower location. Then she glowered at Oliver. He was still looking at her as though she'd said something asinine.

"What?" she snapped.

His dark eyebrow arched even further up his forehead. She tried, for a moment, to pretend it made him look stupid.

It didn't.

"You're gonna sleep on the floor?" He moved across the room, eyeing the large bed with a bemused expression.

"Thought that was obvious."

He tilted his head. "Why?"

There was a challenge in the glint in his eye. She glared at him. The heat grew.

The day had been as difficult as every other since Alice died. And tomorrow they'd make their way to the Wasteland. It'd take nearly a full day just to reach the edge of the toxic cloud—which said something for how high the damn thing was. No wonder planes went around.

Part of her wanted to accept the challenge. To fight, either with words or with her fist sunk into his gut. Then again, there was another way they could defuse the tension. She sucked in a breath, pulling air into her chest slowly and deliberately as she tried to banish the urge to tackle him.

Oliver was watching her, waiting for an answer.

"Someone needs to watch the door," she growled. She strode to the vacated space in front of the dresser. Oli made no move to get out of her way, and her arm brushed against his chiseled chest, not quite as tanned as his arms but difficult to avoid staring at nonetheless.

"You don't trust Noah?"

Jamie ignored him for a moment, brushing through her long blonde hair with her fingers so it would be easier to braid. Then she caught sight of him in the mirror, waiting for her answer. "I don't trust anyone," she murmured.

The words were meant to sting. To burn him the way even a simple touch burned her. To dig like thorns the way his salute to their commanding officer had dug into her that day. A salute, an about-face, and then he was gone, striding down the hallway while she stood still, waiting for the extra punishment that came from what she'd said to such a high-ranking official. Words she'd spit in defense of the way she had felt for the man who walked away.

But Oliver's expression didn't change. He kept watching her, almost as though he hadn't heard her. He had, though. He had the same genetically heightened hearing she did.

She looked away, knowing he'd seen her check, and bit the inside of her cheek with frustration.

She properly ignored him while she braided her hair and tied it off with a spare band she found in the top dresser drawer. She shrugged off her jacket and folded it gently across the wood. Then she plunged her hands into the lukewarm, slightly dirtied water. Her wrists and forearms stung. The mystery bruises and scratches, likely from traipsing through the woods, ached. They shone red and blue across her pale skin.

She scrubbed her fingers, loosening the dirt from the creases in her skin and scraping it from under her fingernails. Should have done it before she braided her hair, but as she was about to go through a nuclear fallout site, a little dirt wouldn't hurt.

"I think we're safe here," Oliver said quietly as she finally finished and crossed back to her make-shift bed.

"I don't think we're safe anywhere."

"What about Vic's place?"

Jamie shot him another glare, not entirely sure why she was hell-bent on so much hostility after they'd worked together so well during the day. Part of it was to shake away the desire she pretended not to have. Part of her wondered, hoped, that if she was mad enough at Oli before she fell asleep she'd dream about him instead of Alice.

"Well," Oliver said, folding down the remaining blankets and settling himself between the sheets. "There's plenty of room if you change your mind. I'll stick to this side."

Jamie plunked onto the ground. She folded the comforter, keeping one side under her and draping the other across like a sleeping bag. She punched the pillow a few times, then laid back and stared straight up at the ceiling. "I'm good here, thanks."

A few seconds passed before the bedside table lamp went out. The silvery glow of nighttime filtered in through the slitted window above the bed. The curtains didn't entirely close, casting shadows across the far wall.

Jamie exhaled through pursed lips. The build up of rage within her was reaching a tipping point. Fear mingled through the anger, occasionally skimming the surface with horrid thoughts of what would happen if Oliver went berserk. Or if she did. Or if they died before they got to Vic.

What would her sister think? If no one came after she'd sent that letter?

What would she think when Jamie showed up without Alice?

These thoughts kept her in bad company as sleep slowly took her. And with sleep came the dreams.

Nightmares.

She was back in the ring, but it was Vic this time. Vic, who she beat almost every time they sparred because her older sister couldn't break from training if her life depended on it. But this time was different. Vic was older than Jamie remembered, a scarred and bloodied version with blackened eyes. She grinned at Jamie before attacking. There was no order, no thought, no strategy. Only violent, painful strikes.

Jamie was trapped. Cornered as Vic pummeled her with body shots. She tried to dart away. Vic snatched her hair, pulled her close, and got an arm around her neck.

Jamie flailed. Fear flooded her veins, sending logic from her mind as she thrashed with all her might. There was a snap.

A crack.

And then Vic was gone, and Jamie was the one with her arm around someone's neck. And Alice's wide eyes were staring up at her as pain laced her forearms.

"Shhhh."

Jamie jerked, coming to just enough to recognize the voice behind her was not a threat.

Hands were on her wrists. She studied them through a sleepy haze. They were strong, scarred, and familiar.

His grip was firm, but not painful. Her own fingers were odd, tight. Something wet dripped from her nails.

She half-rose. "Oli?"

"It's all right, Jamie." His voice was so quiet. Like he worried they'd wake someone up. "Go back to sleep. I'm just gonna hold your hands for a bit."

It might have been the word sleep that dragged her back down. Or just the fact that she'd not gotten a decent night since before the fight.

Either way, her eyelids drooped, weariness pulling her head back to the pillow as well.

She took in a breath and felt him do the same at her back. The blanket was between them, muting the warmth of his body. But his steady inhale and exhale provided a metronome for her to follow. She sank back into darkness, his arms still wrapped around her.

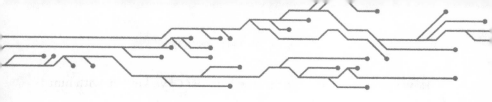

15

SPARRING

J AMIE WOKE TO SUNLIGHT streaming through the crack in the curtains. Her hands were before her, a darker set of fingers wrapped around her wrists, pulling them close to her chest. Oli's arm was a weight on her side, his deep breaths warm on the back of her neck.

Her dreams had eased after the one Oliver had interrupted. She studied his hands. The short nails cut to nubs every few days. The pale scars that lightened his honey brown complexion. His grip was loose, and she moved one of her hands, tracing up his forearm until she reached the little tattoo they all shared. The identification that was the only real sign she was older. He had different letters, the initials of a different designer. The numbers were what mattered though; her's was lower.

He didn't have as many tattoos as she did, but a handful of new designs decorated his skin.

Oliver stirred, his next inhale cut short as he shifted a little, pressing closer to her.

Jamie hesitated. She trailed her fingers across his skin like she used to. His steady breath returned.

How many times had she dreamed of this? Of waking up with him holding her? Beside her?

And what was so bad about it? So wrong that she'd refused to share a bed with him even just to sleep? What could it possibly hurt to let herself feel him with her hands the way she had only once before, and with her heart the way she had for years?

Tears burned and beaded in her eyes. Desperate desire poured in rivulets, dripping down her cheeks and soaking into the pillow beneath her head.

Jamie used every ounce of her Unborn genetics to remain quiet as she cried. And, when Oliver finally woke a few minutes later, her eyes were dry.

"How'd you know?" Jamie's hands were planted on her hips. She watched Oliver lift one of the bikes with ease, carrying the thing out of the shed so they could install all the equipment they needed for the journey.

Noah shielded his eyes from the sun. It already shone high overhead.

Floor or not, sleeping under a roof with an actual pillow and blanket had been enough to keep both Silvers asleep longer than usual.

"You've got your secrets, and I've got mine."

Jamie scowled, a flash of heat searing her fragile nerves. "What secrets? Oliver told you everything that led us here."

An Organic followed Oli out of the shed, hefting two metal cylinders and a roll of thick nylon cord.

"Sister?"

A low growl rumbled up from Jamie's throat. She shot a glare at the Gold. "What about her?"

He raised an eyebrow. "I didn't know they made Silvers with siblings."

"Aren't we all related in a way?"

"Yeah?" Noah huffed out a wry chuckle. "He your brother?" He jerked a thumb toward Oliver, and Jamie snarled through clenched teeth.

"No." Her hands clenched, the ghost feeling of wraps around her knuckles made her wish she could try her skill against Noah's. How long would she last against a Gold?

Worth ten of you. That's what command had said every time she questioned the wisdom of sending a Silver to do something beyond impossible.

Still, she'd last a few rounds. Do some damage. Make him think about his words before he said them.

"Jamie."

She swallowed down her anger and met his eye.

"I'm joking." There was an apology in his tone, as though he knew he'd stirred up trouble by being an ass.

"It's fine." Jamie bit the words out, but as she spoke them they became true.

It was fine. Fine for him to joke, for her to have a sister, for her history with Oli to be different. She inhaled, rolling back her shoulders and relaxing her hands. Her mouth curled into half a grin.

"Vic, the one we're trying to find. She *is* my sister. Not in the way Organics might think of it, but we are sisters."

Noah gave a soft nod and, with no help from her required for what Oliver was doing a few paces away, she continued.

"The three of us, me, Alice, and her, were all born nearly at the same time. Our creator had some kind of special funding, and we spent the first five years or so away from the normal facilities. Didn't know Silvers trained in blocks of twelve until we were ready for specialty training. Even when we got sent abroad, we managed the same base assignment." She huffed a sigh, a flash of gray hair and a weathered, aged face jumping to the front of her mind. "I'd bet a steak dinner it was Angela's doing. Science experiments, daughters, whatever we were to her, at least she wanted us to stay together."

Noah let silence fall for a few seconds before he looked out at the haze to the west. "Yet the one still living is across the country. A world away."

Jamie's fingers went to her ribs. To the single tattoo the girls had kept from everyone else. The word *Rodina*, scrawled in Alice's tidy script. A reminder that they were what the word meant – family.

"The war ended." Jamie shrugged. "Things changed." She bit the inside of her cheek, watching a scraggly tree in the distance as it shook in the wind.

If Angela had still been around maybe she'd have been able to keep the girls together. But she was long dead by then. Jamie had cried as much as the others when they found out—right after they'd been shipped out. Years later she'd been glad her caregiver wasn't around to be disappointed by the way she'd turned out.

Noah's dark eyes, flecks of gold barely visible in the right light, intruded on her gaze.

She raised an eyebrow and pursed her lips at the calm expression on his face. "What?"

"I find it interesting. You were so close, but you appear unfazed by the separation. By the death."

The phoenix on Jamie's neck flared. Heat raced through her, sending a buzz into her ears and a red haze across her vision. Her hands were up, feet spreading as she adjusted for the rocky terrain.

Her fist flew before she realized what she was doing.

She caught him off guard, and her knuckles slammed into his cheek with enough force to break the jaw of an Adam.

But Noah wasn't an Adam.

His head whipped to the side, and when he came back up, he was grinning with blood seeping from his gums. "Ahh, so there is a part of you that cares."

Another surge of fury pounded across Jamie's shoulders. She let out a strangled cry and swung again.

This was stupid. Foolish.

Pure.

No audience. No showboating. No pandering to Organics who spent more than she made in a week betting against her.

This was just her, blind anger, and decades of skill.

Behind the rage, a bud of relief began to grow.

Noah blocked the swing. He shoved her arm back. She leapt aside as he kicked at her middle. The blow still made contact, but it was glancing.

Jamie exhaled, circling the Gold. He watched with wary eyes. Blocked another two jabs but didn't see her leg in time.

Her knee caught his thigh in a sensitive spot. She grinned at the sound of pain he made. She kept circling.

He caught on to her pattern faster than most. On her next swing he snatched her arm.

She flew—over his shoulder and onto the rocky dirt with a thud. The oxygen burst from her lungs and refused to be replaced.

She rolled. A foot slammed down where her arm had been seconds before. Leaning back, Jamie planted her hands behind her shoulders and shoved herself upright.

She got her feet under her.

A massive fist smashed into her face.

Immediate daze had her blinking rapidly to clear her vision. She threw a few more punches, listening for Noah's heavy tread but unable to hear through the ringing in her ears.

She shook her head. The daze cleared.

She shook it a few more times, locking the Gold's position as strands of her hair fell across her face. He watched her, wary but with a satisfied expression suggesting he thought this was done.

She staggered a few steps, leaned to the side, and kicked.

Her foot connected with the big man's chest. He fell back, the unexpected nature of the attack enough to drop him onto his ass.

Jamie returned to her stance, fists at the ready, and looked down at him.

Noah was laughing.

She let out a breath, panting a bit and drenched in sweat from the heat and the fight. Her face burned. Her knuckles stung.

Her heart sang.

Jamie straightened as the Gold waved a hand, still chuckling, the other hand rubbing his chest.

Oliver stood a few paces away, a heavy wrench clenched in his hand and a wild, scared look vanishing from his face as Jamie caught his eye.

He scowled at her, then rolled his eyes and turned back to the bike. The Organic helping took a few more seconds to stare before returning to the job.

Jamie crossed the distance she'd sent Noah with the kick and plunked down beside him.

"What was that?" she demanded. There was no anger in her voice, though she still hadn't quite caught her breath.

"You tell me. You threw the first punch."

She pursed her lips, side-eyeing him with a dry expression.

He let out another rumbling laugh. "You've heard what they say about only children: we like pushing buttons."

She snorted.

He clapped a hand on her shoulder. "I didn't have what you did, Jamie. Part of me envies it. That comradery of fellow Unborn, that family, it might have made my war a very different thing."

Her nose itched. She rubbed at it with the back of her hand, wincing as she caught some of the newly forming bruise that ran from her upper lip to her cheekbone.

She'd had a family, that much was true. But her units had never run quite the same way the other Silvers' seemed to. There was so much loss. So much turnover when it came to the Coppers under her command.

"You have it now," she murmured.

"Yeah." He nodded, taking his hand back and resting his arms on his knees. "And I'm about as terrified of losing them as you are of not finding your sister. I know you care, Jamie. It's written in everything you do, everything you say. I haven't been through what you experienced in that ring, but I can see the weight of it on you. The weight of the loss. The weight of a leader."

The muscles in Jamie's jaw twitched.

"Leader. Right," she murmured, shaking her head. "I think I'd need a lower fatality rate among my subordinates to be called a leader."

She fisted her hands again, the already scabbing knuckles breaking apart and bleeding again.

They matched her forearms now. The gashes and bruises she'd been giving herself, unknowingly, in her sleep. The marks of her unconscious effort to wipe the snap from whispering across her skin.

"What's the first rule in sparring?"

Jamie's brow furrowed. She darted a glance at Noah, but he was still staring out at the town.

She let out a breath through her lips. "Be light on your feet. Keep moving."

He nodded.

Back down the dusty road, Oliver called for them to look at something.

Noah shifted, letting out a groan as he rose to one knee. His hand went to her shoulder again as he spoke. "It's hard to be light when you carry so much with every step. You might consider letting down the load, or at least finding someone to share it."

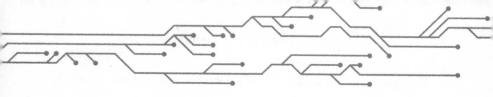

16

Δ GHOST

THEY LEFT LATER THAN Jamie would have liked, but still with enough time to reach the edge of the wasteland before dark.

Their bikes were laden with things they'd shed as they went. Two extra gas cans, oxygen tanks, full body gear, and enough food for them to load up on calories before they entered the nuclear zone.

As Trish had said with a weak chuckle when she passed over their bundles of food, it would be unwise to eat anything once they were inside the cloud.

South, Noah had told them. South until they reached the remains of a wide, asphalt road. It would take them as straight as possible until they got to the other side.

Jamie released one of her grips, flexing her hand and shaking the tingling out of her arm. It had been a while since she'd been on something like this. In the war it had been a thicker beast with metal plating ahead of the front tire to let her plow through debris.

Oliver had done well fixing up the old things. All that time sneaking into the military garages when he should have been training had paid off.

Though the seat was about as comfortable as a concrete stool.

"My ass is numb," Jamie grumbled a few hours later when they'd finally stopped for the day. She kicked out the stand and gently settled the bike into place. The ground was rocky, dense with a layer of fine dirt that puffed under her feet with every step.

Through the dust covering his face, Jamie caught Oliver's grin. He covered the chuckle with a cough. She shoved him anyway.

"What?" he said with another laugh.

"You know what," she growled, but a smile threatened at the edges of her mouth. His laugh was like his singing. A sound she'd never be able to hear without smiling.

"Besides the ass, how are you feeling?"

He was looking at her arms.

After the scuffle with Noah, Jamie had gone to Trish to get something cold for her face. Oliver had come as well, insisting she put bandages over her forearms.

Not that she needed to. Not with how quickly Silvers healed. Already the claw marks she'd made in her sleep the night before were scabbed over and beginning to scar. Small wounds were like that, quick and easy to heal. Larger stuff though, that was a different story.

"I'm fine." She clenched her jaw, fighting the instinct to turn away and start setting up camp. Instead, she faced him with a nod. "Thanks. The bandages will help tonight."

He blinked, those silver eyes becoming guarded.

Jamie twisted her lips, then moved past him and grabbed her sleeping mat. "It was a good idea."

She felt his lack of movement, heard it in the silence that settled in around them. There were no creatures here. No trees or birds or beasts or even insects lived this close to the Wasteland. It was unnerving.

She turned around, flipped her mat open, and spread it onto the ground with the bikes on either side. They'd set up close to the vehicles with a small fire.

"Are you ill?"

Jamie glanced up.

Oliver's arms were crossed, his biceps thick as he leaned on one leg and raised an eyebrow.

"No," Jamie said with a scowl.

"I've never once heard you say I've had a good idea."

Jamie ignored the flash of heat that came with his words.

They weren't true. He'd had many good ideas. Stowing away in the stairwells, bringing an extra set of rations on missions, and locking the door to the room they'd found that night.

It was that memory which brought the blossom of warmth to her stomach. His voice, husky and breathless: "We should lock the door." Her own, whispered back with urgency: "Good idea." Before he'd flipped the bolt, she'd laced her fingers through his, and they'd tumbled backward onto a set of shoved together cots.

Jamie swallowed down the biting words that leapt to mind. Instead, she rose and met his eye. "That's not true. I've said it before."

She kept his gaze, holding it as the flame in her grew brighter, hotter. Not with anger, or fear, or blinding rage. No, it was something else that glinted in her eye.

Her grin spread as that something reflected back at her from Oli. He swallowed, memory hitting him the same way it had hit her. His cheeks darkened, the caramel color taking on an amber hue as he wet his lips, then looked away and moved toward his own supplies.

Jamie huffed out a sardonic chuckle before starting on their fire. Good to know she wasn't the only one fighting a biological response.

Her arm bandage caught on a protruding shard of metal on the back of her bike, and a little voice sounded in her head.

Not just biological, Jamie. You've got history. That's only going to make it harder to ignore.

Jamie's hands trembled at the echo of Alice's voice in the back of her mind.

She spun around, then shook her head with a grimace. It sounded so real. As though Alice had been with them, ridden behind Jamie on that damn dirt bike. As though she was only a few feet away, sparking a flint to get them a fire to keep them warm against the desert chill that crept in when the sun went down.

Her heartbeat thudded in her ears.

Was it because Jamie hadn't dreamed about her anymore that night? Was she going to have her sister's whispered words... what she *would* say if she were there... in her head forever?

Or was her mind tired? Playing tricks.

That was it.

Jamie had imagined Vic's voice barking orders after too little sleep on missions. And, though she'd never admit it aloud, those pretend orders had saved her life once or twice.

That's what this was. Lack of sleep, strain, the nerves of going into a nuclear fallout zone in the morning.

Jamie kept these thoughts running as she got the fire going and dumped their rations into a tin can to warm up before they ate.

Most of Trish's food would be consumed at first light. Right before they darted into the hazy smog that lay between them, Vic's little safe haven, and answers.

Jamie stared up at the night sky, one hand on her satisfied stomach, the other propped behind her head. The cold had settled over them like a blanket, but the combination of fire, blankets, and Unborn resilience kept the worst of it at bay.

She'd be able to sleep tonight, even with how bright it was here.

"You remember that outpost to the east?" Oliver's low murmur reached her across the low crackling of what was left of their fire.

Another smile split her lips.

She was doing that a lot lately. Those damn kids in the Switch had started it, their adorable blonde mops of hair and their scurrying little feet.

The sound of Alice's voice in the back of her mind had darkened her mood. But it was hard not to smile at the memory he was referring to.

"Come on," he said when she paused a little too long. "You remember. The one with the eggs?"

She snorted, surprise pushing her into a laugh. "Yeah, the eggs. I completely forgot about the eggs."

"How could you possibly?" he demanded, amusement in his voice.

She picked at the edge of her shirt. "I remember the mission, Oli. But the eggs aren't what stood out."

He went quiet, and it was her turn to pull a memory out of him.

"It was the first time you sang to me." She closed her eyes, sinking into that morning, so many years ago. "We cleared it, found and ate the eggs, and then had a full day before we had to leave. We watched—"

"The sunrise," Oliver finished.

Jamie nodded, shifting so she could look at him through the flickering flames. "I'd never heard that song before."

He turned his head, meeting her eyes as firelight reflected across his silver irises. "It's an old one. I don't know if I got the tune right, but I found it in a stack of books before we got shipped out."

"I like how you sang it."

He swallowed and opened his mouth.

Jamie whipped up as the roar of an engine sounded in the distance.

Oliver was a half-second behind her. He dumped a stack of dirt onto their fire and threw his blanket over his bike.

Jamie did the same with hers, keeping a sharp eye on the twin points of light approaching from the south. They finished the work of covering everything valuable, then stood side by side, watching the vehicle approach.

"Just one," Jamie murmured.

The lights looming in the darkness were too even to be a set of bikes. They moved up and down with every jolt and jerk over the rough ground.

"How big, though?" Oliver's body was tense. Any sense of sleepiness was gone from both of them.

"Who has access to a car these days?" Jamie said through clenched teeth.

"I'm more worried about who is driving at this time of night."

"Good point."

They might have tried to hide, but the five miles this close to the haze were deserted in every sense of the word.

Jamie's hope that whoever it was would go wide and miss them by a quarter mile was quickly dashed. The roar of the engine grew louder and louder until headlights flashed across their faces and a wide military transport truck skidded to a stop a few yards away.

Dust flew up, clouding the brightness of the lights. A figure stepped out of the cab, and Jamie immediately recognized the epaulets on the military jacket.

She squared her shoulders on impulse.

"Hello," Oliver called, staying where he was but turning slightly and shielding his eyes from the light.

The engine and headlights shut off, and the figure clicked on a flashlight.

Jamie's sight adjusted within a few seconds. The figure was a man, dressed in a field uniform. A lieutenant, if his pins were to be trusted. And Organic, symbolized by a patch on his sleeve. Which meant that, though she and Oliver were captains, if it had been wartime, this man would have rank.

The flap at the back of the truck opened; the sound of tarp hitting metal echoed in the silence of the night.

Jamie shifted as two figures joined the LT, flanking him. Her mouth went dry at the sight of one, then two, then three more. They were men, or at least carried the appearance of men. But their faces were blank, no expression to be found. Their eyes were glinting, whirring, metal. And several of them had not been given the full humanification treatment—metal arms and cybernetic joints glinted in the faint moonlight.

Jamie's fingers found the edge of Oli's arm and she squeezed his wrist for the brief shot of comfort it gave.

The lieutenant stepped toward them, the cluster of Uniforms behind him following suit with heavy, clanking footsteps.

17

LIEUTENANT

"**U**NBORN ON THE EDGE of the Wasteland... interesting."

Jamie's spine tingled as she suppressed a sneer. She pressed her left thumb into the center of her right palm.

Robots surrounded them. Actual, literal robots. Not half-genetically-engineered organic bodies like her and Oli. No, Uniforms were something else entirely. Unable to act on instinct, unable to use humanity in their judgment—hell, judgment was questionable, too. The things around them, dressed up with skin and clothes so they'd be less terrifying to the population, acted on orders alone.

Which meant if the lieutenant sitting on the rolled up sleeping mat across from her found out they were intent on breaking the law, or if he just decided he didn't like them, she and Oli would have one hell of a fight on their hands.

Hence, suppressing her sneer. She gave a tight smile and looked to Oliver to respond.

Oliver stacked a few more sticks on the fire he had just relit. Flames crackled, warming the three of them. A pot of water sat just beside the fire, and a single bag of tea floated on the top.

The dozen Uniforms had not circled them. That would have ensured a threatening presence. But nine stood near the truck and the others flanked the Organic.

"We were headed to the crossing up north, sir." Oliver dusted his hands and settled a few feet from Jamie.

She wanted him next to her, the warmth of his leg pressed against hers for the reassurance that she wasn't alone. But strategically, they needed to be further apart.

Lieutenant Corvick grinned, his pale skin and white teeth reflecting the firelight. He was young, young enough that Jamie doubted he'd ever been deployed overseas. He'd probably finished training and gotten those butter bars on his shoulders a few years after the war ended.

"You haven't heard about the new regulations, then?"

Jamie ground her teeth.

Steady.

She almost flinched. But the single word in Alice's voice reminded her of the multitude of stealth missions her friend had undertaken. Missions that required a slow trigger finger and careful subterfuge.

Jamie let out a breath and, pulling a mask from deep within, flashed as much of an easy smile as she could manage. "Regulations? We know about going through the proper checkpoint for Unborn."

Oliver stirred, but she didn't look at him.

The man before her tilted his head before nodding. "These just came down the line; it tracks you wouldn't know. But they'd have told you at the checkpoint. Good thing I came along." He smiled again, his lips curling a little too far and exposing his gum line. "Might have saved you two some time."

"Time?" Oliver asked, his voice mild.

Jamie wondered if Corvick felt the tension winding around the fire. She was a passable liar. Oliver was the better of the two of them by a mile, but Alice would have taken the lead here. Wraiths were known for not being seen, but if they did get caught on a mission, they could bluff their way out better than anyone Jamie knew.

The lieutenant reached out and inched the pot of water closer to the flames. "Yes, it's quite a ways for you, and I fear you won't hear favorable news should you continue your journey."

"Why is that?" Jamie murmured.

He twisted to the side, stretching his arms with a grunt. "Unborn aren't allowed to cross."

Jamie furrowed her brow and parted her lips slightly. "What?"

Oliver mimicked her confusion. "Why not? We were hoping..." He swallowed, selling the disappointment. "We were hoping to see some old friends, sir."

Jamie fidgeted with the sleeve of her jacket. "Is there anything else we should know? Any other new Unborn regulations?"

Corvick heaved a sigh, looking between the two of them. "Did you happen to register your movement with the bureau when you left... where are you two from again?"

It was almost a stale taste on the air, the way his question hung between them. A trick. A gimmick to get the Unborn to slip up.

Jamie spoke with the certainty of truth. "I'm from Philadelphia, but Oliver came over from the coast. Boston area, right?"

He nodded.

"So, not together?"

"We fought together," Jamie said before Oli could respond. Her tone carried a strand of defensiveness she couldn't tuck away. "And now we're traveling together."

There was a pause.

"Friends, then?"

Jamie's lip curled. She gripped the fraying clasp of her zipper and jerked it up and down a few times. She needed *something* to do with her hands or they'd become fists at her sides.

"Like she said," Oliver's voice carried a hint of disobedience as well, "we fought together. Old war buddies, you could say."

Corvick chewed his lip, then nodded. "Any other war buddies of yours around here?"

At this, Jamie's reaction of surprise didn't need to be faked. She shot a glance at Oliver. "No, just us. Though there are a lot of Coppers in Philly. Are you looking for someone?"

Corvick looked past them, and Jamie was reminded of the number of Uniforms on either side of their fire. She tilted her head, listening. There, the faint clinking of boots on the ground. At least one of the Uniforms had moved behind them.

The hairs on the back of her neck stood on end as a chill ran up her spine. She exhaled slowly.

The lieutenant picked up one of three tin cups at his side and tapped his fingernails across the surface. He turned his bright blue gaze to meet her silver one. "I am, in fact. A Silver. Caused a lot of trouble out west, and now she's on the run."

Jamie sat very still. Ringing began in her ears, but she forced it down. Forced her heartbeat to remain calm so it wouldn't drown the words she desperately needed to hear.

Corvick straightened, his chest protruding like a proud peacock. "I was chosen to get word to the crossing ports. Warn them of the danger and sniff out any illegal crossings along the way. We've had reports of one a bit north of here."

Oliver leaned forward, resting his forearms on his knees. "Like we said, we've been headed north. We haven't seen any other Silvers during our trek, but we mostly keep to ourselves, sir. Any word on what this one did?"

Jamie swallowed down the flare of anger at the way he spoke.

Part of the game.

Jamie closed her eyes, pinching them tight for a moment as she willed Alice's voice to leave her mind. Now was not the time to be hearing ghosts.

"Everything okay?" Corvick was staring when she opened her eyes.

"Yeah, just a headache. It's been a long few days." Jamie rubbed her fingers across her forehead. "Do you have a description? Or even an ID number? We can keep an eye out on our journey."

Corvick let loose a high-pitched chuckle, his grin turning cocky. "Obviously I have a description, or you'd both have been arrested on sight."

Jamie stuffed her hands into her jacket pockets. She'd avoided it so far, wanting them out and ready in case the Uniforms were given orders to attack. But her anger, her discomfort, and her fear were all reaching a staggering peak.

"You said a woman?" Oliver said, pulling the lieutenant's focus away from her.

"Yes. Silver, obviously. Tall, with dark hair, angular features. Skilled fighter, with the training of the leadership circuit." He looked at Jamie.

She refused to give in to the urge to touch her blonde hair. It was braided down her scalp on both sides, twin snakes that draped well past her shoulders.

"And a series of tally marks in a line down each arm."

Jamie could barely breathe. She met Corvick's daring gaze, holding herself together through sheer desperation as he put the finishing touches on a perfect description of her sister.

With the calm that only comes in the eye of a storm, Jaime shrugged one shoulder, using the movement to slip her arm from the sleeve of her jacket.

She leaned toward the fire, showing off the X's marking her from shoulder to elbow. "It's a common style among Unborn. They can mean a bunch of different things."

Corvick nodded. A flicker of disappointment shadowed his expression, but he visibly relaxed as she pulled her jacket back on.

"What do yours symbolize?"

Oliver inhaled. He had to know, had to sense the urgency coursing through Jamie's veins. Vic wasn't just a destination for them now, she was in danger. She was being hunted.

Jamie pushed the thought down and flashed her teeth at the Lieutenant again. "I got one for every kill."

His youthfulness showed in the widening of his eyes and the blanching of his skin, but he recovered quickly. He cleared his throat and reached for the pot of water almost sitting in the fire. "You must have been deployed near the end of the war." He looked up when he was finished pouring his tea. "To be able to track them all."

"Up to a hundred." Oliver's voice was not smooth or soft now.

Jamie shot a look at him, surprised at the lack of restraint on his face. He was staring at the lieutenant. A furrow marked his brow, and his muscles were tight against the constraints of his coat.

"Sorry?" Corvick looked at Oliver over the lip of his tin cup.

"She didn't track them all, just the first hundred."

A bit of tea dribbled from the man's mouth as he darted a glance at Jamie. He returned focus to Oliver quickly and wiped his chin with the back of his sleeve. Jamie was convinced she caught the scent of his fear-tinged sweat even through the smoke of the fire.

"Well, if that's what *this* Unborn was tracking, we should have little trouble bringing her in." Corvick raised his tin cup. Then he waited, watching them both.

Oliver reached, with slow and steady movements, and took up the matching cups. He poured from the pot, filling Jamie's to the brim and leaving only a few swallows for himself.

Jamie took the offered cup. Her heart hammered in her chest, but she drank when the others did. Warmth seeped down her throat and pooled in her belly. But it wasn't the warmth that came from Oli's laugh, or little feet scampering, or Alice's excitement over fresh baked bread.

It was molten and dark. As though the hot water fed the pit of black that had been growing since Alice's death.

She remained still, silent, and seething as Oliver engaged Corvick in meaningless conversation. Her fellow Silver lauded the lieutenant's accolades, shared names of Organic officers they both knew, and showed more than a surface-level interest in Corvick's military goals.

Eventually, after the stars overhead shifted position and the tea had been drained, Corvick stood.

He stretched, cracked his neck, and smiled down at the two Unborn. "It was good of you to share your fire and your time. Where will you go now?" He eyed the still-covered dirt bikes.

Oliver shrugged a shoulder, standing as well. "South, most likely. If we can't go west, maybe we can find some friends near the wetlands."

"Be sure you get registered when you find a landing ground. Unborn can't be wandering anymore."

Oliver nodded. "Yes, sir."

Jamie clenched her teeth and stared into the fire. She heard, rather than saw, Lieutenant Corvick return to his truck. He scrambled into the cab, the sound followed by heavy clunking as Uniforms joined him in the cab and bed.

Her eyes were tired, lids heavy, neck aching. But she did not let down her guard or her focus. She cocked her head just enough to better catch Corvick's words as the truck engine turned over.

"Good timing. We'll get to that shitty dump before dawn. They know something there, and I'll be damned if I'm going to let someone else find that hybrid before I do. It'll mean a double rank promotion if we bring her in."

Jamie closed her eyes. The truck revved. A moment later puffs of dust coated their little camp as the lieutenant and his Uniforms sped away into the night.

18

Small Miracles

"**D** *AMMIT*."

Jamie looked up as Oliver's boot slammed into the pot by the fire. It flew into the air with a clang, the bouncing of the metal echoing in the empty air around them.

That temper he kept on such a tight leash was reaching the end of its tether.

"He's going to the Switch," Jamie muttered. Her disgust for the Lieutenant churned like spoiled meat in her stomach.

"I know," Oli snapped.

She met his eye. "Vic is in danger."

His lips pinched together, and he exhaled a heavy sigh. "I know."

"We'd lose a day."

"I know, Jamie." This time almost a whisper. "But—"

She stood, zipped her half jacket to the neck, and pulled a knit cap over her hair. "We don't have a choice."

His eyebrows drew together, body tense.

Jamie strode to her bike and ripped the tarp off the top of it. "He can't know we're behind him. No lights."

Oliver's lips parted. He watched her movements, almost holding his breath.

Jamie finished securing her things and turned to him. His face was barely visible in the dying firelight. The moon above them was a thin sliver. Stars speckled the sky, but even they were dim so near the Wasteland.

Still, she could make out every crease of his skin. Her mind filled in the spaces she couldn't see from memory.

"We don't have a choice, Oli. Not with how badly that man wants a promotion. Not with that many Uniforms under his command. Not even a Gold..." She shook her head. "We can't risk the chance that Noah can't take them all."

"There would be collateral damage even if he could."

Jamie looked into the silver pools of his eyes. She knew what he was thinking, knew he was seeing the same devastating memories they both shared.

They finished loading up the bikes.

"Slow," Oliver said as he started his engine. "The Uniforms will spot us if we go around."

Jamie exhaled through flared nostrils and clenched her handlebars. "Let's go."

They dumped the dirt bikes a mile from the Switch. Dawn crept along the horizon as the two Unborn crept toward town.

They'd kept a good pace, the lieutenant's truck a dot in the distance for most of the trek. Even so, the five-minute difference between his arrival and their own sent nerves crawling down Jamie's spine.

They reached the lip of rubble that separated the western edge of the Switch from the stretch of nothingness between it and the Wasteland.

All was quiet, but instinct told Jamie it would not be for long. She tapped Oli's shoulder and gestured to the first row of boxy homes.

They moved. Stayed low and crossed the space in seconds. Jamie pressed her back to the edge of the structure and leaned her head around the corner. Still silent. Still that calm of pre-dawn.

The hairs on the back of her neck stood on end, and she wished Noah had given them weapons before they'd left.

Then again, if they'd been caught with them...

Oliver froze beside her. Jamie glanced at him and he tapped his ear with a finger.

She listened.

In the distance, someone screamed.

She was up. Up and running with Oli's footsteps pounding behind her. Not tactical like Alice. Not strategic like Vic.

No, Jamie was a different breed. Designed for ambush missions. For close combat, heavy casualty, barely-make-it-home-alive missions. She was built to destroy everything in her path, and she embraced that intent.

The two burst out of a narrow alley onto the main road. The inn was ahead of them. Trish stood just outside the doorway, clutching the baby to her chest with the gaggle of children clinging to her legs.

Over two dozen townsfolk were clustered in the street. Four Uniforms surrounded them, weapons aimed at the people, blank gazes carrying no hint of mercy. A pile of guns were strewn across the ground. Not the sleek, shiny things the Uniforms carried. These were the sawed off shotguns, hunting rifles, and handguns that had been trained on Jamie and Oliver at their first arrival.

The robots turned as one, glinting red eyes fixing on the Unborn.

"Corvick?" Jamie directed to Oliver as she moved one way and he the other, flanking the group.

His words were clipped. Short and to the point. "Don't see him. Or Noah."

Jamie nodded. She pursed her lips, fists at the ready as the Uniforms closest to her shifted, facing her and then back to the civilians. Their weapons flicked back and forth. A smirk split her lips. No judgment. Only orders. The trick was finding out which orders took precedence.

And after their evening tea with the lieutenant, Jamie was pretty sure she knew what would be at the top of the list.

She gestured to the nearest machine. "Hey, tinman," she called out, using her practiced Valhalla ring voice. "Good to see you again. You don't happen to know where your boss is, do you? Because I came here to kill Lieutenant Corvick."

Across the crowd, Oliver's eyes widened.

As one, the Uniforms surged toward her.

Jamie scampered.

Shots rang out, eliciting screams and rapid scurrying. Half of the townsfolk darted toward their weapons. The rest sprinted to safety.

Jamie reached an alley, bullets peppering the dirt at her feet. She leapt, grasped the edge of a drain pipe, and clawed her way to the rooftop.

Seconds later, the four Uniforms marched into view, weapons trained down the long stretch between buildings.

Jamie exhaled a single whispered curse. And jumped.

She landed on a Uniform in the middle. She latched her leg around its neck and swung her entire body weight backward.

The thing flipped as her back hit the ground. She released at just the right time. The Uniform slammed into one of its fellows. Metal crunched as both tumbled to the ground.

Jamie flipped to her feet. A gun swung her direction.

She leaned, grabbed the muzzle, and jerked the thing forward, then sharply back again. The butt of the weapon slammed into the Uniform's shoulder, but the pain of the impact jarred her as well.

She grunted, her elbow seizing, but she didn't release the gun. She kicked at the knee joint. The Uniform buckled. As it went to one knee, it swung.

A flesh covered metal fist impacted her gut with a whole new level of force than she was used to. Closer to Noah's punches than she'd have liked.

She flew backward, yanking the weapon with her as her hand clenched on instinct.

Her back smacked against another Uniform. She forced in a breath. Pain laced through her torso as her lungs expanded.

She fell forward as a mechanical arm came from behind to pin her in place. It was too late.

Jamie rolled, then kicked out again, landing a direct hit on a joint. As she did, a thick boot stomped onto the gun, and it slipped from her fingers.

The silence of the fight, no utterances of pain or exertion from the Uniforms, unnerved her.

The one in front of her swung. She leaned out of the direct path, but just the glancing blow split her cheek. Her mouth filled with blood.

The two on the ground had risen. They surrounded her as she crouched, fury in the heavy breaths she pulled into her chest. Only one still clutched its gun, but there were four of them.

Now would've been a good time for strategy.

She spit blood onto the ground and looked up. A shadow moved behind the Uniform in front of her.

Jamie grinned.

A blast like a cannon sent a spray of oil, metal shards, and other bits she didn't care to identify spewing across the alley.

Oliver cocked the shotgun in his hands as the Uniform fell, its head entirely obliterated.

Jamie spun. Her foot caught the ankle of one of the remaining three enemies, and she took it to the ground.

Another blast sounded above her head. She sank her fist into the Uniform's eye socket. It dented.

She growled, already hissing with pain as her knuckles split on the metal skeleton of the machine before her. Another strike. A third. With the fourth, the Uniform stopped moving.

She rolled off, springing to her feet in time to avoid the boot coming at her face. It caught her waist instead. She slammed into the brick wall behind her with a cry of pain. Her hands instinctively clutched the pain below her ribs.

Oliver leapt. His arms latched around the head of the last standing Uniform. He twisted, all the rage and despair he'd kept a secure lock on exploding out of him in a roar of effort.

The Uniform's head detached from its body with another spurt of fluids and wires. The body slumped. Oliver tossed the head to the ground.

He rushed forward. Jamie straightened with a moan, squaring up for the next attack.

But Oliver was looking at *her*, coming toward *her*.

Her heart leapt into her throat for a brief moment. Then she saw the silver of his eyes, his open palms, and the fear etched across his face.

His hands landed softly on her cheeks. He stooped, briefly meeting her gaze before he scanned her body. "Are you okay?"

Jamie swallowed. Her breath came in quick gasps, heartbeat thundering even faster than it had been a few seconds ago. Her skin flushed where he touched her.

She put her fingers on his wrists and gently pulled his hands away. As she did, the bloody wreck of skin that was her knuckles caught her eye.

She avoided looking, keeping her eyes on Oli instead.

"I'm okay." She moved him back a step to get a view of his whole body. "You?"

He nodded. The fear faded from his features, but the tense pinch of his brow remained. "We're not done."

"I know." She spit again, a glob of mucus and blood landing on the dirt between two mechanical bodies. "We need to find Noah."

She straightened again, unable to hold in a gasp as pain latticed across her ribs and torso.

"Shit. These things are—"

"Another level, yeah." Oliver stooped and grabbed two of the Uniform's weapons. He passed one to Jamie. "Not too bright though."

She nodded. "Small miracles."

She took another few seconds to breathe. The dust at their feet had turned to mud from the oil still dripping out of the Uniforms.

The weapons were as high-tech as the things designed to use them. Jamie frowned down at the gun. She'd have preferred her standard issue, but anything was better than hand-to-hand against a walking sheet of metal.

The cool morning breeze stung against the exposed nerves on her knuckles.

They hurried from the alley. The street was mostly deserted. A handful of Organics stood like sentinels in front of the door to the inn.

Jamie limped toward them. To her surprise, not a single one trained their weapons on her or Oli.

"They taken care of?" a gruff voice barked. A thick man with flaming red hair and bright green eyes hefted his rifle across his forearm, holding it with the skill and knowledge of someone trained with firearms.

"Those four," Oliver replied. "Where is Noah? Where's the lieutenant?"

"Where's Trish?" Jamie craned her neck to see over the cluster of people. Just inside the door she spotted a petite brunette woman holding the baby. The children were tucked under one of the tables. A stone-like weight dropped into Jamie's stomach.

The man frowned, looking around as well, concern blazing in his eyes.

"She went to find Noah." The brunette stepped forward, her voice soft and high like a little mouse. "He was cleaning weapons in the shed. She said he could help."

Jamie pursed her lips. Frustration roiled through her veins. She met the eye of the redhead. "Keep everyone here. If any more people show up, put them in the inn. If you spot Uniforms, bar the door with every piece of furniture in the place."

The man scowled.

Oliver took half a step forward, meeting his eye with a not-unkind expression. "Uniforms can go one for one against a Copper. These newer versions are on par with Silvers. You do *not* want to fight these things. Keep these people safe; that's the priority."

He'd fought. That much was clear as the man straightened and jerked his head in a nod. He'd probably been one of the last squads of Organic soldiers on the front line. Which made him older than he looked.

Jamie swallowed down a bitter taste on her tongue. Her mind flashed to a different time, a different cluster of soldiers before her.

Ones who took her orders, whether they thought she was worth giving them or not.

With a final scan of the group of Organics, she stepped away. Her feet found purchase on the hard packed dirt of the road. Her fingers caressed the semi-automatic in her hands.

"Ready?"

She glanced beside her. Oli's weapon was at the ready, his face set, his breath even.

He nodded. "Let's go find a Gold."

19

DIBS

THEY TOOK DOWN ANOTHER two Uniforms on their way to the shed which had stored their bikes. Townspeople hurried past. Only a few changed course when Oli called for them to make for the inn.

"Ammo?"

"Low," Jamie growled. She checked her clip again, irritated that she hadn't taken an extra off the metallic bodies they'd left in the alley. "Wish we had a few more Silvers here for this. You're right about these new versions."

"Yeah, this'd be a different fight if we had Vic or James."

"Or Katya," Jamie said. She shook her head. Wishing didn't change the fact that they were tackling this mission solo. Vic's location was no longer a mystery. But the rest of the Silvers and Coppers they'd fought alongside may as well have been on a different planet.

The Switch was a small town. Small enough that it barely took a few minutes for Jamie and Oliver to get to the shed, even with how carefully they moved.

It was empty. Signs of a struggle were evident in the torn apart Uniforms and the bullet holes peppering the old car and the far wooden wall.

"How many Uniforms do you think a Gold can handle alone?" Oli asked in a low voice as they moved east, further into the outskirts.

"We've dropped six. Looks like Thomas took care of at least two."

"Hard to tell how many there were at the shed."

Jamie inclined her head. The body parts in the shed had been shredded past the point of identification.

"Four left, maybe more." Oliver repositioned his weapon. He'd drawn his blade, holding it in his left hand as he steadied the point of the gun with his arm.

Jamie wanted to run. To charge forward with guns at the ready. But she'd gotten lucky that first time, and she knew it. If the Uniforms had been given different orders, she might've gotten a bunch of innocents killed.

So they went slow and stayed out of the open.

It was eerily quiet.

The low wall circling the town came into view, only one set of homes between them and the rolling hills they'd traveled through to reach the Switch.

They slunk along the side of a long-parked trailer home. Oli snuck a glance around the corner. Jaime took half a step to join him. His hand flew out, briefly touching her torso before he lifted a fist.

She nodded and moved back. A few seconds later Oliver switched places so she could assess what he had seen.

A string of curses went through her mind. She bit her tongue to hold them, and her anger, in check.

On the other side of the trailer they hid behind was a dusty circle of run-down, rusted out vehicles. Noah stood in the center, his shirt ripped and knuckles bloodied.

He faced them—well, faced Corvick. The lieutenant's pistol was aimed at Noah's chest. Uniforms clutched his arms on either side.

Jamie frowned for a second. Even injured, he had the ability to rip them apart before the bullet left the chamber, so why—

"Shit," she breathed.

Oliver leaned in, his chin just above her shoulder as he looked out.

Trish was on her knees to the south of the dingy clearing. A bruise welled across the left side of her face, blood dripping from her nose. Her gaze was distant, dizzy. A Uniform stood behind her. Its hand gripped the back of her neck.

They were far from Noah. Too far for him to act, which had to be why he hadn't yet. A single move and the machine behind Trish would snap her neck without a thought.

Literally.

"Ideas?" Oliver asked, his voice nearly silent but mild as though they were discussing the weather.

They stepped further back, pressing against the silver plating of the trailer.

Jamie bit her lower lip, flexing her free hand. Her gaze stuck on the ruddy, rocky ground for a moment. She knelt and picked up a rock the size of a small apple. She studied it for a few seconds. "You remember that border crossing?"

His brow furrowed for a second. "The hostage negotiation?"

"Yep."

His full lips curving into a smile. "You want dibs?"

Jamie bared her teeth. "Corvick."

"Okay. I've got Trish."

"Thirty seconds," Jamie said as she pocketed the rock.

He nodded.

They split up.

Jamie skirted forward, staying low and using the rusted-out vehicles between her and the lieutenant to keep out of sight as she counted.

The weapon in her hands was a comfort. Like having an old friend around. Her knuckles ached from digging through the metal eye socket of the Uniform she'd taken down. Pain laced across her torso. Her breath hitched for a second as she stifled a groan.

Crouched running was not ideal for quick healing.

The low rumble of voices helped cover Jamie's boots on the dirt. She hesitated, knelt behind a tire, and listened intently to the conversation going on between Noah and the Adam pointing a gun at his chest.

"... an Unborn here," Corvick was saying. "You're hiding her, and I can't have that. Give her to me, turn over the illegal arms, and I'll think about sparing the ones housing traitors who turned their weapons on a military officer."

Noah's voice was tighter and deeper than usual. "There is no Silver woman here."

Corvick scoffed.

Jamie glanced under the car. The lieutenant moved forward, stepping closer to the Gold.

Seconds ticked by.

"There must be," Corvick insisted. "Nothing else could destroy my Uniforms so efficiently. My scouts were torn apart."

He took another step, and Jamie moved. She climbed slowly. Used one hand to pull herself up and planted her boot on the shards of a broken window.

Her head poked over the top of the truck. She pulled the rock from her pocket, still counting seconds in her head.

Noah shrugged and made to step forward before the Uniforms holding him jerked him backward. "Are you certain?" he asked, narrowing his gaze on Corvick. "Humans are quite tenacious."

It was a wonder the lieutenant hadn't realized who—what—he was really speaking to. Noah's dark contacts glinted with flecks of gold as the sun hit them. Then again, the concept of Unborn disguising themselves in such a way was unheard of.

But if Corvick got much closer...

Jamie's mental count hit thirty. She leaned back, aimed north, and chucked the rock.

A full three seconds passed until a loud clunk sounded behind Corvick. He turned; the Uniforms who had flanked him mimicked his movement. But he'd stepped away from them. Toward Noah. Toward her.

Jamie scrambled the rest of the way onto the roof of the truck, tightened her grip on her gun, and launched herself into the air for the second time that morning.

It was a gamble going for Corvick first. But he needed to be unable to speak. So he couldn't give orders, and because Jamie had wanted to break his jaw since he'd opened it the first time.

She and the lieutenant went sprawling into the dirt. He coughed. Spit dust from his mouth.

Jamie whirled on her knees. Rose to her feet. Trained her weapon on one of the flanking Uniforms and blasted a hole into its chest. A split second later she completed her turn with a full kick at Corvick's face.

Her boot made contact with a disturbingly satisfying crunch.

The man let out a wail like a dying animal and fell to his side in the dirt. His hands clutched at his ruined teeth, blood flowing as free as a babbling brook.

One of the Uniforms reached her.

It grabbed the hood of her jacket, catching a handful of hair as it ripped her backward.

She yelped. Pain burst in her scalp. She flew, soaring over the thing's head as it flung her to the ground. Her head cracked against the hard-packed earth. Ringing split her ears.

Her vision blurred.

The force required to put her down so effectively mixed a bead of fear into her swirling storm of anger. Oli was facing off against two of them.

Put it down.

She rolled, pushed to all fours, and nodded at Alice's non-existent voice. Put down the Uniform, then see to Oli.

He could handle himself. Jamie knew it.

Knew it and fixed the thought firmly at the front of her mind because if she turned to look... if she spent a single second distracted, the machine swinging at her would rip her head from her shoulders.

She danced. Danced like she was back in the ring, balls of her feet, gun loose in her hand until she could get enough distance to raise and fire. This close and the Uniform coming at her would have a hand around the muzzle before she properly aimed.

Sounds caught her attention. Shouts, a scream, crunching metal.

She narrowed her focus.

The Uniform she'd blasted a hole into stirred on the ground. The one in front of her swung again. Its fist came far too close to her ribs.

Jamie feinted. Made to go left and went right instead. Earned just enough space to take advantage of her surroundings again. Her foot planted on the sturdy edge of an empty tire. She came down with both hands around her weapon. The butt of the thing crashed into the weak joint between the Uniform's neck and shoulder. The gun stuck there.

The Uniform pummeled her side, but she held on, prying the weapon deeper. Grinding metal pained her ears. She jerked.

At the sound of the pop, Jamie dropped her entire body weight onto the Uniform's arm. She, and it, fell to the ground. The gun clattered down as well. Ruined.

"Shit." Jamie rolled again.

She came to her feet just as a pair of ebony hands closed around the Uniform's neck.

Jamie panted, drawing short bursts of air through her nose and trying not to stand too straight for the hurt radiating across her torso.

Noah was a sight to behold.

The Gold wasted no time. He was not strategic the way Vic would have been, nor graceful like Alice. If anything, he reminded Jamie of herself. But stronger. Stronger than she'd ever guessed or been told.

The gap between her and a Copper was one thing, further than a Copper and an Organic. Comparing the distance between Copper and Silver with Silver and Gold felt like comparing the distance between the earth and the moon with the moon and the sun.

Part of Jamie was glad she'd never truly fought one. And she understood the military's desire to keep Golds separated from each other.

Noah shredded the Uniforms. Scrap metal seemed an appropriate term for what they became as he strode across the little battlefield.

"Jamie."

Another spike of pain splintered through her as she turned too fast. Oli was there. Leaning against Trish and wincing. But there. Alive.

Some internal recognition of how much that meant to her sent alarm bells blaring through her head. She ignored them as relief drove the pain from her body.

"Oli," she breathed the word, and hurried to him. His leg was wounded, bloody and not quite supporting his weight.

Trish was crying. Tears glistened against her shiny red puffed-up cheek. She passed Oliver to Jamie, her eyes saying everything she couldn't form into words.

Jamie swallowed and nodded once. "You're okay?"

Trish nodded back. Her hands trembled. She glanced at Corvick, still writhing in pain on the ground.

Jamie's features tightened. Her gaze darkened as she took in the pathetic wriggling mass of unearned authority.

She looked back at Trish's swollen face.

"Was that him?" Jamie met Trish's eye and did not need to specify her question.

Trish's slender, calloused fingers briefly touched her face. She nodded.

"Jamie," Oliver muttered.

"Yeah." Jamie tightened her grip, adjusting his arm over her shoulder to better carry him. "In a second."

With little choice in the matter, Oliver limped along beside her as Jamie crossed to the lieutenant. A few paces away, Noah finished dispatching the final Uniform. He turned to look at them both.

Jamie kicked Corvick onto his back. He stared up at her, those baby blues filled with tears as he whimpered something unintelligible. Her lip curled in disgust.

"I don't think you needed to hit her," Jamie murmured.

Corvick's eyes widened even further. Fear was as thick in his expression as the blood was on the dirt around him.

She released Oliver, and he grunted as she leaned down to give Corvick a better view of her face.

"I know that Silver. The one you're looking for. She's good at not being found." The corner of Jamie's mouth twisted into a smile that hinted at pride. "But just in case, it'd probably be better if that message never got delivered."

He grunted, pleaded something that she couldn't make out through the broken bones that had once been his jaw.

Jamie settled her boot against his neck for a quick kill.

A surge ran down her spine and through her limbs. A rush of anxiety, of fear.

She pulled back, breath coming heavy as the snap that had killed Alice reverberated across her forearm again. The bandage under her sleeve was heavy, stifling.

"Hey."

Jamie blinked and looked up.

Noah stood before her. Blood and grease speckled his shirt. His face was dark with the trauma of a war long past and violence not forgotten. He held out a pistol.

Jamie frowned for half a second before recalling that Oliver had filled him in. Had told him the whole story of Alice and the darkness and the ring. She took the gun.

"You want me to—" Oliver got half the question out. The rest was cut off by the gunshot as Jamie put a hole in the lieutenant's forehead.

20

The Wasteland

"**W**E'VE GOT THIS."

Jamie pulled her jacket back on, wincing as the fabric scraped across the myriad of bruises across her torso and arms. "Are you sure? We could—"

"Stay?" Noah raised an eyebrow. "No. I think we both know you don't have that kind of time."

She met his eye.

"The one he was looking for, she's your sister?"

Jamie's jaw tightened automatically. She relaxed it with a swallow and a nod.

"We don't want to leave you exposed," Oliver chimed in. He sat half a pace away, which was about as far as Jamie was comfortable with him being after the heightened fear of the fight.

Part of it was the mission. Knowing she needed him not only to get to Vic, but to get the revenge they both needed. Part of it was their friendship. She'd known him longer than just about everyone. There were a handful of Silvers who had joined her, Alice, and Vic at the start of their tour. Oliver was among the few still standing.

And there was a part of her, a very small, neglected part, that worried he might die before she forgave him.

Trish had done a decent job patching his wound, but it continued to sluggishly bleed through the thick bandage. The Uniform had nearly taken out his leg. A large gash across his calf, deep enough to expose the white of his bone, had required staples to close properly.

She glanced at him before looking back at Noah. "He's right. If anyone comes looking for that fu—"

"We'll be all right," Noah interrupted. His voice was slow and steady. A sharp contrast to the alertness in his eyes, the edge of his movements. "We know how to clean up a mess. If anyone *does* comes searching for the lieutenant, they won't find a trace."

He put a hand on Jamie's arm. She looked at it, then him. There was knowing in his gaze. An understanding of the urgency she felt. The desperate, driving pressure to get to the person who needed her most.

She exhaled. "We need more gas."

He gave it to them. Gas, food, water, and, just before the two Silvers prepared to ride off again, Noah passed Jamie a long blade. Its sheath was black, detailed with golden lines that matched the handle. The knife itself was a solid eight-inches. Long enough to do more than a little damage in her hands.

"Why give it to me?" she asked, her voice thick with gratitude.

He grinned. "I have a feeling you'll need it. And he already has one." Noah jerked a thumb at Oliver, who was attempting to find a comfortable position to ride with the lower half of his leg almost immobile.

Jamie fidgeted for a few seconds, uncomfortable and uncertain. *Thank you.*

She almost flinched at Alice's familiar nagging tone. Then she inhaled and gave a sharp nod. "Thank you."

Noah nodded back. "I understand the need for revenge. Use it well."

They still had to go south. Jamie clenched the handles of her bike, fighting down a snapping remark when Oliver reminded her that the quickest way through was the best idea. Both for their own health and for their time.

A road was necessary. A straight shot through what would otherwise be nearly impossible terrain. Even if getting to it added several hours to their journey.

Jamie seethed the whole way.

There was no stopping to rest this time. Even with their injuries and nightfall fast approaching. Instead, they gulped down their meals in silence, swallowed enough water to give them both stomach aches, and filled their gas tanks.

"Six hours for the first leg," Oli said.

Jamie didn't respond. She was mid-wrapping a thick scarf around her neck and the lower half of her face. Goggles went on over her eyes, a scarf covered her braided hair, and a helmet was next. She tucked the ends of her braids into her sweater, not sure what a toxic nuclear haze would do to them, and not wanting to find out.

Every article of clothing was tucked in. No piece of skin exposed.

Jamie had even rolled up her jacket and secured it at the bottom of her bag. She was pretty sure they'd have to burn their clothes on the other side.

"Jamie."

She glanced over. Oliver looked the same way she did, every scrap of golden-brown skin hidden, a heavy pair of goggles barely letting her see those silver eyes, and a thick scarf muffling his words. His left leg was wrapped tight. Riding was just about the worst thing he could do for the wound, apart from walking. But they had little choice in the matter.

That fact did not ease her worrying.

"We *have* to stop."

Her lip curled under the fabric. "I know. Gas."

"No." He stepped in front of her bike. His coverings didn't manage to hide his wince.

Jamie released the handles, sitting back and staring at him with a furrowed brow.

"We have to stop for oxygen," he said. "I know we can go longer. And I know you want to. But if we don't get clean air at least a little, we don't make it to Vic."

Jamie clenched her hands. She didn't like having so much fabric between her fingers. Wraps were one thing, doing their job to protect her knuckles in the ring. But the gloves covering her hands now were thick and bulky.

She clicked her teeth; a sound he probably didn't hear past the scarf. "I'm not trying to get us killed before we get there, Oli. Six hours."

He met her eye, a tricky thing to do with both of them wearing goggles. But he must have seen her sincerity, or at least the truth of not wanting them to die before they arrived, because he gave a sharp nod and returned to his own bike.

He swung a leg over with a grunt and started the engine. Jamie did the same.

A wide four-lane highway stretched before them. The hazy wall of the Wasteland was about a mile away. Final bits of reflecting sunlight painted the thing in hues of red, orange, and pink.

Jamie leaned forward, wincing as her body squalled its dislike of the movement. Still, a smile split her lips. She turned her head toward Oli, shouting so he could hear her.

"Hey."

He glanced over.

"You realize what this is, right?"

She couldn't see his usual furrowed brow, but he shook his head.

She gestured a hand behind them, and then toward their destination. "*This*. We're riding into the sunset. Cowboy."

He threw his head back in what she recognized as exasperation. Jamie barked out a gleeful laugh, revved her bike, and sped forward with Oli close on her tail.

Her amusement at his expense did not last long.

It was only Jamie's experience as an Unborn soldier, her training from birth, her missions that barely skirted death, and the significance of the tattoo on her ribs that kept her going after the first two six-hour legs.

Everything hurt. Every inch of skin, the inside of her lungs, her eyes, all of it burned. A ceaseless fire that relented to nothing and no one. Not until they got to the other side. Not until they got away from the hollow husk-like remains of what had once been.

They passed too many towns. Too many homes still standing. Ghostly shadows of a foreign world. A foreign time.

They passed divots too. Massive craters that had been the epicenters of bombs dropped. At one point the road before them crumbled into one of these pits, leaving only a few inches of asphalt to navigate for nearly half a mile. They'd have gone onto the dirt, but fear of losing the track was too great.

The painted yellow lines and somewhat smooth dark gray path beneath them were the only things stopping them from becoming completely and utterly lost.

The sun did not shine. The sky brightened in the day and went dark at night. The mundanity of it made Jamie's eyes itch.

They were in a liminal space. A purgatory.

Jamie shuddered as they passed a half-destroyed sign offering a detour to a park. She knew, vaguely, where she'd been created. All Unborn were imagined, drafted, and crafted in the U.S. On "good ol' American soil," as one of her first commanders had liked to say.

Most of those facilities had been in the midwest. They'd been the targets of the nuclear strikes.

Jamie, Alice, and Vic had all said goodbye to trainers, cooks, and younger Unborn when they were shipped overseas. Jamie liked to imagine the ones who were Organics, the ones who just worked in the facilities, had been on trips back home, maybe near the coasts. That they'd, at least, been spared.

In reality she knew the truth. They had all perished. Succumbed to—hopefully—quick deaths at the hands of the enemy. Everyone except Angela, their creator, who had traveled with them to their first base only to die just before they shipped out to the front line.

It had been a motivator for their first few years of war. Avenge the ones who never made it past those five-Cal days. The little ones, who never knew life beyond the gray walls, the rows of beds, the days of tests and training and pushing. Always pushing. To be better, faster, stronger.

Jamie's front tire thumped over a tree branch, and she shook her head to return her focus to the road. Oliver was a little ahead of her and didn't notice the swerve as she'd adjusted.

She swallowed, the acrid taste of death on her tongue even after a short break to fill their gas tanks and inhale fresh oxygen from the canisters strapped to their bikes. They didn't dare eat or drink. It was bad enough breathing.

"One more burst," Oli had said.

She'd heard the pain in his hoarse voice, even through the many layers. Weariness dragged at both of them. Unborn could go days without sleeping, and they were. But they'd been up a full twenty-four hours before entering the haze. If they had been in normal conditions, able to eat and drink, able to stop for more than five minutes at a time...

Jamie glanced at her milage reader. Another four hours. Maybe. If they didn't run into any more spots where they could only go 10 miles per hour. And when they came out the other side?

Noah hadn't given them any input on the west coast. He'd never been there.

It would be new territory for them.

Jamie unclenched her fingers, shaking out her left hand before settling it over her chest for a few seconds. Vic's letter was there. Folded and tucked into the lining of her sports bra.

They had coordinates. They had a destination.

They'd get out of this. Get cleaned up. Get a night of sleep.

And then Jamie would find her sister.

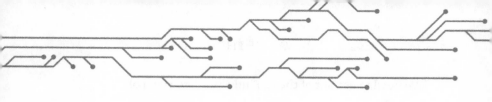

21

One Small Part

THE WORLD OF SEPIA-TONED haze ended with such severity Jamie worried for a second that she'd passed out and was dreaming.

She hit the brakes, rear wheel skidding sideways as she rubbed her sleeve across her goggles to stare, transfixed, at the sight before her.

Miles ahead, but still close enough to catch her breath, the ruddy gray tones shifted to green. Sprawling hills rolled up and away, growing to giant heights as they became mountains. Towering, rocky cliff faces and snow-capped peaks stretched north and south as far as the eye could see.

Jamie had seen mountains. Seen regions of snow and rock and evergreens. But this felt different. New.

She glanced at Oliver. He'd stopped as well, staring the same way she was at the beauty before them.

She wanted it on canvas. Wanted the brush strokes to carry the weight of the snow, the sunlight casting shadows across the rocks, the way the tarnished Wasteland eased into something beautiful.

It took a moment of enjoying the scenery for Jamie to remember the constant burning across her body. She winced at the discomfort.

"We need to get out of these. Find a place to clean off."

Her voice was muffled still, but she didn't want to remove the scarf. Not without taking the time to take everything else off as well.

Oli pointed a gloved hand ahead. The road continued; the asphalt was even more faded here. Sprigs of grass shot through the cracks. Sunlight poured across everything. It would be blinding when they removed their goggles.

Jamie took off, leading the way this time as they rode on. The road stayed straight longer than she expected. It was a good twenty miles until they hit the hills. There, it twisted and turned, steep inclines and sharp drops as they made their way into the mountains. Thick trees and sharp rock walls seemed to grow up on either side of them as they entered a twisting canyon.

Within half an hour, she was drenched with sweat. The suffocating weight of her helmet, the heavy sweater, the thick tape wrapped around her legs where her boots met her pants, was all somehow worse than her still stinging lungs.

But there... She slowed to a crawl, inching her bike forward until she reached the broken metal rail that had once served to stop cars spiraling out of control when they rounded turns too fast. Below them, some sections roaring with white rapids, others calm as a surface of glass, a river snaked through the mountains.

They'd built the road to follow it, Jamie realized as she knocked down her kickstand and took a few dazed steps forward. Her head spun, exhaustion, dehydration, and very likely radiation poisoning all coming to a head now that she'd stopped moving.

They were maybe thirty feet above the rushing water. But it wouldn't take much to get down, assuming her vision stopped blurring. There was a gradual decline of thick brush and scraggly trees.

Oliver stepped up behind her, his presence felt without her needing to turn.

"Here?"

She nodded, and blinked hard a few times, forcing herself away from the edge of unconsciousness.

They moved the bikes as far from the road as possible without risking them crashing down the cliff into the ravine below. Then they stripped.

Jamie started with her helmet. Still gloved, she unclipped the thing and tossed it to the ground. Her goggles and scarf came next; the fresh air hitting her face was like a burst of adrenaline. By the time she ripped off the tape, kicked her boots into the pile, and pulled her shirt over her head, her lungs had adjusted to the nontoxic air.

She sucked in breaths as though she were meditating, filling every inch of her chest with each pull, and exhaling until there was nothing left.

She spread her arms and tilted her face toward the sky, letting the sun beam down on her exposed skin. She'd need to change underwear, but that would be after she washed some of the sweat and muck from her body.

Jamie strode across the dirt pull-off where they'd parked, tugging the letter from Vic out of her bra and stowing it safely with her pack. When she turned, Oliver had lit a match and set it to their pile of contaminated clothes.

The fire was not what caught her eye.

Jamie exhaled, her lips parting as a surge of rage chased away the joy of the sunlight.

Oliver's left leg, the one the Uniform had injured, was a mess. A single, massive bruise ran from the edge of his black briefs down, past his knee, to the middle of his shin. A dirty, bloodstained bandage was wrapped around his calf. The wound needed to breathe, be cleaned, and re-bandaged.

She stared at it, brow furrowed, skin buzzing with a cold that seeped into her bones. If the blow that had done such damage had been aimed at his chest, or his head... a lump formed in her throat.

"Holy shit, Jamie."

She blinked and looked at his face. He stared at her with a matching expression of angry horror.

"Wha—" Jamie stopped asking as she glanced down at her own body. Her torso, from the band of her bra down to her hipbone was a match for his leg. Dark purple and blue, with the sickly fading green of days-old bruising at the edges. "Oh."

"Your arms look better at least." He strode toward her, leaving the fire to burn out behind him as he took her hands in his. His thumbs briefly hovered over the scabs covering her knuckles before he turned her hands over to look at her forearms.

He was right. The days of no sleep—no nightmares—had given her time to heal. There was minimal scarring, and a few faded yellow marks from the bruises she'd given herself.

"Why didn't you say your leg was that bad?" Jamie asked. She tilted her head, pulling away from him to get a better look.

"We needed to go." He shrugged. "It's not like we had the opportunity to change bandages the last couple of days."

She scowled.

Oliver grinned. "Do you wanna talk about my leg, or should we go rinse off?"

The dry, chalky taste on Jamie's tongue demanded they do the latter. She looked back at the fire. It was dying quickly. Their clothes were ash. The helmets nothing more than lumps of molten plastic and shards of metal.

She bent and scooped a handful of dirt and rocks off the ground and walked to the fire. Her knuckles stung as bits of smoke drifted up and caressed her skin.

She dumped the earth onto the flickering flames.

They found an inlet a few hundred yards upstream. A small channel had been carved out of the rocky earth, water drifting gently here. The only ripples on the surface came from the low-hanging branches of a drooping willow.

Jamie glanced back the way they'd come. The road was out of sight, but their tarp-covered bikes were just visible.

A splash jerked her attention back to the water. She shrieked as frigid droplets landed on her skin. Oliver came up for air, throwing his head back and spewing a mouthful of water at her.

She shrieked again, glaring as he burst into belly-deep laughter. The sound took her away from the horror they'd just ridden through. Took her from the bruises patterned across her torso. Took her from the gut-clenching fear for Vic's life. The guilt for Alice's. The questions and confusion and anger roiling within her mind.

His gaze lit on her, silver eyes framed by long black lashes.

"You understand I can't let that slide," Jamie said with a grin that she tried to turn into a scowl.

He smirked, his gravelly voice making her overly aware of how little they were both wearing. "Show me what you've got."

She scoffed, took a few steps back, and then cannon balled into the water inches from him.

The shock of the cold was quick. After it, the caress of water was like a soothing balm against her sore muscles, a cleansing sting on her scabs, a numbing ease to the tension running through her bones. She sank. Knees to her chest, arms curled around them.

She was a stone. A rock drifting down through the water and hitting the bottom far too quickly. Bubbles slid from her nostrils. Her hair unstuck from her back, sweat washed away by the cold encompassing her.

She could sleep here. Eyes closed, body freezing, mind finally quiet. Something stirred near her. The sharp clack of rocks hitting together underwater brought her from her moment of peace.

Jamie opened her eyes, blinking rapidly to ease away the burn of the water.

She lost a burst of air as laughter sprang from her lips. Oli hovered before her, his eyebrow raised, head cocked as he surveyed her.

He leaned toward her, and without the worry of his wound in front of her, Jamie couldn't avoid the intoxicating sight of his bare chest and arms. The strength of his shoulders, the shape of his neck and jaw as sunlight filtered in through the glistening water.

She rose, breaking the surface and inhaling another breath of fresh air. The cool water was not enough to stop heat pooling at the bottom of her stomach. She licked her lips as he surfaced as well, standing and shaking his head. Droplets flew from his shaggy black hair, over an inch long now and flopping across his forehead.

The sight stirred another rush of warmth, almost a burn, through Jamie. She'd never seen his hair this long. Never seen the scruff on his jaw so dark.

"You're..." Oliver swallowed. His gaze darted across her body before returning to her face.

Jaime blinked. She focused on his words, an immediate mistake as the shape of his lips caught too much of her attention. Her breath felt too shallow.

"You're okay?"

That brought some sense back to her. She frowned. "Yeah. I'm fine. Tired."

He nodded. "We should sleep."

A sinking disappointment, thick like sticky syrup and heavy like stone, put pressure on Jamie's chest. She ran her tongue across her teeth and fought the instinct to agree and leave the water.

Instead, she clenched her jaw and drew a breath. On the exhale, she stepped forward.

"Do you want to know why I didn't share that bed with you?"

Oliver's eyes went wide. He glanced around, as though there were any risk of someone hearing them.

Jamie kept her gaze on him. Watching the small movements of his face. The little twitch of his eyebrows and lips. The way his throat bobbed when he swallowed.

Part of her wanted to turn away. To leave the water, get dressed, curl into a ball all alone and fight her nightmares by herself. But it was the same part of her that carried all the weight from that time. The weight of the killing, the deaths, the fallout with Vic. All of it.

And it would never leave. That piece of her that refused to be called a leader because of the lives she'd lost. The piece that stung when Noah had talked of comradery because she'd had a family but never a connection to those soldiers who depended on her. The piece that knew what happened that day with Oliver was just as much her fault as it was his.

It'd be simple to keep hating him, blaming him for walking away. It was what had kept her from joining him at the inn. And it was the darker side of her that had wanted to sleep with him, to use him out of spite instead of anything else she might feel.

But she was so tired. And that piece of her, after all they'd been through—in the war and the past week—felt smaller somehow.

"It would have been so easy," she murmured. "To give in to that craving to touch you again."

Oliver was frozen, as though he thought if he moved he'd startle a wild animal.

"But I was *so* angry."

He flinched. Barely a movement, but she caught it.

A smile ghosted across her face. "I blamed you for a long time, Oli. And part of me still does."

He opened his mouth, but she raised a hand and shook her head.

"Not for us getting caught. And not for what happened with me and Vic. Not anymore. It was you walking away; that's what still hurts."

"Jamie." He whispered it. Whispered her name in a way that sent a flutter through her stomach. "I'm sorry. But you should know—"

She cut him off, her words equally soft, only audible because they stood so close. "I don't want to know, Oli. I don't want to care about why it happened the way it did. I..." Her jaw went tight, her hand briefly clenched at her side. "I can't live with hating you."

His lips trembled.

Jamie stepped forward. They were inches apart now. The warmth of his breath caressed her cheek. She kept his gaze.

"I can't convince myself to be angry with you anymore. I don't *want* to be angry anymore. I want—"

But he knew. He knew what she wanted. Always had. And damn if she wasn't good at making her needs, her intentions, known. But words weren't required here.

He broke her sentence with a kiss. Gentle at first, a brush of lips almost as hesitant as their first, so long ago.

Her hand circled his neck, fingers lacing through his hair and pulling him closer, deeper. He clutched her waist, another half second of hesitation before he brought her to him.

The heat of them both chased away any remaining cold.

They had done this once before. In a cramped, dark room on uncomfortable cots with the fear of repercussions in the back of both of their heads. This... this was different.

Jamie was mindful of his leg, but when he gripped her thighs and lifted, she willingly wrapped her legs around his waist. The weight of her was lessened by the belly-deep water they stood in. He shifted, moved them toward the river's edge and leaned his good leg against a solid rock.

His fingers bit into her flesh as he dug deeper into the kiss, and she returned the favor, clutching his upper back as his muscles rippled under her hands.

Her arms tightened around him. She pulled her lips away to kiss his cheek, his jaw, his neck. She bit him, just hard enough to elicit a gasp which brought laughter bubbling from her.

He slipped and, with a splash, both of them hit the water.

Laughing even harder, Jamie took his hand, slung his arm over her shoulder, and the two stumbled to shore. To a patch of moss-covered ground that was both soft and firm. Jamie put a hand to his chest, pressing just enough to convince him to lie back.

His voice was coarse, silver eyes looking up at her as though she'd never been seen before. "I can't get over the way you laugh."

She grinned, settling over him with a hesitance she wouldn't normally employ.

She moved her hands, tracing the shape of his arms, his chest. Her fingers danced lower, and his breath hitched.

"How's your leg?"

"I'll manage," he said through gritted teeth.

She laughed again and again. Her body and mind shifting between the soft warmth of the humor they shared to the searing heat, first of him under her as she rocked to the gentle lapping of the river, and then of the turn, him above, fingers exploring every part of her.

They laid side-by-side afterward. Jamie's breath slowed, her heartbeat steadying as the glow of the sun dried their bodies. She leaned in, his arm curling around her as she rested her head on his chest.

She traced the pattern of ink across his shoulder. Jumbled thoughts returned to her as the minutes ticked by.

And he must have felt it. Felt the exhale as her mind began to sort through their next steps. The obstacles in their path. The foes yet to face.

He tucked a strand of blonde hair behind her ear and pressed his lips to her forehead. Then he began to sing.

Jamie smiled against his chest. The words were simple, the melody of his own making. An old poem or lullaby he'd found on a mission. A song for the night, for the stars.

She closed her eyes, letting his voice wash over her. By the time he reached the second verse, she was fast asleep.

22

WARM WELCOME

T HERE WAS COMFORT IN pulling on her favorite jacket, lacing up her boots, and twisting her hair into twin French braids.

Jamie flexed her arms, clenching her fists enough for a light sting to whisper at her freshly healed knuckles. She stretched, whole body singing with the delight of being well rested.

They'd gone another round after waking up. Quicker, but no less pleasurable. Sleep had been necessary, as anxious as Jamie was to get back on the road. It had been sound, at least. No nightmares. No waking to bloody arms and painful bruises.

They'd caught fish in the river, boiled water over a small fire, and when they had enough provisions to satisfy the thought of a few days on the road, they prepared to set out.

"We need to find a town," Oliver said. He finished folding the tarp that had covered his bike, neatly stuffing it into the pack strapped to the back. "I think we've got about half a tank of gas left, each."

Jamie eyed the way his muscles tightened under his shirt, and then tugged the note from Vic out of her bag. "If we can find someone who knows where this is, maybe we can barter work for more gas."

"Or walk if we have to."

She nodded. "She's somewhere up north. Not near the coast, not south. But these aren't the coordinates I studied back in the day."

Oliver let out a snort. "Too true."

He put up his kickstand and walked his bike to her.

Jamie grimaced at the heat flushing her cheeks. There was no reason for her to be red; not after everything they'd shared only a handful of hours ago.

Oli tilted his head, brushing a thumb across her cheek. "I think the sun got you a bit."

She glowered, unable to stop a smile quirking the corners of her mouth. He leaned in and gently pressed a kiss on her cheek.

Jamie's lip curled into a full-on grin. She reached out as Oli went to step away, snatched the front of his shirt, and jerked him back to her.

She dove into the kiss, well aware it would be a good long while before they were able to have a moment like this again. She poured the passion of wishing they had more time by the river into the pressure on his lips.

After a few seconds, she patted his chest and gave a gentle push. She smirked at the slackened look on his face as he pulled away.

She revved her bike. "Okay then. Time to move."

They left, roaring through the canyon and then over and under and across wide sweeping roads and bridges that carried them past the mountains. As lush and green as the area was, they found little in the way of human settlements. Jamie almost slowed at a couple farm houses, but the sight of shotguns leaned against the wall outside the door had her speeding up instead.

It made sense for the families here to keep themselves stocked with illegal weapons. It was unlikely the government or military made it this close to the wasteland with such mountainous terrain in the way. Raiders were probably the big danger out here.

Which made Jamie think of Noah, of Trish, of the children in the Switch. And then that turned her down a train of thought she'd been avoiding. One that had started when she'd seen the life Noah had built. A peaceful life, but one with purpose.

She daydreamed for a few quiet moments. Her mind drew up a small home, time and space to paint, a cool stream, and Oli's warm hands on her each night.

A cold claw squeezed around her heart. Jamie sat up on the bike, one hand keeping her steady as she pressed a palm to her sternum. It felt wrong. Wrong and selfish and horrible to be happy, even for a moment. To dream of things that might be possible. A life that could be more.

Alice was gone. Dead and gone, and the ghostly echo of her neck snapping still lived in Jamie's bones.

She'd have laughed. If Jamie had been able to talk to her, to tell her she was finally doing that thing Alice always told her to—*forgiving*.

She was finally moving past hurt to address the feelings underneath it. Of course, that's not what Alice would've laughed at. She'd have laughed when Jamie's face went red talking about Oliver. She'd have giggled with glee when Jamie told her about the river, about the way his scruffy beard had tickled. She would've taken Jamie's hand and pressed it to her heart. She'd have encouraged her to follow that pull, that call for a peaceful life. A life with love in it.

Tears streamed down Jamie's cheeks. The wind chilled them, practically turning them to ice before she was able to wipe them away.

You're allowed to be happy.

Jamie gritted her teeth. It was a memory, that's all. A memory of one of the hundred times Alice had said those words to her after the three sisters were separated. The two of them, alone on the ratty carpet of a storage room they'd found to sleep in. Jamie had pulled Alice close, tucked her smaller frame in tight to keep her warm.

"What if she's not okay?" Jamie had asked. "What if something happens to her and we never know?"

Alice shook her head, curling her fingers around Jamie's jacket. "She's Vic. Nothing can hurt her."

But that wasn't true. Jamie knew it then, and she knew it now. They were strongest together. All three of them.

Life would've been... maybe not easier, but better if Vic had been with them, if they'd had their unfaltering leader to show them the way...

No.

Jamie leaned forward onto her bike again, shaking her head to try and drive away that voice.

It would've been better because we would've been together. We figured out the way ourselves, just like you're doing now. Vic is a leader because that's who she is, not because she ever needed, or expected us to follow.

Jamie snorted and shook her head again. The distant echo of Alice's voice faded in the back of her head.

That sealed it. She was going crazy, or she was haunted. No middle ground after hearing those words in her mind. Because of course Vic expected them to follow. Expected Jamie to follow, to fall in line, to stand up straight and accept any and all orders no matter how stupid they were.

Jamie exhaled through clenched teeth. She'd done all right, hadn't she? Finding work, scraping together enough for the little apartment she and Alice had shared. She'd made good choices. Not always the smartest or the best, but good.

Until she'd turned Oli away.

That anger in her bones, the bitter taste that perpetually lived on her tongue, had been what got Alice killed.

Jamie gazed out at the stretch of highway before them, her stomach churning. Partially because they'd gone nearly three days with no food and then consumed half a dozen fish. Mostly because if they found Vic healthy and whole and waiting for them... she'd have to find a way to explain what happened to Alice.

A faded green sign announced a town twenty miles away. Jamie slowed to a stop, brushing her finger across the gas gauge to wipe away the dust and heaved a sigh at how close the needle was to empty.

Oliver caught up several seconds later, and Jamie winced at how in her head she'd been. She should've known he was so far behind.

"How're you looking?" she asked.

He raised an eyebrow and bit his bottom lip.

A heavy chuckle bubbled up from her chest, but it died quickly. He read the anxiety on her face and cleaned off his own gas gauge.

"Nearly out."

"Think this town is still standing?"

He shrugged, a furrow in his brow as he stared out at the horizon. They'd hit another stretch of nothing. Desert for miles, the rolling hills of the mountains long gone.

"We'll be damn lucky if we get there on fumes."

Jamie nodded. "Not many other options." She looked to the horizon as well. To the sun beginning its dip back to the earth.

They needed food, water, and gas. And beyond that, they needed to get to Vic. There were miles still, probably hundreds of them, between Jamie and her sister. There was no way to know if Vic was alive. If she was all right. If the military types had already caught her.

Jamie's mind sank into a spiral of awful thoughts as she and Oli made for the town.

Their luck didn't carry them all the way there, but they ran out of gas with only a half-mile or so before the cluster of buildings. They dismounted and pushed the bikes along.

The closer they got, the less hope Jamie held that they'd find any sort of useful supplies.

The term town was a bit of an overstatement. The rundown shacks had the look of the Switch, but without that underlying sense of well-fed, well-cared for people.

Wooden slats made crooked walls, panels of aluminum served as flat roofs, and most of the doors were simply yards of fabric strung along openings.

Organics, as rundown looking as their homes, watched them carefully. Jamie's hand went to the blade at her waist, sheath tucked into her pants, hilt hidden by her shirt. She pushed her bike along with one hand, keeping pace with Oli while making sure to have an eye on their backs.

She wished they still had the Uniforms' guns, but they were too large to be easily concealed. And if any kind of law enforcement caught sight, she and Oliver would have a whole new set of problems to deal with.

There was no town center here. Only a brick well and a sudden increase of bodies watching them.

Jamie slowed to a stop a few steps behind Oliver. A chill ran down her spine, that old battle precognition kicking in as people surrounded them.

"Hello there," Oli called out. His voice fell low and flat against the dirt around them. He glanced around, trying—Jamie knew—to pinpoint some kind of leader.

She did the same and came up empty. Each face looked as much like the last as it did the next. Tired people, guarded and suspicious and hungry. The makings of raiders and bandits if they had access to weapons. Which Jamie doubted, given that none were currently pointed at the two of them.

"You'll have better luck up the road. Thirty miles to the next town." The gravelly voice belonged to a hunched woman with dirty gray hair and a scar running down the left side of her face and neck. It looked like a chemical burn.

"Better luck with what?" Jamie said, her tone sardonic. "You don't even know why we're here."

"To fill those guzzlers," the woman responded, her voice equally snarky. She glared at the two of them and gestured to the bikes. "We don't have fuel here. Or enough food to share. And I doubt you'll find either further on."

Jamie's mouth opened before she thought better of it. Oli's hand went up, and she fell silent, seething, but grateful he was fine handling things of the talking-to-hick-Adams variety.

"We would never ask for a gift of such a kind. Though we were hoping to trade. Perhaps for water, instead of food? It sounds like we still have a while to go before we can stop for the night."

"Damn right you do." A man spoke up this time, from the other side of the grouping.

Jamie caught his gaze in time to see the anger splayed across his face. Her nostrils flared, adrenaline beginning to flow in preparation. The man looked away.

"We don't need no hybrids here," the old woman said, her eyes still on Oliver. "You lot take more than your share."

Shouts went up at this. Calls of agreement, shouts of jobs being stolen, food being hoarded.

Jamie moved closer to Oliver, wary of the way he was leaning on his right leg. Fast healing or not, his injury needed more time before it was back to normal. Which made her less inclined to teach these Organics a lesson in manners.

A glass bottle shattered against the body of Oliver's bike.

Jamie grip slid from the handlebars. Her bike tilted sideways, thudding to the ground as her fingers wrapped around the hilt of her blade.

Oliver dropped his bike as well and threw up his hand. He walked forward slowly, as though he were in an enclosure with dangerous animals.

Jamie's lip curled into a warning grimace as he spoke.

"Hold on now, we don't want any kind of trouble. We're moving on."

Sunken, hungry gazes did not flicker with any sort of alteration in motive at Oli's words.

Jamie gritted her teeth. "We can take 'em."

The old woman's eyes widened for a brief second before a snarl twisted her lips. "Of course a bottle-bred resorts to violence."

"Your man threw the first stone," Jamie spat. "Get your people in order before someone gets hurt."

The crowd encroached enough that their way was blocked. Jamie shifted, ready to draw her blade.

Oliver glanced at her. "We can't kill these people."

"What do you suggest? The tanks are empty," she said through clenched teeth. "Are we walking the bikes or leaving them?"

More movement. The Adams drew even closer.

"Seems it'd be easier for you to leave them," one of the crowd said.

Another called out, "Your kind don't need 'em anyway."

"Jamie." His voice was deep and quiet, his words only for her ears. "We have to go. Now."

A low growl rumbled in the back of her throat. He was right, of course. Because if they did engage, people would die. And if Unborn were responsible for killing Organics... there was enough trouble for their kind at the moment.

Jamie knelt, warily keeping her gaze on the approaching people. They'd slowed, but a few at the front tightened their grips around heavy tools.

She unstrapped her bag and slung it across her shoulder. Beside her, Oli did the same. She caught his wince as he stood, and another flash of anger roared through her chest.

They had little to carry, but leaving the bikes stung. Even if it had taken thirty miles to find gas, it might have been worth lugging the things across the desert if it meant getting to Vic faster.

The crowd parted before them, hissed threats and spits in the dirt their only goodbye. Jamie stayed a step behind Oliver. She was wounded, same as him. But if these assholes decided to test how much they knew about Silvers, they'd face her before they landed a blow on him.

No one tried anything, though jeers followed Jamie and Oliver well past the edge of the worn-down huts that made up the little town.

They made it at least ten miles before needing to stop. Oliver slung his bag onto the ground and plunked down on a long-fallen bit of concrete wall.

He stretched out his leg, wincing again as he pulled his pants away from the bloody bandage underneath. A furrow marred his brow, and a scowl cut into his smooth skin.

Jamie set her bag down a tad more gently. It was odd for that sort of thing to get to him like it did her. His temper was as hot as hers, but it was usually buried deeper.

"What a welcome," Jamie said dryly. She threw her arms out, baring her face to the blinding sun. "Thanks, west coast, we appreciate the warm greeting."

She peeked an eye at Oli. He was still sullen, hands clenched in front of him, gaze on the dirt rather than her attempted antics to rouse any sort of smile.

"Hey." She sat beside him and put a hand on his uninjured leg. "What is it?"

He scoffed. "Are you serious?"

Jamie bristled. "No, I asked the question as a joke. Ha-ha. Never mind." She made to stand, but he wrapped his fingers around her wrist so gently that she paused.

"I'm sorry," he muttered.

She raised an eyebrow but sank back down. "You understand that I'm also incredibly pissed about the bikes?"

Oliver nodded.

"And at the notion that those assholes thought they had a shot at taking us down?"

Another bob of his head.

"And what the hell is 'bottle-bred?' Who thought that sounded like a good insult?"

He didn't smile.

Jamie leaned out to get a better look at his face. "That's not what's bothering you."

Oli met her gaze. The wear from the road showed in the lines on his face, the bags under his eyes, and the dust in his ever-thickening beard. He swallowed, then faced his hands and picked at his nails.

"It took a long time for me and Cade to find work," he murmured.

Had the highway been in use, with cars zooming by in all four lanes, massive trucks carrying a surplus of food and wares, a never-ending parade of traffic, she wouldn't have been able to hear him.

But there were no cars. No food. No bodies except their own and the buzzards that had been flying overhead for the last hour. Jamie was able to hear every word, even with how quietly Oli spoke.

"We got help from the UA for a while. It was enough to keep us fed, but we were living on the street. There were moments of kindness. A roof over our heads every once in a while but... it was hard. Harder than the war in some ways."

Jamie nodded, thinking briefly of her own experience with the way people looked at her and Alice when they first arrived. Their experience with the Unborn Assistance program had been a little different. Jamie had thrown something of a tantrum when they'd refused to give any information about Vic's whereabouts. Resulting in both her and Alice being banned.

"I just—" Oli broke off, his jaw tightening as he grimaced. "We all thought it would be different, right? And after that," he gestured to the town they'd left behind, "it seems like we had it easy. At least in Boston they didn't *hate* me for being Unborn. They didn't dismiss us because of how we were created. They used us, of course. Manual labor that goes harder and faster than anyone else. I could take a day's worth of work and get it done in an hour. But I still busted my ass, and I was respected for it. I worked harder than anyone else on those docks and no one denied it, Organic or Unborn."

Jamie bit her lip, thinking of the many times she and Alice had hidden away on the construction site, taking an extra break because they'd already done more work than half the Organics put together.

"You've got a better work ethic than me," she said with a light laugh.

Oli shook his head and darted a side-eye at her before returning his gaze to his hands. "I don't think that's true. You pick and choose what to care about. That helps narrow your focus, makes it so you excel at those things."

"We're Silver, Oli. We excel at a lot. That was kinda the idea behind the design."

He snorted. "That's not what I mean." He looked at her, head on this time, and she lost her breath at the sincerity in his face. "You have the skill to ride through things you don't like doing and focus on the important stuff. I..." He sighed. "I have trouble with that. If I'm not giving my all every time, I'm doing something wrong."

Jamie opened her mouth, an ache clenching at her chest for a moment. She took his hand. "You're not, though. You're not doing anything wrong by getting a damn break every now and then."

Oli nodded. "Yeah. I *know* that. But convincing myself to go easy is..."

"Not so easy?"

"Yeah."

They fell into a comfortable silence for a while. Birds cawed in the distance, scurrying creatures kept close to the ground, shaded from the scorching sun by ruddy rocks and scraggly brush.

Jamie kept Oliver's hand. She traced her fingers along his calloused palms, over and around his scarred fingers, and eventually up his arm to the small tattoo in the crook of his elbow–GS:CXCV. Gary Scott 195. A different designer. A different facility that raised him from test-tube baby to pre-teen before sending him off to the base where they'd shared training prior to being shipped to the front lines.

Her thumb rubbed across the letters, dark even against his rich brown skin. She plucked at his sleeve. Her hand rose higher, tickling the hair at the back of his neck, following the edge of his scruffy jaw, and finally turning his head toward her.

He met her eye, that slightly metallic glint catching the sunlight as he studied her face.

She leaned in, face tilted up to meet him. Their lips touched in a whisper of a kiss. Jamie pressed harder, her tongue dancing across

Oli's full lips, chapped like hers from the sun and the wind and the trek. She sank into him, and he caught her.

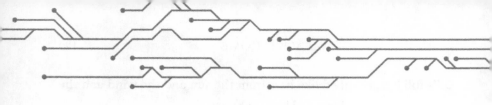

23

A Good Sign

T HEY REACHED THE NEXT town that night. Even with their slowly
healing injuries they were able to walk farther and faster than
most.

They eyed the run-down, sad structures from afar. Jamie scouted
closer and caught the tail end of a fist fight between two men, arguing
over rations.

She and Oli moved on.

They slept off the road, a tarp below them to put distance between
their bodies and the cold desert ground. Another was flung over the
top, and the two stayed warm by pressing close.

Waking at dawn, walking until they found a chance at food, and
then continuing on until nightfall became their routine. They lost
weight. Jamie felt it on herself, her musculature wilting away with
the lack of training and nutrition. She felt it on Oli when they sank
into each other's arms each night.

Early in the morning on their fourth day crossing the west, they
found a city. Not a town, a full, sprawling city with twisting roads,

suburban areas, and a handful of towering skyscrapers. Still stand-ing–mostly.

They stood on a low ridge. Just high enough to get a view of the rocky landscape that led to the city's edge and the set of towering mountains on the other side.

Jamie eyed it with a frown. "How are we playing this?"

"Orders?" Oliver looked over, his gaze scanning her torso where the awful bruise was fading to yellow. It was covered, but just as she had kept a careful eye on his leg, he'd checked her injuries frequently. "We can say we have orders to get to these coordinates." He gestured to the city before them. "There has to be something military here. Maybe a UA."

She nodded. "We should find a place to wash up first. Something tells me we don't smell great."

"You don't like the way I smell?" He pulled a grin from her with the over-exaggerated offense in his voice.

Jamie gave him a playful shove, then took her blade from her waistband and tucked it into her backpack. "Hide yours too. We can't afford to get detained."

He did the same, and they made their way forward.

The first few neighborhoods of empty houses were a familiar sight. People didn't live on the outskirts, not when the protection of num-bers was available to keep raiders at bay. Then again, Jamie wondered how often raiders even approached a city like this. It had been a rare event back east.

Patrols walked the streets. Organics, in groups of four with a com-bination of military and police uniforms.

Jamie pulled the loose strands of her hair in front of her face and kept her head down.

Beside her, Oli pulled on a sweatshirt—though the morning was already hot—and tugged the hood as far as it would go down his

forehead. They walked slowly, keeping pace with the steadily growing numbers of Organics on the street.

They were ignored for the most part. Only a few curious children
looked twice, and while one's eyes went wide as they met Jamie's
gaze, whatever they whispered to their parent was hushed away.

"There are..."

"No Unborn, yeah." Jamie's jaw was tight. "We need to skip the
bath. Let's try to find a grocer, grab some supplies, and ask about the
coordinates."

"Preferably one on the far edge of town?"

She nodded. If Unborn were banned from this city for whatever
reason, she wanted to be as close to their exit as possible before
getting recognized as a Silver.

It was a long walk through a strangely intact place. There were a
handful of rundown buildings here and there, a few streets where
garbage was often dumped which led to a specific stench that followed them a ways. There were burnt out cars, beggars, and broken
glass. Stretches of highway overpasses sank into neighborhoods. But
for the most part, the city was whole.

Open-doored restaurants wafted scintillating scents, stirring
Jamie's already tight-with-hunger belly. She thought of the minuscule amount of credits in her bag. They would go farther at a grocer's,
getting things that would sustain them for the rest of their journey.

Still, she couldn't help deep inhales each time they moved past an
outdoor dining area where steaming plates were set upon tables in
front of happy, clean, Organics.

"Eyes down," Oli muttered urgently.

Jamie didn't jerk, she lowered her head with ease and wiped at her
pant leg as though she was looking at dirt instead of hiding her face.

A patrol strode past, their boots thudding against the
sun-bleached pavement. Jamie and Oliver kept their pace and, after

a few tense seconds of wondering, they turned a corner and seemed to be in the clear.

"Are they looking for Unborn, you think?"

"Who else?" Jamie muttered. She swallowed. They'd reached the skyscrapers, and a tingle of claustrophobia made her stomach clench even more. "I haven't seen a single Copper."

"We're getting close," he said. "The highway picked up not far after these." He gestured to the towering structures around them.

"Do you want to risk patrols? Or keep going and hope there is *someone* friendly to Unborn in those mountains?" Jamie couldn't keep the bitter bite from her voice.

Oliver shook his head, running a hand across his scruffy black beard. "I don't know that we have a choice but to risk it. We can't keep going on squirrels and barely edible plants."

Jamie heaved a sigh. She clenched her hands, breathing through the radiating anger that threatened to drive away reason. "And we need to know which way to go. We can't keep blindly heading west."

He nodded.

They reached the far side of the city and found a cluster of small shops built together and somewhat separated from the nearest neighborhood.

"I'll go in first," Jamie said. "Keep watch."

Oli's brow furrowed.

"Come get me if a patrol comes by," Jamie elaborated.

He grimaced, but he bowed his head and leaned against the tall pole of a shattered streetlight. "Be careful."

Jamie strode toward the shops. Dusty windows advertised clothing, infant necessities, boots, and general goods. She aimed for the general goods, keeping her eye line pointed at the sidewalk while listening intently.

At the door, she paused. A familiar shape drew her attention. There, at the bottom of the left pane of glass, a small symbol was drawn into the dust. A circle, with a diamond in the center.

It was almost... it could have been the symbol for Unborn. The symbol sewn into their dress uniforms, patched onto their combat gear, and shared among them all, Coppers, Silver, and Golds. The one thing, besides their origins, that bound them together.

Or maybe it was someone drawing random shapes into a dirty window.

Jamie bit her lip, then pushed the door open. The interior was dim. Lit by the front door and windows as well as a single hanging light over a counter in the back.

The store appeared empty. Jamie wandered the narrow aisles, pulling a handful of items and carrying them in the crook of her arm. She aimed for protein and calories, choosing a couple bags of jerky and a few pre-packaged pastries.

Water would also be smart. She and Oli could boil from streams as they went, but bottles at least would let them carry some on the road.

She dumped her goods onto the counter, raising an eyebrow at the empty space where a worker should be. A tarp hung over a doorway a bit further back.

"Hello?" Jamie called, barely controlling the snappish anxiety in her tone. She wanted to get this done and move on, preferably before a patrol wandered by.

"Ope, hello there!" A cheerful voice sounded from behind the curtain. "Sorry. I didn't hear you come in."

Jamie blinked.

The person pushing past the tarp was short, stout, and smiling hard enough that Jamie's cheeks hurt just looking at it. They were somewhat androgynous, with bright colored pants and a black tank top. Their hair was shaved close on one half of their head, a zigzag design creating a pattern above their ear. The other side was long, braided into segments and dangling well past their shoulder.

Age was as tricky as gender.

"Hi." Jamie fiddled with her hair, dragging more strands in front of her face as she stepped to the counter. "I want to get this and water, if you have it."

"Oh yeah, I can do that for you. I'm Hector, by the way. Happy to help with whatever you need!" The jovial tone showed no signs of calming.

Something about it, about the way the shopkeeper danced around the counter to a closed cabinet Jamie hadn't opened and fetched an armful of plastic water bottles, made Jamie speak.

"You have something on your window. Some kid drew in the dirt or something."

The flinch was almost imperceptible, but Jamie was looking for it. Hector fumbled as they set down the bottles and one thudded to the ground at Jamie's feet.

She stooped, picked it up, and rose to meet their gaze. Hector backed away, bumping against the wall beside the tarp.

Jamie's pulse raced, a brief second of fear that she'd have to chase this person down and silence them ran through her blood.

"You're Unborn."

Jamie nodded. "You know what that symbol means."

Hector swallowed, then bobbed their head in the affirmative.

"You know what putting that on your window insinuates?" Jamie cocked her head, studying them closely.

They'd calmed, the initial surprise brought on by her eyes fading into excitement.

"I hope so," Hector said. They returned to the counter and began stacking her items by type. "You came in, that's a good sign."

"You're not going to call for anyone?"

"No." They frowned. "This is a safe place. At least, as safe as I can make it."

Jamie nodded, turned on her heel, and strode to the front door.

Hector called after her, but she ignored them. She pushed the door open and scanned the parking lot for Oliver. He was still perched at the light, arms folded across his chest.

She stuck her hand out the door and beckoned. He joined her inside a moment later.

"What's wrong?"

Jamie shook her head and walked back to the counter and Hector. "This place is safe for us?"

The shopkeeper's eyes were wide, darting between her and Oli with unbridled excitement.

"Yes," they said. "You can stay as long as you need."

24

Hope

THE INITIAL JOY OVER finding a roof under which they could rest was somewhat dimmed by the story Hector told them.

It was impossible for a city to completely outlaw Unborn because they were technically citizens and, therefore, had a level of rights no matter how hard Organic senators tried to change that. However, it was not impossible to make the entire area so inhospitable that they'd leave on their own.

Regulations had been passed almost immediately after the war. Unborn were relegated to the worst and hardest jobs. The UA had been protested until every Organic worker there had quit. Shops refused to sell Unborn food, restaurants refused to serve them, wage theft and frequent police harassment was common.

Curfews were put in place, limits on where Unborn could live, when they could assemble, how they could travel... all designed to chase away any who had found themselves there. And it worked. The handful of Unborn still living in the city had been driven out a few years prior.

From what Hector knew, they were settled in the mountains to the west.

"Why though?" Oliver demanded.

They sat in the back of the little shop. A corner lamp illuminated enough of the space to keep them out of total darkness. The room was for storage. Two of the walls were lined with shelves and full of boxes of nonperishable items. A stack of blankets was piled into the corner, which the three of them had spread across the hard floor to make for more comfortable seating.

One of the non-shelved walls was decorated with images. Small and large pictures, both photographs and drawings, as well as a decently large map of the United States pre-bombing.

Hector had given them food and water and watched with wide eyes as they scarfed everything down like ravenous animals.

Jamie's attempt to give them the remainder of her credits was met with a cheerful laugh.

So, she and Oli filled their bellies with the only fresh food offered (apples and a hunk of bread) and stored a fair amount in their bags for later. Jamie hadn't realized how thirsty she was until she downed her third water bottle and Oliver reached over to stop her from taking another.

While they ate, Hector talked. And when they were satiated and Hector's story was done, Oliver's eyes glinted with fury.

"I don't know," Hector said with a shrug. Their wide eyes dimmed, sadness drawing their lips into a deep frown. "I trade with the Unborn who left. They grow food as decent as anyone, and they've started bringing in materials for other things, too. Clothes and woodworking, that sort of thing. I like them fine. My parents were advocates against the resolutions. They, and a few others, started marking their shops with your symbol. In case others came."

"I still don't understand why," Oliver muttered. "Why treat us like this? After everything—" He broke off, but Jamie heard empty screams and the shatter of bombshells in the silence that followed.

Hector shifted. They moved to pick up the remains of their lunch with quick, jerking movements. After a few minutes of quiet shuffling, they glanced at Oli. "I think they were scared."

"Who was scared?" Oliver snapped.

Jamie put a hand on his back. They sat together, facing Hector with a pile of wrappers and apple cores on the ground between them. Jamie rubbed little circles at the top of Oli's shoulder blades.

Her mind went to the Unborn in Carter's club. The ones who took drugs to battle the shame of the only work they could find. She thought of Alice, of the blind darkness that had taken her friend.

Her arm stung, and she was struck with a brief but intense urge to scratch off the chunk of skin that had been in contact with Alice's neck when she had died.

Jamie swallowed and leaned her forearm against Oliver's back. The pressure, the heat of him, drove away some of the cold sting.

"The people here," Hector said. "There were rumors after the war. People talked. Talked about how strong Unborn are. How the things they did..." They hesitated, fiddling with the ends of their braids. "It made them monsters."

"The war didn't make us monsters." Jamie's voice was low. A growl of words that came more from her soul than her throat. "Humans did that when they built us."

Another long round of silence followed her words. Oliver's hand found her leg, and he gave a squeeze. Then he turned to Hector.

"Do you have any mode of transport? Any vehicle we can use?"

They shook their head. "I'm sorry, I don't. You're welcome to anything useful in the shop."

"We can pay—"

"No." Hector threw up a hand. "Please. My parents left me this place, and I want to keep their legacy. They did what they could. And I want to do that too." Their jaw tightened. "When things are wrong, bad, people have to do something. Or it just keeps getting worse."

Oliver stood, and Jamie followed his movements. He held out his hand, grasped Hector's with practiced gentle firmness, and shook it.

"Thank you."

Jamie nodded. "If we run into those trading partners, we'll tell them of your kindness. They might cut you a deal next time."

Oliver turned a raised eyebrow and skeptical expression her way. She ignored him.

"I do have one thing to ask." Jamie turned, pointing to the map nailed to the wall. "Can we get a look at that?"

They made it out of the city and into the mountains with no issue. The food and water Hector had given them would last until they reached Vic—if they were careful.

"Four days," Jamie said between panting breaths.

They marched uphill, following the steep inclines and declines of the old mountain road that took them north.

Oliver glanced at her but remained quiet.

She looked at his leg. It would be fully healed by the time they reached the coordinates Vic had provided, assuming nothing attacked them before then.

Towering trees surrounded them. The heat of the sun was muted by their trunks and branches, leaving sections of evening where Jamie shivered with every step before they made camp.

They'd found no sign of the Unborn living tucked away up here, though many trails diverged, dirt and gravel paths that led away from the road taking them to Vic. If things had been different, maybe they'd have explored. Searched for their brethren and inquired about the logistics of such a peaceful sounding life.

Tawny colored boulders, bigger than tanks, lined sections of a river that ran through the mountains. The road didn't follow it, but they intersected at times. Always with the warning sound of rushing water to let them know well before they found it again.

There was no bathing this time. No wasting frivolous moments along the water's edge. No hesitation or pause in their trek.

Jamie let Oliver hold her wrists each night, wrapped around her like pretty paper around a present. He kept her from shredding her forearms in her sleep. Yet even with his warmth behind her, the nightmares returned.

These were different. No longer the echoing snap of Alice's neck. Instead, Jamie was faced with a hundred scenarios of how she'd find Vic. Dead, tortured, imprisoned. Or alive, happy, and at peace until Jamie arrived. Until the moment Jamie would have to tell her the truth.

So maybe she didn't need Oliver holding her. Maybe she'd have cried in her sleep and that would have been all. But the feeling of him with her each night and morning was something she could not voluntarily rid herself of.

It helped that the little voice which sounded so much like Alice in the back of her head kept telling her it was okay. Telling her she was allowed these little moments, tiny slivers of contentment.

She hadn't told Oli about the voice yet.

They talked about other things as they pushed forward. Old missions, old friends, what Noah and the others at the Switch were liable to be up to, if they might ever return to the east coast, how they'd get there.

They avoided Alice and Cade. It seemed their last conversation had been enough for both of them to want to put some distance, however artificial it was, between themselves and the pain.

As much as he was helping her each night, Jamie noticed that Oli was also less tired in the morning. As though he were sleeping better as well.

The fourth day saw them exit the mountains. There was no lessening of the trees. They were still encompassed by vast and high greenery, but the landscape was now dotted with fields and pastures as well.

Anxiety crept down Jamie's back as they trudged along the road. It was well worn and potholed. Sprigs of grass and weeds overcame large sections. A handful of downed trees along a stretch of it suggested there had been a recent storm.

Jamie was glad they missed it. She was also glad for Oliver's hand as they neared civilization and staring eyes.

"Seems like this, at least, is about the same as on our side of the country," Oliver murmured as another farmer tucked a child away at the sight of them.

"Yeah, and they aren't grabbing pitchforks like I was worried they would."

He snorted.

Jamie had fished out Vic's letter that morning. She'd memorized it before they'd reached the Switch. But as they grew closer and closer to the destination that had been nearly two weeks coming, she found herself checking the coordinates nearly a dozen times, certain she'd somehow messed up and they were still days and days away.

She slowed her pace as the sun inched closer and closer to the horizon and unfolded the yellowed and frayed scrap of paper.

Oli's hands blocked her gaze. He put two fingers under her chin and gently lifted until she met his eye.

"We won't make it there tonight," Jamie muttered, her lips twisted to the side. Her nose itched, the burn of tears in her eyes infuriating her almost as much as Oliver clearly clocking them.

"It took longer getting through those mountains than we anticipated," he said, moving his hand to cup her face.

She leaned into his palm and sniffed. "I wanted to get to her tonight."

"Nothing stopping us."

Jamie raised an eyebrow. "We have another forty miles to go."

He nodded, pulling away and shifting his pack to his other shoulder. "We'd better get moving then. I plan on stopping at least for a few hours, but if we keep going, we can at least make it by morning."

An odd sensation welled up in Jamie's chest at his words. Some bittersweet clenching of her chest that reminded her of the fear she'd felt when they'd faced the Uniforms together. When she'd seen his injured leg. Maybe even when she'd seen his glinting silver eyes on the other side of the fight ring cage, after five full years apart.

She swallowed the feeling down. "I'm surprised you want to get there so badly."

He shrugged and turned, long legs striding confidently down the road. The wound on his calf had healed well with the supplies they'd received from Hector. There would be a scar for a long time; he was lucky he hadn't lost the leg. "I've never had an issue with Vic. We only had those couple of missions together."

"Then why—"

"The sooner we get there, the sooner we get answers. And maybe..." He swallowed. "Maybe if we get those answers, get justice for Cade and Alice and the others... Maybe there's something else after. Something for us."

"The revenge is for us," Jamie growled.

Oli nodded. "Yeah. But maybe something else after."

She didn't respond, though she felt his gaze off and on for the next few miles.

You could give him some hope.

Jamie gritted her teeth. Foolish as it was to talk to the ghost of her friend, she couldn't help responding. *You come first, Alice. I take out the ones who took you out, and I'll deal with Oli after that.*

Oohhh, deal with him? Jamie swore she heard a lilting chuckle. *Like you did at the river?*

She picked up her pace, blushing. Hope for Oli would mean hope for her, and she didn't think she could face that until Alice was avenged.

They stopped twice. The first time to eat and drink their fill. The second to light a fire and warm their hands for a while. The nights were cold, colder than they'd been in the desert before the wasteland.

Dew coated the grass, the morning sun turning everything a stark gray as they rounded a bend and came upon a small town. It wasn't like the city they'd passed through. No abandoned buildings on the outskirts, no clear signs of destruction by raiders. Nor was it the hostile village of Unborn haters who had practically stolen their bikes.

Jamie's lip curled in a scowl at the memory. How much sooner might they have arrived with a little gas in those engines?

She bit back the anger. A fair bit of it came from nerves, another chunk from how tired she was. And as kind as Hector had been, nonperishable rations weren't exactly an ideal diet with how long they'd been traveling.

Her boots were frayed, the concrete beneath becoming sharper with every step. They'd changed clothes a few times, but had nothing that wasn't coated with a heavy amount of muck and odor.

A flash of memory, of crisp cut pants, silver gleaming from shoulders and chests, hair slicked back into neat buns at the base of the neck... Vic had always been the one to make sure they were within regulations.

Not just within but exceeding. Not a button left unpolished. Not a single wrinkle. Except Jamie.

That thought, along with the uncertainty of what she would find, caused a spike in her anxiety.

She moved ahead of Oli, scanning the town for anyone with metallic eyes to answer her questions. There was no sign of Vic. No sign of the sanctuary she'd mentioned in the letter.

"We're here," Jamie muttered as they reached the center of the town. A fairly large hotel took up half the block to the south. A few small restaurants and shops seemed well equipped considering the state of economic depression in most towns of comparable size.

Oliver looked at her.

"The coordinates," she said through clenched teeth. "This is it. I don't see any damn Unborn, do you?"

He shook his head. "Let's not jump—"

"I'm not jumping, Oliver," she snapped.

He blinked, eyes widening a fraction before he narrowed them and raised an eyebrow. "No need for that, Jamie. I'm on your side, remember?"

Guilt crashed like a wave, but she could do nothing but nod.

"Excuse me," a voice called from behind them.

Jamie whirled, squinting in the dim morning light.

A man strode toward them, Organic, tall with dark hair and overalls. He'd been up early, given the dirt on his clothes and the sweat on his brow. Grudging respect boiled in Jamie's blood.

"Can I help you folks?" His voice was light enough, though an underlying concern laced his tone.

"Just passing through," Oliver replied.

The man paused, looking them over. Then he nodded. "Well, you look like you could use a good night's rest. If you decide to stay, the hotel here is nice, and if you're short up on credits I'd be happy to have you come by the farm and do some chores in exchange for a hot meal."

Jamie's hands trembled and the burning returned to her eyes. She blinked. Clenched her hands. Took a breath.

"We're looking for another Silver. A woman. She's—" Jamie had to hesitate to steal her nerves. "She's expecting us."

The man's eyes went wide, his bushy brows nearly touching his hairline. "Ahhh, well, that's a different story, isn't it?"

Jamie met his eye, her jaw tight and her stomach knotted into tight coils.

His head dipped in a slow nod. "I think I can help you folks find who you're looking for."

25

Untouched Leader

T HEY CAME UP OVER a ridge and were faced with a gorgeous sight. Sprawling, fenced-in fields. A big red barn, horses visible as they munched on an early morning breakfast of hay. Patches of trees scattered the landscape to offer the animals shade. And at the end of a long gravel drive, a massive multi-story ranch house that had seen better days but was clearly cared for.

"This... this must be the place." Oliver's voice was careful.

Jamie hated it. Hated the way he was looking at her every few seconds as they strode down the hill. Hated the way the grass licked at her boots, dew soaking the cuffs of her pants and adding yet another bit of filth to mar her meeting.

"Yeah. We'll see." Her voice was careful, too. A careful control over the blistering anger that had sparked so suddenly and violently within her that she almost didn't understand it.

But she did understand. The rage came from what her imagination was telling her Alice would say if she could have seen all this. She'd have loved it. And Vic...

A low growl rumbled in Jamie's throat as figures exited the house. A handful of them. Mostly Organics based on the build. And one Unborn she'd have recognized anywhere.

Vic.

Vic, who had been enjoying this... this haven for who knew how long. Vic, who hadn't found them until it was too late. Vic, who was so good at giving orders—*get here*—and so utterly terrible at breaking them.

The fury grew as one of the men took a place by her side. He was tall, stocky build that spoke of laborious work and a head of blond hair shaved close at the sides.

Vic liked her space, so who was *he* to get so close?

Not just close. Close and armed. Vic too, handguns held loose at their sides as though Jamie was a threat. As though she and Oliver were encroaching on something they weren't allowed to be part of.

Jamie's hand clenched. She gripped the strap of her bag to keep from reaching for her knife.

She should have been relieved. But she couldn't feel anything beyond the fury.

She had to get control of this anger. This solar flare of rage that threatened to burst from her and burn everything.

Vic didn't like fire.

She likes you though, Alice's voice whispered through the back of Jamie's mind. *Try to remember that.*

Jamie's forearm itched. Her fingers tugged up her sleeve, nails digging into the skin before she realized what she was doing.

Oli put a hand on the back of her elbow as they walked.

The scratching stopped.

They slowed a few paces away from the welcoming committee. Jamie spared a glance at the man beside her sister—not bad looking for an Organic with those brilliant blue eyes—but her focus narrowed in on Vic.

Vic looked... Vic looked almost the same as she had that day.

Slim, dark hair not quite as long as Jamie's, tall angular features a contrast to both her sisters. But there was more, and Jamie's Unborn eyes caught the new ink on her arm—she'd been with other Unborn at some point. The way she held herself—injured. And the way she didn't frown as Jamie had approached, though her steely gaze had darted past nearly a dozen times in a vain search for Alice—still needing to be in control.

So before Vic opened her mouth, Jamie spoke, unable to keep the acid from her tone. "Well, you certainly found yourself a nice place."

She gestured to the sweeping fields. The other Organics had moved away, collecting tools they were likely to use for the day's work.

Oliver stirred at her side, but she ignored him.

"Is this why you never came to find us?" A snarl curled Jamie's lip. "Too busy living the high life?"

"Hey—" The blond man took half a step forward before Vic's arm flew out to stop him.

Jamie's nostrils flared.

She's keeping him safe, Alice whispered again.

Jamie shook her head and scoffed as she eyed the man. "Ahh, got it. Too busy *playing house.*"

She laughed, knowing the sound would grate against Vic's ears the same way her stone-like countenance grated Jamie's nerves. "Don't tell me you're *sleeping* with an Adam. Can he even keep up?"

At this, Oliver did more than stir. His hand found Jamie's lower back and he brushed his fingers softly across the gap where her jacket didn't meet her jeans. His touch was like a cool splash of water on the sizzling anger within.

Vic spoke, her voice drawing Jamie's gaze again. "You could try giving people the benefit of the doubt before you go off spewing your wild assumptions."

Jamie frowned. There was something... in the words themselves, so mild compared to the tongue-lashing Vic was capable of, and in the way she spoke them. Her long fingers danced across her chest and the hint of a wince creased the edges of her eyes.

More hurt than Jamie had originally thought.

Oliver cleared his throat. "Maybe we can take this inside?"

Jamie huffed out a humored breath as the blue-eyed man looked to Vic for confirmation. Vic jerked her head toward the door, and the man led the way as the four of them trudged inside.

Well, Jamie trudged. Vic limped.

"What the hell happened to you?" Jamie asked, her voice tight. The Alice question was coming, and she was pretty sure she'd rather face a dozen Uniforms than talk a feelingless Vic through the most traumatic moment of her life.

Her sister let out a pinched breath. "It's a long story."

Heat flared again in Jamie's chest. "Seems like we've got time," she muttered, unable to keep the bitter edge from her voice.

They were brought into a sitting room. Furniture lined the walls, comfortable seats layered with dirt, grass stains on the carpet, and a generally warm and welcoming atmosphere.

It was still just the four of them, and Jamie wondered where the other Unborn were in this 'safe place' her sister had written of.

Oliver perched on the arm of a plush chair, his gaze fixed on Jamie. He wanted to ask questions. To get to the heart of why they had come so far. But he'd let her and Vic go their round first, and she appreciated the sacrifice.

She crossed to a window, unable to watch Vic pretending not to be in pain any longer. And unwilling to notice the way the man who joined them kept looking at her sister. As though she were a full moon rising after half a night of darkness. As though she were the only thing lighting his way.

Vic had given some part of herself to this man. Some vulnerability she'd never offered up to Jamie, no matter how many times she'd tried to talk. Tried to fight. Tried to cry. To scream. To do anything to connect.

It had all been so much easier when they were young.

"Quite the operation here," Jamie muttered as she stared out at a view Alice would never get to see.

The man spoke, strain in his voice. "We have a lot of help."

His words were a match. A spark. All that was needed for the solar flare of rage to burn molten in her core.

"*Help*, huh?" She turned, staring at Vic.

"Jamie, I—"

But it was too late.

"You could have written sooner," Jamie snapped. Her forearm itched again, and she balled her hands into fists. "You could have come to find us. Hell, we'd have come to you if we knew where you were. But no. Not a word. Nothing. Nothing from our fearless, untouched leader."

"I did write." Vic's voice was barely audible, and the softness, calmness of it only served to set more of Jamie's heart ablaze.

Sarcasm dripped from her voice. "Oh, that's right. You did. Five years later." Her breath was short. Ragged.

And pain took her then. In that moment, as she wished Vic was healthy and whole so they could fight out some of this anger, a nearly unbearable weight pressed against her. Because the last time she fought a sister—

Jamie's very bones ached with grief. "We looked for you. We *waited* for you."

Vic watched her, that steady gaze not matching the pain in her voice. "Jamie."

"We waited for you to find us, Vic." Tears burned at the corners of Jamie's eyes. She bit them away, drawing blood in her cheek and letting the metallic taste replace some of the pain with more rage.

Vic was still standing there. Standing and watching and still not asking about Alice, though she knew. She *had* to know. Jamie wouldn't have come without their sister.

"I didn't know."

Jamie's growl cut across the words. She turned to the window, ready to slam her fist into the glass if it meant not slamming it into Vic's perfect, smooth jaw. Then the words sank in.

Jamie's frown deepened, and she spun back to face her sister. "Just like we waited for you to put that damn goody-two-shoes reputation to work and *keep us together*." She spit the final words.

"I'm sorry," Vic whispered.

A piece inside of her broke. Because this wasn't Vic. This wasn't the woman who *knew* everything, was *never* wrong, and sure as hell wouldn't *apologize* to a subordinate behaving the way Jamie was behaving.

She shook her head, unable to hear the words. "Sorry for what? For not finding us?" Her voice trembled. "Or for not looking?"

"That's enough." Vic's Adam took a step between them, his lips in a thin line as he shot a warning glare Jamie's way.

Her breath caught at the concern on his face. She pushed past it, looking around him at her statuesque sister.

"You were too busy playing house with your new *rodina* to bother with us. And then that letter came..." Shuddering anguish ripped through Jamie, and all she wanted, all she needed in that moment, was for Vic to feel it, too. For her big sister to tell her it was okay for the pain to cut so deep. "A day too late." Blood coated the inside of her mouth as she bit through more of her cheek, but it didn't stop the tear that escaped. "Too late, Vic."

Vic's eyes closed. She released the breath she'd been holding with whispered words. "I didn't know."

Jamie's brow furrowed. She swallowed at the sudden splash of emotion across her sister's face. The quivering lower lip, the tears dripping down her face as she opened her eyes again, forcing Jamie to meet her gaze.

"I didn't know where you were." A desperate inhale. "I didn't know how to find you. I didn't know what to do or say or try to keep us together without making things a thousand times worse."

Jamie's anger melted into fear at the way Vic held her body, as though she was trying to keep the pieces of herself from falling apart.

"I'm so sorry," she gasped.

Jamie took a step, but the blue-eyed man beat her to Vic, catching her as she sank to the ground with shuddering sobs.

Jamie watched, eyes wide as Vic looked up at her with naked emotion, finding a way to apologize again through the sobs.

"Jamie." Oliver's voice reached her through the haze of dying fury and burning concern.

She glanced over at him, his face as pained as hers as they watched the strongest Silver on record break into pieces before them.

We are as strong as those around us. It's been five years. None of us has that strength anymore.

Jamie gave a light shake of her head to rid it of Alice's voice. She stepped forward, offering a brief nod to Oli before addressing the Organic.

"I think Vic and I need some time alone."

26

Sisters

"Fight nights?" Vic raised an eyebrow, the look so similar to the one she'd worn when they were teenagers and Jamie showed off her first tattoo, that Jamie almost snorted in spite of the heavy air of tension between them.

They were alone, at least. Oliver had gone with Hunt—the Organic Vic was infatuated with. There had been promises of a shower, clean clothes, and food. All of which Jamie craved, but none could come before explaining what had happened to Alice.

They sat on either end of the couch. Vic held herself carefully, even after the break, the eruption of emotions Jamie had always wished were there but had rarely seen. There was something cathartic in the knowledge that she wasn't the only one dying inside.

"Yeah, fight nights," Jamie said. "Good money, even with the assholes running things taking a cut off the top of the bets."

"Bets?" There was a strain in her tone that brought up Jamie's hackles.

"It's not like there were a lot of options, Vic. Especially not right away. I don't know how they did things out here, but my options were fight, whore, or starve. I chose to fight."

Vic's lip curled, and Jamie bit back the piercing anger that flared once again.

"Go ahead and look down on me for it. It's fine. I'm used to it."

At that, Vic flinched, and Jamie realized she might have read the look wrong. Maybe the curled lip and judging eyes weren't for her, but for the circumstances their people had been forced into.

She swallowed, clenched her hands, and continued her story.

She told Vic about her and Alice's life out east. Told her about Oliver's arrival, the bitter anger she'd carried, and how dismissive she'd been of his warnings.

She watched Vic's face grow more horrified with realization as she described the match. Jamie versus Alice. Valhalla versus the Hummingbird.

They both smiled as Jamie said the name. It had been fitting.

"She came at me hard, but it was normal until..."

"Her eyes went dark."

Jamie's lips trembled, tears blinding her. She nodded. "I'd never seen her like that before. She wasn't fighting to fight. She was trying to kill me, Vic. She almost did. But I got a hold of her, I begged her..."

She broke off, gritting her teeth as tears dripped down her cheeks. Her hands were clenched so tight her knuckles went white.

But she owed it to Vic. And owed it to Alice to tell their sister what happened.

"I *begged* her to snap out of it. I had her in a hold, to knock her out." She looked at Vic then, begging again, this time with her eyes as she stared at her big sister. "I didn't mean to... she was fighting me so hard. She wouldn't stop, and her neck... it just..." She looked away, her words broken by the sobs she'd only let out in her sleep before that moment.

Vic's face was a mirror of pain, her own tears painting streaks down her cheeks. She reached out, took Jamie's hand, and squeezed it.

Jamie's breath hitched. She returned the pressure.

Vic's calloused hand was a balm on the open wound still wrenching Jamie apart. They were broken. The trio of fighters, the Silvers who couldn't be stopped, the sisters who had made a family out of an experiment, love out of pain. Cut down to two.

"It wasn't your fault, Jamie." The words came out a whisper, but the sincerity behind them had all the strength Jamie knew Vic possessed.

She's right, you know.

Jamie didn't look at Vic, but she bobbed her head to show she'd heard.

Vic spoke again, louder this time. "There's something bigger happening. Someone is making Unborn go dark."

Jamie swallowed and wiped away her tears. "We figured as much. Some kind of military operation."

Vic gave a stiff grin, and then filled Jamie in on her side of things. The last five years hadn't been uneventful for the eldest sister either. She'd formed a community, pulling together Unborn in her way, and making a place for them.

Not quite how she put it, but Jamie read between the modest and self-deprecating words.

It hadn't been easy, but it had been a life. A peaceful sounding one, between the police and Organics hassling every Unborn they saw.

Then... the worst had happened.

217

Jamie had already heard, already knew from Oliver's report that the entire village had been slaughtered. But hearing it from Vic's lips was worse.

"I broke out of it, Jamie. There's something different about me."

Jamie's brow furrowed, her jaw tight at the hurt in Vic's words.

"I came to with my hand around someone's throat. And when I let him go, he went and tore apart one of our friends." She shook her head. "There was fire everywhere, and I didn't recognize a single soul. So I ran."

It was Jamie's turn to take her sister's hand. Vic squeezed her fingers, the pressure concerningly weak.

"I was alone, watching Uniforms stalk through the remains of my home. Then I remembered Max. That Silver I had a few missions with near the end of the war. He'd mentioned a place." Vic gave half a grin, taking her hand back to press it to her ribs with a wince.

Jamie's gaze dipped to the bandages her sister was no longer trying to hide.

Vic explained how she'd found the ranch, almost by accident. She'd met Hunt, the Organic who owned the land and offered a sanctuary for Unborn.

She told Jamie about the bunker beneath them. The safe haven she'd written about, where the effects of this Unborn darkness couldn't reach. She told her about a colonel with a power complex, a man named Linus who'd been hunting relentlessly for her, and a general with ties to bigger fish, bigger problems for them all. She told her of the threat they posed to the safety of the ranch, and how reliant they were on Uniforms to do a soldier's job.

"Uniforms did this to you?" Jamie's face twisted in painful memory of the damage the robots had done in the Switch.

Vic grimaced, a familiar expression she'd often used when something was out of her control. "You know no one else could've except a Silver. And probably more than one."

Jamie huffed out half a laugh of agreement. She thought of Noah striding down the street once Trish was safe, tearing apart Uniforms where they stood. "Or a Gold."

Vic met her gaze, but Jamie shook her head and gestured for her to continue.

"The problem is that even though I took out this general, there are others."

Jamie stood, crossing to the window yet again as Vic told her of the news they'd received the night before of another massacre. Another village of Unborn destroyed because something, someone, had flipped a switch.

The sun had risen high now. The fields of gold held a greener hue in the full light of day, and the trees in the distance swayed with a gentle breeze. Idyllic. That's what it was.

It would make for a good painting.

They talked a while longer, even joking a few times in a sisterly way that eased the ache in Jamie's chest.

There was a chance, according to Vic. A possibility of getting coordinates off the dead general's hardware. They might find the ones responsible for Alice.

And when they did—

"How we doing, ladies?"

Jamie jolted, her gaze darting to the doorway. Oliver walked through, crossing to Jamie without taking his eyes from her. She gave a small nod and brushed her fingers across his palm as he stepped around to stand beside her.

Then she attempted to muffle her scowl as the Organic came in as well.

Vic might've been in love with this Hunt person, but damn if Jamie didn't still need to vet his weak ass.

Still, he was careful with her sister. His voice was gentle as he asked if Vic was okay.

Jamie waited for that answer as well. For all their hours of conversation, there was still a string of tension between them just waiting to be plucked.

Vic met her eye with the slightest upturn of her lips, then faced Hunt. "I will be."

The feeling of real water, with the pressure to scrape the grime from her skin and the heat to create steam felt as though it washed years of exhaustion from Jamie's life.

She tried to shut off her mind and focus on the feel of the water pounding across her back, but it was nearly impossible.

Moments after the men had come in, a boy had darted into the room and given a rundown of his prowess hacking into confidential government servers. Putting aside the fact that he was barely a teenager, and absolutely still a child, there was no denying that he'd done it. He'd found the location of the trigger being used to make Unborn go rabid. The kill switch, as Vic had called it. A button some stranger pushed to destroy Unborn lives.

Jamie bared her teeth in a grin, lifting her head to let the water into her mouth only to spit it out again. She did that a few times, chuckling to herself at how protective Vic had been when the boy had entered.

He was the orphan child of refugees. It made sense that Vic might be worried about Jamie and Oliver's reaction to seeing someone who looked so much like an enemy combatant.

Another difference between the east and west coasts. Jamie had seen her share of refugees in Philly. Some outcasts, some hated for their skin the way she was hated for her eyes, but all living the same dreary lives as everyone else.

There was something about that protective instinct that warmed Jamie's heart. Vic *had* changed. More than she thought possible.

Of course, some things never change.

A fact made clear by the reaction Vic had had when the rest of them informed her she wouldn't be allowed to ignore her multitude of life-threatening injuries and join them in taking down the bad guys. The moment had increased Hunt's standing in Jamie's eyes. The way he'd point-blank refused to back down when Vic insisted she go.

She'd finally caved, but part of Jamie was sure that was only because her punctured lung and broken ribs were acting up.

So the plan had been set, the mission parameters put in place.

Jamie shuddered, though the water was still plenty warm. She didn't enjoy the thought that she'd be facing down a number of Uniforms soon enough.

They'd spend two nights at the ranch, talk to this doctor person, and have a few decent meals. Then, they'd collect some gear and avenge their friends.

Her pruney hands clenched into fists, and she looked at her forearm. White scars lined her skin. The bruising was gone, and she hadn't pressed hard enough to bring blood forth when they'd arrived.

Telling Vic about everything, almost, had eased the urge to scrape the memory from her bones. She pressed her forehead to the concrete. The voice was still there. She thought it would have left, faded into the darkness of her mind when she told Vic how Alice had died. But their sister still whispered to her.

For how long?

Until it's done.

Jamie eased her head back from the wall with a shallow nod of understanding.

She had to get out. Needed to dress and go see the resident doctor about some sort of serum that could supposedly prevent Unborn from going "dark," as Vic called it.

Footsteps entered the bathroom, and Jamie glared at the shower-head. The bathroom was separate from others, not a line of stalls, but it wasn't overly private either.

"I'll get out when I'm done," she said with a grumble. The water was still hot, and she had planned on at least two minutes under the relaxing spray for every day on the road.

"I didn't come to get you out."

The heat from the water sank through her skin and into her belly at Oliver's low drawl.

She gave a coarse chuckle. "I thought I'd gone over my time."

"Nope. You've got as long as you want." His voice was closer, just outside the stall door. "You've certainly fogged up the place, though."

Jamie's lips twisted into a crooked grin. "Figured we deserve a good chunk after everything."

"We?"

She exhaled through her lips, brushed her soaking hair back from her face, and flicked the latch on the shower door.

It swung open.

The angle of the showerhead kept most of the water inside, but a few drops splattered onto Oliver's shirt and pants. He stared, un-flinching and unabashed, at her body. At the water dripping down her curves.

Heat rushed to her cheeks and lower as his eyes clouded over with something scorching and primal.

She bit her lower lip, enjoying the hitch in his breath, the way his eyes darted to her face. The way he took half a step before looking down at himself.

"I'm fully clothed."

Jamie snorted. "Good observation."

Oli glanced around the bathroom. The door had no lock, just a little strip of metal to flick into place that might offer them some privacy. He turned back to her and raised an eyebrow.

"You sure?"

"Dress down, soldier," Jamie murmured, her voice rough, body already burning with the thought of his hands on her again.

He laughed, darted to the door, and did up the latch. By the time he'd moved the four paces back to her, he'd stripped his shirt, pants, and shoes.

"I've already been in here a while." Jamie reached out as he came closer, her fingers grazing his thick pectoral muscle.

He met her eye, that dark bushy brow crooking up again as he took another step. She was close now, a breath away.

"Why does that matter?"

Jamie grinned. She reached up, cupped the back of his neck, and pulled him to her. "Just that we don't have much time before the hot water runs out."

He chuckled again, the husky sound of his voice sending another burst of heat to her stomach. "You're saying we should hurry?"

"Well, maybe not *hurry*, but I don't want to waste any time."

And she went to her toes, smashing her lips against his with the force of everything she felt for him. He pushed in. Her back hit the concrete wall with a satisfying sting.

Oli used his foot to pull the door closed, refusing to take his gaze from her.

When his lips found hers again, it was like they were two pieces of the same puzzle kept apart for too long. When his hands found her skin, it was like he was feeling her for the first time again. And when they both found release, shuddering against each other as the water pounded down, it was like the world exploded into stars.

27

DOC

THE TRIP TO THE doctor's was less fun than the preceding shower. Oli went with her. A fortunate thing as her nerves built with each step down the spotless bunker hallway.

Something about a childhood of shots, experiments, and nonstop tests made her less than comfortable around people with a medical degree.

"Armory after this?" Oliver was grinning, walking with a jovial stride that kept a smirk on Jamie's face. "That Hunt guy said we can take what we need when we leave. I figure we plan the mission tonight, get everything packed, and then spend tomorrow relaxing."

"That would mean specs come before armory," Jamie said. "We have no idea what we're going up against."

She glanced up and down the hall.

They'd run into a surprisingly small number of Unborn as of yet. There had been a few when they got down into the bunker, Coppers who'd watched their movements with wary eyes.

Jamie knew there was another Silver there; Vic had said as much. Apparently the man was something of a surrogate father to Niko, the orphan kid with too much skill and time on his tech devices.

"We're getting that brief over dinner," he reminded her.

She rolled her eyes. The stiff and polite way in which Hunt had invited the two of them to dinner with Vic's new little family was another reason it seemed her sister and the Organic were perfect together.

He had a stick up his ass too.

"Hey," Oli said with a grin, catching her expression. "Food is food, and with how the outside of this place looked, I'm betting they've got good grub."

Jamie grumbled a sound of agreement.

"Plus, Vic is too messed up to slap you when you piss her off."

Jamie opened her mouth, a half-offended laugh echoing down the hall. "*When* I piss her off?"

He shrugged, and Jamie would have come up with something clever to say, but they were at the door they'd been told about, a little plaque labeling it as the medical wing.

Oliver gave a rap with his knuckles, and a second later, a woman with frizzy blonde hair and a wrinkled white coat flung the door open to greet them with a smile.

Oli smiled back. Jamie forced her mouth out of its perpetual frown.

"Come in, come in." The doctor gestured them forward with all the calm of someone who thought they were in control of a situation.

Jamie fought the urge to bare her teeth.

The room was sterile. Same colored walls as the rest of the concrete bunker, but with enough light for surgery and a scent of cleanliness that sent shoots of anxiety through Jamie.

She clenched her hands.

"Thanks for seeing us, doctor," Oliver said. He glanced at Jamie and took a half step, shifting so he was in front, his body blocking half of her from sight.

Her pulse steadied.

"Thank you for seeing me." The doctor gave an easy smile. "And it's Morgan, or Doc if we want to be fancy."

Jamie huffed a chuckle. Vic was right—this one wasn't like most of the Organic researchers they'd known back in the day.

"Good to meet you, Doc. I'm Oliver; this is Jamie." Oliver looked around the room. "We won't waste your time. Vic said you have some sort of serum to stop us going rabid."

The woman held up a hand, shaking her head enough for the corkscrew curls framing her face to sway back and forth. "I don't want to make promises I can't keep. This is a new serum derived from what I know of Vic's ability to fight off the control that takes over. We've been able to test it on Coppers, once. But we don't know how long it lasts or if it will work twice."

"Or if it works on Silvers," Jamie murmured.

Doc nodded, meeting her gaze. "I am confident in my work, but there are differences among you. Copper and Silver were not built the same, and clearly there are discrepancies within ranks as well."

Jamie gave a slow nod. "Alice turned; Vic didn't."

The doctor's face contorted into a brief look of pain. "I'd hoped... Vic spoke of you and your sister. She'd hoped the woman who created you all had given you two the ability to fight off the dark as well."

Jamie's breath caught. A brief, split second reaction that she smoothed over. But Oli heard. His hand found her wrist, and he gave a quick squeeze.

"We assume you'll want to run some tests," he said.

Doc turned her attention to him. "If you'd allow me, it would be very helpful. They'll be quick, nothing that'll take much of your time."

They agreed, and the doctor set them up on neighboring cots. She started with Oli, doing the usual battery of tests to check heart rate, oxygen levels, and more. She didn't touch his calf, but her fingers hovered over the gnarled scar where the Uniform had hurt him.

"When was this?"

Oliver glanced at Jamie, twisting his lips into a frown as he thought.

"A week and a half?" Jamie threw out. "It was on the other side of the wasteland."

"So two weeks, maybe, because it took almost three days to get through," Oliver added.

Jamie nodded. She looked to the doctor, whose eyes had widened, a hand now pressed to her chest.

"You went *through* the wasteland?"

Jamie's cheek twitched. "Yeah. We, uh... we ran into a lieutenant who was hunting for Vic. Figured if word had reached our side of the country, she was in real trouble. There wasn't much time to waste." She gave half a shrug. "There also weren't enough credits to get us across the safe way."

The doctor recovered quickly, smoothing her jacket and returning to Oliver's vitals. "You Silvers really have an entirely different kind of strength."

Her words startled Jamie, who'd been expecting something about their creation, or how they were closer to Uniforms than they wanted to believe. Instead, it seemed as though the woman was relieved.

"It hurt," Jamie murmured, grimacing at the admission. "Going through. It burned."

Oliver nodded. "The whole damn way. We set fire to almost all our gear when we made it out."

Doc gave a soft smile. "That was smart." She finished with Oliver and moved her equipment to Jamie's cot. "I'm pleasantly surprised at how quickly an injury like that," she gestured back to his leg, "healed. Because Vic's injuries are severe."

Jamie nodded as Doc wrapped a blood pressure cuff around her arm. "They'd have to be for her to let us go on this mission without her."

"Let is a pretty strong word," Oliver said with a laugh. "She wasn't happy about it."

Doc sighed with a shake of her head. "I'm glad you talked sense into her. An Organic would not have survived the journey home. I doubt a Copper would have."

Jamie bit her lip, falling quiet as she thought of the numerous injuries they'd all taken turns sustaining in the war. None had been enough to put Vic out of commission for more than a week or so. But what she'd faced to keep the ranch safe was a different kind of battle.

Uniforms were dangerous up close.

When Jamie had taken on four in that alley in the Switch, Oliver had showed up with a sawed-off shotgun. If he hadn't...

Distance would make all the difference when they reached their final destination.

Doc finished her preliminary tests and drew blood from both of them. She returned from placing the blood vials in a refrigerated cabinet as Jamie pulled on her jacket.

The doctor sighed. "I'd like to do one more scan on both of you."

Jamie turned, adjusted her collar, and raised an eyebrow.

"Radiation poisoning."

Oliver let out a low hiss of an exhale through pursed lips. "Right."

"We feel fine," Jamie said, her tone more snappish than she meant it to be.

Doc took her words in stride. "I understand that, but there could be residual effects that we won't know about for years unless we test for them."

"What would you require?" Oliver's hand found Jamie's lower back again, the warmth of his palm seeping through her shirt. She leaned into it ever so slightly.

"The blood test will give me some answers, and if you're comfortable with it, I can do a quick scan with this." She held up a thin bar that was familiar to Jamie.

The techs during their training days had used similar tools. Hand-held devices that could read a number of different things.

"Yeah." Jamie grimaced. "Let's get it done. I'm hungry."

Doc worked quickly, having the Silvers stand as she ran the wand up and down their torsos, around their arms and legs, and around their heads.

"I'll have results tomorrow morning."

Oliver offered his thanks.

Jamie zipped up her jacket. "How much serum do you have? How many Unborn will we be able to bring?"

Doc scratched a spot on her forehead. "If you leave tomorrow, I'll have six vials."

"We hope to stay two nights," Oliver said. "There is planning to be done."

"Good." She strode to her desk and thumbed through a couple of papers. "I can get another batch going tonight. I will try for a dozen."

Jamie swallowed down a biting remark and instead offered a stiff, "thank you."

They left, another chunk of time having gotten away from them.

A Copper waited for them at the end of the corridor. Jamie took up her usual position in front, and Oli fell into place behind her.

The woman was tall. Dark skin and beautifully braided hair with copper beads that accented her eyes.

"Claire," she said by way of greeting. "I'm here to show you around a bit."

"We require an escort?" Jamie flashed her teeth, the smile not reaching her eyes.

Claire grinned back. "You sound like Vic."

Oliver cackled. Jamie's jaw went slack for half a second before she gave a begrudging nod to the Copper.

"We don't need a full tour," she said. "We're supposed to meet Vic and her Organic for dinner."

Claire's eyes widened and a laugh bubbled up from her as well. "I won't tell Hunt you called him that." She turned, leading them down a series of identical halls.

"Wouldn't matter if you did," Jamie grumbled. "Not like he can do anything about it."

Claire tilted her head in a way that could have been agreement or skepticism.

"So, do you like it here?" Oliver asked, darting into the conversation, likely to keep Jamie from saying something that would get them kicked out of the bunker for the night.

"I do." Claire glanced back at him. "I liked it before too, but it's changed having Vic around."

"Changed how?" Jamie took a few quick steps to catch up. She'd lollygagged at an open door, the scent of well-appointed seasoning driving sharp hunger through her stomach.

Claire shrugged. "Things were good, but we were in survival mode. It felt like those gaps in the war."

"Negotiation limbo," Oliver said with a nod.

Jamie shook her head. Those had been some of the hardest weeks. They'd spent their time cleaning, sparring, planning, and finding ways to stave off boredom. Not able to fight, to rescue prisoners, to do anything other than secret missions—which were Alice's forte anyway—because the bigwig politicians were pretending at peace. The negotiations had never lasted more than a week, and each time the violence erupted again, it was more bloody, more brutal, more merciless.

"Yeah. Not quite that tense, but there was definitely a question of what comes next. It didn't feel like this place had reached its purpose yet, you know?"

"And it does now?" Jamie asked with a raised eyebrow.

Claire laughed again, leading them through a large rotunda to a narrow hall with a ladder at the end. "It feels like it's headed that direction. Hunt has plans. New ones, that I don't think he'd have thought of without your sister."

Jamie blinked. She turned, facing the Copper at the bottom of the ladder with a furrow in her brow.

Claire's expression was mild. "She's talked about you plenty. In case you didn't know how important you are to her."

A burst of emotion slammed through Jamie, threatening to take her legs out from under her. She smoothed her features, offered up a nod, and then gestured for Claire to lead the way up the ladder.

The Copper shrugged and headed up, her boots clanking gently against the metal rungs.

Oliver put a hand on Jamie's shoulder. She met his eye, reading the unasked question and replying with a nod. She was okay.

He went up the ladder. Jamie followed, realizing as she did that it had been a while since she'd asked him the same question.

28

DINNER

T HE COMMOTION IN THE kitchen was startling given how few people were actually in the room.

They were in the dining area of the main ranch house. A massive oak table with seats for a dozen and scratches all across the wood sat in what would be the kitchen if all the food weren't prepared in the bunker below. The countertops looked as if they were used for holding weapons and farming equipment, not chopping vegetables.

Niko, the teenage tech wiz who had found the location of the base they'd be infiltrating was hurriedly wiping down the table with a questionably gray cloth. Hunt stood behind Vic, who looked heated at being forced to stay in her seat rather than help with dinner preparations.

A man identical to Hunt in everything except facial hair, Silver eyes, and the ability to stand, sat in a wheelchair at the head of the table. He watched them, his gaze heavy with the weight of knowledge. He'd been in the war. He knew the kinds of things all Silvers had done.

But the knowledge didn't hamper his friendly manner.

"Max, I assume," Oliver said, striding the distance and putting out his hand.

The Silver grinned, scrunching his bushy mustache as he reached out and took Oliver's forearm.

Jamie smirked. "Yeah, Vic, way to make introductions."

Her sister bristled for a fraction of a second before Niko darted forward.

"This is Max," he said, his words coming quickly. "And Max, this is Oliver and Jamie. Jamie is Vic's sister, but not quite sister, but close enough."

Vic put up a hand, the smile on her face as real and bright as the light from the setting sun streaming in through the window. "Thanks, Niko. Jamie likes to poke fun."

Niko glanced at Jamie. She stuck out her tongue.

He looked affronted for a moment, then grinned.

Food appeared a few minutes later, cutting through the somewhat stiff talk as Oliver and Max chatted about innocuous things, Hunt stiffly but politely asked Jamie boring questions, and Niko checked in with Vic often enough to make Jamie set an imaginary clock in her mind to see when Vic would tell him to shut it.

The meal before them made Jamie glad they were taking an extra full day at the ranch. Meat, fresh meat that had been cooked in the fat of the animal and seasoned to perfection, potatoes smothered in cheese, roasted broccoli, fresh rolls, and little lemon bars for dessert.

Jamie and Oliver inhaled their food. Oli worked a little harder at behaving with somewhat decent table manners.

Jamie scooped pieces of everything onto her bread and ate it like a sandwich, sopping up the juices with the final roll from the basket. She had *not* asked if anyone else wanted it.

Hunt excused himself halfway through the meal and disappeared for a few minutes. He returned, kissed Vic's forehead, and ten minutes later, another round of food was set down by a grinning Claire.

Jamie met the man's striking blue eyes across the table and gave a shallow nod. Her respect was rising. A frustrating thing, as she would've loved to be able to tease Vic about a list of faults when they returned.

If they returned.

The thought soured her mood, even with a full belly and the relief of being done with medical tests. A dozen syringes. A dozen chances to not turn on each other.

Or a dozen Unborn on the mission.

Conversation bubbled among the well-fed group. Oliver and Max had reached a comfortable stage and now shared old war stories. Much to the wide-eyed interest of Niko and the occasional warning look from Hunt or Vic when talk turned a bit too dark.

Jamie was silent. She played with her fork, flicking the tines hard enough to earn little notes of music. She pulled forth memories. Missions of a variety of natures with a mix of variables. And a mix of soldiers. Different Unborn with different skill sets. Many who would be very useful on this sort of operation, if she could find them.

Several long minutes passed before she looked up from the table. Vic watched her, those identical silver eyes calculating and wary. Jamie's brow furrowed for half a second, then she made a writing gesture to her sister.

Vic muttered something to Hunt. He stood, left the room again, and returned quickly with a pad of paper and a pen.

Oliver and Max had devolved into a dirty-joke-off. Each's face lighting with glee as the other belted laughter over their antics.

Vic attempted to soften their language a few times but gave up after Hunt joined them with a few jokes of his own.

Jamie would have tossed her own brand of dark humor into the ring, but her mind was spinning. Analyzing, calculating, and planning. The paper filled with scribbles. Ideas for taking down Uniforms, names of people she wanted to find, and equipment they'd need along the way.

Eventually the laughter dissolved, jokes and people spent of energy. Max leaned back in his wheelchair looking between Jamie and Oliver.

"You two came quite a ways to leave again so soon."

Niko's eyes widened. He pulled a foldable tablet out and began typing furiously.

Jamie grimaced at the distraction but capped her pen and looked at the Silver. The man carried an older look than the rest of them. Maybe his injuries. Maybe his inability to run from the memories of the war. Maybe a mix of both and the world they lived in, had combined to put gray in his hair and wrinkles on his face.

Whatever it was, the shift in topic only added to the effect.

"We came for answers," Oliver said, his voice quieter than it had been all evening. He glanced at Vic. "Seems we've found them."

Max's voice was steady. "You came for revenge. The both of you."

Jamie's fingers curled into a fist on the tabletop. The movement drew Vic's gaze, and Nikos'. Hunt and Oli continued to watch Max.

"That, too," Oliver agreed.

Jamie clicked her teeth. "We came to make sure Vic was okay." She smirked. "I don't know if that's exactly what we found."

Vic glared. Hunt stifled a snort.

"But you're alive," Jamie said to her sister, the smirk fading into a thin line. "And so are the people responsible for Alice." Her gaze darted to Oli. "And Cade. And the rest of our kind who have gone dark." She met Max's gaze. "That needs to be rectified."

There was silence for a moment, then the man nodded. "Niko has the details of the facility's location. You're headed south."

Niko leaned across the table, flipping his tablet around and revealing a map of the west coast.

Jamie cringed internally at the distance they'd have to go. She heaved a sigh, then looked at Niko and pulled her pad of paper close again. "What've you got?"

What he had was a damn lot.

Vic had handled a large piece of the puzzle. Based on the intel she was able to collect, and the deep dive into covert files Niko accomplished with said intel, their enemy had the capability of turning Unborn dark at any time.

"It's an old Marine base," Niko said, his accent licking through the words with how quickly he spoke. "In an uninhabitable zone. They've got access to satellites." He shook his head, dark hair flopping across his forehead. "You wouldn't be able to make Unborn go dark without being close normally. There are only certain times they can access other places. But with the equipment they have—"

"They can hit anywhere on the west coast," Jamie interrupted. Her lips pressed together, the raw fear of losing someone else to the mindless violence thundering in her chest.

Hunt leaned forward, his arms resting on the table as he folded his hands together. "We don't know how long it will take for the people doing this to realize what Vic accomplished. When they do, it's likely the facility Niko found will up their security."

"And very possible they'll come after you," Oliver murmured. He and Hunt exchanged a look.

"We can handle ourselves here." Max folded his arms and leaned back in his chair. "The serum works on Coppers, and we have plenty of ways to fend off unwanted visitors."

Vic cleared her throat and all eyes turned to her.

A ghost of a grin flashed across Jamie's face. So much hadn't changed.

Still, her sister was in bad shape. They'd been at the dining table for a while. The sun was gone, and her face had taken on a shiny pale pallor.

Jamie frowned.

"The ranch will be fine," Vic said, her voice quieter than Jamie would have liked.

Hunt's face matched her own concern.

"What I'm worried about is the two of you taking on a mission of this size on your own. Two Silvers is..." She threw up a weak grin as she met Jamie's eye. "Formidable. But it won't be enough."

Jamie nodded. "Agreed."

She ignored the surprise on Vic's face and turned to Niko, ripping a sheet from her little notebook. "You can find just about anybody, right?"

The boy grinned as his slender fingers took the paper from her hand.

29

PARTING

J AMIE STARED OUT THE window, absently braiding a section of her hair. It was thinner now. She'd noticed it after the wasteland and, as much as she wished it didn't matter, she was saddened by the lack of luster it once had.

It might grow back. Or it might be one of the prices paid to make sure Vic was alive.

She glanced at the bed against the far wall of the room. It was large, wider than anything she'd ever slept in, and decorated with more pillows than a regular person needed.

They served a purpose at the moment though, nestling Vic into a comfortable, slightly inclined position so she could sleep without lying flat.

She found a good place.

Jamie closed her eyes for a second, turning back to the window before she opened them.

The sun was setting. It was odd—how many sunsets she'd seen on this journey. She hadn't had the opportunity to watch them as much in the city, or during the war.

This was a good place to watch the sunset.

A good place to watch it rise.

A good place to heal.

"Leaving in the morning?" Vic's scratchy, sleepy voice was soft, but reached Jamie across the empty room.

"Yeah." Jamie took a deep breath and let it out as the last bit of color left the horizon.

"Niko found everyone?"

Jamie left the window. She crossed to the bed and sat at the old wicker chair beside Vic. "Not everyone. But enough." She shook her head. "I was surprised with how many died between discharge and now. And a handful are on the east coast."

Vic swallowed. "Anyone—"

"No," Jamie interrupted. "No one from the main squad. Apart from Cade and Alice."

An exhale of relief, and then Vic's expression darkened. "You'll be careful, Jamie?"

There wasn't concern in her tone. It was almost a question, but not as much as it was an order.

Jamie leaned back, folding her arms over her chest. "You worried, big sis?"

There was a flash of irritation, then Vic chuckled with a wince. "How have neither of us changed in five years?"

Jamie's eyes widened, as did her smile. "I don't know about that. Time was you'd give orders instead of asking."

"Time was you listened to most of them."

"As far as you know," Jamie said with a wink.

Vic stuck out her tongue.

Then, almost simultaneously, they both sobered. There was an absence in the room. Lighthearted taunts missing from the conversation. A tinkling laugh that should have been with them but wasn't.

Tears magnified Vic's eyes. Jamie reached across the bed and took her hand. Vic squeezed, that lack of pressure still concerning. Especially after hearing the list of injuries she was healing from.

"I'll be careful," Jamie murmured, looking down at their entwined fingers. "I don't plan on leaving you alone, Vic. And I told her—" Her breath hitched. Vic squeezed harder, tears sliding down her cheeks. Jamie shook her head and tried again. "I told her a long time ago that I'd try for happy, and it seems like this is a place where that would be possible."

"You're coming back, then."

Jamie bit down on her bottom lip and gave her sister a shallow nod.

"Doc says she needs to rest."

Jamie didn't turn, didn't look away from Vic at the sound of Hunt's voice from the door. Instead, she stood and leaned in, planting a gentle kiss on Vic's hairline.

"I'll be back for my *rodina*. Promise."

Vic released her hand and wiped at the tears on her cheeks. "I'll hold you to that, Captain."

Jamie's mouth twisted into a sardonic smile as she straightened. "Oli told you."

"Yep."

She shook her head. Then she turned from the bed and crossed to the door. There was a moment of hesitation as she and Hunt sized each other up yet again.

Then Jamie sighed and said in a perfectly neutral tone, "If she's not in perfect health when I get back, I'm going to rip your arms off."

Hunt blinked. Alarm flashed across those crystal blue eyes. Then he grinned. "I'd be worried, but even if she's still injured she can take you."

Jamie snorted, strode past him through the door, and made her way into the deep bunker where Oliver was waiting in their room.

"Here's the layout." Niko pressed a foldout tablet into Jamie's hands. It was small, the size of her palm when all folded up. His fingers twisted together once the device left his hands. "Don't turn it on yet, though. Wait until you're a lot closer so you don't waste the battery."

Jamie raised an eyebrow at the twig of a boy telling her how electronics worked. "Yeah, I know, kid."

He shrugged, completely unbothered by her tone. "You won't have a way to recharge on the road."

"Yeah."

Oliver snorted behind her. Jamie jabbed with her elbow, but he darted to the side and avoided the strike.

"You know how to find your friends?" Niko glanced past her at Oliver.

It was predawn, and a handful of Organic ranch hands were assisting them in packing up three horses. Oliver was cinching saddles and checking reins.

They'd both been given a detailed lesson in horse riding and care the day before. Jamie had trotted around the ranch and hadn't fallen off. Which had boosted her confidence enough for her to let go of the frustration she felt at not getting to take the ranch's only truck.

Two horses would carry the Unborn. The third was loaded down with food, tactical gear, and weapons.

It would be a cross-country trek. With the exception of a couple stops to find more of their kind, they'd be avoiding roads and cities with vigor. The weapons alone were enough for the two of them to be hung without much of a trial. Add on rising tensions between Unborn and Organic... It would be better to not be seen.

Jamie patted her left jacket pocket. "I've got my map right here," she said with a softer smile than usual.

The kid had passed it to her the night before after another 'family dinner.' A hand drawn map of their route to the old marine bunker, each destination of an Unborn on her list marked with a star.

It was a thing of beauty, and it made Jamie want to see more of his art. Made her want to pull him aside and ask about technique, color, style.

Instead, she'd folded it up with a nod of appreciation. There would be time to look at it on the road.

"I'll see you when you get back?"

His voice, tremulous to match his twitchy hands, said it like a question.

Jamie ran her tongue across her teeth, then glanced around conspiratorially. Niko did the same.

She leaned in.

He copied her.

She muttered, just loud enough for Oli to hear because he was so close to them, "Vic came back after taking down half a dozen of those robots."

Niko nodded, his eyes wide.

Jamie grinned. "I can count on one hand the number of times she's beaten me in a fight. Out of hundreds. Yeah, kid. You'll see me when we get back."

He glanced at the Organics who had just finished packing up the final horse. Almost like he thought he'd get in trouble for Jamie shit-talking Vic.

"Don't let Max practice arm wrestling too much." Oliver planted a hand on the kid's shoulder.

Niko let out a shallow laugh. Then, without another word, he turned from them and the dawn light and hurried back into the house.

Jamie sucked in a breath and released it slowly through pursed lips. "Time to get going."

She and Oliver mounted their horses. Hers was a dappled gray, spots of black and white coating its neck and a coarse tangle of black for a mane.

"Careful with them." One of the Organics, a redhead with a strong jaw and oversized forearms patted Jamie's mount. "We need these three back."

There was something in his tone that soothed the bristles his words brought forth in Jamie. They'd only been there two days, barely, as they'd spent much of that first arrival day with her in heated conversations with Vic. Yet, there was something about this place...

"I wish we could have stayed longer," Oliver said as they clopped over the grassy hill and toward the large arched gate at the open end of the ranch. "I could use a few more of those dinners."

Jamie's mouth curled into a half-smile. "Yeah, and another shower or two."

She snorted at the flush of his cheeks.

They made it out of the ranch and away from the road. The sun rose to their left as they began the long journey south.

30

Stakes

T HE JOURNEY AWAY FROM the ranch was startlingly easier than getting there had been. Jamie understood the concept. Big animal carries you and all your supplies and has great endurance—that
would speed up a trip.

But she and Oli were Unborn. Their endurance more than matched
that of a four-legged beast. She'd underestimated the impact the
horses would make.

The difference came from not having to lug the multitude of guns
and gear on their backs the whole damn way and resting as they rode
half the day.

When the sun dipped below the tips of the trees and Oliver suggested they stop for the night, Jamie was ready to keep going.

Until he pointed out the danger of a twisted leg on the first day of
the trek.

It would be a problem with the horses, to be sure. But there was an
added factor neither of them had had much chance to discuss. Doc
had told them the radiation from the Wasteland wasn't likely to have

any overly deadly repercussions, but their accelerated Silver healing was stunted, at least for now.

Injuries this early in their trip could mean failure. Whether they'd heal as quickly as they were used to once more than a week sat between them and the Wasteland was a question yet to be answered.

Jamie grumbled, but accepted the logic behind his words. The two set up a quick camp, walked the animals to a nearby stream for some water, and then tied them to a close cluster of trees with plenty of grass nearby for munching.

Light splintered through the woods to the west. The ocean was there, somewhere. Jamie had a vague idea how far it would be to see sand, a beach, water crashing against the shore.

Much too far to divert from their mission. Though they'd end up near enough when they got closer to the base they were after.

She took a bite of the thick sandwich Claire had packed for them. There were over a dozen of the things, bread freshly baked the day before, rich cheese, thick cuts of meat.

The flavors turned ashen in her mouth as her gaze caught on a small bundle strapped to the front of the pack horse's gear.

Her fingers reached for her boot, where a prepped syringe was filled with what Doc hoped would be enough serum to bring her or Oli back if one of them went dark. Jamie scratched her leg and pulled her hand away from the spot.

Oliver had another of their dozen doses. They'd planted them privately. Each not wanting to know where the other's was—in case some part of them was left when the transition happened. In case they knew enough in that state of violence to destroy the other person's only hope at getting them back.

Jamie looked at the half-eaten sandwich in her hand and the apple she'd been shining on her pants for the last ten minutes.

"This doesn't feel right," she muttered.

Oliver looked over. He lounged against the trunk of a large tree, his torso only half the size of the towering thing. His food was already gone, and his hands now fiddled with a paring knife and a hunk of wood. He'd just started humming something when she interrupted with her dark thoughts.

"What doesn't?"

Jamie shook her head. "This." She held up her sandwich. "Tell me of another mission where the stakes were this high and we stopped for the night to eat a sandwich."

Oliver raised an eyebrow, tilting his head at her. "Are you upset we have food, or upset we aren't moving faster?"

Her jaw clenched, though his tone was mellow. And the truth was, she couldn't point out the problem. Couldn't blame the food, or the logic of resting the horses and themselves, or the distance they had to travel. But it didn't feel right. It didn't feel like...

"It doesn't feel like the war," she finally said, her voice soft.

A crease settled between Oli's eyebrows.

Jamie set her food down on the brown paper it had been packed in. "I just," she sighed. "We're back in it. Back in a fight, with an enemy we can see. And it feels..." She grimaced. "It feels like we should be on a transport, getting dropped into enemy territory, going in guns blazing."

Nerves jangled in her stomach, and she clenched her hand into a fist.

"There's something," Oliver murmured, his gaze no longer on her but on the blade in his hand, "truly rattling about going into this fight knowing we could turn on each other at any moment."

A lump caught in her throat.

He continued staring at the knife, the silver of the metal so similar to both their eyes. The defining features that marked them as not just warriors, but elite. Specialty fighters with no waver in loyalty, no fault in capability.

"I think it doesn't feel like the war," Oliver said, "because it's not. In the war there were countless Coppers, hundreds of Silvers, plenty of bodies to take up the fight if we fell. This has higher stakes because, if we don't *do* this, if we fail..." His fingers clenched suddenly around the blade, and he winced.

Jamie stood and strode over to him. She plunked beside him on the leaf-coated ground and took hold of his wrist.

His fingers loosened, the inner edge of two of his knuckles wet with blood. He looked at her, brow still furrowed, full lips trembling. "If we fail, Cade and Alice are never avenged. And the rest of our kind faces the same fate they did."

She spread his hand, assessing the damage with the care and attention he'd had with her forearms what felt like months ago. It had barely been more than a week.

The slices were skin deep. Even slower than usual healing they'd be scabbed over by morning. Still, the drip of blood on the blade caused a falter in her breathing. Like a premonition of what was coming.

"So." She forced out a weak chuckle. "Stakes are higher, we have basically no support besides what the horse is carrying and any Unborn crazy enough to join us on the way, and if we fail, our kind might be wiped off the face of the planet."

The despair on his face, the pain etched into the weathered lines of his dark skin, faded for a moment as incredulity took their place. "Well, when you go and say it like that—"

She shook her head, pursing her lips and shrugging. "Sounds like a bad idea. I say we go to the beach instead."

He didn't fall over laughing, but he smiled, and a bit of life returned to his eyes. "I'll take you to the beach after this."

It was her turn for incredulity. "Yeah? On our way back to the ranch or..."

He closed his uninjured hand around one of hers. "I'm serious, Jamie. When this is done, we don't listen to the rules anymore."

She arched an eyebrow.

He rolled his eyes. "*I* don't listen to the rules anymore. We do what we want when we want. We go wherever you wanna go." He swallowed, his jaw tightening a fraction. But he didn't look away. "I'll be with you when this is done. No walking away."

A shadow of memory flickered across her mind. The long hall, the commander's screaming fury, the embarrassment and anger. The sound of Oliver's footsteps fading.

It was gone in a blink. That memory, and the pain that came with it even after she'd insisted to herself that the anger was pointless. The hurt hadn't been gone before, she realized. Though she'd moved past the blame and bitterness, there had still been heartbreak.

She didn't respond. Couldn't, because the brunt of her emotions would have been blatantly audible in her voice. Instead, she scooted closer, put his arm around her shoulder, and leaned her head against his chest.

They reached the first mark on her map the next day. It was difficult, picking and choosing which of their old friends was close enough to join them. More than a handful were on their current side of the country but not on the way to their destination.

Still, the desire to charge in with a full contingent of capable Unborn was overpowering. If the threat of going dark didn't hang over them with every step, she would've considered taking the detours.

But this stop was close.

And familiar.

Jamie shook her head as she and Oli, walking the horses, turned down one of the dirt paths they'd skipped by on their way through the mountains so many days ago. "If we hadn't been in such a hurry—"

Oliver grinned. "Yeah. But it'll be nice to see her now."

The dirt and gravel road took them up a steep incline. Towering forest pines lined either side. Scraggly bushes encroached on the trail, though it was clear that the road was used frequently enough to stop nature overtaking it entirely.

"Think she'll join us?" Jamie asked, looking up the road.

A fair distance ahead of them, just visible around a slow bend, was a shabby wooden gate connecting two towering rock cliff faces on either side. The gate barred their way ahead.

"Has she ever said no to a fight?"

Jamie snorted. "Have any of us?"

He didn't say anything, and she almost winced at the reminder that she had said no to him. That she'd rejected his request for help, and in doing so, had sentenced Alice to her fate.

Oliver sucked in a breath as they came to a stop before the gate. It stood tall, but his height allowed him a glimpse over the top.

"What do you see?"

"More road."

Jamie scowled.

Oliver waved his hand, gesturing to someone Jamie couldn't see from her shorter vantage point.

"Someone's coming," he muttered. He stepped away from the gate, drawing the horses with him, and Jamie followed.

"Unborn?"

He nodded. "Copper."

Not Katya then. Jamie's mouth twisted in a grimace. It would have been nice if the first eyes that spotted them were familiar ones. But they were Unborn. With any luck there wouldn't be an issue.

A head popped up at the top of the planks of wood.

Jamie raised an eyebrow, trying to keep down her laugh.

The Copper looked young, likely fresh out of training at the very end of the war. With the rapid growth they'd experienced, he could very well have been only sixteen or seventeen.

His wide copper eyes matched his brows and identical colored hair. Every inch of his face was coated with freckles, as though the sun had taken one look at him and decided tanning was never to be in the boy's future.

He stared down at them for a few seconds.

Jamie shifted.

Oliver glanced at her, then handed over the reins.

She took them, her scowl back in place.

"Hello," Oli said in a clear, calm voice. He stepped forward with his arms open. "We were hoping to find some fellow Unborn in these mountains. We'd heard there are friends here."

The boy's gaze darted to Jamie, then back at Oliver. "Friends of who?"

Jamie cocked her head. Clever question.

"Friends of soldiers," she called, cutting off whatever Oliver had been about to say.

The boy's gaze met hers, and she rethought her opinion on how old he was. A youngling wouldn't have that kind of analysis in his eyes. No, this man had seen war.

"'Fraid that's not specific enough to let you through."

Jamie took a step, sidling up beside Oliver with the horses trailing behind her. "What sort of specifics are you looking for?"

Beside her, Oliver sighed.

"Name? Rank?" She held out her arm, gesturing to her inner elbow with the other hand. "Unborn ID?"

Oliver held up a hand. "Let's start with names, yeah?" He gave Jamie a pointed, 'settle down' look.

She rolled her eyes.

The Copper turned his attention back to Oli as he spoke.

"I'm Oliver. This is Jamie. We're looking for a friend of ours. A Silver."

The young man glanced at Jamie again. "Why?"

This time Oli cut her off, stepping again so he was in front of her and looking up at the Copper. "We need her help. Have you heard about the incidents going on in Unborn villages and towns?"

A chill went down Jamie's spine at the way the young man's lip curled in what appeared to be disgust.

"You're here to fight. To bring trouble."

A low growl sounded in the back of her throat.

The horses stirred restlessly.

"We'll only bring a fight if one is necessary to find our friend," Jamie hissed through gritted teeth.

Oliver groaned this time, an audible sound that was accompanied by him turning to grimace at her. "Can you *please* let me do the talking? Hmm?"

She gave him a scathing grin.

"You can't take anyone from here," the Copper called down. "None of us knows anything about the attacks. We aren't involved."

"Neither are we," Oliver replied. His even tone shifted, taking on the deeper resonance he used when in command of a unit. "In fact, we're trying to stop them happening."

The Copper didn't respond. He just watched them, those calculating eyes taking in everything from their horses to their boots.

"Her name is Katya," Oliver continued. "We fought together in the war. If she is here, she *will* want to speak with us."

At this, the expression on the Copper changed. His wary eyes widened, brow narrowing for a split second before he smoothed his features. He scratched his chin.

Jamie gritted her teeth.

"Katya."

Oliver nodded.

The man inhaled, then blew out the breath through pursed lips. "You haven't gone rogue? Either of you?"

A bolt of worry thundered through Jamie's chest. She stepped forward again, planting herself beside Oli for a second time.

"Do you mean going dark? Rabid?" She raised her free hand and gestured across her eyes.

He nodded.

"No." Her fingers tightened around the reins, and she wished she was holding Oliver's hand. "But we've lost friends to what's causing it. And we're on our way to make it stop."

He sighed and looked from her to Oli and back again. Then he gave a light shake of his head and disappeared behind the gate.

Jamie let out her breath, frustration flaring.

There was a screech, a high-pitched whine of hinges as the gate inched open. It stopped just wide enough for the horses to get through single-file.

Standing before them, a head taller than Jamie had guessed, was the Copper.

He wore a faded gray button up shirt and a pair of long blue jeans. He ambled forward, his lanky form slowing to a stop at the edge of the gate. He stuck his hands into his pockets.

"I'm Tucker. Welcome to Respite."

31

Respite

I T WAS LIKE SOMETHING from a woodland storybook. Jamie recalled her small red and bruised fingers opening a faded cover with small furry creatures. It had been one of the first things she'd read.

And here it was in front of her, a picturesque village nestled into the mountains. Small homes built of wooden beams, paths of rock and gravel to avoid stomping through the wide array of greenery nearly everywhere.

They appeared to be practical plants. A handful of people, Unborn and Organic alike, wandered with baskets, plucking juicy red tomatoes, rainbows of peppers, and even...

Jamie swallowed, eyes wide at the row of strawberry plants only a few feet ahead of them.

"Horses this way," Tucker said with a jerk of his head.

Oliver took two of the reins and followed the Copper around the far side of the first large cabin. Jamie trailed behind with her mount. It was easier to tear herself away when she registered the many eyes watching her intently.

The feeling of being analyzed every place they went was starting to chafe.

The gravel path they followed led to a covered stable. Tucker introduced them to an Organic man with flowing blond hair almost as long as Jamie's. He helped them unpack the horses with only a raised eyebrow at the many weapons.

"Leave those here." Tucker gestured to the guns.

Jamie, who had been mid-holstering one to her hip, glared.

Oliver nodded. "They'll be safe here? Not that we don't trust you, but—"

Jamie's scoff cut his words short. His lips tightened, but he didn't look at her.

"No one'll touch your stuff," the blond man, Dwain, said. "I keep the animals, and I'll make sure of it. You have my word."

There was something soothing in the twang of his voice, though that only served to make Jamie more suspicious. Still, there were plenty of creatures in the stable, which probably meant he stayed busy here.

A dozen stalls had been constructed, short fences functioning as deterrents rather than actually designed to keep the handful of goats and sheep in their pens.

A light layer of hay covered the ground. The horses were given feed bags, immediately dipping into them and the water trough against the back wall.

Jamie's stomach twinged with guilt at how hungry and thirsty the animals were. They'd given rest and sustenance when possible, but it was a long trek through the mountains.

"Dwain can handle your belongings," Tucker said. He leaned against one of the thick posts holding up the roof. His lanky arms were loose at his sides. "You wanted to see Katya."

Oliver exchanged a glance with Jamie, and she gave a brief nod.

"This way."

They followed him to the other open end of the stable, out and down another path that wound through a series of cabins. The interiors had to be small, one bedroom in most, maybe two. A larger building, narrow but long, with windows covered by thin panels of fabric, seemed to be the center point of the village.

Respite was nestled between two rocky cliffs. The entire village was small enough for Jamie to see where the buildings stopped. To the north, opposite of the way they'd come in, a field of tall grass stretched a quarter-mile before another cliff rose up to block the way. Small trees, barely saplings, grew up in a grid pattern along one side. A few goats prowled at the farthest edge, mowing down the vegetation.

The road they'd followed up from the gate took a few extra bends before reaching the village itself. It kept Respite hidden, but offered limited actual protection.

Jamie frowned as they walked, eyeing the high ridges around them. "Do you have someone on the gate at all times?"

Tucker looked back at her. "Not all the time."

"How do you know if someone is coming?" Oliver asked.

He sighed. "Katya will answer your questions, if she's in the mood."

Jamie chuckled at that. A fair response for someone who didn't know them. And a good sign that it was the Katya they were looking for.

Tucker led them around a bend.

Jamie broke into a wide grin, a flutter of joy dancing through her.

Sitting on a minuscule front porch, hands preoccupied with a set of wooden needles and a ball of pink yarn, was Katya.

She still wore her hair in a long black braid. Her olive complexion was darker than it had been from more time in the sun. Mono-lid eyes were decorated with touches of some kind of colored powder, reminding Jamie of how fond Katya had been of make-up the few times they'd gotten a chance to use it. And her slender frame had more build now. Practical muscles meant for tilling earth rather than carrying heavy guns.

While not part of the squad Jamie had trained and bunked with, she and Katya had run more than a few missions together, often with Oliver or Cade as their seconds in command.

Silver eyes darted up from her work, and Jamie was relieved at the smile that crossed her friend's lips as well.

"Well, shit," Katya yelped. She dropped her yarn and darted toward them with arms outstretched. "What the hell are you two assholes doing here?"

Jamie let out a laugh, pulling the much shorter woman into a tight squeeze. Oli went next, wrapping Katya in a one-armed hug and resting his cheek on her hair for a moment.

"Looking for you, smart-ass," Jamie drawled, unable to keep the mirth from her voice.

Katya cackled and punched Jamie's arm.

"This is crazy. I never thought I'd see you two again," she said, eyes glinting with excitement. She leaned around them, glancing back the way they'd come. "Where are the girls? Cade?"

The bubble of happiness in Jamie's chest popped. She reached out, and Oli took her hand.

Katya's gaze followed the movement. She raised an eyebrow.

"Cade is dead," Oliver murmured, his voice tight.

Jamie squeezed his hand.

"Alice, too," he continued.

Katya's face pinched into a flash of grief, followed by a weariness that suggested they weren't the first to deliver such news.

Jamie put a hand on her shoulder. "Vic's all right. And pretty close, actually. Some Uniforms messed her up. That's the only reason she's not here right now."

Katya bared her teeth. "You took care of them?"

"We weren't there," Jamie said. "We got placed on the east coast."

"She finished the job, though." Oliver clenched his fist, and Jamie had a brief dream of a future where they went back to Boston and somehow found the actual Uniforms who had killed Cade.

It was a pipedream. And an unnecessary one. They were on their way to take down the people who were actually responsible, not the robots simply filling out their programming.

"Good," Katya growled.

Jamie gazed around the peaceful village. "You've had some experience with 'em then?"

Tucker stepped forward before her friend could respond. "Katya, did you want to get them settled in with some food? I'll get Logan. You can fill them in somewhere a bit more private?"

Jamie released Oliver's hand and turned to stare at the Copper. They weren't in a secluded space, but once the handful of people there had seen Katya embrace them, they'd gone back to their business.

Katya's nose twitched, a sign of irritation she hadn't broken—and a good tell that made it easier to beat her at poker. She nodded. "Yeah, let's get you both some food."

"I won't say no to that," Oliver said with a grin.

Jamie grunted an affirmative and followed as, once again, they were led down winding paths. They went back the way they'd come, to the long building at the center of the village.

Katya shoved the door with her shoulder and held it as everyone traipsed inside.

Jamie blew out a breath, shaking her head at the sight before her.

The building was one massive room with a set of swinging double doors at the far end. Tables lined it in rows, awfully familiar to old mess halls.

But this was something entirely different.

The roof had been outfitted with glass or translucent plastic, allowing beams of sunlight to both warm and brighten the space. Windows had been set into the walls—thick ones, with large wooden shutters ready to close from the inside.

Plants grew along the walls, hanging from baskets, in pots on the ground, and some even sat on shelves that seemed to only serve the purpose of holding the little green things.

All of it was enough to impress, but the scent was what took hold of Jamie.

Similar to the meals she and Oli had shared back at the ranch, but there was a richer sense to the smells here. As though the spices had been baked into the wooden beams above them. Years worth of community meals.

There was almost an echo of laughter through the hall, and a flickering vision of what might have been—what could have been—took hold of Jamie. If she and Alice and Vic had been together, maybe they'd have found a place like this. Maybe they'd have made one.

"So, what are you filling us in on?"

Jamie blinked, ripping her gaze from the nearby window where she'd been watching a small tree sway in the wind.

She looked to Katya. "Yeah, and why didn't Tucker want you talking in front of anyone else?"

Katya puffed her cheeks and blew out a sigh. "Come on. Food is this way."

Jamie and Oliver exchanged a furrowed glance and followed their old friend.

"It's only happened once, about three days ago. And it didn't affect everyone, but we lost the one who went rogue."

Jamie sucked a breath in through her teeth.

She was perched on the edge of the kitchen counter. It was a long wooden thing lining most of the room the double doors led to. A brick oven made up the farthest wall, a back door beside it which was currently closed but likely opened during cooking hours to let out the heat.

Oliver stood beside her, leaning his hip against the counter and gnawing on the final edge of his third cob of corn.

The two ate their fill while Katya explained the incident that had caused Tucker's immediate suspicion of them.

A Copper had gone rogue, as they called it. He'd ripped a sapling out by the roots and torn the throat out of one of the goats. Fortunately, he'd been in the field and not a more populated area.

Katya had been the one to take him down. The Coppers in Respite had kept the Organics safe, and she'd pinned the man to the ground. Their leader, a man named Logan who Jamie and Oli had yet to meet, had delivered the headshot to end the violence.

Katya did not cry during her tale. Jamie heard no falter or hesitation as her former subordinate debriefed her as though this had been a mission in the war, not a member of her community going crazed and being executed.

But there was a tightness to her voice, a shudder in her shoulders as she gave them the gruesome details, that told Jamie how important this place was to her.

"Have you heard of others?" Oliver murmured. His fingers drifted across the countertop until he reached Jamie's hand. His fingertips tickled the back of her hand, up her wrist, and back down before he covered her hand in his.

Katya nodded. "Our contacts in the city nearest us..." She glowered. "It was already difficult trading with them, but now they're scared. There have been more reports. Whole villages of Unborn—"

"We know," Jamie said. "It happened to Vic's."

Katya fell quiet, chewing on her bottom lip as she pondered.

Jamie shifted her hand, intertwining her fingers with Oli's and giving him a squeeze. The story of the execution had to be hitting him harder with how Cade had died. Killed for something he'd had no control over.

"How did you get here?" Jamie asked after a moment of silence. "How does a place like this exist?"

Katya gave half a shrug, crossing to them and stacking their dishes. Oliver made a move to help, but she held up her hand and shook her head.

She went to the large basin sink—one of the only metal things in the building—and dripped a small amount of water into it. She spoke as she scrubbed.

"A lot of us started out in the city, and it was real rough going right from the jump. But there were plenty others stationed further away. Dropped in smaller towns with no need for them."

"Or want," Jamie grumbled, thinking of the town that had cast them out without a second thought.

Katya gave half an eye roll and a short nod. "Or want. But we found this place when they drove us out. A few Organics came along." She stacked the clean dishes on a flat cloth and turned to look at them, drying her hands on her pants. "Enough who have actual life skills to help us build something."

"What? You didn't learn woodworking as part of that rigorous Unborn training I've heard so much about?" A new voice joined the conversation, sounding from the other side of the double doors.

Jamie slid from the counter, planting on the balls of her feet.

An Organic pushed into the room, and a grin split across Katya's face.

The man was broad with a square chin, bushy sandy blond beard, and a violet hat that clashed horribly with his creamy complexion. He looked older, maybe mid-forties. And he surveyed Jamie and Oliver with an air of someone entirely unconcerned with their presence.

Jamie's grip on Oli's hand tightened.

Tucker trudged in behind the man, sliding sideways until he stopped at a corner and leaned back with his arms crossed.

"Jamie, Oliver, this is Logan." Katya moved forward, bridging the gap between them. "He runs Respite."

"Mostly," the man said with a chortle. "Katya does the heavy lifting. Literally."

Katya shook her head with an eye roll, but Jamie caught the glint of pride in her gaze. "Logan is the one who managed the majority of our building materials. He's half the reason we have running water most of the time, and the entire reason we can still trade with the city."

He waved off her words with a meaty hand. "Solar panels are next. I get *them*, and you can give me all the credit you want." He stepped toward Jamie and Oliver with his hand outstretched. "It's good to meet you."

Oliver went first, releasing Jamie's hand to shake Logan's. "Back at you. We knew there was a settlement of Unborn in these mountains, but this isn't quite what we expected."

"It's amazing what happens when you put our kind to work on sustainable things," Katya said dryly.

Jamie snorted. She took Logan's hand after Oli, giving him a firm handshake. "It's an impressive place. We've seen something similar, but not quite as communal as all this." She gestured vaguely.

Logan smiled. "It was a lot of work and continues to be. There are plans to fill out a few spare corners of space, open up a separate lot for more goats, extend the chicken pen, and—"

"Logan," Katya broke across his stream of thought.

He blinked at her. "Right." He turned to Jamie and Oliver. "Tucker tells me you two came for a reason. To find our friend, here?"

Jamie gave a sharp nod. "A bit more to it, but finding Katya was the first step."

His bushy brows came together in a curious expression. "What's the next?"

32

A Challenge

"**I**T'LL BE A CHALLENGE." Oliver stood with Logan, leaned onto the table as he gave the other man a detailed account of the plan. "We have another place on the way to our target to check for old friends who might be able to help. We need as many Unborn bodies as possible."

"Twelve at the most," Jamie corrected.

Katya raised an eyebrow. "Why the limit? You've said you don't know how many Uniforms will be there."

Oliver sighed, a tired exhale as he straightened and crossed his arms, looking at Jamie. She met his gaze, the weight of the answer heavy on her chest.

She turned to Katya. "Going dark, that rogue, violent switch, it's also what killed Alice and Cade." Jamie pushed away from the counter and pulled a capped syringe from her boot. She gave it a little shake. "This is the only thing we know of that *might* be able to stop it."

Katya's round face blanched. She swallowed, a hand clenched at her side. "Do you know what causes it, then?"

"Somewhat," Oliver said with a nod. "They put something in us when we were built."

Jamie grimaced. "A switch, or something. There's a doctor where Vic is. She was able to create a formula to block whatever triggers it."

"It hasn't been tested?" Tucker asked. He crossed to the table, staring down at the map of the west coast Logan provided when the planning had begun.

"Not on us," Jamie muttered. "It works on Coppers. At least, it works once. We don't know if it's a one-time thing or not. And we don't know—"

"If it'll work for you," he cut across her, glancing at Katya as he did. Jamie's lip curled, but she nodded.

"And you only have twelve of those." Logan pointed to the syringe Jamie still held.

She planted her boot on the bench seat beside him, tucking it back with a furtive look at Oliver. "Yep."

"Well, shit." Katya clicked her teeth. "A challenge might be under-selling it, Oliver. Going up against the enemy without being able to completely trust each other?"

"I trust you," Jamie snapped, her voice harsher than she meant it to be. She softened her tone. "I trust both of you." She looked to Katya and Oliver. "If someone goes dark... that's just another factor we deal with when the time comes. We all know well enough that nothing goes as planned with something like this."

"Don't you think it's a little different," Tucker murmured. "If it's our own people turning against us mid-mission?"

"You plan on coming, too?" Oliver asked, his dark eyebrow raised.

A stir of irritation went through Jamie. Oliver had been correct when he said they needed as close to a dozen Unborn as they could get for this. But she didn't know Tucker. And as much as she trusted Katya and Oliver, a random Copper was a different story.

"He is," Logan said, rising from the table with a grunt. "And so am I."

Katya opened her mouth, but Jamie beat her to it.

"We don't need an Organic ride-along."

The big man raised an eyebrow and straightened his violet hat. "I'll choose not to take offense to that. You might not need an Organic most of the time, but this is sort of a special circumstance, don't you think?" He tapped his temple, cocking his head.

Jamie pursed her lips, eyelids fluttering closed in a moment of annoyance.

"Fair point," Oliver said. He gripped the corners of the map and folded it along the crease-lines. He looked up and met Jamie's gaze, her eyes wide with a meaningful stare. He shrugged a shoulder. "Even one person who can't be controlled could be a huge boon."

"You think he'd be able to get a syringe into one of us if we went dark?" Her tone was low, a deep warning growl.

"I think we stand a better chance of him trying than all of us losing ourselves with no one there to help."

Katya nodded. "Logan can handle himself, Jamie."

Jamie scowled. "Have you gone up against Uniforms?" she asked, directing her question to Logan. "Have you seen what we can do?"

The man didn't flinch away from her stare. "I haven't. But I've seen what Katya can do. And I've seen what Tucker can do. And if there is a way to guarantee that my friends stay who they are... I'm not going to sit here and do nothing when there's a chance I can help."

Frustrating respect came with his words. Jamie gave a sharp nod. In her periphery, she spotted Katya giving Oliver a knowing grin. As though the two of them knew the impact of Logan's words and what Jamie's response would be to them.

"Fine. Come along. But we only have the three horses, and we are going to try to recruit more Unborn along the way. It's not going to be a quick trip."

Tucker cleared his throat. Jamie glanced at the man, noting how pale his skin was around the myriad of freckles.

"We can probably speed things up a bit," he said. "If you're okay leaving the horses here."

They only spent one night in Respite. As much as Jamie would have enjoyed another evening on a comfortable bed, a full belly of hot food, Oliver snuggled beside her without one of them needing to keep watch, they didn't have the time for such luxuries.

Still, the welcome given when the rest of the village was introduced brought a fuzzy sort of warmth to Jamie's chest that she didn't want to leave behind.

It was a peaceful place. Logan's big plans for expansion, solar panels, a radio tower, a more refined water filtration system, all suggested it would remain that way. Secluded from the rest of the country. A safe place for Unborn and Organics to live in harmony.

If Jamie and Oliver could stop the darkness. If they could end whatever had lost them both their closest friends. If they could finally get revenge.

Jamie rolled a strawberry through her fingers as her butt bounced up and down in the bed of the rusty blue pick-up truck. They'd left the horses with Dwain in Respite. The man had seemed overjoyed at the notion of caring for the beasts.

Logan drove, Katya by his side in the cab. Tucker and another Copper who had volunteered for the mission—Stark—sat in the back with Jamie and Oliver.

There were blankets set down, half the material covering the gear they'd brought from Vic's place as well as three ten-gallon gas canisters, the other half cushioning them all against the metal of the truck bed. Logan had brought everything Respite could spare to get them all the way to the base, and hopefully back.

The main road was going to be faster, and they had an Organic with them to do the talking if they ran into trouble, but Jamie's stomach stirred at the thought of being stopped.

She plopped the red berry into her mouth, leaves and all. The flavor coated her tongue, fresh and juicy and a reminder of what might be… if they succeeded.

Jamie folded the pale blue handkerchief over the remaining strawberries. The girl who had pressed it into her hands as she finished loading weapons was maybe twelve. A smaller child had clutched her sleeve, staring up into Jamie's silver eyes with wonder.

There were families at Respite.

The knowledge stuck with her.

Darkness fell. They'd been on the road most of the day, stopping only briefly to relieve themselves along the way.

Oliver reached across her lap and tugged a blanket over both their legs. His hand brushed across the top of her boot. A well of worry deepened in Jamie's stomach as she thought of the syringe still there.

He'd seen it. They all had. And at some point, she'd have to find a new hiding spot. The fear that she'd need it, that one of them would turn and they'd have to do the worst to maintain the mission, thrummed through her with every beat of her heart.

Warm skin, soft but thick with callouses, caressed her hand. She unclenched her fist, allowing Oli's fingers to brush across her palm, a soft tickle that settled the anxiety in her chest.

The trees overhead faded away with every mile. It wasn't long before they were replaced with stars.

Katya took over behind the wheel sometime in the night. When the moon was full and bright above them, fields of grass and rolling hills rising and dipping on either side.

Jamie dozed. Her head lolled, slumping against Oli's shoulder every now and then until he repositioned to hold her against him. The dozing turned to deep sleep, and with the dive into her subconscious came fresh nightmares.

This time it was Katya's neck against her arm. Then Tucker's, Stark's, Logan's, and finally Oliver's. She jerked with each break. Pain reverberated along her arm.

Her eyes snapped open.

Oliver had fallen asleep with her arm pinned behind his. The eastern horizon was tinged with gray. On the other side of the bed, Tucker was asleep, his arms folded up behind his head as he stretched those long legs as far as they went.

Stark was awake, his copper eyes keeping watch at their rear.

Jamie shifted, gently pulling her arm out from behind Oli and easing the blanket higher on his torso when he stirred.

She crossed her stiff legs and stretched her arms. "Anything new?" Her voice was low, loud enough to be heard over the rumbling of the truck but hopefully soft enough not to wake their companions.

Stark glanced at her and shook his head.

He'd been quiet so far, similar to Tucker in that way, it seemed. Logan was always ready with conversation, Katya too, but the Coppers held a more stoic countenance.

"Do you know how much longer we have?"

"No," he said, adjusting his blankets as his breath fogged the air between them. "But it can't be far to the outpost you spoke of."

Jamie's chest tightened, and she gave a shallow nod.

They sat in silence for a while. The wind whipped by, the sun steadily brightening the sky as miles passed.

"How many do you plan on accompanying us?" Stark asked as the first true rays of golden light split through the gray. The vegetation on the mountains behind them shifted from black to green.

Jamie ran her thumb across her knuckles. "We can only take six more. And I had originally thought as many as possible would be best." She shook her head. "But the idea of a full dozen, any of us able to go dark at any point..." She sucked in a breath through her teeth.

Stark nodded, his dark corkscrew curls flopping across his forehead. "I'm wary of adding to our numbers. Tucker and I... we've had our own issues with fellow Unborn."

Jamie cocked her head, her eyebrow slightly raised. "Before people started going dark?"

He tugged at a few loose strands of the blanket covering him. Then he glanced up, his copper eyes fixed on the horizon. "The ranking when it comes to Silvers seems like it's pretty cut and dry. But things got a little more complicated, a little less clear, on the field for Coppers."

Jamie clicked her teeth. She recalled a handful of more crowded missions where Silvers butted heads about who was in charge. Usually after the commanding field officer was killed. But the arguments were usually short-lived. Chain of command was what it was, no matter who thought otherwise.

"We took a garrison in our second year, but once we occupied, the enemy reinforcements arrived and we were pinned down. We were stuck there for almost two months, and our Silver..." He paused, the ache of loss splashing so vividly across his face Jamie was certain she'd be able to draw it from memory even years from then.

"Died."

Stark grimaced. "She was torn apart."

Jamie's frown deepened.

"Wolves." His hand clenched into a fist. "She took a squadron of soldiers hunting, to stave off our starvation. Only Tucker returned."

"And it was wolves that took her down." She didn't ask it, didn't question his words. But there was skepticism in her tone.

"That's the official story," Stark muttered. He glanced at their sleeping companions. "Tucker and I, we were trained by her. Practically raised by her. The others weren't part of our original squad."

Jamie's stomach sank. Her mind turned to the Coppers she, Vic, and Alice had trained. The boys and girls going through their five-cal days, bodies growing far too fast. Minds, too. They'd run their Coppers through a thousand drills, harping on every wrong move, every step that would get them killed in the field.

They'd done everything in their power to keep those men and women alive.

And still she could count on two hands the number she *knew* had survived the war.

"What actually happened?" Jamie's voice was low.

Stark bit his lip. His gaze sank to his hands as he pressed a thumb into his palm. "One of the Coppers in the contingent decided he'd be a better fit to lead. He was a big one, a cocky bastard who liked being the one to get information out of people."

Jamie's lip twitched into a scowl. "I know the type."

Stark nodded. "He made sure it was mostly his friends on the hunt. Our Silver didn't make it back, but Tucker made sure he didn't either."

"Wolves," Jamie murmured.

Stark met her eye. "There wasn't much trust for other Unborn after that. Respite is the first place since..." He ran a hand along his jaw and tried again. "Respite gave us the opportunity to trust people again. Unborn and Organic."

A comfortable silence fell again.

The morning sun eventually woke Tucker and Oli. Katya stopped the truck so they could refill the tank and switch drivers. Jamie took the wheel, Oliver sitting beside her while the others stayed in the bed.

Their trek continued south, but at a heavily marked fork in the road Jamie took a right to take them west.

Oliver ate his share of their breakfast, passing her strawberries every now and then as she concentrated on the road.

When he'd finished, downing a swig of water and wiping his fingers on his pants, he cleared his throat. "If we don't find Christian, do you want to try someone else, or are we going straight to the base?"

Jamie exhaled, her thoughts jerked from the road, their mission, and what they'd have to do to accomplish it. "I, uh...." She blinked the fog of distraction from her eyes. "We can do this mission just the six of us. Those Coppers know their stuff."

Oliver glanced at her, and she looked over just long enough to meet his gaze before focusing back on the road.

"What?"

He chuckled. The sound sent a little rush of something warm and sweet through her chest. A ripple of pleasure at the knowledge that something about her brought a smile to his face.

"You're losing some of that sharp edge."

The pleasure melted, her smile going with it as a scowl took her features. "What's that supposed to mean?"

He raised both hands, still grinning. "Nothing bad."

When she didn't respond, and her expression didn't change from disgruntled annoyance, he sighed.

His voice held nothing but sincerity when he spoke. "The list of people you trust has always been short, but I think after the war it also became permanent. As in, unable to be added to. Seems like that's changing a bit."

Jamie chewed the inside of her lip, her chest uncomfortably warm with an anxiety she couldn't shake. "I trust them as much as any of us can trust any Unborn at the moment."

"Yeah." He nodded. Then he pointed toward a shape in the distance. "Is that it, you think?"

33

UNFAIR

J AMIE HAD HOPED TO find Christian in a small town only a hundred miles or so from the coast. Niko's map had labeled it as his discharge location.

Staring at the piles of rubble and scorched wood, Jamie now hoped that her friend had never set foot here.

The town was gone. Each building had been destroyed, obliterated with what looked like heavy artillery. After that, whoever did it had torched everything left. The stench of burned wood, the acrid scent of melted rubber, and the horrifying recognition of charred corpses made Jamie wish she'd skipped breakfast.

She drove slowly down the cracked and ruined road. They passed caved-in buildings, foot-high walls of concrete the only sign of the shapes they'd once formed. When they reached a T intersection, someone thunked on the top of the cab.

Jamie stopped the truck and threw it in park.

Everyone got out. Jamie passed the keys to Logan and, with a nod from Oliver, took one of the guns from under the blankets. She chose a handgun to go with the blade already at her side. Good for close quarters.

"This was a—" Katya began.

"Full town?" Jamie muttered, stepping around bits of rubble as she moved away from the truck. "Yeah. According to the map we got a few days ago, this was a standing town."

"A few days ago..." Logan's voice was pained. Tight with sadness even as he went for a weapon as well.

Fear bubbled in Jamie. Fear that they knew all too well who was responsible for this... *what* was responsible. Uniforms on orders, or Unborn on a rampage. Either possibility made her lips press tight with fury and settled a cold weight of certainty onto her chest.

Christian was very likely dead. As was anyone else who had the bad luck of calling this place home.

She felt Oliver step up beside her, sticking to his usual position just behind her left shoulder. "He might have gotten out. Might have been long gone before any of this happened."

The warmth of his voice almost chased away the cold. But something in his tone drew her eye, and she saw on his face that he didn't dare to hope there was any truth in his words.

She shook her head. "We should go."

Katya, already several feet from the truck and beginning to scour the ruins, turned abruptly, her dark eyebrows narrowed. "We should search for survivors."

Jamie's jaw tightened for a fraction of a second. She inhaled, forcing her muscles to relax. "Look at the wood, Kat. It's not smoking. The ground is dry, there's been no rain. This happened days ago, at minimum."

Her friend snarled, the sound echoing across the rubble.

"Perhaps we can spare a few minutes," Logan said. He stepped between the two of them, his big hands holding a semi-automatic.

His gaze was alert but soft as he looked at Jamie. "To rest, eat a quick bite, before we get back on the road."

Tucker and Stark watched as well, and Jamie felt the eyes of them all on her. On her like they'd been in the war. On those rare occasions when command wanted the job done bloody rather than done right. When they'd put her in charge rather than Vic.

Some young lieutenant had made the mistake of repeating the general's words within Jamie's hearing. *If we want them to come back, we send AF178. For sending a message, and getting the job done no matter the cost, we send AF179.*

The words echoed in her ears as she gazed out at the destroyed buildings that had once been homes. She'd razed villages. Towns like this. She'd given the order to send metal cylinders filled with explosives to end the safety, the comfort, and the care once created by four walls and a hearth.

"Jamie."

Not a question, but Oliver's voice in her ear was enough to bring her back to the present.

She straightened. "Five minutes."

Katya's nostrils flared.

"I don't like it," Jamie said, her voice sharp. "This place feels miles from safe, so we stay *five minutes*. Then we head to the base. And we get this done."

Tucker gave a sharp nod. Stark turned with him as the two strode toward Katya and spoke in low murmurs.

Oliver put a hand on Jamie's shoulder. "It's the right call."

She exhaled, forcibly unclenching her jaw yet again. She didn't respond, but she leaned into his hand for a second.

When he pulled away, it was to join Katya and the Coppers. The four of them began a quick and efficient search of the area.

Jamie stayed beside the truck, her gaze constantly roaming, her heartbeat thudding in her ears.

"Seen this kind of thing before?" Logan leaned against the hood, his large frame throwing a shadow over Jamie's torso.

She glanced at him then continued her scan of the horizon. It was rippled, like canvas torn where a beautiful skyline should have been.

"I've *done* this kind of thing before," she muttered. There was a darkness to her voice, a chill that seeped through her words. She didn't look to see Logan's reaction.

"What was the protocol afterward? Stick around for a few days, or move on?"

Jamie blinked, a jolt of surprise at his question briefly halting her thought process. "It... it depends. If we're taking the territory, we stay. If we're clearing an area of enemies..." She shuddered. "That's more a slash and burn, then hit the road thing."

"No way to know which this was," Logan said. His tone was not judgmental, nor was it forgiving. It was a statement of fact and not a question.

A piece of Jamie still flared with the need to defend herself. She swallowed it down, attempting to put calm into her voice. "Exactly why I don't want to stick around to find out."

"Yeah. I'd rather not tangle with anything before we have to."

At this, Jamie did look at him. "Any*thing*."

Logan pushed off the truck and did a slow circle, keeping a watchful eye on their surroundings. "I'm hoping it wasn't one of us who did this."

She cocked her head, an eyebrow raised. "One of *us*?" she parroted him again.

He met her skeptical gaze. "Humans."

They left at the five-minute mark despite Katya's protests. She, Oli, and the Coppers had only searched a third of the demolished town. No one else made a fuss, but experience had taught Jamie that this needed to be handled sooner rather than later.

So when Katya climbed behind the wheel, Jamie left the men to the back and jumped in to join her.

Her fellow Silver didn't look at her as they pulled away from the ruined town. It would be just the six of them. They didn't have time to try a different mark on her map. Everything else was too far off the path to the base. And with the threat of going dark accompanying every ticking second on the clock, Jamie would rather risk it with the six of them than spend an extra two days finding reinforcements.

"Just us then." Katya's eyes remained on the road, but the bitter tone in her voice permeated the cab.

"Yep."

"And you don't see a problem with leaving that town the way we found it?" She spoke through gritted teeth. "You don't have an issue leaving our friends buried in that mess?"

Jamie's hand clenched into a fist at her side. She filled her lungs with a breath that did not calm her the way she'd hoped it would. The bubbling anger she'd kept at a simmer since releasing some of it at Vic was growing unmanageable.

Partially because of the fear that accompanied it. Partially because she was jealous of Respite, of the peace her friend had found while she and Alice had struggled for scraps. And partially—mainly—because the war was supposed to be over. She'd done her time fighting. They all had.

"We don't know Christian was there when it happened. Hell, Kat, we don't know *when* it happened, *why* it happened, or if the ones who did it are still there somewhere. Waiting for people to try and mount a rescue so they can kill even more."

Katya growled. Her fingers tightened on the wheel, knuckles going white as the muscle in her jaw worked overtime. "How likely," she practically breathed the words, exhaling them in a hiss that drove pain through Jamie's chest, "do you think it is that Christian, or any other Unborn in that town, would've left?"

Jamie pressed her fingers to her temple. "You left."

"I was kicked out of my discharge city. That's not the same."

"You've seen what happens," Jamie snapped. "You know what we're trying to do here, and spending half a day searching for survivors isn't the best use of our time."

"Right," Katya said, shooting a pointed glare at Jamie. "I forgot. With you, it's about completing the mission, no matter what we have to give up to do it."

A barrage of faces sped across Jamie's vision, and the buildup bubbled over. She slammed the side of her fist into the window. Not hard enough to crack it, but hard enough to send a sting through her arm that settled her anger and stemmed her nerves.

Katya jerked, her breath coming shallow. She darted a glance at Jamie.

"I don't like it any more than you do," Jamie growled. She rubbed her hand. Her thumb pressed against her knuckles, driving away the urge to punch the dashboard. "I lost Alice, Kat. I lost Alice, Oliver lost Cade, and Vic lost her whole damn community. We don't have time to play hero for a single town in shambles."

Tense silence fell between them. Katya's jaw was tight, her knuckles white on the steering wheel.

Jamie blew out a sigh. "I get it—"

"I didn't know he was so close," Katya interrupted. She shot Jamie a quick look. Tears glistened in her eyes. "It wouldn't have taken any effort to go get him, bring him and anyone else to Respite. But I didn't know he was there."

"Oliver was in Boston. Not close, but close enough, you know?"

Katya nodded.

Jamie picked at the seat cushion. "They didn't do us any favors, dropping everyone in random-ass cities. Not telling us anything about where the others were."

"Scared." Katya's voice was tight. The regret in her tone shifted back to anger, but it didn't feel directed at Jamie any longer. "They've always been scared of what we are. Even during the war."

Jamie's gaze drifted back out the window as they passed through a cluster of scraggly trees. "It sounds so childish in my own head," she murmured. Ahead, the road twisted through sandy cliffs. They'd be at the ocean soon.

"What does?" Kat prompted after a moment of silence.

Jamie rubbed her knuckles again. "How unfair it all is. After everything we did..." She shook her head, her mind drifting to the multitude of times she'd been scolded for questioning commands. "Complaining never gets anything done."

"Not for us," Katya said with a chuckle. "Remember that major who threw a bitch-fit over his sleeping quarters."

The memory of it drove away her darker thoughts for a moment. She snorted and let out a laugh. "Did I tell you what Alice did the next time he was due to come inspect?"

"No." Katya's grin grew. "All the details. Tell me it was painful."

Jamie laughed again and launched into a detailed story involving a harmless garden snake, a nail file, and a very uncomfortable mattress.

As the two talked, sharing tales of their time in the war and after, a familiar voice whispered in the back of her mind. *Focus, Jamie. This isn't going to be easy. Don't lose sight of what you might have to do to complete this mission.*

It was Alice's voice, but the words felt wrong. Too much like what their old handlers would say before assignments.

She thought of Stark and Tucker... of the bond they'd had with their Silver. A bond she'd had with perhaps a few of her Coppers, but one that did not come naturally or easily.

They lost too many, too quickly, for there to be any sort of real relationship.

How many times had she gone off mission to try and protect them? How many times had she nearly lost her life to keep them safe, only to be reprimanded upon return to base and lose half the squad to a transfer?

At some point, she'd stopped trying to make those connections. She'd had Alice and Vic, and that was enough. Oliver, too, for a short time at the end there. Everyone else was a waste of time. Of effort. Of heartache.

And hadn't it been that way for the others too? Vic had been given different Coppers every year or so. A new troop for the lead Silver to train. A green squad for her to sharpen up and pass off to someone with less skill.

Alice had never run a squad. Her missions were solo for the most part.

An ache, like pressure expanding in her sternum, caused an internal wince. She, Vic, and Alice had been closer to Golds than she realized. Isolated.

If it hadn't been for Angela, would the three of them have been allowed to stay together for so long?

Unfair.

Alice's voice again, echoing the sentiment Jamie felt as Katya talked about a troop transport missing spark plugs so they could stay at a hidden oasis for a few extra hours.

34

Rebel

T HE REST OF THE day passed without incident. They switched drivers frequently. Everyone rested as much as possible.

They'd arrive at the edge of the Uninhabitable Zone in the early hours of the evening. In the meantime, they passed through a handful of towns. None larger than the one that had been destroyed, and none with any visible Unborn.

None they felt comfortable stopping in, even with Logan in their party.

Nerves were on edge, not only among their group, but also buzzing in the air whenever they passed through inhabited spaces. Jamie didn't know if it was the way these people always viewed Unborn, or if rumors of mass slaughters had reached this far south. Either way, she was glad they didn't have to stop.

The ocean sang to their right as they followed an old highway down the coast. Sea spray sometimes danced on the wind, putting a salty taste on Jamie's lips when it was her turn in the bed of the truck.

The colors of the water stole her attention over and over. She wanted the images to stay in her mind, to stick in her brain the way horrific scenes from the war seemed to. She wanted to see them painted. Wanted to describe every inch of the scenery to Niko and see what the kid could do with his pencils.

She glanced into the cab through the little back window. Oliver sat behind the wheel, Stark beside him holding a map now that they'd gotten so close to their destination.

It had only been a matter of weeks since Oli had returned to her life, but her world had changed so much. *She* had changed so much.

Was it the weight of everything? The threat of her kind being turned against each other, slaughtered for something they couldn't control that had finally unlocked her ability to forgive?

Or was it losing Alice? Not knowing if she'd find Vic alive.

Being alone.

Jamie shook her head, breaking her dazed-out stare at the reflection of the clouds on the window.

That wasn't it.

She ran her hand along her forearm. Her heart was heavy with the weight of what was coming next. But she found a breath of relief with the realization that the intensity of her feelings for Oli weren't due to circumstance.

She'd loved him when they were young. When the words were unfamiliar and left unspoken because of what they would mean. When part of the reason for their connection was because it was another way to break the rules. Another way to rebel.

Logan barked out a laugh at something Katya said, and Jamie blinked away her distracting thoughts. Tucker rolled his eyes at whatever the Silver had said. Jamie joined in, chuckling along as the other two continued exasperating the Copper.

The horizon darkened. Clouds began to cover what little blue was left in the sky.

Oliver slowed the truck, and Jamie rose, planting a hand firmly on the top of the cab to stand for a view ahead of them.

Her stomach lurched.

It was labeled an Uninhabitable Zone because it, like a handful of other locations in the States, had been bombed to oblivion during the war. Part of her had thought that was an exaggeration. The Wasteland was one thing, but she'd lived the last five years in a partially bombed city. It wasn't uninhabitable in the slightest.

This was different.

The wreckage started early. Miles and miles before the actual zone was cordoned off. Fractured homes, vast stretches of rubble with no sign of greenery or wildlife, pockets of ground where explosives had carved craters in the soil. Jamie's nose twisted in disgust at the sight of a half-melted school bus. Even so many years later, the acrid smell of outlawed weapons of war churned her stomach.

A mile in and Jamie understood why no vegetation was growing. The scent was in the air, high on the wind above them. Clouds coated the sky as far as the eye could see, but they offered no hope of rain. Only the promise that no light would be found in this place.

"You'd think they wouldn't need the signs," Logan muttered as they passed the first row of warnings.

Jamie nodded. "But this was one of our largest military installations. Anyone who knows anything about prewar knows they could find something valuable here."

He shook his head. "With the restrictions on firearms, I'm surprised people would risk it."

Tucker gave a derisive snort. "There's more than just guns in there, Logan. A lot more."

"And these assholes we have to deal with have access to it all," Katya growled. She met Jamie's eye. "Good thing you brought us some toys too."

Half a smile flickered across Jamie's face. "Thank Vic when this is over. She's the one who got us the guns."

"Oh, I mean to," Katya said with a grin. "Now we know there is another safe place for Unborn? There's gonna be some fun meet ups."

"You want another go at her."

Katya nodded before Jamie finished the sentence. "I want another go at her. Yes."

Jamie laughed and gripped the edge of the truck bed as Oliver slowed to a stop. "She's gonna kick your ass. Again."

Katya opened her mouth, brow furrowed in a half-offended, half-surprised expression. But Logan's bark of laughter interrupted whatever she'd been about to say.

"Let's keep it quiet." Oliver followed his own instructions as he gently closed the driver's side door. "I don't like how empty it is here. Feels like something is watching us."

Jamie nodded. "We only have an hour to sunset, and I imagine it will get dark here quicker."

The others circled around, attentive eyes on her as she spoke.

"Set up camp. Two of us can continue on and scout the base. We're all familiar with the exterior layout, correct?"

Everyone uttered sounds of agreement. Jamie had powered on her tablet from Niko for a few brief minutes the evening before. They'd scoured the design of the facility, committing it to memory before she'd shut it down again to save the battery.

"If we're dealing with Organics or Unborn, we should approach at night and use the darkness to our advantage."

"And if it's all Uniforms guarding the place?" Stark asked.

She grimaced. "Then the light won't matter, and we go in when we have the best visibility."

"I'll scout ahead," Tucker said.

"Good plan." Katya winked. "You can't cook worth shit anyway."

Logan chortled, then composed himself and looked at Jamie. "Are you okay with me joining him? Or do you want an Unborn for this?"

Jamie put her hands on her hips, surveying the road ahead. "We're close enough to the base, and there's enough time before sundown that you'll be able to see. You can go."

She turned to Tucker. "Stay clear of anything that moves. We have schematics of the interior; we just need to know their perimeter defenses. Don't get too close, and don't be seen."

"There's no reason for anyone to think we're coming," Oliver added. "Surprise will be our biggest asset here. So let's maintain it."

Tucker nodded, straightened, and saluted.

Jamie returned the gesture on impulse, blinking afterward with surprise at how quickly her body moved to respond. Beside her, Oli had done the same. He looked less startled about it.

She smoothed her features and gave Tucker a quick grin. "Be careful."

He and Logan left. Jamie watched them jog away with a familiar tightness in her chest. They'd reach the fence-line that surrounded the base rather quickly.

The rest of them got to work setting up a camp. It would be more than a simple shelter for the night. It would also be their primary fallback location. A spot to meet up if things went wrong.

The secondary location had been decided on earlier. A cliffside overlooking the ocean. They'd passed it a few miles before they hit the Uninhabitable Zone.

"I'm surprised you let them go," Oliver murmured at her side a few minutes later. The two hefted a thick slab of metal, leaning it against the side of the truck to help disguise their vehicle from view from the road.

"It's just a scout," Jamie replied, her voice equally low.

He leaned against the metal, crossing his arms in a way that high-lighted his biceps and forearms. "I can count on one hand how often you've delegated a piece of a mission."

"Lies." Jamie scowled. "I delegated all the time."

His dark eyebrows rose. "When you *had* to. When we had to split up forces or something. Or if a handler was there, and you knew you'd get in trouble going out yourself."

"Even then," Jamie said, her scowl turning to a rebellious grin.

He nodded. "Even then."

Oli pushed away from the truck and the two went about draping tarps and stacking rubble to continue the illusion that would hope-fully keep prying eyes from their little camp. The scent of cooking meat lingered in the air as Katya and Stark worked on preparing their meal.

"It's trust, right?" Jamie said it like a question, but she wasn't really asking.

Oli paused and met her eye.

"That's how Vic brought so many back each time," she murmured. "Because she trusted her Coppers enough to let them handle things. She didn't split focus."

"Jamie—"

She shook her head. "I know what my track record looks like, Oli. I know I lost more than most."

He put a hand on her arm, gently holding her in place like he did at night to stop her from clawing gouges into her forearms. "You are the *only* one who thinks of it that way."

Jamie's jaw clenched, and she had to remind herself to inhale. She didn't pull away from him, but she felt cold. Cold and overwhelmed with the fear that this would go the way nearly all of her missions had. With a body count she could barely live with.

Oli glanced at the truck, made a face that said he figured they'd done good enough, and pulled her away. Not toward the dug-out fire and their friends, but across the road and down an incline until they were far enough to not be overheard by a Silver's enhanced ears.

"Jamie—"

"It was hundreds." She interrupted him again, her vision blurring with tears that had picked the least optimal time to fall. "Hundreds of Coppers stationed under me, Oli. And I tried…" Her voice caught, her throat locking as though an icy hand was wrapped around her neck.

"Jamie." His tone was more forceful now. He took hold of both her arms, stooping to meet her silver gaze with his own. His brow was furrowed, and it took Jamie a moment to realize he was not only concerned, but also surprised.

"They gave you every impossible mission on the books. They assigned you the deadliest encounters." He was incredulous, as though this was common knowledge she should have already had. "The most gruesome kill zones. You were given suicide missions almost every time, and you came out of all of them alive."

Her cheeks were wet. Wet and salty as the tears slid to her lips and jaw. "Everyone had hard—"

"*No*," he interrupted her this time, his voice low but fierce. "No. We lost soldiers. We led people on difficult missions. We failed at times. You were given *suicide runs* by command almost every time. Because they knew you'd get it done. The fact that you survived, and that you brought back *anyone* is a testament to your skills as a Silver and a leader."

At this, she snorted. She pulled one arm free, wiping her tears away with the back of her hand. "Leader. Right."

The sincerity on his face shifted to frustration. He glared at her. "Listen to me, Valhalla."

She winced at the nickname.

"You can mope about it all you want. But the rest of us know the truth. Even Vic. You remember why you got demoted the first time?"

Jamie shook her head. "You weren't even there."

"No, but I heard about it. Before I ever met you, I knew who you were."

She frowned, a warm bubble in her chest driving away some of the cold. "I didn't follow orders. That was the first one."

"*What orders?*" he demanded. His tone left no room for her to avoid the question.

She swallowed. "They wanted us to pull back. To retreat from the city."

"Why?"

"Too many casualties."

"And?"

Jamie hesitated. The official reason, the one marked on every scrap of paper she'd been made to sign when she'd been demoted after barely a year in the field, stated that the city was unwinnable because of superior firepower. She'd refused to leave, endangering the lives of her soldiers, herself, and the comprehensive campaign for the region.

The truth—a truth very few people beyond herself and her handlers knew—was that by the time orders for a retreat had been sounded, over a dozen of her soldiers had been captured.

The enemy had pinned them, cut off escape, and through the loss of a lot of Organics, had managed to take them. The soldiers had been deemed casualties. And Command had decided to shell the city to pieces rather than let the enemy keep their hands on Unborn.

Jamie refused to leave.

The sight of her men, strewn open across operating tables as though they were clocks and the doctors tinkerers trying to see how they ticked, still stirred nausea even a decade later.

She and her team had saved over half the captured soldiers. They'd lost a few on the way out, and blew the facility to bits to ensure the city wouldn't have to be destroyed.

That was the first time Command had demoted her, and the first time they'd relieved her of her unit. The men she'd saved, the Coppers from her squad who had volunteered to go into that den of horror with her, all transferred before she'd even said goodbye.

Her heart ached with the memory of it. The lives lost, and the pain of what she'd seen that day.

"How do you know about that?" she murmured, her chin quivering as she tried to breathe past a fresh wave of tears.

Oliver's fingers caressed her jawline. He planted them under her chin and raised her head, forcing her to meet his eye. "Because the soldiers you saved that day went on to tell the story. You have a reputation, Jamie. You always have."

Her frown was one of confusion. She took his hand, squeezing the fingers with her own trembling ones.

His cheeks creased as a smile took his lips. "Before you were Valhalla, they called you Rebel. The Coppers sent to serve under you knew what was coming. They knew it wasn't your fault. And they knew their best chance of survival was to let you do what you do."

Jamie gave a half-hearted scoff. "Stir shit up?"

He leaned in, his lips brushing her cheek as his breath warmed her ear. "Break the rules."

35

ΛLONE

I T WAS A COLD night. The clouds overhead should have locked in the heat of the day, but it felt as though all the warmth was sucked out to sea when darkness fell.

Jamie tucked in beside Oliver, warm rations in her belly and heated nerves buzzing in her head.

His fingers traced the intricate designs of her tattooed arm, following the curling vines and thorns from her inner elbow to her wrist and back. When goosebumps raised the little hairs on her arms and she pulled on her jacket, he switched to drawing circles on her palm.

Her mind ran through thoughts and plans, ideas for how to breach, logistics concerning their ammunition and firepower. And every now and then, when the talk subsided and things got quiet, she thought of what Oliver had whispered to her that evening. That she was known, not for the lives lost as she'd always believed, but for the ones she'd managed to keep alive.

The darker it got, the more stressed Jamie became. Her steadily increasing anxiety was slightly lessened by the return of Tucker and

Logan. The men had scouted well enough and came back unscathed and certain they hadn't been spotted.

The base was guarded by Uniforms. Half a dozen of them patrolled the exterior fence-line. The interior was likely the same—overrun with Uniforms and only a handful of Organics to control whatever device caused Unborn to go dark.

Any question among the group of whether or not Niko's intel was correct melted away with the news.

The six of them sat for a moment, then Katya spoke.

"Distance shots. Silvers sniping from that ridge you saw, Coppers and Logan at the fence ready to cut it so we can go in when the robots are dealt with."

Jamie nodded.

"I'm not as good with a rifle as you two." Her gaze flicked to Katya and Oli. Then she looked at Stark and Tucker. "If either of you is proficient, it might be better to have you both on the ridge as well. Head and body shots don't do as much as you'd hope with Uniforms. You'll want to aim for the neck and arm joints. I'll be by the fence with Logan." She gave a nod to the Organic.

His eyes were hooded with the weight of their mission, but he nodded back.

"I can shoot," Stark said with a crack of his knuckles. He glanced beside him where Tucker leaned against a truck tire. The wiry Copper had eaten his share of dinner and was gnawing slowly on a strip of jerky.

Tucker nodded. "I'll go with you two." He gestured to Jamie and Logan. "It'd be good to have three on the ground anyway, in case Uniforms make it past the snipers."

"What, you don't think I could hold them off?" Logan grinned as he said it, but only Katya managed a chuckle.

"Gotta try and be quiet about it," Oliver muttered. He pulled his arm from around Jamie, leaving an opening for the cold night air.

She moved as well, scooting away as she opened her pack and removed the tablet Niko had given her. She unwrapped the cloth keeping it cushioned as Oli continued.

"If we can breach before they know what's going on..."

"That'd be ideal," Logan finished. He stroked his beard with a nod. "We have no notion of the numbers inside?"

Jamie clicked the little button at the top of the tablet, unfolding the compact screens as she did. They opened like an origami shape to about the size of a large book.

Niko had been correct: the battery was already at seventy percent after their short usage the night before.

There were two files. One was the exterior layout they'd consulted previously. Jamie clicked the other, and a flickering picture appeared on the screen. It sent a pang of hurt and a thrill of righteous motivation through her.

It was the three of them. Her, Vic, and Alice. Just after they'd arrived at their first real base after training.

Alice was in the middle. The smallest, and the one to insist they pose together. A shock of white was already streaked into her hair, the result of a simulation gone wrong. Her arms were looped around Jamie and Vic's waists, one on each side as she tugged them together.

Vic looked nervous, Jamie realized. Happy, satisfied to finally be in the action, but there was fear behind her eyes.

Behind all of their eyes.

Jamie wore her usual mischievous grin. She hadn't adopted the paint in her hair yet. One hand was jammed into her pocket, the other circling around Alice. She'd pinched Vic a second after the picture was taken. And had been rightly tackled to the ground for it.

Alice had watched, cackling with laughter as Jamie and Vic burnt off some of the pent up steam in their systems.

Jamie ran her hand down the side of the tablet. Where had Niko found this? This relic of a time when they'd imagined pictures of their efforts at war would be put in history books. When they'd dreamed of homes where the happy memories could be on display.

The image faded, jarring Jamie from her recollections as schematics for the old, defunct Marine base appeared on the screen.

She scanned the blueprints for a long moment, the sounds of the other's continued discussion barely registering in the background of her mind.

She squinted.

A blinking red light in the top left corner caught her attention. The words *Satellite NOT in position* were visible in small type beside the light.

On the other side, taking up an inch of space all down the right side, were small boxes. Six of them were green, the rest gray. There were three dozen in total, in rows of twelve. Above them, in identical font as the satellite message, was the word: *Uniforms*.

Jamie shuddered. She could do nothing about the threats they were about to go up against, so she turned instead to what she could focus on.

The blueprints showed a multi-story facility, but it wasn't the levels above ground that were of interest to her. From what Tucker and Logan had said, most of the exterior was as ruined as the rest of the Uninhabitable Zone.

No, Jamie's interest lay in what was underneath. She scrolled down, coming to the meat of what Niko had uncovered in the short amount of time he'd had before they left the ranch.

A network of tunnels, extending over half a mile in some places. This was where they'd find their answers. This was where the forces behind Unborn going dark were lurking.

This was where they'd find revenge.

"It looks like there is a large source of energy being used here." Jamie pointed.

She handed the tablet off. Logan took it first, then showed the spot to the person next to him. They passed the device around the group.

"That'll be it," Katya said. Her analytical gaze, always the strategist, devoured the blueprints. "Looks like most of the rest of the facility is defunct."

"Does anyone have a pen?" Logan asked.

Jamie blinked and stared at him, her eyebrow raised.

He gestured to the tablet in Katya's hands. "It's a maze down there. You all might have photographic memories, but that's not exactly the norm for Organics."

Stark dug through his bag for a moment before passing a thick black pen to Logan.

"Right," Katya said, lightly rolling her eyes.

Jamie stifled a grin.

"As I was saying," Katya continued. "It seems like everything left is underground, but none of it seems all that liveable."

"That's what I was thinking too," Oli agreed. "We might be missing something. There are only a handful of sleeping quarters."

Tucker cut in, his brow furrowed, "But there has to be Organics. Uniforms don't have the programming to run something like this."

Oli nodded. "Exactly. The question is what kind of intelligence we're working with. The hope is to eradicate this problem. But..."

"This might just be a band-aid," Jamie finished for him.

The others looked at her with varying degrees of confusion and concern. Logan handed over the tablet. Jamie shut it down and elaborated.

"We don't know if this is the only place like this."

Stark uttered a low grunt.

Jamie glanced at him, then continued. "It might be. Vic nearly died for the information we're going off of. But there are still a lot of questions unanswered. This facility is what caused the destruction of her village." She met Katya's eye. "And the death of our friends."

"Then it doesn't matter if this is the end or not," Tucker murmured. "This place needs to be destroyed. If there's another, we'll take it out too."

The group gave nods of approval.

"So." Katya flexed her fingers, glancing at the dark tablet in Jamie's hands. "Intel gathering is part of this. We need to find out how. How are they doing this?"

"And who." Oliver's voice carried a coldness that caught Jamie's attention. "I want to know who is pulling the strings on this whole mess." He looked at Jamie. "Vic found a lot, but I think there's more to this."

"If we can add to what she knows..." Jamie left the thought unfinished.

He was right. But collecting intel had been Alice's forte. Jamie was more interested in setting fire to everything that would burn.

You've got to find the fuel first.

She exhaled, the sound enough to draw Oli's gaze even as the others continued discussing the plan.

She wondered, not for the first time since they'd left the ranch, if she should tell him about Alice's disembodied voice living in the back of her mind. But what could he do about it anyway?

He held her arms that night. Curled around her, pressed against her, his hands keeping a gentle but firm vigilance around her wrists.

Unwelcome thoughts appeared when the talk ended. Fears, familiar ones she'd had since her first days of training, resurfaced.

Death surrounded her. Always had.

Angela had told them about the failed Unborn. Test tubes beside theirs going dark, the organic matter removed to make room for a new attempt. Since before she was born, death had lived beside Jamie.

But they'd survived. She, Alice, and Vic had lived. Had made it through training that took the lives of the weakest Silvers. Had gone to war, been shot, tortured, walked through miles of ice, gone days with no food and water, and still... still came out of it together.

And even when Alice died... as painful as the thought was... Oliver had been there. Jamie hadn't been *alone*.

This mission.

Jamie swallowed, her eyes glistening with tears as she looked up at the black and gray, cloud-covered sky.

Vic was at the ranch. Alive and happy and content with the people she'd found there. The stories she'd learned. The lives she'd become entwined with.

Jamie squeezed her eyes closed, pulling her arms closer to her torso and, in doing so, tightening Oli's grip on her.

If she lost these five. If she lost *him*.

She sucked in a shaky breath, easing it through trembling lips to keep it quiet.

If she lost him, it would change the meaning of the word *alone*.

It took her a long time to fall asleep.

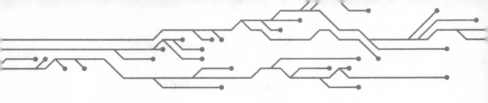

36

THE FENCE

A SPRIG OF DRY, long-dead grass brushed against Jamie's cheek. She scrunched up her nose, blowing out the side of her mouth to get it away.

Rock and rubble dug into her stomach, thighs, and arms. Beside her, Katya shifted with a nearly silent grunt.

"I know we've had worse," the other Silver whispered, her voice nearly inaudible against the chilling wind that bit at their exposed skin. "But this is ridiculous."

Jamie pinched her lips together to keep in a chuckle. The years after the war hadn't been easy, but she'd gotten used to *not* lying on cold, hard earth in near silence while watching the monotonous movements of enemy combatants nearly five-hundred yards away.

They were on the ridge. A natural barrier that kept the base from what had once been a bustling street that led to beachfront properties. The thick fence that had helped keep the base private was no more. Huge sections had fallen. Their group walked right over it.

Of course, when they'd neared the top of the ridge, they'd switched to crawling on their bellies. It was slow work. Necessary to ensure the hypersensitive sight of the Uniforms remained on something besides them.

Oliver was several dozen paces to the left. He managed a spot with fairly good cover from a bit of stone.

Jamie was glad there was no sun. The dull light was less likely to glint off the scope of his rifle.

On the other side of them, Stark lay in a similar position.

The three snipers were prepared. All that was left was for Jamie to join Tucker and Logan on the ground. They'd wait for the signal, and when most of the Uniforms were felled, they'd go in.

She hesitated.

The morning was still cool. It would grow hot eventually, given the temperature the day before, but for now, in the calm of the early hours, it was mild.

Her mouth was dry anyway. The sweat of adrenaline, anxiety, and anticipation drenched her lower back and hairline. There had been no paint, but thick clay-like mud served to mute the brilliant blonde of her braid.

Valhalla, at it again.

Unfallen.

Jamie nodded to the ghostly voice's murmur in the back of her head. This time... this time would be different. This time they'd all be unfallen.

A flicker of painful reality struck her at the thought. A reminder that that was not how the world worked.

She ignored it.

Logan and Tucker waited in the agreed-upon location. Jamie took a minute to check her gear—as many guns as she could fit on her person without blocking access to the large blade at her right. Another, much smaller, knife was tucked into her left boot.

A syringe was strapped to her forearm. She'd taped it there, cap in place to keep it from piercing her skin, the feel of the plastic a slight reassurance. Ready for the split second of time she *might* have if one of them started to go dark.

Her second one was in her right boot. Less accessible, but also less likely to break in a fight.

The men on either side of her were also loaded for bear. Logan's eyes were narrowed, his forehead pinched in a tense look. The hatchet dangling from his belt loop had a more sinister appearance in the gray landscape.

Tucker was steady. A revelation that Jamie had not expected but appreciated greatly. His breathing was even, his hands loose at his sides, his gaze on the corner of crumbling dirt and rock where they'd round and sprint to the fence when the time came.

Jamie licked her lips. She checked that the tablet strapped to her thigh was secure. She'd checked it moments before the climb to the ridge. A dozen of the boxes on the right had gone green. The rest remained gray, and she hoped with every fiber that the ones in green were the ones active, rather than the ones charging.

They'd find out shortly.

The scouting done the evening prior had paid off. They had given themselves the perfect amount of time to prep before the first patrol came along the fence line.

Not that Jamie could see them. But she heard the shots.

Her stomach tensed as the Unborn on the ridge above hissed to each other. Their words were inaudible, but she could picture them sharing information, calling targets.

The Uniforms returned fire.

She winced as bullets slammed into the dirt above them. They were around the side, but the impacts still sent showers of earth soaring into the air and raining down upon them.

Tucker glanced her way at the end of the first fifteen seconds.

His fingers brushed against her sleeve. She looked at him, expression tight with worry.

"Stark is a good shot. And I know Katya is. Oli?"

She blinked, then nodded.

"One more volley, then it's us."

Jamie's chin rose. She gave another, sharper nod. The calm from the Copper seeped into her veins. She inhaled, and the stench of gunpowder brought a stinging nostalgia to her heart.

She unholstered her sidearm.

Logan released his ax.

Tucker pulled his blade from his side.

When the next wave of Uniforms hurried toward their fallen fellows and the shots began and the call came for them to rush the fence, the three sprinted with everything in them.

Jamie got there first.

The fence was intact. Behind it, robotic limbs bled oil as shots rang out from the snipers on the ridge. They'd taken down four. Another two moved with inhuman speed toward them along the fence line.

A bullet hit one. Its arm joint exploded in a shower of sparks and sheared metal. It kept running.

Jamie swallowed down her fear as it lifted the remaining hand. It got closer. Closer. Another blast from the ridge behind them and then—

It was close enough. Jamie took aim and planted two shots into the thing's face. One in each eye socket. The combination of her hit and another bullet to the chest, and the thing joined the pile of spare parts.

"Help here," Logan grunted out.

Jamie whipped in his direction. He'd cut through the fence and was tucking clippers back into his belt. The chain link was old. Rusted in places and reinforced by twisted strands of razor wire.

It wasn't opening.

Jamie crouched as further shots perforated the remaining Uniform. She scurried to the Organic, and he moved aside. She took hold of the fence on both sides of the cut.

She yanked it apart.

"Through, quick." Jamie jerked her head for Logan and Tucker to go through first.

Logan darted into the gap with Tucker close behind.

Jamie followed, still bent in a low crouch. "Find cover."

The two men nodded and moved away. Speed was pivotal here. The snipers would be climbing down from the ridge. With any luck there were no more guards on the exterior.

The group needed to be together to breach the tunnels. The thought of losing someone in the maze-like network was nearly as terrifying as what they'd find when they got down there. And, while the Unborn had memorized the tunnels the night before, there was still the possibility that the facility had changed since those blueprints were made.

"Incoming," Tucker hollered. He'd found enough cover that Jamie couldn't see him. She hoped the Uniforms wouldn't either.

"Shit," she hissed.

She glanced over the edge of the pile of bricks she crouched behind. The enemy weren't sticking to the fence line anymore. Three Uniforms charged toward them, down the center of the relatively flat rubble. They moved with a synchronicity that was disturbingly familiar to the way she'd once fought alongside her sisters.

One leaped straight over a mound of burnt branches and slabs of wood. Its heavy metal legs left a divot in the ground when it landed. Another crouched, took aim, and peppered the bricks serving as her shield with bullets. She jerked back behind cover.

"Concentrate fire," Jamie called out.

The distinct lack of shots behind them suggested their snipers were already working their way down the ridge. It seemed as though the Uniforms knew not to hug the fence. Did that mean their programming allowed learning? Or did some Organic already know they were there and was pulling the strings?

She released a breath. "Ten o'clock first."

When the barrage slowed, she took another peek. They were eight-hundred yards out.

Seven hundred.

Four-fifty.

Damn they were quick. Self-preservation had not been hardwired into these things. They continued forward, ignoring any option for cover.

In a break of shots, Jamie took their chance.

"Now!"

As one, she, Tucker, and Logan rose and unloaded their weapons into the Uniform furthest to her left.

The impacts did not drive it back so much as slow its impossible speed. Still, the storm of bullets managed to penetrate the human-like exterior of the thing. It ran on, mechanisms still firing for a few seconds before it thudded, face-first, into the dirt.

The other two machines kept shooting. The sound of a true, pinned firefight pulled memories from Jamie's core.

The snipers needed to get to them, but moving through the fence while getting shot at was not ideal. And Tucker and Logan couldn't get a shot off with the Uniforms now so close to them.

She narrowed her eyes, swung around the side of her brick pile, and ran with the speed of a Silver.

The Uniforms did exactly as she'd expected they would. They followed her movement. Bullets shattered the ground at her feet. She bobbed, weaving in and out of chunks of stone and piles of debris.

Pain seared her side. Experience told her it was a graze. Adrenaline let her ignore it.

The Uniforms didn't bother with cover. They marched forward without hesitation. But the drive to take her and the others down split them. One continued straight, drilling bullets into the stone pillar Logan now crouched behind.

The other turned as Jamie sprinted in a wide arc. But, as fast as he was, she had muscle to push her forward. Flesh and bone and blood pumping. Each beat of her heart a reminder that she'd lived this long—survived this much.

She was close. Barely twenty yards. The red glint of the Uniform's mechanical eyes were trained on her.

Her first shot hit right between them. It wouldn't take the thing down, but she didn't need it to. Instead, the brief second of time given to her by the distraction of a shot to the forehead allowed her to slam into it with all the momentum of her sprint.

It flew backward. Her shoulder screamed displeasure.

She took two rapid shots at the arm joint as the thing doubled over. The Uniform's standard issue light machine gun dropped into the dirt.

Jamie did not stop moving. She gripped the metal shoulder of the humanoid machine and, in half a second, it was on its back. She emptied her clip into the base of its spine.

The Uniform collapsed with her still clinging to it. She breathed heavy, shallow breaths as she clambered to her feet. She did not straighten until she heard a call from Tucker.

"Clear. Jamie?"

"Good here," she called back, standing and wincing as she rolled her shoulder. "Logan?"

"Alive," he hollered. The man emerged from hiding, his face pale. "Those bastards are quick."

Jamie nodded. She strode toward them. "Fingers crossed those were the last of the ones above ground. Eyes toward the entrance, though."

"Yeah," Tucker grunted.

Jamie surveyed the horizon before them. She could follow the fence line a damn far distance before the smog of the Uninhabitable Zone obscured it from view. There was no sign of additional Uniforms on the way.

But something itched at the back of her neck.

"Jamie..." Logan's slow, hesitant tone made a shiver run down her spine.

She turned.

Logan was a good ten yards from her still. Tucker stood between them, facing the expanse ahead. The Copper's head twitched. Little movements, like he was trying to shake off a fly—or having a seizure.

Jamie's breath left her lips in a cold exhale. She met Logan's eye even as she bent, one hand going to the cuff of her boot.

"Tucker," she said, her voice softer than usual.

She pulled the syringe from its hiding spot and popped the cap off the needle.

Her voice made no impact, but the soft thunk of the cap hitting stone beneath her feet caused him to turn.

Emotion hit her like a freight train. She could barely breathe, barely move as the sight of Tucker's clouded black eyes shunted her back to the fight ring. Alice's face swam before her, feral and furious. The dull itch in Jamie's forearm flared to a painful intensity.

And then the Copper moved.

Jamie shrieked with fury as Tucker turned and sprang at Logan. Why he didn't go for her first, she didn't know. Maybe because she was the more challenging target.

It didn't matter, because she knew what he could—would—do to the Organic in their group. A spray of dust and pebbles followed the force of her boots pushing away from the ground.

She wasn't close enough.

Logan cried out as Tucker rammed into him. Both men went down in a spiral of limbs. Tucker got atop his friend and a flurry of blows knocked Logan's head side to side.

Jamie launched herself at the Copper. The two flew to the side as she attempted to use one arm to keep him pinned, the other straining to find flesh to puncture with their only hope of getting him back.

This was not like any fight with a Copper she'd experienced before. Tucker was wild. An animal pinned by her body. His short nails were still long enough to scratch, and deep lines of red soon marred her arms and face.

She was at a disadvantage. Because even though her Silver engineering should have made it a very uneven match, she was trying not to kill him.

She couldn't block with the syringe in her hand, and his fist connected with her jaw. She spat a glob of blood, pressing harder into his chest with the arm that had him pinned.

If he'd stop flailing for half a second—

She saw the opening. With no hesitation, Jamie jammed the needle into Tucker's neck. The liquid drained from the tube.

He didn't so much as flinch. But with both hands free now, Jamie was able to lean into keeping him secure.

He continued to fight, straining and lashing out, but silent. It was the silence that dug into her. The unnatural quiet was the biggest difference between an Unborn going dark and an actual rabid animal.

The thought brought nausea to her stomach.

Voices pulled a fragment of her attention, and Tucker slipped an arm out of her grip. He swung at her side this time and hit her forgotten graze wound.

"*Shit*," she groaned.

She grabbed his arm again, but as she did, it went limp in her grasp. Tucker went slumped. His head twitched again, the same spasm as before.

Footsteps told her the rest of their group had arrived.

That, or she was about to die at the hands of surprisingly light-footed Uniforms.

"Jamie?" It was Katya, and the breath of relief Jamie let out was accompanied by a muffled sob.

She swallowed the emotion, the pain, and the fear that had been clenched in her heart since Tucker's eyes had gone dark. Fear that the others had turned as well.

"I've got him," Jamie responded. She didn't look up. Didn't take her focus or effort away from keeping the Copper pinned to the ground.

However, as she stared down at the man, his seizing stopped. The black in his gaze faded, like clouds passing after a storm, revealing the copper sheen she was so used to.

He gasped, a difficult act with her planted firmly on top of him, and jerked.

On impulse, Jamie shoved him even harder into the dirt.

"Hey." Oli this time. His voice was right by her ear, the familiar callouses of his hands on her arms. "Jamie, I think he's back."

"What if—"

Katya interrupted, her tone nearly as gentle as Oli's. "There's enough of us, we can put him back down if it didn't work."

Jamie shuddered. "Logan–"

"Stark is with him. He's alive," Katya said.

Jamie nodded. She was trembling. She let Oliver help her up, leaning on him as she stood once again.

Tucker remained on the ground. He stared straight up at the foggy haze of gray above them. His breathing was shallow, and there was something Jamie recognized in his face. A look she'd seen on soldiers before. One that brought dread to her heart.

It was that look which pulled her out of her own state of shock.

"Tucker." She put a hand on Oli's chest, and he released her, stepping away.

The Copper didn't move.

Jamie said his name again, more force behind her voice.

When he refused to move a second time, she knelt beside him. He did not look at her.

She closed her hand around his jaw and jerked it to face her. The move itself startled him out of the hopeless, despondent expression he'd been wearing.

"Get up, soldier." She gave his head a little shake, then lightly slapped his cheek. "We have work to do."

It took several long minutes for Tucker to be able to continue on.

Logan was another story. The man had survived his first bout with Uniforms only to be pummeled half to death by one of his closest friends. His face was a swollen mess of bruised and bloody flesh. His left eye barely opened. He'd lost three teeth, and when he spoke it sounded like he was trying to hold twenty marbles in his mouth.

"You have to stay," Jamie said. She hissed a second later as Oli rubbed a finger of ointment across the not-as-small-as-she'd-hoped gash along her side. It had been the sopping wet blood in her shirt that had brought it to everyone's attention in the first place. The fact that it hadn't yet begun to scab put truth to Doc's warning about their lessened healing abilities.

Logan glared at her. At least, she assumed that was the expression. It was hard to tell. He lifted the ax from his belt and gestured it at her.

She shook her head.

Oli slapped the bandage onto her side, gave it a pat that drew a curse and a wince, then grinned as he handed back her sticky, damp black t-shirt.

"It's not up for discussion, Logan." She turned to the man, giving him her full attention now that her wound was patched. "You nearly died. And you sure as shit can't fight right now. Going into those tunnels is going to mean actual close-quarters fighting. Hand-to-hand with machines capable of taking down Silvers."

He mumbled something along the lines of "that didn't matter before," and Jamie uttered a low growl.

"It matters now. Injured soldiers leave the field."

He gave her side a pointed look.

Her lip curled in frustration, and she stood.

Oliver and Katya exchanged a glance Jamie chose to ignore as she stalked toward Logan. She gripped the front of the man's shirt, noting the wince of pain just from that.

"You don't want to sit out because you're injured? Fine." She pulled him forward, her nose less than an inch from his as she poured every ounce of authority she could muster into her next words. "You'll sit out anyway. Because I'm telling you to, and in this little group," she shook him, earning another wince and a grunt of pain this time, "I'm the commanding officer. You'll do what you're told, or I'll handle you the way insubordinates are handled on the field."

The mutinous look on his face shifted. As though her words reminded him who she was—what she was—and what she and the others had already been through in their short lives.

He looked down and nodded.

Jamie released his shirt. "Besides, our getaway will be a helluva lot faster with you sitting over there," she pointed toward the main entrance they'd learned of while scouting, "with the truck, waiting for us to come out. We won't have to walk as far, and the truck will do better on actual roads."

The man's swollen eyes welled with tears. He stood and pulled the ax from his belt loop. With another, more accepting nod to Jamie, he limped to Katya.

Jamie's brow furrowed in befuddled realization as the man handed Katya the handle of his ax.

She took it. Logan bent. Katya stood on her toes. And the two shared a shadow of a kiss, his wounds allowing for nothing more.

Jamie turned away, her lips pinched together and eyes closed. No wonder Respite was so carefully crafted for equality between Unborn and Organics.

She opened her eyes a split second later. They needed to move. Not soon so much as immediately. It was almost a certainty at this point that the people in the base knew they were coming.

Speed had not been the ally she'd hoped.

Oliver came to her side. His fingers brushed a trail down her arm and he briefly squeezed her hand. "You did the right thing."

"I know." She exhaled through pursed lips. "We should check on Tucker and Stark. They need to get ready to go."

"Any idea why it was only him?"

Jamie shook her head. "I don't know why it was only Alice either. Or why it was everyone when it happened with Vic."

Oli tilted his head back, stretching his neck as he looked up at the clouds. "We were counting on Logan."

"I know." Jamie put a hand on his arm, giving him a squeeze before stepping away. "We have to hope Tucker is immune now. Get Katya ready. We need to go."

She left him nodding in agreement as she made her way toward two figures in the distance.

Stark had taken Tucker the minute the Copper could stand again. He'd pulled his friend away, muttering in a low voice while the Silvers patched up Logan. The two still stood apart from the rest.

Jamie was not quiet as she approached. Gravel crunched under her thick boots, drawing their gazes when she was still a good distance away.

Stark leaned in and murmured something to Tucker. The other man shook his head. He clenched his trembling hands.

Jamie reached them. She tilted her head, studying the Copper who had tried to kill her barely five minutes prior. "How're ya feeling, Tucker?"

The tears in his eyes broke her heart. He looked at the ground, and the shift in angle highlighted the bruises across his face. He likely had a large one across his chest as well from where her arm had kept him on the ground.

He didn't respond.

Stark met Jamie's eye, and she read his sorrow in the glinting Copper. The pain he felt, empathy for his friend aching in his bones the way it ached in hers.

"Tucker," Jamie murmured. She took a step closer. "Logan is all right. He's alive. It could have been much worse."

She saw a brief flash of the man's temper as his glare fixed on her before he looked away. "I couldn't... I don't even remember what happened." He lifted his hands, surveying the bruised and bloody knuckles. "I know we handled a wave of Uniforms. Next thing I know, you have me on the ground and everything hurts. I don't... I don't remember hurting Logan."

Jamie couldn't respond. Her throat was stuck, her heartbeat too loud in her ears.

I didn't feel it.

Her breath hitched as the voice in her head whispered gently.

Didn't know what happened. My last memories were the cheers of the crowd, and the dance we did.

"You don't remember any of it?" Jamie whispered the words.

Stark's eyebrows drew together in a frown as he watched her.

Tucker shook his head. "Nothing. Not even you injecting me, but that's what happened, right? You saved me?"

She gave a shallow nod.

Silence fell for a few seconds. Tucker picked at the scabs already forming on his knuckles. He stared at the ground.

"So," Stark finally said. "Next move?"

Jamie broke her gaze from the skyline and bit the inside of her cheek to pull herself from the fight ring and Alice's cold, black eyes.

"We stick to the plan. Logan is going back for the truck. He'll be waiting at the main gate." She glanced at Tucker. "So now we have a better escape plan."

"But we still need to go fast," Stark confirmed.

Jamie nodded. "Fast and careful. I'm betting we missed our window to get underground before they realized what happened. But we've got this." She patted the tablet at her thigh. "And given that we've only come across Uniforms so far, I'm betting these people underestimate Unborn."

Stark nodded. "Let's get to it then." He gave Tucker half a side-long glance. "We're ready."

Jamie's gaze flicked to the other Copper, but she didn't question his sure statement. "Good."

As early morning shifted to mid, Jamie and the other Unborn walked one way. Logan limped the other.

The syringe strapped to Jamie's forearm had survived the encounter with Tucker. Her skin tingled with its presence. A twin to the itch that danced along her right arm.

Revenge was coming. She felt it in every step toward where Niko's map said the entrance would be. She wanted to hold Oli's hand. To ask if he felt Cade's presence with them as they marched to end the lives of those responsible for his death.

But her weapon was drawn. Held loose at her side the same way the others held theirs.

Tucker's hands had stopped shaking. The years of training kicked in, sending his guilt and fear deep into his mind to deal with later. When it was done.

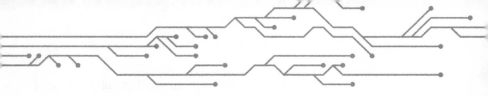

37

Underground

I T WAS LIKE WALKING through ancient catacombs.

Thick metal plates covered a hole in the ground, flat against the earth, cellar style. At one point, it had probably been in the bottom layer of a well-fortified building. It was in the center of the base, and the crumbling walls and piles of rubble around suggested at least a three-story structure.

The group was careful but quick as they dismantled the Uniform keeping guard. And then it was a matter of hefting the doors open, cracking a glowstick and tossing it down, descending at least twenty feet into thick, inky black.

Jamie went first. Her boots hit the concrete ground with a thud. It, like everything else they'd encountered in the Uninhabitable Zone, was dry. Dry and dim, even when they pulled out flashlights.

This was a maintenance tunnel. A shaft that connected with the facility itself, but had not been the primary entrance point when the buildings around them were still standing.

"Is it secrecy?" Stark whispered when the last of them were all within the tunnel. "Is that why we've made it this far? They don't want to alert anyone to their presence here, so they have minimal numbers?"

Oliver shrugged, but Jamie frowned.

"Let's move away from the ladder and check the tablet again."

They did so, walking a hundred feet and following the tunnel as it took a sharp left turn. The floor was graded down, taking them another story or more below the surface.

Jamie pulled the tablet from its holster at her hip. The battery was at fifty percent. The icon for the facility popped up, but the list to the right caught her attention first. A handful of the boxes were green, the majority of the rest gray. But there were seven now marked in black.

She swallowed. The implication that there were nearly twenty Uniforms in the facility—powered up or not—was not a friendly one.

She murmured the information to her friends, their expressions mirroring the terror of fighting those machines in close quarters. She felt a flutter of relief that they hadn't brought Logan down here.

They did a quick refresher of the map, eyes and ears alert for any sign of movement on either end of the tunnel they were in. All was quiet. Still and dark.

Haunted.

Jamie clicked off the tablet. They were not far from the doors that would lead them into the actual facility. Their target, the one room surging with energy output, was half a mile south of their current location.

She'd half hoped that when they were closer, the map would somehow show the location of the Uniforms patrolling the halls. Little green icons or something they could avoid. But that was not the case.

They carried on, moving forward with cautious, silent steps until they reached a metallic gray set of double doors. There were no windows and only one handle.

Jamie stopped and, though it caused her gut to clench, turned her back on the door so she could properly face her people.

"This is it. Priorities: intel and destruction. Take every scrap of paper you find. Tablets, keycards, flash drives, anything loose that fits in your bag, grab it. We'll worry about tracking devices when this place is a pile of ash." She turned to Katya. "Speaking of which. We each have enough explosives to take out whatever device is causing this?"

The shorter Silver nodded. "Given the heat signature coming off the room... once we get an explosion started, it'll take care of itself."

Jamie sucked in a breath, planting her hands on her hips as she surveyed the others. "Okay. Timer starts now. Five minutes to find anything you can and meet in that main hall that leads to the device. We set the charges and get out. Ten minutes total. If that fails—" she couldn't help a glance at Oli as she said it—"we all meet topside. Do *not* be down here when the time runs out."

Tucker and Stark nodded. Katya gave a wicked grin. Oliver saluted.

Jamie rolled her eyes. "Two teams. Break quick for those office-type looking rooms. And watch your backs. Uniforms are prowling."

They waited, watching her with the expectation that she'd turn and begin the heart of the mission. But she hesitated.

She looked at each of them, the pressure of the syringe against her skin, the splintering echo of Alice's neck snapping in her ears.

Jamie exhaled. "Be careful. Stay close to each other and, first sign of something off, use your syringe. If this..." She broke off, the words stuck in her throat. With a grimace, she carried on. "If this is where it ends, so be it. We're fighting for Unborn now, not on the orders of some general in a safe room. Not for the lives of millions of people across an ocean. Not for a war we had no part in starting. This is for us. For *our* future."

They each met her gaze in turn. The dedication and conviction she felt mirrored back at her with each metallic glint of their eyes.

She reached out one more time to squeeze Oli's hand. Then she went to the door, gun drawn, blade at the ready, and a dream of what their lives might be without this darkness fixed in the front of her mind.

They took down another Uniform in the first twenty seconds of breaching the door.

Tucker's lockpicking got them in quick.

The combination of Oliver's machete and Katya's borrowed ax handled the Uniform before it had done much damage. Still, Jamie snarled at the way Oli favored his barely-healed leg.

"Nicked it," he replied when she whispered if he was all right. "Right along the scar."

She was tempted to tell him to stay to the rear of the group. But part of her knew it was a selfish command, and the rest of her knew it would be a foolish request. The ones in the back weren't any safer than the Unborn leading the charge.

So she kept quiet, leading them all down the disturbingly stark, barren halls. The scenery had changed after they'd gone through the door. Where dirt and brick kept the tunnel on the other side intact, this area had been constructed carefully and with the intent of housing—or at least officing—high-ranking military officials and researchers.

The walls were slates of gray metal, pressed with rivets that looked as though they served an aesthetic purpose rather than a structural one. The floor was tile, a checkerboard pattern of gray and white that made Jamie dizzy when she looked at it too long. Fluorescent lights beamed down. As with everything else around them, the lights showed signs of how long this place had been buried beneath a decimated base. Half were burnt out, singe marks on the plastic covers that held them in place. Many flickered on and off, the eerie effect causing an extra layer of sweat to mat the hair at the back of Jamie's neck.

She rounded a corner, following the map in her head as they hurried deeper into the facility. When they hit the first major fork, the party split ways. Katya, Tucker, and Stark turned left. Jamie and Oliver went right.

The lack of any Organics on guard—men and women with the ability to think critically and raise alarms—was a bad sign by itself. Add on the musk in the air, the layers of dust on the edges of the hall floors, and the general quiet, and Jamie was beginning to worry that this was the wrong location.

Maybe those Uniforms were left by someone scouting the Uninhabitable Zone a few years ago. Maybe they'd find nothing here.

Jamie barely finished pushing down the awful thoughts when a door ahead of them opened.

She jerked back, throwing up her arm. Oliver froze.

There was nowhere to vanish. No corridor to disappear into. No door to slip through.

An Organic man in a coat walked into the hallway. He was older, maybe mid-fifties, with a hunched frame and thick glasses.

Jamie's hand was around his throat before he got half a step.

He looked as though he wanted to scream. She squeezed, and his eyes bulged out, even larger because of the bend of his glasses.

"Are there Uniforms in that room?" she hissed, jerking her head toward the door he'd just come through.

He could barely move his head, but her hand was locked tight enough that she felt his jaw turn side to side.

"If you utter so much as a squeak I will end you. Understood?"

A nod this time, and a single tear streaking down his face.

Jamie released his neck. "What is that room?"

Oliver moved forward, passing the two of them and scanning the hall.

"My..." The man's voice was ragged, either from her near strangulation or fear. "My office and quarters."

Oli glanced back, and Jamie gave a sharp nod. He swooped forward, gun at the ready as he pulled open the door and moved inside.

Jamie returned her attention to the man she had pinned. "Where are you going?" she growled. The familiar heat of anger rose in her chest.

His jacket, keycard lanyard, the mousey way he flinched at every word, reminded her too vividly of the researchers tasked with testing her and the other Unborn.

Some had been just as afraid as he was now. Terrified of their own creations.

It took the man a second too long to answer, and Jamie shoved his chest. He knocked against the wall, wincing as his head cracked against the metal.

"I was—" His words were jittery, spoken in a rush to avoid more of the pain promised in Jamie's expression. "I was sleeping. I didn't see the alert. We're supposed to go to the staging area."

"How many Organics?"

His eyes, a dark sort of murky hazel, glanced side to side, as though he thought help was coming.

"Um—"

"Um? Are you so incompetent that you don't know who you work with? Or are you stupid enough to try lying to me?"

He swallowed. "Five. There are five of us most days. Four on research and one military type. They switch out every so often. But we doctors are here around the clock."

Jamie's lip curled as disgust channeled through her veins. "Doctor? Interesting choice. I thought doctors helped people."

He had the gall to look ashamed, and it made Jamie hate him more. She blinked, trying to push down the rage bubbling within her.

But he knew. The look on his face. The way he rubbed his sweaty palms together. The way he kept glancing at her eyes. He knew what he was doing here. What their "research" really was.

Jamie inhaled. Her grip on her weapon was tight. The other hand shook with anger. "Were you here when the village went dark?" She tilted her head. "Were you the one who pushed the button, or turned the key, or did whatever it is that robs us of all agency and control? Or were you just in the room, watching?"

"I..."

Jamie clenched her jaw. This man had answers. Information she wanted and needed. And yet...

"Did you know there were children there?"

He met her eye, the fear in him nearly clouding the response to her question. His lack of surprise was answer enough.

Jamie plunged her blade into his gut.

Oli stepped out of the room as the man slid down the wall, a final exhale coming out as a whimper before his eyes went dull and his breathing ceased.

"What did—"

"That village," Jamie said through clenched teeth. "The one you told me about... with the kids."

Oliver looked at the body again, then back to Jamie with a nod. "I got everything I could find. Keep moving?"

She knelt, lifted the edge of the man's coat, and wiped her blade clean. When she stood, some of the rage bubbling inside had simmered down. When she spoke, her voice was low. "Yeah. He said something about a staging area. That's where all the Organics were supposed to be headed. Heavy sleeper here was running late, so I imagine all our fishies are in the barrel."

He huffed a chuckle and shook his head. "No shooting them until we get more information. We need to know if this is the only place they can activate the kill switch or whatever it is."

Jamie gave half a shrug as they continued walking. "This was all Niko could find."

"And no offense to the kid," Oliver muttered with a grimace. "But I'd rather get that intel myself than go off of whatever he found on his illegal search through military records."

It was her turn to chuckle before they both went back to the operational silence required to sneak through an underground facility guarded by Uniforms.

After another few minutes there was still no break in the monotony of the identical halls. Jamie even paused at one point to pull out the tablet and double check that they were following the correct path.

The little red light alerting her to the fact that a satellite was NOT in position was blinking now. She frowned at it.

On the other side of the screen, the check boxes were still there. Three more had gone from green to black.

Jamie exhaled and tilted the screen toward Oli. "I was hoping we'd have picked them off a bit more by now," she whispered. "I don't like the idea of facing down the remainder all at once."

Something heavy thudded out of sight ahead of them.

"I don't think that'll be a problem." Oliver shifted his grip on his gun.

Jamie clicked the little button at the top of the tablet and slid it back into the holder at her thigh. In one fluid movement she also pulled her gun from its holster. Her blade was still clenched tight in her hand.

Glinting red eyes locked on her silver ones for half a second. The emptiness within them made her skin crawl.

The Uniform was at the end of the hall, where the map said a sharp turn and a door to the final corridor before the central area, which she assumed to be the staging area the researcher had spoken of, would be waiting. The machine adjusted to the sight of them. It raised the mechanical arm holding a gun.

"*Go*," Jamie snapped.

She launched herself forward. With the speed and ferocity of someone built and raised to destroy, she sprinted down the hall. Bullets whizzed by her ear as she darted left and right, rapid, unpredictable movements only slightly too quick for the Uniform's corrections.

Or maybe not too quick.

A bullet caught her arm and the force of it swung her into the wall. She crashed hard, her head dancing off the metal as she let out a yelp.

It was enough to slow her down. Not stop her.

A shot rang out from where she'd been standing seconds before. The Uniform's chest concaved as the thing stumbled a few steps backward. Before it righted itself, she buried the muzzle of her gun into the crease of its neck. Two rapid shots tore through the internal mechanisms.

Her blade finished the job. She stabbed into the shoulder joint of the arm holding the gun. With a strained grunt, she leveraged until the entire arm popped out of place and clattered to the ground.

The body of the Uniform followed a second later. Jamie darted forward, checked around the turn, and then slumped against the wall buzzing with relief at the lack of further enemies between them and the door.

Oliver's footsteps echoed through the hall behind her.

"*Jamie*," he hissed, concern lacing his voice.

She heaved another breath and holstered her gun. "I'm okay." She pulled up her sleeve with a grimace. Not at the clean entrance and exit wound from the Uniform's bullet, but at the broken syringe, cracked pieces still taped to her arm.

The miracle cure dripped down her arm, mingled with the blood from her wound, and plunked like droplets of rain onto the tile floor. Wasted. Like she had dumped a clip of ammo while the enemy bore down upon her.

Her stomach clenched with fear.

Oliver rounded the corner with a curse. "What are you—dammit." He rushed to her side, already pulling strips of gauze from a pocket of his cargo pants. "I knew you were hit. Scared the shit out of me, Jamie."

Her fear melted away as the dark, dry humor of battle drew a smile across her lips. She chuckled. "What? One through-and-through? Come on." She stuck her tongue out at him. "We've both had worse."

He paused in the act of wrapping her arm to glare at her.

"Not without our normal healing, we haven't."

She rolled her eyes but said nothing.

When he was done, the bandage tight enough to stem the bleeding until her body began healing itself, his fingers brushed against the jagged remains of her syringe.

"That's unfortunate."

She snorted. "You've got a way with understatements, Oli."

He laughed, and a seed of hope grew, blossomed, and wilted within her. Her expression sombered. She pushed away from the wall and shifted her blade back to her dominant hand.

"One more down. And we'll be meeting up with the others soon."

He nodded, reading her change in tone and adjusting the way he'd always been able to on the field. "Hopefully they had better luck with intel."

She gave a begrudging nod. "Should have kept that asshole alive for a few more questions."

Oliver checked his weapon and then closed his fingers around the pull handle of the heavy double doors before them. "Nah. You got enough." He jerked his head at the backpack slung across his shoulders. "And I got the rest."

The corner of Jamie's mouth twitched. "Ready?"

He squared his stance. She did the same, prepared to run again should the door open to a set of Uniforms.

"Ready."

38

DARK

AFTER WHAT FELT LIKE endless rows of empty rooms, Jamie and Oli met up with the others. Their friends were equally bruised, though they'd had better luck finding intel.

Or simply had a better grip on their tempers.

"Satellite makes sense," Oli was saying in a hushed tone.

Tucker nodded. "Explains how they can hit a group at once, thinning the herd. But I don't understand the one at a time part."

"Maybe has to do with the research," Jamie muttered.

She glanced around the corner into the wide central area. The final section of offices, the mess hall, and meeting rooms before they'd reach that glowing source of energy output on the map. The location she assumed the Organics had been told to hurry to.

"How so?" Stark asked as he reloaded his gun.

Jamie met his eye. "I don't think this is about making us all go dark. Whoever is behind this has something else in mind. There's enough hate already, so the motivation to turn Organics against us isn't there. And the more of us they do this to, the more likely it is that other people get hurt."

"You think they're trying to figure out how to control us." Katya's rage vibrated in her voice. She'd sustained a large gash across her cheek, and her left hand looked as though it had been crushed by something. At least two of the fingers were fractured, if not entirely broken.

Jamie nodded. She gestured to the Coppers, both uninjured, and to Oliver who had also gone without much damage so far. "The Uniforms are good in big groups, on the field with nowhere to hide. And they'd be devastating against Organics. But for anything one on one with a Silver, or," she gave a nod to Tucker and Stark, "two on one with Coppers, and they struggle. Not to mention the utter inability to adapt on the fly."

"We're soldiers," Stark said. "How hard would it be to reinstate the Unborn division and get us back to work if they needed us to fight?"

Oliver shook his head. "They don't." He let out a breath, brow furrowed in deep thought. "This," he gestured around with his free hand, "none of it is sanctioned by the government. Can't be, or they wouldn't be this worried about secrecy. And, like you said, they'd just call us back in."

"The people behind this want Unborn for something else," Tucker muttered.

Jamie nodded.

Katya met her eye with a glint of understanding shining in her silver irises. "So all of it... the villages, our friends..."

"Tests." Jamie clenched her jaw. "Experiments. For some greater purpose we still don't know about."

Oliver's frown turned to a deep, hardened scowl. Jamie put a hand on his arm and some of the anger in his face subsided. He met her eye with a nod.

"We end this," Jamie said. "End their ability to keep doing this to our people. Then hopefully we find some answers in what we've collected."

The others exchanged nods and grunts of agreement. Jamie pulled out the tablet again. The satellite was now "in position." A disconcerting fact that drove a rush of added urgency through her.

The number of Uniforms had dropped the expected amount given how many Katya and the other two destroyed, which only served to confuse Jamie.

There were still so many mechanical soldiers, why weren't they on? Why weren't the Organics sending them to swarm the Unborn? Take them out before they got too close?

"Everyone have their C4?"

Nods all around.

"Good," Jamie said with a heavy breath. "Let's do this."

She slipped the door open, stepped into the hall, and froze.

It was as though her limbs were no longer connected to her mind. She felt her head twitching, felt the strain in her muscles as she tried to move. And then her vision began to blur.

Realization struck and if she could have screamed, she would have. Would've let out a sound so desperate it would've driven any hearing creature mad. Instead, she watched the far end of the hall as her sight narrowed down to a pinpoint. Figures stepped from the rooms. Half a dozen. And then everything went dark.

Jamie became aware as she was flying through the air. Her body slammed into the door she'd just stepped through, and she slid across the floor until she hit the wall of the corridor.

She blinked, dazed, and stumbled to her feet with vertigo threatening to take her back to the ground.

She swallowed, forced her lungs to accept as much oxygen as they'd take, and pressed a palm to her forehead.

Pain reverberated across her body. It felt as though every inch of her had been pummeled. Her gun was gone. A slice marred her shoulder and chest. A smaller cut was gouged into her thigh. The wrappings around her arm were loose and frayed.

It took several long seconds for realization to click into place.

When it did, her blood went cold.

She lunged away from the wall. Stumbling feet took her through the door, her frantic gaze searching for the others, for answers.

The near silence of the skirmishes in the long, wide hall was as unsettling as the sights themselves.

The area was large. Nearly twenty-feet wide and a good eighty-feet long with doors spaced along both sides. It looked as though it should have held soldiers on break, people eating snacks from the mess hall, tables and chairs and comfy couches and all the things one would expect to find in such a place. But it was stark and empty.

Over halfway down the hall, Oli fought with his back to her, barely holding his own against two Uniforms.

Closer, Tucker was fighting as well. Katya and Stark were on him. He was pinned to the wall, dodging every other blow and becoming bloodied far too quickly.

On the tile floor a few yards from the three skirmishing Unborn was a single syringe.

Jamie dove for it as Tucker sent Stark spinning away with a blow to the face. The Copper—eyes no longer with a glinting metallic sheen but as dark as she'd feared—caught sight of her. He shifted targets, launching with grasping hands aiming for her throat.

Her fingers latched around the syringe.

Stark landed on her. A fist found her gut. Another flew towards her face.

Jamie crossed her arms, holding tight to the syringe, and rolled. Stark's fist cracked the tile in two.

She went to her knees, fluid movement only slightly hampered by pain, and slammed the needle into the man's thigh. It punctured the thick cloth of his pants and sank deep into his flesh.

She jammed the plunger and left the syringe dangling out of his leg as she scurried backward to avoid his flailing arms.

"Shit," she hissed, glancing again at Tucker barely managing his fight with Katya. She'd meant to get the Silver with the serum.

Too late for it now. She was out of the cure. Stark—already shaking his head as though ridding it of a haze—and Tucker would handle Kayta. Oliver needed help.

She moved down the wide hall, more a lobby than a corridor. Doorways shot off on both sides, leading to research and exam rooms, more offices, a small mess, and a set of barracks-style rooms.

The room that mattered, the one that drew Jamie's gaze even as she pulled the spare gun from her ankle holster and trained it on the Uniform most exposed, was the one at the far end. According to their schematics—which had been correct so far—that door led to the room where they'd find the transmitter.

Her quick eyes caught sight of a couple of Organics cowering just inside one of the offices. She barely spared them a glance. They were not the primary concern.

She took aim, striding across the tile floor with purpose in her steps. Her bullets burrowed deep into the metallic skull and chest of the Uniform who had circled Oli to take him down from behind.

The other slammed its fist against Oli's face. Jamie winced and picked up her pace.

Barely a second later Oliver buried his blade into the thing's eye socket. Already damaged, it swayed a few seconds before it fell.

Jamie let out a shallow breath of relief. Her lips parted in a grin.

And then Oli turned.

"No, no, no, no," Jamie muttered the word. A chant on repeat as dread sank through her bones.

Oli's reassuring smile was gone. As was the silver of his eyes. Dark pools of mindless violence surveyed the area before they landed on Jamie.

He stalked toward her like a predator, all instinct and no feeling. It was as though he didn't notice the pain in his side, the gash on his arm, the swollen bruises on his face.

Jamie took two steps backward, angling to catch a glance at the other Unborn. Tucker and Stark were together now, trying to pin down Katya. Two more Uniforms walked through the distant door they'd all come through.

And Oliver was between her and the transmitter.

She clenched her jaw. Most of these doors were dead ends. But the one leading to the barracks-style sleeping quarters looped around. Logan had pointed it out when he'd sat studying the map so closely.

Jamie pinched her lips together. She slid her gun back into the holster, reaffirming her grip on the blade she'd been given so long ago. At the start of her and Oli's journey. When they'd been allies and old friends, and maybe something more, but nothing she'd have admitted to back then.

He drew closer.

She stepped again, putting herself just before the door to the barracks.

She didn't dare take her eyes away now, not with Oliver so close. The Coppers would fix Katya. They'd handle the Uniforms.

They'd have to.

She had to trust that.

When he was within arm's reach, she bolted. She'd always been faster. The fastest, besides Alice. His footsteps pounded along the corridor behind her as she whipped around turns, taking a roundabout trek to their destination.

Empty bunk beds flew by on either side as she ran. There was no time to stop. Any falter or hesitation, and he would catch her. And if he caught her, they would fight. And one of them...

A furious growl erupted from her throat. She reached out, snagged her hand on the rail of one of the bunks, and yanked it hard. The thing crashed to the floor behind her, but she did not stop to see if it had slowed him.

The satchel on her back thudded against her with every step. She was close.

If she destroyed the thing, the transmitter that must have caused them to go dark once they passed through the last barrier of heavy metal doors, Katya would come back. Oliver would come back.

Tears burned in Jamie's eyes as she flung open another door, took a hard right, and bolted down the last corridor. That was how it worked. That *had* to be how it worked.

Because she was out of syringes.

39

GLADLY

JAMIE PRACTICALLY FLEW INTO the room. The heat from the multitude of computers would have told her this was the place even if she hadn't been following the map in her mind.

She slammed the door closed, threw the deadbolt, and then hefted a large metal desk against it.

That might hold him for a moment.

"Huh."

Jamie whirled. Sitting at a row of monitors was a dark skinned Organic man with close trimmed hair and a similar lab coat to the man she'd gutted in the early section of the tunnels. His face was smooth save the wrinkles at the edges of his eyes.

"So, you knew exactly what you were going for," he muttered. He leaned back in his chair, arms resting at his sides as though he could not hear Oliver slamming against the door.

Jamie inhaled through flared nostrils, but her attention was torn.

Across the room, past the man and the monitors and a single large black box with a long silver antenna and a multitude of buttons and labels, was the door to the central lobby area she'd come from.

Her friends were gone from sight, as were the other Organics and Uniforms.

A part of her was desperate to shoot him and run. Drop the charges, hope they went off, and go find her soldiers.

But this wasn't gaining ground in some war of politics. This was a fight for the survival of every Unborn.

This was a fight for a real future. Not a promise of some dream that would never come true.

End this.

Jamie crossed to the door and closed it.

"Who are you?" she said, walking back around the monitors and facing the man.

The rows of screens behind him showed angles all over the underground complex and the surface. A quick scan showed that the exterior cameras were limited to the main road in and out of the old base. Jamie had specifically orchestrated their entrance to avoid such surveillance. A whisper of pride breathed across her skin, tugging her chin a fraction higher as she surveyed him.

The man spread his arms. "No one important, I'm sure." He had a lilt to his voice, an accent she couldn't quite place.

"The lab coat begs to differ." Her voice was low. There was something else going on here; had to be for him to sit there with no weapon in sight and no Uniform protecting him.

He ran a hand across his smooth chin. "In the grand scheme of things. I'm a small fish, Silver."

"Are you responsible for Unborn going dark?"

"Ahhh, interesting terminology. I like that. 'Going dark.' Can I use that?"

Disgust and anxiety warred across Jamie's face. Her jaw was tight, her body tense with a heightened awareness of the explosives in her bag—and the ticking clock that was Oliver's attempts to get past the door.

"What do you call it, then?" She took a step forward, forcing her expression into one of curiosity. She glanced at the black box in the center of the monitors. The antenna was twisted, coiled and tall, and reminded her of the comms devices they'd used in the trenches during the war. "It accesses a satellite, right?"

He let out a surprised chuckle. "You really do know your stuff. How did you find out about that?"

"How did you get access to it?" Jamie reached out. Her fingers brushed the top of the black device and, for the first time, the man twitched.

He settled back into his chair, pulling back the air of nonchalance even as he carefully watched her hands. "How did *you* get around the failsafe?"

Jamie sighed and shook her head. "We don't have time to both be asking questions."

He chuckled. "You might not, but I've got all the time in the world."

Her pulse thudded in her ears. Oliver slammed into the door yet again. The lack of a grunt, a call, a shout of pain, was almost worse than hearing the impact of his body against the door.

She pretended not to notice, still analyzing the transmitter. "If he gets in here, he won't stop with me. You've got those squishy Organic legs. You won't get far."

The man laughed. A full laugh this time, high and twisted as he leaned back and then forward, slapping his knee. "Ohhh, that would be nice for you, wouldn't it? If you could at least count on him killing me in his rampage after he finishes tearing you apart."

Realization dawned, and Jamie shook her head slowly. "Something stops them going after you. After all of you?"

He nodded. "Anyone we choose, really. It's amazing what a few key experiments can uncover. We've had..." His smile caused nausea to rise in Jamie's stomach, the metallic taste of vomit coating her tongue. "Pivotal advancements in the last few weeks alone."

An experiment. Jamie wasn't sure if the rage in the voice still whispering in her head was hers, or Alice's, or both. It didn't matter.

The memory of her sister's eyes, inky pools of black with no thought or control, caused a strange sort of stillness within her.

"If I destroy that..." Jamie aimed the point of her knife at the transmitter.

Worry flashed across his face for a brief second.

"They'll be released from this 'failsafe' rampage?"

He scoffed. "That would be poor planning on my end."

Jamie swallowed down her disappointment. She still needed intel, and time was running out. "Military base," she murmured. "Military satellite?"

He shrugged, but his smug expression suggested she was correct.

"But you're not working for the United States government. *We* worked for them. And for the military. All it would take is orders, and plenty of Unborn would flock back to their makers."

She frowned down at him. "So there *is* some other entity involved." She waved a limp hand at him. "You didn't set this all up. There'd be more security."

His smile faltered.

"But you are worth protecting. Or maybe it's just the technology." She flashed a pitying, scornfully apologetic smile at him. "I'm sure this is all quite expensive."

"Oh, I'm worth protecting," he snapped. "I designed this." He jerked his chin at the transmitter. He huffed. "There are usually more Uniforms guarding the place."

"It was already built into us then," Jamie said, not quite asking a question as much as confirming. "You just created a way to access it."

"They did make you clever, didn't they?" He sighed. "But not clever enough."

He reached, and it was almost slow motion the way Jamie followed the course of his hand toward the button on the desk. It would reset the transmitter, or release the rest of the Uniforms, or open the door and let Oliver in.

Any number of things that *could not* happen if she was going to succeed in this mission.

She was faster than him. Faster than any of them, and it was foolish of him to try. His hand hit the floor and there was a half-second delay before the screaming started. He clenched the stump of his arm, blood pouring over everything, staining his bleached coat from the sleeve up.

Jamie leaned in, one arm on the back of his chair, the other clenching the grip of her knife with trembling fingers.

"You flipped that switch and murdered my best friend. You're responsible for hundreds of innocent lives—lost."

He scoffed through the pain, wincing and speaking through clenched teeth. "Innocent is a bit of a stretch. You've all killed." His gaze flicked to the door and back to her. "You'll have to kill again before the day is over."

Rage surged within her. She moved her face closer, pressing the point of her blade into his torso.

As the knife sank through the folds of his clothes, the flesh of his chest, and the bones of his ribcage to find his heart, she grinned with all the righteous viciousness of revenge.

"Gladly."

40

UNFALLEN

J AMIE WITHDREW HER BLADE and flicked her wrist. A shower of blood cascaded across the tile. She sheathed her knife and searched the man's body, relieving his corpse of a data tablet, communications device, and a handful of papers. She stuffed them all into her bag and dug out the C4 and detonator.

Oliver thudded against the door again. It was loosening at the hinges.

He'd still be lost. Gone from her until she could find the others and hope someone still had a syringe. If she could get past him. If she could avoid a fight in which one of them would surely...

Her gaze flicked to the dead man in the chair, and she shook her head.

She knelt with the explosives. The wiring underneath the computers would do the trick. Crouching to reach it sent a flare of pain through her various injuries.

"Oli," she called. "You have to break out of this."

There was a pause, and then another slam. Her fingers worked quickly, pressing the C-4 into a bundle of wiring just below the transmitter.

"Dammit, Oliver!" she shouted, her voice breaking.

Tears burned in her eyes. She hoped the others were out. Hoped the Coppers had gotten Katya back. That they hadn't all fallen at the hands of the Uniforms. That they'd reached the surface and found Logan.

Because she was looking at two options. Set the charge and blow herself and Oliver to the next life. Or put it on a timer and have to fight him. Kill him.

Like she'd killed Alice.

He rammed the door again. Splinters of light came through the growing gap in the door jam.

Jamie clenched her jaw. Tears ran down her cheeks. She leaned onto her knees, gaze catching on her bloodstained hands.

She thought of her reputation. Valhalla in the ring. Unfallen.

Unfallen in the war as well. A rebel. Not allowed to keep people from dying. Not allowed to die herself. And not allowed to love.

She clenched her hands and then finished tucking the wires of the detonator into the C-4 to a backdrop of Oliver's body thudding over and over against the thick metal door.

They wanted her to kill him now. These bastards causing the dark. They wanted her desperation to live to outweigh whatever loyalty she had.

She gripped the remote for the detonator in her hand and stood.

They underestimated that reputation she'd built. Because when faced with one *correct* course of action, when had she ever not found another way?

The hinges splintered. The door crashed to the floor.

Oli's wild gaze scanned the room. He fixed on Jamie. She did not hesitate.

With a grunt, she kicked the chair holding the dead body. It rolled across the tile. Oliver ran forward, slamming into it and careening to the side.

Jamie didn't wait to watch him fall.

She ran.

The gash on her thigh clipped and caught on a shard of metal from the doorframe. She yanked it free and pain reverberated down her leg. Still, she ran.

The lobby-like hall was still deserted. By the time she reached the metal doors leading to the rest of the tunnels, the sound of Oliver giving chase reached her.

It wasn't like running from the enemy, an all out sprint with the desire to leave them panting in the distance. She had to make sure Oli kept up with her. Stayed just far enough ahead that he couldn't reach her, but not so far he might get lost in the maze of the facility.

The way back felt oddly short compared to their venture into the belly of the beast. She'd hoped she'd run into the others. Had hoped they might be on their way out, perhaps fighting Uniforms at the exit.

But there was no trace.

There was a plan, Jamie reminded herself. They knew the time limit. They'd be gone by now. Out of the tunnels. Safe.

Unless they hadn't gotten Katya back. Unless the Uniforms had taken them.

Her stomach sank, a vision of her friends' bodies discarded down some distant hallway setting fire to her hope.

She blinked. A dizzy spell sent her careening sideways. She slowed for a fraction of a second too long.

Hands grabbed her.

Oliver wheeled her around and sent her spinning into the other side of the hall. Her body slammed into the metal wall. She grunted, hissing in pain as the gunshot wound on her arm ripped open.

Jamie scrambled. Her feet slipped on something wet.

Oliver's fist surged toward her, and she ducked to the side, frowning at the ground.

There was blood. More than made sense for...

Oliver kicked. His boot hit her thigh, and she screamed. The sound reverberated around them, echoing down the empty halls.

When had she sustained such an injury to her leg? Why had she not noticed until now?

Adrenaline and anger. Two powerful motivators to keep someone moving.

Now, as she realized the extent of the bloody gash opening her left leg from the midpoint nearly to her hip, those motivators faded.

The ground was wet with her blood. Her boots sloshed and her heartbeat thundered in her ears, each thud sending more life draining from the untended slice. It would not clot on its own. The damage was too severe. And her Silver healing was–

She moved again, ignoring the growing despair of her thoughts. She dodged another blow from Oliver. Her hand trembled, but she kept hold of the detonation remote.

His body was unable to keep up with the unfettered craze that had taken him. He may not have been able to feel his injuries, but his movements were sluggish.

Jamie swung with her free hand and clipped his jaw.

She rolled away, pushing off the wall to propel herself forward.

They had to reach the door. The exit into dirt tunnels. The ladder that would take them above.

Fear breached her defenses. The terror of what trying to climb would look like with her body the way it was.

Yet she had to. Because without her playing bait, what would get Oliver out of the facility?

Her breath came in short bursts as she hobbled down the hall. Her vision continued to blur, a horrifying similarity between this and going dark. But she knew blood loss. She knew pain. Her body recognized this with a sense of calm.

It had been a long time coming, hadn't it?

The door loomed ahead. Jamie's lips twitched into a smile as she neared. Oliver's thunking steps were still behind her.

She shifted her grip on the remote. She shouldered the door open.

Darkness greeted her. Pitch black that was at once heavy and cool on her skin. She pushed forward with her eyes closed, dragging her fingers along the dirty brick wall.

Oliver was not far behind. The sound of him scrambling through the door, a second of hesitation as he adjusted to the dark, and then his footsteps coming towards her.

She led him with heavy, panting breaths. Hisses of pain on each exhale.

Her fingers hit a metal rung, and she opened her eyes. Light cascaded down upon her. The opening was above, dingy gray light streaming in to chase away the darkness.

With a gulp, Jamie began to climb.

Far too quickly, Oliver was beneath her. He climbed faster, hand over hand as he caught up and latched his fingers around her ankle.

She clung to the ladder. Exhaustion filled every ounce of her. Pain radiated across so much of her body it was difficult to tell where the worst of it was.

She had nothing left. No energy to fight him. No capability to do more than hold tight to the metal rungs and hope he'd keep climbing after he killed her. Hope he'd make it to the surface before the blast reached them.

Jamie squeezed her eyes closed. She leaned her forehead against the metal. Her fingers loosened, and the remote slipped an inch before she caught it.

She clenched her jaw.

Unfallen.

That title might not last much longer, but damn if she wasn't going to finish this. Her people had given too much to continue being used. Respite deserved a chance to thrive. Vic deserved the peace she'd found.

And if Jamie finally fell... she'd do it under the sun. Not in a dirty tunnel covered in rubble.

She jerked her leg. Her boot, wet with blood, popped from Oliver's grasp.

Jamie wrenched the final piece of her determination from its hiding place within and pulled her way to the top. The light was blinding, even through the haze of smog above them.

She had no capacity to stand. Instead, she dragged herself away from the opening with her forearms, the remote trembling in her shaky grasp.

Oliver emerged from the tunnel before she'd cleared more than a few inches. He stood tall, wavering slightly, but able to walk.

His shadow covered her, blocking the sun from her face.

It made for a nice painting, she thought as her eyes drifted closed. His silhouette, with the cloudy sky behind. It looked like it might rain.

A smile took her lips.

Her thumb found the little red button at the top of the remote.

She'd like to feel the rain again.

Jamie pressed the button. Everything went black.

41

Down the Hill

I T WAS IMPOSSIBLE TO tell how much time had passed when Jamie found consciousness. The sun was still above the clouds, but its exact position was difficult to pinpoint. She was looking at the sky, though—an oddity as she was certain the explosion would have at least covered her body in dust, if not buried her completely.

She was also moving.

Jamie groaned, fear hitting first, followed quickly by confusion as she recognized the arms carrying her, the silhouette of the man clutching her close to his chest.

She was cradled like a babe, her arms tucked in, head leaned against his bicep as she bobbed a little with each slow footstep.

"Hey, go easy now. I don't want to drop you, so don't wiggle too much."

The sound of his voice broke her. And, though she desperately wanted to see his eyes, see the silver reflected back at her, it was enough to hear the rumble of his words. Enough to feel the beat of his heart as she pressed a hand to his chest. Enough to have his arms squeeze just a little tighter as the tears poured from her eyes.

"How di—" She choked on the amount of dust in her mouth.

"Water." Oli grimaced down at her. "Hang on."

He carried her in silence another few hundred yards. The longer he walked, the more Jamie had time to think, and the harder it was not to leap from his arms and demand answers.

When he finally set her down and pulled a canteen from his bag, she downed several gulps in rapid succession. When the immediate thirst was quenched, Jamie rinsed her mouth, choosing to swallow down the dirt water rather than waste it.

"What," she panted, wiping her mouth with the back of her hand, "the hell happened?"

Oliver looked at her, his face a marred mess of cuts, bruises, and bloody mud. "I was hoping you'd tell me. Last thing I remember was us getting to that door. You going in and..." He bit his lip, hands twisting together for a second before he met her eye. "You went dark. Only for a second before—"

"Were you the one who injected me?"

He nodded. "I hit you in the neck and then... it all sort of goes blank from there."

Jamie leaned back against the half-standing brick wall Oli had found for her to rest against. Her leg was a mess. A cinched strip of cloth and a stick formed a tourniquet that had stemmed the bleeding, but even her Silver healing would have struggled with this wound. And who knew when that might kick back in.

The rest of her was in bad shape as well. There were bullet wounds, slashes, and a multitude of other scrapes and bruises she'd received without knowing where or why. But, as the water filtered through her system, recollection filtered through her mind.

"You went dark, too," she murmured. "I think everyone did, except Tucker. I came out of it flying through that same door. If I hadn't..." She shuddered.

Oliver swallowed and looked down at his hands. His knuckles were a mangled mess of skin. "Did I—" He clenched his hands and fresh scabs broke, rivulets of blood seeping between his fingers. "Did I hurt you?"

Jamie shook her head. "You didn't get a chance. I'm faster than you, remember?"

His surprised laugh was a blessing to hear, but it only brought a shadow of a smile to Jamie's lips.

"Where are the others?"

Oliver's brow furrowed. "I didn't see anyone else. There was fresh rubble when I came to. You were..." He paused. Tears grew in his eyes. "You were half buried. I thought—"

"I know Stark came out of it. I got a syringe in his thigh. But they were both trying to get Katya back and then there were Uniforms, and I had to—" She almost choked on the words, fear and bile twisting in her stomach. "I had to get the transmitter. I... I don't know if they..."

"Let's get to the rally point," Oliver said. "They'll meet us there if they made it out."

Jamie gave a shallow nod.

It was slow going. Oli carried half of her weight, but pain still laced every step. She refused to let him cradle her like a baby any longer. Not just for her pride, but also the injuries he'd sustained.

"Logan should be at the main gate, right?" Oliver grunted after they'd gone half a mile at an annoyingly slow pace.

"That was the plan," Jamie replied.

"What's the plan if he's not there?"

She bared her teeth. "Then he'd have a damn good reason for moving, and we go to the coast."

"Your leg needs attention, Jamie. I don't think we'd make it to the beach."

She sucked in a breath, biting back the harsh words that sprang to her lips. "Yeah, I know. If he's not there, and no one is at the first rally point, we heal up and then meet them," her voice trembled, "where they're supposed to be."

"Jamie."

"No," she snapped. "I know what you're going to say, Oliver, and I can't hear it, okay?" She closed her eyes and stepped harder than necessary on her injured leg. The spike of pain cleared some of the fear from her mind. "Not right now, at least. Just... let's get off this damn base and go from there."

"Okay." He pulled her close, pressing a kiss against her temple that was almost as bad as if he'd continued trying to talk sense into her.

Her relief at being alive, at Oliver's life and his return to himself, diminished the closer they got to the base entrance. It was a shorter route than they'd taken coming in.

Images flashed across Jamie's vision as they walked. Stark and Tucker, trying desperately to pin Katya long enough to save her life. Katya in the truck, reminding Jamie of the lives that had been lost under her command. Logan, sitting across the fire sharing his dream of a world where Organic and Unborn don't just cohabitate, but thrive together.

She thought of Alice and, with a pit in her gut, wondered if that ghostly voice would return. Or if it was gone forever now that justice had been served. Revenge taken.

Would her sister telling her to end it be the last thing she ever heard in that hummingbird voice?

Or would whatever psychosis Jamie suffered keep the memory of Alice alive through the whispers in her head?

She wanted to close her eyes as they neared the entrance to the base.

They hobbled past several rows of tire spikes on the road, and a handful of suspiciously standing light posts that had to be surveillance. Jamie was glad, yet again, for the tablet Niko had given her before they left the ranch. The layout of the base had been invaluable.

The street was clearer than most. Debris had been pushed to the side and Jamie assumed there must have been at least a garage of some kind hidden somewhere in the mess of half-crushed buildings on the base.

A hill rose up before them. The apex of which had once been the barrier keeping civilians from entering. Now a sliding gate stood open at the top.

"I can't." Jamie whispered the words. "Oli, if they were still inside when..."

"They knew the plan," he said. His voice was sure, but his hands shook.

Jamie closed her eyes for those last few steps. The final stretch before they'd have a clear view of the road, the homes that had been destroyed by war, and the ocean she could hear from where they were.

"Finally!"

Jamie's eyes flew open at the sound of Katya's voice.

The Silver sat on the hood of the truck parked at the bottom of the hill. Her arm was in a sling, the red of the cloth matching a burn that cut across her face. Her grin was crooked. The edge of the burn kissed the corner of her lips.

Beside her, Logan looked even worse than he had when he'd left them. More swollen, but alive.

All of them, alive.

Tucker waved from the bed of the truck, laid out on the blankets but able to at least lift his head. Stark sat next to him, also nursing a collection of injuries.

Jamie held her breath. Held in the heat and tears and the relief for fear that she was imagining it.

"They're all..." Her lips trembled.

"We made it," Oli whispered. He pulled her to him, his lips pressed to her hair.

She gave the briefest shake of her head, uncertainty clutching so tight to her chest that it hurt.

"We did it, Jamie." He lifted her chin with bloody, muddy fingers. "We made it."

She met those silver eyes, and the dam broke.

She exhaled, tears streaming down her face as she and Oliver made their slow way down the hill to their friends.

42

WAVES ON THE ROCKS

"**I** THINK YOU COULD paint it," Stark said with a yawn. "We have some brushes and stuff at Respite."

Jamie frowned at him. "I'm not saying *I* should paint it. I was just saying it's a nice view."

"He's right," Oliver called from the low fire he'd just finished lighting. "You should paint it."

Jamie gazed out at the coastline. They sat in a semicircle, the cliffside open ahead of them. High waves crashed against the rocky shore in the distance. It would likely rain that night, and the storm clouds rolling in from the distant horizon had hidden the setting sun a few hours earlier than usual. Dim light colored the water a deep blue and green.

She wondered at the way she'd need to press a brush to canvas in order to replicate the white of the surf, the spray of the sea, the light caressing the bottom of the clouds.

Then she rolled her eyes. "Let's focus on getting back before we think about picking up hobbies."

Katya laughed, the sound turning to a groan as her mouth opened a little too far and pulled the tender skin beginning to scar across her cheek.

They'd been on the road for three days. The truck had run out of gas a few miles north of the Uninhabitable Zone. While they might've had luck sending Logan to get gas from a nearby town, there were none close.

Logan had been near tears when they'd left the thing, but with Katya's soothing tone reminding him they'd come back for it, he was able to walk away.

The trek was slow. Jamie's leg had an infection that was preventing healing, even the normal kind. Where there should be a chunky, itchy scab, she was still contending with an open gash which oozed pus and thick dark blood every time she poked it.

They were still days away. But the promise of medicine, food, clean water, and a comfortable bed when they reached Respite was enough to keep them all in high spirits. Not to mention the unspoken, unending relief at the knowledge that none of them would go on a rampage in the night and slaughter everyone.

"I've got a hobby picked out," Logan muttered from beside Katya.

The two sat close, hands clenched just about every time they weren't working on something.

"Solar paneling for a truck?" Tucker asked before the man had a chance to finish his thought.

Logan crossed his arms with a wince and a grimace. "Yes."

A chorus of laughter echoed around their fire.

"I promise we'll go back for it," Jamie said with a smile. "Getting healed up and getting this intel to Vic are priorities one and two. But the truck is a close third."

"Speaking of which." Oli glanced at the storm clouds in the distance. "We should get through some of this before the rain starts."

Jamie nodded. They'd spent the better part of the last two evenings digging through the multitude of papers and electronics stolen from the base. Most of the tablets were beyond their hacking capabilities—at least without any equipment.

But they'd gained a fair bit of information. Clues as to the machinations of the mysterious group responsible for Unborn going dark. Finally confirmed as being unaffiliated with the United States government.

They'd also found confirmation that the base Jamie had blown to pieces had been the one responsible for every account of the attacks since they'd started. At least, the ones they knew about.

Locations dotted on a map had driven a fresh ache into Jamie. A star marked Philly, and another Boston. It seemed the majority of cluster attacks had taken place on the west coast. But the one-at-a-time experiments had been mostly in the east.

"The organization at large might still be going," Oliver had murmured when they'd uncovered that specific tidbit of information. "But the ones who killed Cade and Alice... they're dead."

"Yeah." Jamie's lips had curled into a snarl. "And they can't do it again. We destroyed the transmitter."

She surveyed the map now, hurrying to find the point she was looking for before the clouds got too close. She bit into a hunk of stale bread. It was slow work chewing with the bruises shadowed across her jaw.

But she finally found the Switch, and she sighed with relief at the distinct lack of a marker in the spot where the town was hidden. It wasn't even on the map. Which likely helped keep it safe from being targeted.

"Jamie?" Tucker's tone was hesitant.

She looked up from her perusal, swallowing the lump of bread still in her mouth. "What's up?"

"I found some correspondence between that scientist guy and someone up north, a few days past Respite. Apparently, there was private money behind a lot of this."

Jamie frowned, recollection fluttering at the edge of her mind. "Okay. There's a money guy up north?"

Tucker shook his head. "That's the thing. They hadn't gotten word back from the people they were working with up there." He looked up at her. "That's why their security was so lax. They sent a commander and a contingent of Uniforms to find out what happened."

Jamie's lips parted, her throat catching. "That town... Christian's town."

Katya made a noise. Jamie glanced at her.

The other Silver released Logan's hand and leaned forward, her eyes lit with concern. "Didn't Vic handle something up there? You said she was injured."

Jamie didn't respond. She didn't trust her voice with the stabbing horror fracturing her mind apart. This couldn't be happening. They'd won. They did it.

It was supposed to be over.

"When did the contingent leave?" she asked, her voice carrying a tremor.

Tucker glanced at the papers. "A week ago. Just before we left Respite, it looks like."

Oliver's hands landed on her shoulders, and she met his gaze.

"We have to go." She spoke the words frantically, half rising before he firmly pushed her back into her seat. "Oli, those bastards are after Vic. She's... she's injured. We can't—we have to get to her."

"Jamie."

"*Oliver,*" Jamie snapped, her voice louder than it should have been. "We have to get to her before they do."

If she'd had full use of her leg he'd have been in the dirt already. As it was, he was forced to release her arms as she hobbled to her feet, frantic eyes wide.

She barely noticed the look he gave the others, or the small gesture of his hand to keep them still as she stuffed a few things into her bag and then turned for the road.

But she didn't make it far. Without aid, her leg would not support her weight for more than a dozen steps.

Tears welled in her eyes. She leaned against a thick wooden post, sucking down breaths as though she was suffocating. And she was. She was suffocating with the fear that she'd have gone all this way, survived so much, and would still lose her other sister.

She felt his presence before he touched her. Felt the heat of his torso as he sidled up beside her to stare out at the road ahead.

"It's been days, Jamie."

She sniffed, anger flashing brief and hot against the blind fear within. "I know that."

He leaned his head around, forcing that dark skin and those full lips into her eye line. "If the Uniforms who destroyed that town were after Vic, they made it to the ranch before we even got to the Uninhabitable Zone."

Jamie gritted her teeth, her hand clenched at her side as she absorbed the truth of his words.

"So, what?" she asked, her voice bitter. "She's gone? And there's nothing we can do?"

"That's not what I'm saying," he said softly.

She met his eye. "What are you saying, Oli? Because I can barely stand, but everything in me wants—*needs*—to go save my sister."

He smiled. "And if they were going to Respite, you'd need to save *them*. That's one of the things I love about you, Jamie."

She blinked, abruptly thrown off and at the same time still trying to hear his words.

"And we *will* go check on her. But the outcome of the contingent sent north has already happened. She either kicked their asses or she didn't. And nothing we do will change that."

The words sank in. The logic of it, the timeline of the demolished town and how long they'd been on the road, and how long they still had to go before even getting to Respite, took her panic and folded it up into a neat little square of terror.

She tucked it away and nodded up at him. "Right. She's Vic. And," she heaved a begrudging sigh, "I can't walk."

"Yep."

They stood in silence for several minutes. Oliver watched the storm rolling in, and Jamie studied the ground as she compartmentalized her fear. She repeated the logic again and again in her mind. The Uniforms would've already reached Vic if she was the target. She was on the ranch, with that sandy-haired Organic and a whole mess of Unborn in a bunker.

And she was Vic.

Jamie ran through the timeline facing them. Another two days—three if she couldn't fight off this infection—and they'd be back at Respite. She'd seen enough injuries in the war to know how messed up her leg was, and how long it would take for her to be mobile without a crutch.

But they had the horses. They had allies, friends. Someone would go to the ranch. A week, she figured. A week and she'd know if Vic was all right.

By the time she'd finished working through it all, the sky overhead had filled with clouds. Thunder clapped a few miles out, the heart of the storm still on its way.

When the adrenaline in her system settled, she looked up at Oli.

"You think she's okay?"

He gave the question the thought it deserved. "I think if anyone could handle a situation like that, it would be one of the old squad. One of us, or Vic."

Her voice was soft. "Are you okay?"

He pursed his lips. "Yeah. Yeah, I think I am. There's a weight..."

"Off of you?"

"Yeah. It's good knowing the people responsible for Cade and Alice are dead. And it's a strange feeling, having somewhere to go." He half shook his head. "Having somewhere I *want* to go, now that this is done."

She nodded, a shit-eating grin spreading across her face. "And someone you want to go with. After all, you said you love me."

He raised an eyebrow. "No, I didn't."

"You absolutely did." She turned, steadying herself by leaning against the post as she poked a finger into his chest. "You said you love me, and you can't take it back."

He gave a low growl.

The sound sent a rush of heat to her belly.

"First of all, no, I didn't." He closed the distance between them. "I said your inability to let people be in danger is something I love *about* you."

She smirked up at him.

"Second." He dipped his head closer, his silver eyes locked on hers, his breath warm on her lips. "I do love you. And I'd never take it back."

Jamie inhaled through parted lips. A drop of water fell from the clouds above. It landed on her temple, running down her face as she whispered the words in return.

"I love you, too."

She closed her eyes, and his lips crashed against hers like the waves on the rocks as the storm rolled in. The rain drenched them both as they stood locked in the kiss.

It was a long while before they broke apart.

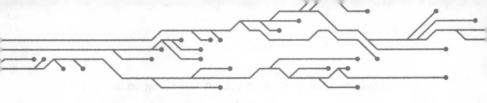

Epilogue

J AMIE HAD NEVER EXCELLED at choosing her battles. And this was no exception.

"Give me the basket."

"You watched all those damn princess movies," Oli said with a wicked grin. "Chivalry is *not* dead, and I will carry these strawberries for you if it's the last thing I do."

"Give me the basket, Oliver."

He shook his head. "How is it you've trained me to hate the full name and love the shortened version?"

She hobbled toward him, her crutch bending slightly with how hard she was leaning on it. Inches from him, and seething at the grin still plastered across his face, she scowled. "Because I paid attention in psy-ops."

That threw him hard enough to break the grin into a gut-shaking laugh. During which time she snatched the basket from his hand.

The sun was high. Respite was in full harvest mode and, though she had been told she could—should—rest, Jamie had volunteered to pick strawberries. One of the only jobs she could do with her leg only just beginning to heal properly.

She sat while picking them and scooched along on her butt to get to the next section when she'd plucked all the beautiful red treats from their plants.

Katya had laughed, but she was the only one. Jamie was not entirely sure if that was because her old friend enjoyed the sight more than the others or if everyone else was too scared to tease her.

Oli leaned in and planted a kiss on her temple. "Fine, carry the basket. But..." He held out his arm.

She rolled her eyes and took it.

He helped her along the garden path toward the mess hall. They passed Logan, face still a bit swollen as he talked over designs for the next expansion with a Copper. Katya, hands full of sweet pea stalks she was attempting to drape onto a new trellis, gave them a nod and then cursed as a few of the stalks fell. A teenage girl darted over to help, hiding her smile as she did.

"They should be back soon," Oli murmured as he and Jamie climbed the short wooden stairs to the large building. "How are you holding up?"

She gave a tight smile and then jerked her head toward the chair swing to the right of the door. "Can we—"

"Of course." He guided them over.

Jamie sat, careful not to put her injured leg between them, and set her basket of strawberries in her lap. "I'm holding up." She sighed and picked up one of the berries, inspecting it closely. "You were right. With how long this is taking," she flipped off her leg, "I'd have slowed them down on the road."

He chuckled. "Or you'd have gone faster and worn out the horses."

"Yeah, or that." She stuck her tongue out at him. Then her expression grew serious again. "If she's not..." She shook her head and tried again. "If she's okay, I want to go see her as soon as I'm healed up."

He nodded. "Of course."

"And if she's not okay." Jamie's voice cracked, but she swallowed down the lump in her throat. "If she's not okay, I know it won't have been my fault. And that's..." She sucked in a deep breath and exhaled slowly. "That'll be enough."

He wrapped an arm around her shoulders. "I'll be here, Jamie. When we find out, and when we go see them, and when we come back and get that little cabin Logan promised. I'm not going anywhere."

She leaned her head against his chest. "I know." She took a bite of the strawberry and spoke with her mouth full. "You want my strawberries."

He shook his head with another laugh. "Yeah, I do. Gimme one."

She kept the basket away for a few seconds before the inability to run hampered her winning the game. But the sight of Oliver stuffing six strawberries—greens and all—into his mouth at once was worth losing.

She folded over with laughter and, when he'd finished chewing and finally swallowed, the two shared a long, slow kiss.

Tucker and Stark had been gone four days. They'd have reached the ranch by now, given information if there were still people to give it to, and gotten as much as they could if not.

Oliver was right on two fronts.

Vic was a capable fighter, and her desperation to keep people safe mirrored Jamie's. If she made it, she made it. If she didn't, she'd have taken down as many enemies as she could. Jamie's sister's fate was not up to her. And the outcome, good or bad, was not on her shoulders.

And it was nice, having somewhere she wanted to be. And someone she wanted to be with.

The End.

Turn the page for a teaser of Unborn Rising, the companion in The Leader & The Rebel Duology.

The Leader

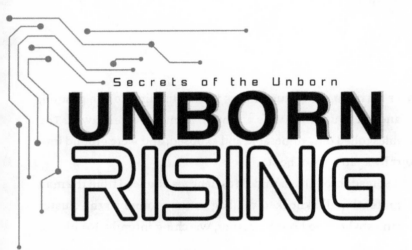

Secrets of the Unborn

UNBORN
RISING

TRACEY BARSKI

JURISDICTION

THE TATTERED BAG OF cucumbers went tumbling to the ground, and the thud drew Vic's attention from a few feet away. The vegetables rolled out, vulnerable and exposed, and were ground into the dirt by a ratty, worn boot.

Heat spread through her middle as her eyes bounced from the man who'd intentionally knocked the bag to the ground to the cluster of Organics who stood on the corner, watching intently. No hint of surprise marked their expressions.

Grim understanding settled within her, and Vic shifted her focus back to the man who'd knocked the bag over.

"Stupid bottle-bred hybrids," he muttered, shooting a sneer at Halle, who was trying to sell her surplus produce—now another casualty of the harassment that had become more and more commonplace.

To add insult to injury, the man flung the smashed cucumbers with his toe, narrowly missing Halle's aghast face. She ducked just in time, then clenched her hands at her sides, expression twisting with rage.

Vic cased the area again. The group on the corner rippled with energy, shifting endlessly, prepared to move when the time came.

Like they were hoping for a fight. Two policemen approached from the opposite corner, their conversation halting as they observed the scene unfolding before them. One crossed his arms and leaned against a light pole, eyes going to slits.

That internal wiring, like a switch had been tripped, fired off inside of Vic, and she lurched forward, wrapping her fingers around Halle's wrist before the other woman could do something she—and possibly the rest of them—would regret.

Halle's head jerked around, blonde hair whipping and barely missing Vic's face. Her nostrils flared as she took in Vic's tight expression that said *not here, not now.*

Even though her chin shifted forward a fraction, defiance warring with submission in Halle's copper eyes, Vic's authority still held, even all these years later. Halle yanked her wrist from Vic's grasp, tensing as she caught sight of what Vic had already been aware of: the sheer number of Organics surrounding the square, including the officers who had no intention of doing a thing about what was happening until it got bad.

The Organic man wouldn't have been that brazen if he didn't have backup. He wasn't a complete idiot, even if he *was* a complete asshole. Having this many of the Unborn in one location was a serious risk if he'd been alone.

Halle crossed her arms, glaring at the bully who'd harassed her as he moved on. There were fewer Unborn at the market that day than usual, but a current of frustrated awareness rolled through those who were present.

Vic straightened, working to catch the eyes of the others. The number of Organics surrounding them might've been an even match for the rest of the Unborn who were there, but the police officers were her concern. Experience had taught her exactly whose side they'd be on. Considering every last one of them was an Organic, it was no surprise. Unborn were barred from even applying.

Which was typical. And such a waste.

Some of the other Unborn watched Vic, tuned for a signal she wouldn't give. The war might have been over, but they were fighters by design. Even in her own body, her genetic coding calculated odds, looked for weaknesses, and organized her squad for maximum damage.

Instead of entertaining those thoughts, she held incredibly still, her gaze following the man who joined his comrades, his hands curling and uncurling into fists, over and over. The group's desire for a fight was palpable, the malice plucking at their restless bodies. Something else had likely pissed them off—lack of food, depressed economy, crumbling infrastructure—and the Unborn were their scapegoat, as usual. It was easy to blame Vic and her people.

The police officers might land on the Organics' side during a scuffle, but starting something needlessly was still frowned upon, and they were cautious of those eyes on them, too.

Small mercies, she thought.

Halle's lip curled as she watched the group of Organics, and the sun caught the metallic glint in her irises as she sent Vic a scalding stare.

Vic gave her head a slight shake. The others caught it, too. Some of them shifted, frustration snapping their movements tight. The rest continued to watch her, wary of what might come next, not sure they wanted to start something, either.

And all of it was a weight that pressed around Vic, one that was stifling and uncomfortable against her skin. But as far as she knew, there weren't any other Silvers among their number, no one who could give her backup as the former leaders of their kind. So the decision remained hers, though the war was over and any official authority a Silver had once had was revoked. At least on paper.

A ripple of uncertainty crested first through the Organics spread out along Old Market, ending with the gang of instigators that lingered on the corner, their attention going to the west. The flame of unease caught as the Unborn became aware of what had spooked the rest of the bustling population.

Uniforms, gray and starched, flashed between bodies, and a stab of apprehension spiked Vic's blood. Even the two officers who'd been casually watching the crowd straightened and adjusted their own uniforms, shifting with discomfort.

Vic's eyes snagged on a small child who was jostled in the crowd and fell to the ground, his shrill wail getting lost in the anxious murmuring of the crowd. Vic's whole body twitched, and she took a step in that direction. Then an Organic woman snatched the boy up and clutched him close in her arms, darting out of sight.

Vic didn't want to find out what was next on the list of bad luck and turned to help the others pack up.

"I've got it," she told Halle, who'd bent to retrieve the bag at Vic's feet.

Halle said nothing, but her gaze lasered behind them toward the dispersing gang of Organics. Halle was more of a hothead than most, reminding Vic of Jamie. She pushed down the cold finger of guilt in her gut when she thought of her old friend, and put her hand on Halle's arm, urging her back toward their little village away from the city.

The Organics began to spread, breaking off from the larger gathering to slink back down alleys and into stores that had withstood the war, watching warily as the gray-uniformed contingent filtered through the mass of people.

Once Vic was sure her people were well on their own way out of sight, she split off and took a roundabout way back to what used to be a main thoroughfare for auto traffic. She hopped over a long-ago downed stoplight and scrabbled over a pile of brick rubble to get to a closed-off alley most people would avoid, sliding in the dirt as she reached the bottom of the crumbled concrete.

She started to brush herself off then heard the robotic-sounding footfalls and froze, pressing her back against the brick wall, stilling her breathing.

Flashes of memory assaulted her, kicking her heartbeat into an erratic rhythm as the veritable army marched past the opening between the two bombed-out buildings.

Images of when she'd been behind enemy lines, trying to sneak her way back to safety, danced across her mind. A time when she'd lost most of her squad to a sniper hiding in the rubble of a supposedly annihilated town.

Her pulse throbbed in her ears, and she fought to keep the oxygen flowing in and out. The pads of her fingers dug into the rough texture of the wall behind her, ripping the top layer of skin.

Pay attention, she ordered, clenching her jaw.

Air huffed through her teeth in bursts as she took in the sheer number of bodies that marched past, movements mechanical and precise. The sound of their footfalls reverberated in her chest, triggering a rattling unease that vibrated her bones.

So many. That wasn't good.

As soon as the last row of gray uniforms passed from view, she moved to the opening of the alleyway, climbing carefully over the heap of broken concrete that had kept her so well hidden.

An urgency sang in her veins to get back to the village. If the others had gotten back already, they might have informed the rest of the Unborn, but she wasn't sure they had the same sense of foreboding she did. She'd feel better once she was sure nothing was amiss among her people.

But this was not normal, and she wasn't the only one who was nervous. The way people reacted at the market earlier meant something was happening that didn't sit right with anyone.

She slid down to the street, wincing as small chunks of debris tumbled down behind her like concrete crumbs, making a ruckus she wasn't anticipating.

Sticking to the shadows and hidden pockets on the path home seemed like the wisest course of action as the marching bodies disappeared around a corner, heading—she assumed—to the more intact part of the city. Some of those buildings had been miraculously spared the obliterating bombs that had peppered almost every city in America. And those that weren't had wealthy patrons to finance the restoration process. It was a false veneer on a deteriorating city that mirrored the country at large.

As she walked into the less recognizable outer edges of the city, she wondered if the Uniforms were being put up in one of the hotels in the midtown district, which led her to thoughts of who might've been pulling the strings there. Political power had once been drawn from the will of society—or at least had pretended to be. These days, no one attempted to hide that it was all about the money.

On the outskirts of the city was a suburban graveyard, its tombstones formed by the jagged pieces of what used to be houses that had once lined these cracked streets for miles. It was all that was left of the families that used to thrive here.

Now it was a haven for thieves and thugs, and Vic kept her eyes open for whoever could be lurking. Most would've trekked to the Old Market, probably to harass her people and steal from their own, and wouldn't be back until closer to nightfall. But that was assuming the Uniforms hadn't scared them home early.

The first few shacks at the edge of her shanty village came into view, a mockery of a suburban "development" that had been named Edge Wood because of its nearness to a thick forest. Squat little wood buildings barely large enough to hold more than a bed and a tiny kitchen—if you could call it that—was the government's gift to their bedraggled, lab-created army. Thanks for ending our war; here's a storage shed to live in.

The outer band of buildings were only a small step above what the Unborn had and housed the poorer of the Organics who didn't seem to mind living close to Vic's kind. Maybe it didn't bother them because their proximity to Unborn gave them a measure of protection from the crime that plagued the rest of the city. The whole area had been dubbed the Edge as if to separate it from what was the legit part of town, and even the whispers from the city-dwellers mentioned it with disdain.

Vic saw more families in the Organic part of the Edge than she generally did in the city, proving that life persisted even when the world was a crumbling mess.

A cluster of children sat on the sagging steps of one Organic house, watching her silently as she worked her way toward her village. Their faces were dirty and suspicious, but the littlest waved at her when she offered a small smile. Casting a final look behind her, Vic cut between two of the shacks in the outer row of her village to make her way to the center of the Edge where many of the Unborn congregated.

Fire pits made little craters in the dirt path at regular intervals, offering a space to gather and connect. The gardens that were meticulously cultivated to keep the community fed rested in rectangular boxes between the shacks that lined the main walk, giving everyone access. It was a community-wide rule that everyone helped maintain the produce and could take what they needed.

"Hey, Vic!"

She turned, the familiar voice drawing a smile to her face, though a low-level anxiety continued to bubble in her chest. It made her recheck her surroundings, just in case.

The only people milling around were those between jobs or whose work kept them in the village. She brought her attention back to the man who'd called out to her.

He stood under the eave of a nearby shack, leaning on the carved walking stick that acted as his left leg, which was missing from the hip down. His dark hair fell to his shoulders, unchecked now that he wasn't required to keep it at regulation length.

"Hey, Coop," she said, slowing to lean against the crooked beam that held the eave up.

His one good silver eye glinted as he grinned. "You look a little spooked."

She lifted a shoulder, unwilling to burden him with her worry about the Uniforms until she got a better read on the situation. Her gaze shifted to the activity down the row of shacks, though Coop's attention stayed on her. Halle was coming out of her own place right then and caught sight of Vic, her expression tightening before she turned away.

"You been causing trouble?" Cooper asked.

Vic glanced up at him, though his knowing look was trained on the other woman now. Cooper had fought in the war years before Vic had. He'd lost his leg and vision in one eye in a blast that had knocked out half his platoon. Though Unborn didn't age the same way Organics did, he was at least a decade older than Vic was. And yet he didn't seem to wear the mantle of his rank in civilian life the way she did.

"I was literally uncausing trouble." The humor didn't infuse her tone the way she'd intended, and her attempt at a smile was brittle at best.

Coop noticed and squinted at her.

She sighed. "We had some push-back from the Organics for being at the market."

"Let me guess," he said. "Someone was picking a fight. And instead of letting them have a what-for, you tugged on those reins, and our little bucking bronco didn't appreciate it."

She gave a mirthless laugh and stuffed her hands into her jacket pockets.

"Listen to me, Victoria."

Her glare snapped to his face at the use of her full name.

"The war's over. Those bars on your sleeve mean nothing here. And if Halle makes a decision—"

"That would affect everyone around her?" Vic interrupted, the heat spreading through her chest and tingling down her arms. Her hands clenched in her pockets.

Coop raised a brow, his expression mild. "You don't have to protect everyone all the time, Vic."

She turned her face away, fighting the urge to argue, to deny the truth of his words. And she fought herself, the inner voice that told her that's what she was made for.

"Good talk, Coop," she said instead, pushing away from the post.

"Hey, don't go getting offended on me." The sound of him shuffling forward—a soft footstep, then the thunk of the wooden cane—pulled her attention back to him.

"No offense taken, Cooper. I just have some other things to do," she lied. "You alright? Need anything?"

He narrowed his good eye on her. "I've got all I need, Cap."

She waved him off, choosing not to push back on that last little jab.

But it sat in her gut, heavy and churning, for the rest of the afternoon.

Acknowledgements

Tracey has to come first, because this is her world. My involvement started during a road trip when she told me of an old story she'd once imagined. A world where super soldiers had already won the war. A world where love can overcome the rest if one works hard enough for it. As usual (and you'll already know this if you listen to our podcast), I went from 0-60 with excitement. We talked plot lines for several different books in this world, and Tracey stunned me by insisting that I write this one. My friend, I'm unbelievably honored that you've let me play in this sandbox with you. I love the world you've made, and I'm overjoyed that you've let me help build the Unborn universe. Thank you.

My husband is next. This book is dedicated to him, and it's fitting given that Oli is my hubby-insert character. Darling, we've been together since we were 16. This life we share brings me unending amounts of joy. Your passion, dedication, and work ethic are something to strive for. I cannot tell you how much I appreciate you and the life we've built.

Last, but not least, YOU BEAUTIFUL READERS!! Seriously, thank you so much for the support you have poured into this book, duology, and series. Tracey and I are so grateful. It's a cliche for a reason: we couldn't do this without you.

ΔBOUT THE ΔUTHOR

C.H. Lyn released her debut novel April 1st of 2023. Since then, writing has switched from hobby to full-blown career.

When not writing, Lyn spends her time taking care of two crazy intelligent little girls, hiking with her family, and baking an array of goodies that sometimes turn out not so good. For more information or to contact the author, visit chlyn.com

ALSO BY

<u>The Old Tales</u>

Song of the Deep

A Voice in the Tower

<u>The Abredea Series</u>

Hope and Lies

Truth and Fury

<u>Miss Belle's Travel Guides</u>

Lacey Goes to Tokyo

Damen Goes to Peru

<u>Spooky Cat Stories</u>

Spooky Cat

One Hell of a Road Trip

Spelling Disaster

<u>Other Works with Tracey Barski</u>

Love is Murder